A GREEN TREE AND A DRY TREE

A NOVEL OF CHIAPAS

*University
of New
Mexico
Press
Albuquerque*

A GREEN TREE
& A DRY TREE

CARTER WILSON

LIBRARY OF CONGRESS CATALOGING-IN-PUBLICATION DATA
Wilson, Carter 1941–
    A green tree and a dry tree / Carter Wilson.
    p. cm.
    ISBN 0-8263-1655-7 (pbk.)
1. Diaz Cuscat, Pedro—Fiction. 2. Peasant uprisings—Mexico,
Southeast—History—19th century—Fiction. 3. Indians of
Mexico—Mexico, Southeast—History—Fiction. 4. Mystics—
Mexico, Southeast—Fiction. 5. Tzotzil Indians—Fiction.
I. Title.
    PS3573.I4568G74   1995
    813'.54—dc20   95-7562
                                                      CIP

CONTENTS

FOREWORD

Francine Prose

HOW TO LIVE WITH A PAST

Carter Wilson's fourth novel, *A Green Tree and a Dry Tree,* is about the life of Pedro Díaz Cuscat—a Tzotzil Indian visionary who spoke in the voice of a saint, breathed spirit into clay idols, and led his people in a holy war against the white landowners and soldiers who ruled the highlands of southern Mexico.

It is about those moments when the line between myth and history disappears; when the myths—which are, after all, only histories which happen over and over again in time—take place once more. The moments when God the Father and the Holy Fool walk the roads of Chiapas; when the Nativity, the Crucifixion, and the Resurrection replay themselves in the valley of San Cristóbal, in the nineteenth century.

It is about the world of mystic vision, in which "it is hard for mere people to see all for everything is visible and always moving. . . . We know everything. We know who will come after. It is blinding . . . because everything shimmers and is every moment all it is." It is about coming back from that world to rediscover the holiness of daily life, of life at peace, of a life full of honey and saints.

It is about the reasons why stories like the story of Pedro Díaz Cuscat survive: because, first, they are *good stories*—full of adventure, excitement, suspense, all those things we love. Because, secondly, they are about things which will always be important to us—God, dreams, magic, families, ritual, greed, rebellion, betrayal, courage. Then, finally, because "maybe tales are not permanent possessions of anyone. For whatever the reason, a story comes to have particular weight for us, its equations are, for a time, our equations. We dream it. And so we bear the story a while, until its burden becomes less."

It is about our parents, our guides, the lessons we teach our teachers: how we take our fathers' lessons and transform them in ways which our fathers could never have predicted, ways which—if we are very lucky—transcend the ways our fathers took.

It is about the grace and power of language when language is used well enough to convey both the simplicity and mystery of its subject:

> I could also see into the depths of things there, into the well-ordered houses where the women made jokes together as they worked, where babies slept without hunger or devilry. In the tree there were swarms of bees and honey. Because there was plenty, in the land of the dead men did not fight. Men and animals knew they were the same as the earth and sky. No one needed to speak because thoughts ran through the sharp air and all wishes were heard. If a woman wanted wool to spin, a sheep would come and stand calmly beside her to be sheared.

It is about all the saints and holy men who have ever tried to describe that other world, who have ever tried to lead their people to a better place.

INTRODUCTION

Carter Wilson

Twelve years after I finished *A Green Tree and a Dry Tree*, historian Jan Rus published some thoughtful deductions about the Spanish-language documents from what is called variously the Chiapas War of the Castes or the Cuscat Rebellion or the War of Santa Rosha—the event on which I based the novel. Rus concludes that the "war" supposedly waged by Mayan Indians against the ladinos or "whites" of the city of San Cristóbal de las Casas in the late 1860s would be much better characterized as a series of retributive raids against the Indians on their own territory, accomplished for the sole purpose of consolidating ladino political and economic hegemony in the highlands. He also calls into question whether the single most spectacular incident in the whole series of events—the Indians' crucifixion of a boy of their own in a drunken public ceremony—ever happened at all. As Jan Rus points out, the ladino newspapers of the time made no mention of putting anyone up on a cross. That "barbaric" deed comes into the written record only twenty years later in a polemical history justifying ladino military actions by Vicente Pineda, a member of one of San Cristóbal's more illustrious families.

Had I had Rus's detective work with the contemporary newspapers in hand when I wrote *A Green Tree and a Dry Tree,* one of the major difficulties of how to think about the main characters would never have arisen. (Notes and other information on the sources I used appear on pp. 287ff.) Whatever the War of Santa Rosha was really like, the leaders of the religious revival that preceded and then precipitated it were clearly a woman and a man from the Tzotzil municipio of Chamula, Augustina Gómez Checheb and Pedro Díaz Cuscat (his name sometimes spelled Cuzcat). Both are those anomalies, people who for one reason or another swim up out of the sea of forgottenness where most human lives are buried into the notice of what we construct as History. Augustina Checheb was said to have been the first to claim some stones in the hamlet of Tzajalemel could speak. (In another version, the stones become speaking clay figures made by Augustina Checheb and Pedro Díaz Cuscat.) At one point she was arrested and jailed in San Cristóbal, and then released. About Cuscat the known facts are similiar, the only additional detail being that he was a *fiscal* of Chamula. In those days a *fiscal* was a collector of taxes, lay teacher of catechisms and go-between in the sometimes touchy relations between the priest in an Indian town and his flock. Cuscat's name survives in some Tzotzil oral renditions of the story, but otherwise he and Augustina Checheb vanish so quickly from the stage that the ladino chronicles, having first demonized the pair, do not even bother to record whether they were ever finally re-captured or punished for their supposed crimes "against the light."

The ladino writers assume Checheb and Díaz must have been charlatans, as do some of the accounts from neighboring Indian towns like Zinacantán where the people never developed any special devotion to the little speaking icons in Tzajalemel. But while an actual human crucifixion does seem well outside the realm of things that Mayans of the highlands might do, the appearance of miraculous talking saints has been a recurrent feature of their religious life at least from the time the Spanish appeared to report on them (and to worry about the little figures stealing paying devotees from the more laconic official images that stay within the precincts of the Church). At the same moment as the Cuscat Rebellion, the much larger and longer-lasting separatist nation forged in open battle by the Maya of the Yucatán was governed by the pronouncements of the Speaking Cross, which was set in the place in captured churches above the altar where Christ crucified had hung formerly. The Speaking Cross was even known on occasion to dictate letters to its more distant adherents among the Cruzob, or People of the Cross. Talking saints persist in Chiapas today. I have never visited one, but I once lent a friend the money to take his wife to get advice about an awful skin cancer from a saint who had appeared north of Chamula, actually not that far beyond Tzajalemel.

Though you could dismiss all the human interlocutors who have presumed to speak for or through these figures as crooks, it is a plain fact that Mayan people have long believed in their prophetic utterances. It is also highly likely that some of the saints' attendants or guardians have been believers themselves, if only intermittent believers. In trying to make up a life for Pedro Díaz Cuscat, and to a lesser extent one for Augustina Checheb, I chose to imagine them as people in the difficult position of being occasional hearers of voices. Thus, for them to resort to ventriloquism would fall into that area of experience where the individual—almost always a person who has become, in Jerome Rothenberg's term, a "technician of the sacred"—operates at a threshold, at some moments ecstatic or possessed, at others not trying to deceive anyone, but employing ritual repetitions consciously in order to re-enter a place already familiar, an automatic state in which the performer has prior faith.

At the time I began writing the novel in 1969, I had been working off and on in Tzotzil and Tzeltal towns for more than five years. As part of a collective ethnographic project on alcohol consumption and then the production of a documentary film about the fiesta of Santiago in Tenejapa, I spent a considerable amount of time talking with the older men who train and then guide participants through their stints in what are called *cargos* in Spanish and in Tzotzil simply *abtel* or "work." As they are undertaken in Chiapas, cargos are an historic adaptation of the European saints' guilds—combined probably with a preconquest Mayan tradition of religious obligation—into a system of amateur year-at-a-time service and extravagant expenditure of the individual's (or individual family's) efforts and funds in making fiestas. In exchange for depleting their resources, the participants receive honor and titles of respect from the community, and the blessings of deities. Taking on a cargo is a duty a person should be prompted to by a dream in which one of the saints asks the man to serve (in some cases, especially with female saints, the obligation falls on a woman). Male or female, the human cargo-bearer mirrors in the world here below the even more arduous work the gods perform bearing us through time in the celestial or spirit world. Some of the old men I worked with were also curers, people with acknowledged special abilities for intervening with the gods in order to return their patients to health. Curers are specialists in "hearing the blood," a diagnostic procedure which involves pulsing the sick person, usually at the wrist and in the crook of the elbow. Curers are also sometimes suspected of turning their gifts to evil purpose, to being witches (this is the charge made against Pedro Díaz Cuscat's mother in the book). Some of the past cargo-holders and guides I got to know were ragged and poor, obviously the worse for the wear of an existence given over to arduous praying and epic bouts of required drinking. But they wore their mysticism—their special knowlege of the relation between human activity and the desires of the supernaturals—with enormous ease and good cheer, and I couldn't help but regard them as people satisfied with how their lives had turned out.

I determined the Pedro Díaz Cuscat I would invent would be brought up from early childhood in the heart of highland Maya religion. He would be someone who would understand this encompassing system even to the level of knowing from personal experience the dangers it holds for those who try to manipulate it carelessly or for their own gain. I also wanted my protagonist to have a strong education in the more transcendant realms of Catholicism. Whether such a training was actually available to

Indian boys in Chiapas by the middle of the nineteenth century I do not know. That would be a matter of chance. A high-level religious apprenticeship had been offered in other parts of the country in the decades after the Conquest, in the period when the fabulous idea that the New World could still become a Christian Indian utopia had its great currency. As in the Tzeltal Rebellion of 1712, in the Caste War of Yucatán many of the leaders of the religion of the Speaking Cross had been sacristans or other assistants to priests. In rebel territory these men continued the recitation of prayers in remembered Latin.

I was less interested in the questions raised by making Pedro Díaz Cuscat a man of split, two-culture knowledge, and more concerned for him to have a personal history in which he was first filled with religious insight of several sorts, then passed through a period of loss, of emptying out, the rejection of everything he had learned, a time of negation in which nothing would seem to matter. These two movements occupy Parts I and II of the book. In the last section, then, it was my hope to present Cuscat as a man in full motion, his actions unimpeded by doubt. Motivation would no longer have to be at issue, for either the reader or the character, who would become in that sense "transparent," known completely to himself and to us.

In the novel's framing story, I wonder somewhat plaintively, Are the Chamula elder Juan Tushim and I the only two people in the world still concerned with who Díaz Cuscat could have been and why the War of Santa Rosha took place? But in fact the urgency on the part of the old gentleman to get his version out before he dies is a stand-in for my own desire to make an occasion of Mayan religious revival speak to the tumult of life in the United States at the end of the 1960s.

It is startling to recall how many of us trusted then that the good news, viable plans for a just future, would come to us from the Third World. Some of the correlations we drew between the mostly middle-class U.S. antiwar movement and the rebellions of the oppressed in other parts of the world and in other times turned out to be self-serving and demonstrably false. Others made some sense. The Mayan rebels of the Caste War in Yucatán had proclaimed, "We are God's sacrifices." And though in the late 1960s I already had a nice little Selective Service deferment as a college teacher, my students, some of them only a year or two younger than I, did not. Their excuses for not having finished their work were that they had been down on the Boston Common burning their draft cards, or that they had been beaten up by the police at a demonstration, or simply that their draft lottery number was so low that they could not sleep at night. I had grown up thinking ours was a benign, democratic society. By 1969, however, the government of the United States seemed like nothing but a brutal machine run by obvious maniacs (Johnson, Nixon) and their cracked minions (MacNamara, Bundy, Kissinger) determined to keep corrupt little tyrants around the world in power even if that meant the sacrifice of the lives of all the young men of America.

Though I had never declared myself a conscientious objector, in the beginning of the struggle over the legitimacy of the Viet Nam War, I took refuge in the pacifism I had learned at a Quaker school. As time went by, like many others I began to realize I wasn't really a pacifist after all. From Chiapas I had some intimation about how Mayan dualism works, especially regarding who is "real" and to be thought of as a person and who is not. On a personal level, writing this book gave me the chance to imagine myself into characters capable of killing other human beings without remorse.

—

A Green Tree and a Dry Tree comes back into print now in large part because of another set of extraordinary events in southern Mexico—the outbreak of the armed revolt of the Zapatista Army of National Liberation (the EZLN). As I write this introduction, almost exactly a year after the Zapatista rebellion, the situation in Chiapas remains entirely volatile, the long-term outcome impossible to predict. But even the extended détente which has ensued between the Mexican government and the insurgents has been instructive concerning how traditional people can survive the modern state. If the ladinos of Chiapas are figured into the equation as a third, independent element (as they must be), the resonance with historical events like the War of Santa Rosha becomes even greater.

Traditional Mayan culture has endured through the last five hundred years partly due to neglect. For centuries before the current resource crunch, indigenous people were allotted only land which no one else wanted. And though ladinos employed some Indian labor, they could only figure out quite limited ways to exploit it. Neglect in turn fed into a conservative indigenous strategy of making their way of life appear poor, unrewarding and even forbidding to outsiders, and of training the young to reject the lures of white society.

Almost from the time of the Conquest a strong moral argument in favor of traditional life, first framed by Bartolomé de las Casas, has affected the way we view the Mayan people. The moral position has always served to appeal to the outside world to intervene against the exploiters of the Indians, whether the threat has come from rapacious Spanish hidalgos or, in the modern period, elements of the Guatemalan army or the *guardias blancas* (white guards), the thugs employed by the cattle ranchers of Chiapas to intimidate peasant farmers. Effective though the moral crusaders have been, they have left many under the impression that Mayan people have never had a good grasp of their own situation. In the time of Pedro Díaz Cuscat the ladinos of San Cristóbal assumed it had taken a traitorous white agitator named Galindo to stir up the Chamulas. In the spring of 1994, the descendants of those ladinos modestly dubbed themselves "Los Puros y Auténticos" (the Pure and Authentic Ones), called for the ouster of their own bishop, Samuel Ruiz, for siding with the Indians, and put themselves squarely on the record as being *against* "human rights." The first response of Mexican President Salinas's government to the EZLN takeovers of January 1, 1994 was to claim that Guatemalan infiltrators were responsible, and the international media have worked to give us the impression that the Zapatistas are entirely the brainchild a green-eyed pipe-smoking interloper named Marcos.

But in fact the Maya do have their own fix on how they have

been dealt with. Historically, they have demonstrated a strong sense not only of their own worth, but also of moral superiority to the whites who presume to look down on them. The evidence is all around. An unforgiving sense of indelible injury issues from an old Zinacanteco flower-seller's account of her own dream about how shabbily a ladino bus driver dealt with her. In her autobiography, Rigoberta Menchú does not forget working in a ladino household in Guatemala City and how, as she says, the *dogs* were treated better than she and the other Indian maid. In this context, the impressive eloquence of the EZLN communiques (as when they legitimize their cause by invoking "our dead, the majority dead, the democratically dead") becomes less suspicious, less foreign, and more a kind of projection—another sort of ventriloquism, if you will—out of an older Mayan voice.

Some well-intentioned observers have taken some pains to point out that the Mayans of the Chiapas highlands are not the same people as the lowland-based Zapatistas. It is true that some of the mountain communities, the more prosperous ones and those which have profited from decades of loyalty to the PRI, Mexico's ruling party, have been suspicious of the rebels. It is also true that some of the Zapatistas are immigrants from other parts of the country. But on the other hand, we also know a large number of them are the younger brothers and sisters of highlanders, settlers who began moving to the jungle over a generation ago because of the terrible scarcity of land in the mountains. To call these people peasants now and deny that they are "Mayan traditionalists" any longer would cynically demonstrate the power of what I have been calling the moral argument in favor of traditional life. The reasoning here would be that if these armed and masked figures coming forth mysteriously from the *selva* are merely other desperately hungry peasants and *not* the living descendants of the glorious *ancient* Maya, they do not deserve any special status in world opinion. They would become then only like millions of other poor people, grist for the fine grinding of late capitalism. And President Salinas's plan for their future, including the loss of what land they do have and their further marginalization, could proceed under his successor, President Zedillo, without further ado.

In periods when they could sense no external authority keeping the whites at bay, Mayan people have consistently resorted to warfare to preserve themselves. The middle decades of the last century were an especially chaotic time in Mexico. The old order of the Spanish colonial empire and the protection of the Church were gone. The liberals, led by the extraordinary Indian Benito Juárez, had had a hard time founding their republic, mainly because of the French armed invasion in honor of establishing an empire for the improbable figures of Maximilian and Carlota. In remote Chiapas, in the absence of other authority, ladino families began consolidating their holdings by claiming land which Indians had thought was their own. Times were increasingly hard, and individual priests started demanding larger payments for the services—baptisms, marriages—they performed in the Indian municipios. In the power vacuum, a traditional form of Mayan worship which, unlike Catholic rituals, requires no oversight by white men caught on and grew dangerously popular. The result was a violent confrontation, probably somewhat less grand than the one I once imagined, but still thoroughly impressive to generations of people on both sides. A hundred years later in 1970 and 1971, as I mention in footnotes [pages 298–99], I found the War of Santa Rosha still quite near the surface in the consciousness of both ladinos and Indians in the highlands.

In addition to Jan Rus's article based on the ladino sources, there are now available several more translated Tzotzil accounts of the War of Santa Rosha. These were collected by my friends Victoria Bricker, Gary Gossen and Robert Laughlin, and I have listed them below as items in a small additional bibliography. I also strongly recommend Kevin Gosner's excellent history of the Tzeltal Rebellion of 1712.

For a number of years author and anthropologist Peter Nabokov for some reason had it fixed in his head that the University of New Mexico Press would be the right publisher for a paperback edition of *A Green Tree and a Dry Tree*, which was long out of print. Friend that he is, Peter made the requisite effort and the idea was taken up with dispatch by Elizabeth Hadas, who has proven to be a completely attentive and encouraging editor. I owe both of these people a great deal of thanks.

ADDITIONAL BIBLIOGRAPHY

Alicia M. Barabas. *Utopías indias: Movimientos sociorreligiosos en México*. Mexico: Grijalbo, 1987.

Thomas Benjamin. *A Rich Land, a Poor People: Politics and Society in Modern Chiapas*. Albuquerque: University of New Mexico Press, 1989.

Victoria R. Bricker. *The Indian Christ, the Indian King*. Austin: University of Texas Press, 1981.

George A. Collier (with Elizabeth Lowery Quaratiello). *Basta! Land and the Zapatista Rebellion in Chiapas*. Oakland, Calif.: Food First, 1994.

Kevin Gosner. *Soldiers of the Virgin: The Moral Economy of a Colonial Mayan Rebellion*. Tucson: University of Arizona Press, 1992.

Gary S. Gossen. "Translating Cuzcat's War: Understanding Maya Oral Tradition," *Journal of Latin American Lore* 3 (1977): 249-78.

Robert M. Laughlin and Carol Karasik. *The People of the Bat: Mayan Tales and Dreams from Zinacantán*. Washington, D.C.: Smithsonian Institution Press, 1988.

Rigoberta Menchú. *Me llamo Rigoberta Menchú y así me nació la conciencia*. Barcelona: Editorial Argos Vergara, 1983.

Jan Rus. "Whose Caste War? Indians, Ladinos, and the Chiapas 'Caste War' of 1869." In Murdo J. MacLeod and Robert Wasserstrom, eds., *Spaniards and Indians in Southeastern Mesoamerica: Essays on the History of Ethnic Relations*. Lincoln: University of Nebraska Press, 1983.

A GREEN TREE AND A DRY TREE

And there followed him
a great company of people,
and of women, which also bewailed
and lamented him.

But Jesus turning unto them said,
Daughters of Jerusalem, weep not for me,
but weep for yourselves, and for your children.
For, behold, the days are coming,
in the which they shall say,
Blessed are the barren, and the wombs that never bare,
and the paps which never gave suck.
Then shall they begin to say to the mountains,
Fall on us; and to the hills, Cover us.
For if they do these things in a green tree,
what shall be done in the dry?

—LUKE 23:27-31

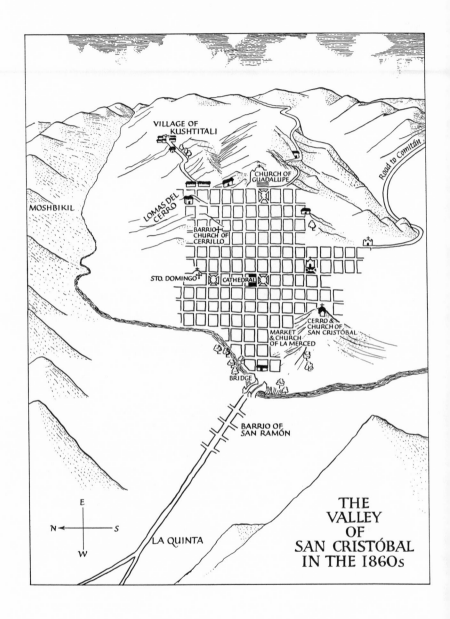

VILLAGE OF
KUSHTITALI

CHURCH OF
GUADALUPE

Road to Comitán

MOSHBIKIL

LOMAS DEL
CERRO

BARRIO
CHURCH OF
CERRILLO

STO. DOMINGO

CATHEDRAL

CERRO &
CHURCH OF
SAN CRISTÓBAL

MARKET
& CHURCH
OF LA MERCED

BRIDGE

BARRIO OF
SAN RAMÓN

E
N ◄——► S
W

LA QUINTA

THE
VALLEY
OF
SAN CRISTÓBAL
IN THE 1860s

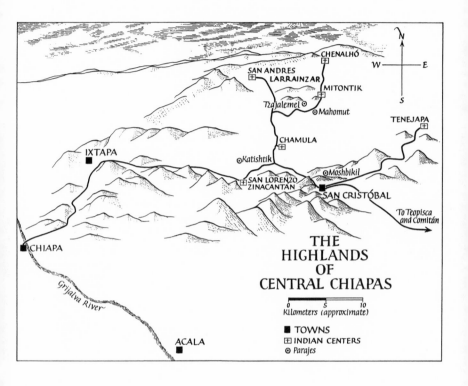

THE
HIGHLANDS
OF
CENTRAL CHIAPAS

0   5   10
Kilometers (approximate)

■ TOWNS
⊞ INDIAN CENTERS
⊙ Parajes

"*Mistakenly people have believed that from father to son the Indian fed on a perpetual hatred for the white race, but this is not correct. Properly speaking the wars they have caused are not caste wars, but what the barbarian hordes coming out of central Asia brought against the Roman Empire; warfare of savagery against civilization, of dark clouds against the light; it is the war owls would want to wage against the sun because its brightness blinds them. . . .*"

—Vicente Pineda,
*Historia de las sublevaciones indígenas
habidas en el estado de Chiapas.*
San Cristóbal de las Casas, Chiapas, 1888.

"*The majority believe in God from cowardice,
only the few believe in Him from fullness of soul.*"

—Maxim Gorky

PART I

THE FLOWER BEARER

1836-1856

1

And what do we know about the birth of Pedro Díaz Cuscat?

I sleep well and dream. It was after noon and hot light broke from heaven again and again in flashes.

We know that once her mother-in-law had felt her and promised it would not happen until after the crazy days and on into the month of Muk'ta Sak (that is, in March by the white calendar), then Rosha gave up worrying for her own cumbersome swelling.

Rosha's sister was outside stooped beneath the grass eaves transferring water to the smaller pots. The older girl, on her knees inside, paused in her own work and brushed a strand of hair away from her face. In a moment she was flooded with the memory of the day her husband had gone away, herself in the crowd of black-skirted Chamula women in the street in San Cristóbal, the women crying, and how as their husbands and sons dismally clumped off down the cobbles Antun Díaz, eyes brimming, drunk, had called back to her *Tools Rosha! buy new tools for planting!* The women had turned to stare at her. *And my animal, Rosha, don't forget my animal in the night!* Then the women had laughed, thinking he was making a joke about having her, not suspecting that this young man who looked as ragged as the others going off to the plantations to make enough to begin was in fact already the owner of something, a powerfully spined black bull. Rosha was remembering that day, nearly half a year gone now, and again, gazing at the machete and the hoe blade black glowing in the dark corner, wondering why she was here, alone except for her sister when, starting up from her knees, she discovered the pain buried so deep inside her that her hands went for her skirt and she was hiking it to find what sharp thing had dug into her stomach when the contrary action began and she fell forward into the white ashes of her fire.

I see them, Rosha's little sister returning with help. They came down the hill to cross the path, Antun Díaz's mother tottering along faster than it seemed possible for an old woman to move, her heavy hands like jaws biting the heat. To her eyes, new from inside, the unshaded hills blanked white in the sun and seemed bare of green life and, luckily, of curious other beings.

No. Above her a fragmented black wheel flapped slowly around. Seeing the birds, Antun's mother let out a dull low whistle. And then, as she scrambled uphill to her son's little house cut under the brow of the ridge, she noticed a boy waiting in the crotch of a dry tree with a slingshot and unboylike patience. It was he who became the messenger of disorder, as all of us are willing to be at times, and later brought with him the pack of children which gathered at the fence, straining to see into the little house, laughing and calling out to the stranger, until Rosha's sister at last turned the door shut against them and barred it from inside.

The old woman performed the man's job, holding the knees and forcing wide the opening. Below her on the dirt floor Rosha thrashed, mouth open and smiling, eyes begging to be released, and called her husband's name, first loud, then in whispers. At first Antun's mother could not understand the pleasure she saw in the girl's face, but then the face became like a water mirror to her and she found in herself the vague remembering of things she had not experienced in many years and then only in the dark, and all the anger against this thin witch her son had dragged home with him from Larrainzar swelled in her and she reached out and struck Rosha, the back of her hand to one cheek, then the palm to the other.

What she coaxed finally from between Rosha's legs looked asleep. Below the soft lump of the head there was a fleshy blue chain impressed into its neck. For a moment the boy baby's being dead, strangled by itself in its own cave, seemed right to the old woman.

In the dream the day passes down to evening in phases, like the more and more peaceful breathing of a person escaping from fever. The children at the fence have called all the insults they know and, disappointed, have gone off home. Though it is late in February, there is the intimation of a winking small frost to come tonight.

Rosha was asleep on the ground swaddled in a blanket. Her mother-in-law moved about in the near dark gathering the filth of the useless birth together and wrapping it all in a rag. She gouged a small pit in the earth floor with the point of the new machete, placed the bundle inside and began scooping dirt over it. Then she stopped. Though she knew to bury what had come out of Rosha to keep bad spirits from getting hold of it and using it against the girl, not being a real midwife Antun's mother had no idea of what to do with the stillborn child itself, whether to bury it also or to leave it in a gully somewhere for the animals to find. She loosened the fleshy cord from around its neck, cut it and tied it off, and put that in the little bundle before closing it and reburying it. And the small thing she took outside and left in the flat moonlit yard of her son's house.

Still later Rosha woke up in the dark. Her sister had gone across the way with the old woman to get food and they had fallen asleep there. Rosha unwound herself from the blanket and crawled outside. Against the mud wall was a tiny lean-to she had prepared for herself and thatched with road grass for the steam-bath they would fix her when she had given birth. But the stones inside were not heated, and there was no one to pour the water.

And so it was, the old man told me, that Pedro Díaz Cuscat's mother happened to find him and to see for the first time the deep collar in his neck which they say he carried with him for thirty-five years, and Rosha took him back inside and held him against herself and, waking and dreaming, prayed to the old saints away in her own town.

Who broke the bars on the pen where her husband's bull was kept at night we do not know, neither that nor what sudden desire for human company brought it forth to push against the door and somehow, delicately, not breaking anything, to move into the little house and settle itself against the woman and her child.

Later the believing people of Tzajalemel where he was born said that the bull must have been Pedro's soul come to save him, for without the animal's great heat Rosha and her boy would have died that night. But when he was a man, Pedro denied that a bull was his soul. His followers would ask him and he would say he had never had the dream which can tell us which animal our soul is. At the end with his tired soldiers, he once said he must have the soul of a rabbit, because rabbits pop up here and there.

"But his people never believed that," Juan Tushim told me. "They thought he was making one of his jokes. Because he was a man who wasn't afraid, as rabbits and men are."

I scrambled over a fence of tangled brush and climbed a hill so steep and dry that the powdery dirt gave way under my heels. I admired the tenacity of the clumps of grass which grew there where not even an Indian would try to plant corn. Farther on of course I found dry stalks, bent over to the ground at this season and so spindly they never could have supported ears. Indians plant corn as superstitious old ladino women cross themselves, in the same spirit of propitiation and with like feelings of there being no harm in trying. Farther south, in Guatemala, I have seen corn growing on slants so precipitous the men had to let each other down to the fields on ropes tied under their arms.

At the top of the hill was another bramble fence where I was met by a skeletal troop of barking dogs. As I was climbing over, I heard scurrying inside one of the three aged houses and then there was a pause and silence. Dusty tall immobile trees shaded the compound.

He came out to greet me in a ragged once-black chamarra without a belt, his hair flaired from his head on the right where he had been sleeping. He wore the high-back sandals of a man who has done cargos, and he carried two little chairs. When I bowed to him and said *"Pasaro,"* he set down one of his chairs and touched me with the back of his hand on my forehead to release me and then he invited me to sit in the shade. Below us to the east was the center of Chamula with its giant church and the dusty plaza larger than several football fields and the three hills with the guardian crosses. The place I stayed and did my typing at night by a hissing Coleman lantern was there and beyond, waiting, all the parajes, the open country where the people lived.

Juan Tushim had worked with me for several days at my house in the village. I had taken from him the sequence of Mayan months and their Tzotzil names, the eighteen twenty-day months and the tricky five-day month. Then he had said I should come to visit him.

After a few minutes he asked if I would mind moving. "Too cold on this side for an old man." So we took our chairs and sat again on the west side of his hill. A woman who seemed a little young to be his wife brought two gourd bowls half-filled with a mixture of whitish ground corn and water called *maȼ'* in Tzotzil. Juan asked if I knew to drink this stuff. I told him I did. Between sips we moved our bowls in little circles to keep the water and the corn flour mixed. Juan rotated his expertly and carelessly, mine sloshed out. Just as we were setting the bowls on the ground, the woman reappeared and took them away.

Juan Tushim cleared his throat. "In your country in the night how many times does a man work it with his wife?"

I wondered if this was the question he had invited me to his house to answer. None of the younger men had ever asked it, though the people I knew in Chamula sometimes seemed more doggedly concerned with the ethnography of my place than I was with theirs. "I don't know," I said. "Once, twice. And here?"

He grinned. "With *my* wife, it was four times every night."

The boast hung there between us a moment. I didn't know whether I was supposed to accept that or laugh at it.

"But she died," Juan Tushim said, nodding. "Now you—you're old not to have a wife of your own. You must feel the bite on you to go back to your country and get yourself one."

"I'm not leaving tomorrow."

"You're not?"

"No."

We sat on that a while. Finally he said, "If I knew how to write things down on paper like you do, I could give better stories than the ones you've asked me for, better than the old month names—they don't even use those now."

"What are the better stories?"

"About when Santa Rosha came to us and spoke, and how old Cuscat went to make war for Her against the people in San Cristóbal. I know that one from my grandfather, and he was even a soldier for Cuscat."

"If you tell that story, I will try to write it down," I said.

"But it's long and maybe you will get tired of it and have to go back to your country before I can finish, even if the end is very good too."

"What if I promise you to stay?"

"Yes," he agreed, "that would be the right thing to do."

Then he was silent. We watched small flurries of schoolboys going along toward home on the red clay road west toward the paraje of Katishtik. I thought Juan had forgotten me. There were the grayish drops of cataracts on both his eyes and I didn't know how much he could really see.

The dogs started up again and a boy of eleven or twelve struggled through the fence, his soft flappy school readers in his hand. Without raising his voice, the old man asked the boy to bring something from one of the houses.

The boy went inside and then came over to us, his face wet with water, and handed a leather tube to his grandfather. He settled between us on the ground, pulling his slick black hair back from his face with his fingers.

Juan untopped the tube, fished inside it and brought forth a curled brown photograph. "My grandfather," he said.

Probably around the time of the Revolution the man had stared at the lens, fixed but not afraid, inviting the camera to take away what it could of him. And in the result he seemed generous and indiminishable.

"I learned what I know from him," Juan said. "At the middle of the day when the sun stops in the top of the sky, my grandfather would not speak, because then God says the names of the sinners, and my grandfather could hear."

We admired the photograph again.

"My grandfather took me once to see a picture in San Cristóbal. A priest gave us the story of it."

"A picture of what?"

"They were killing babies. They had swords, men I was told were soldiers. Yes, and in the door of every house there was blood and some of the little babies were dragged down to the road and their mothers followed them tearing out their hair. It was a very old picture and very good, it showed a lot of people. The moon was shining, and the priest told my grandfather."

"What did he say?"

"He said that when the little Jesus was born the soldiers, the Moors or the ladinos I think, some sort of white people at least, they came and they asked at every house whether the people in there believed the little Jesus had really been born. And if the people inside said yes the soldiers left them alone. But if they said no, they couldn't believe it, then the soldiers said 'All right. Good. Then we'll take *your* baby and kill it,' and that's what happened when the little Jesus was born. But it was only the boys they took, because nobody cared if they took the girls."

I dream less happily, of a week or a short month after Pedro's birth.

In the cold night Rosha had been outside and had heard the shod horse and the silvery tinkle of the trappings, and then she had seen the man going by, north toward the town of Chenalhó, a ladino riding easily with his hand turned inward on his thigh.

When he came into her yard, he spoke like an Indian, voice high in his throat, begging, Can I get warm by your fire? I know you're there.

She could hear his hands feeling for a catch on the smooth-planed surface of her door, the stroking and pressing of his hand.

There's news about your man, señora. Can't you let me in for just a minute? It's very cold.

At last she unlatched for him and then quick, as if burned, she scrambled back to the far side of the smoky fire.

Now do you recognize me?

Though she shook her head, Rosha did recognize him, the snakeskin belt and the flower-stitched leather boots with the tiny spiked stars, and knew him for sure by the chapped redness in his cheeks and the hunched way he moved, a hot country person shriveled by the mountain cold. He had been leaning by the manager's desk the day her husband had made his mark and committed himself to the plantation.

A baby, the ladino said. And more than a year now since your man came to work for us.

No. Not a year.

He seemed not to have heard her. A woman without a husband. What will our dear Jesus say about that?

I have a husband.

What do you think I came all this way to tell you?

He stood up, nearly touching the boards above his head, dug in his pocket for his silver five-twenty and tossed it down between them, saying something more, the manager sorry and there, keep that for yourself.

It was a trick the ladino had well practiced. When the girl went for the coin he could descend on her from above. Afterward he could recover the money. But even when the five-twenty rolled close to her and stopped, this one did not move. So he settled down again, smiling, and stretched his tough hands toward the red remains of the fire.

Let me see your child.

The girl shook her head, no.

Oh let me, he said.

She brought her hands to the knot of shawl at her throat and untied it. She swung the little bulk around and held the naked child out to him.

What a pretty thing, he thought, especially for an Indian baby. How nearly perfect—the woman holding it as she had learned to do with the head forward and the indented flesh hidden in the soft neck skin so ıt would not frighten people—completely smooth and yet the limbs and the little torso, no bigger than the ladino's spread hand, already muscular and strong. With near deference he slid two fingers down the valley between the baby's round legs to the mound above the little penis where a boy is fleshy like a little girl. He ꝕressed and the baby thing throbbed and waved and stood up. Laughing, the ladino pushed again and a good stream of water came out onto the woman's lap. He held it with a two-finger grip, the way in fun fathers grab their children's noses. Gelding Indians is making fewer fuckers without losing any carriers, his boss used to say.

The ladino wondered why the baby so pleased and excited him. Maybe it was at last seeing a savage completely naked. Being a work foreman and forced to speak their grunting talk and to spend his sad life among them, the ladino had put himself to work in more than his share of filthy cunts. He even stood a reputation for liking the Indian girls better. And he had beaten his share of browned backs until they crumbled away from him like land falling into the sea. But as though it was the most important of all things, they always managed to keep some vestige of rag around themselves. In San Cristóbal they still told how, a hundred or more years ago during the uprising, they left Indians out to die in the sun chained to stakes and moaning for their saints to save them, and how in spite of guards posted in the city plaza the other Indians managed to creep up to the dying ones in the night and tie tatters of cloth around them.

Watching the naked child, the ladino had forgotten to peer into all the dark corners or to count the number of breathers in the little house.

He took the baby, laid it aside and grabbed the girl's wrists, holding them tight in one of his own hands while he felt under her and dragged out the machete he had suspected was hidden there. He threw the blade and heard the metal clank against the door behind him, then pushed the girl down onto her back. Whipping his belt loose, he got up over her and tied her hands.

He felt something teasing at his crotch. He started and lifted away, but then looking down, he saw that the woman's teeth could not get him. Rather than angry, her little defiance made him amused. It excited him to want blood, from inside her mouth, from somewhere.

He sat back, held her legs down and pushed up her blue skirt. Strange, he knew she shouldn't be wearing blue, but he could not figure why it was wrong. She had sinewy thin legs and a belly flabby and soft with extra skin. Once they were roped, the Indian girls were easy. They all dressed the same and under the skirt there was nothing, no unusual or newly fashionable or variable buttons and straps to make them laugh when you fumbled or hesitated. He could not see her cunt, but like a soldier finding his rifle in the dead of night, he recognized the machinery by touch and knew where he was. He wedged her legs apart with his knees and she opened to him and from her dark face, from the smile, it seemed that she wanted him. Her arms, bound over her head by the belt, were still, and when he lowered himself she reared to him like a Christian whore.

The ladino hit wrong and then, grunting, he pulled off and felt for the place. Its smooth opening was sticky and unclean like a much-used bottle, but he went in again anyway. Deep inside they were always clean enough, unless they had been stuffing wool or whatever up there to staunch their blood.

The girl's face was surprised, she tightened in the pain, but then she submitted to it and the ladino, settled now in the lap, drawing back and going in again, wished she would fight more. Sometimes with the Indian girls, especially the stronger and younger ones, he could get himself a nearly free time, as dreamy and indefinite a release as he used to have when he was a green boy in the ranches and before dawn would give it to his blanket or some Indian's pile of pine needles or even God's sweet soft earth.

But this one would not fight. Her thin thighs pressed in, nudging him to get on with it, her body telling him it had been a long time since the last and moving him toward it faster than he wanted to go. And then from her eyes it looked as though she was going to find pleasure too. And he hated that, hated the women who enjoyed themselves under him, and even in the last strokes he thought of taking it away from her.

The ladino misjudged Rosha's smiling. In the vague light he could not see reflected in her black eyes the tiny figure standing above him, Antun's mother with the machete hanging between her thick hands. He could not see how carefully and rapidly the old woman judged, he could not know what pleasure the sight gave Rosha, or that her terror at the last moment came from imagining the blade might come down so hard it would tear through the insubstantial white body and not stop until it had pierced her own.

The ladino could not have understood Rosha's face at all. When the awful, virulent force hit him, he had just begun pumping into her and was smiling oddly at the complacent, perfect baby boy who had been left on the floor with its head turned toward him.

Juan Tushim squinted at the sun just about to tuck itself down behind the low hills in the west. He shut his eyes and turned his face up to the light. When I looked again the transformation was nearly complete. The sun had gone and the few puffy sheep of clouds which had been white a moment ago had turned pink.

Then Juan said, "If you know how we watch out for our babies, you must know what his mother did with the little Cuscat."

"But I don't know."

"All right. His mother wasn't a Chamula woman. They say she was from Larrainzar, but who knows if that is right? It *is* true she was a stranger and later cured people, though maybe she wasn't a witch. And all the talk about Pedro Díaz Cuscat not being a Chamula himself came from the mistakes about his mother. If you talk to people who don't know, they will tell you he was a white person, a ladino, and his mother found him on the road near Chenalhó or that she stole him from some ladino's house in San Cristóbal. But people will tell you anything. And they believe what they say because they have said it. And a lot of people, even Indians, don't believe that an Indian could ever do all that Pedro Díaz Cuscat did.

"Well. His mother protected him from losing himself and the bad things getting their hold on him. If she was visiting away from her own house, when she got up to leave she would sweep all around herself with her shawl so no part of his little soul was left behind. She kept strangers from seeing him and fixing a bad eye on him. She bit off his fingernails when they scratched her breasts, and kept them in a little bag with bits of his baby hair she chopped off with her knife. Antun Díaz came home from hot country, he wasn't dead after all, but he must have been thin from working there. Hot country has never been good for us, it gives us fevers, and if we weren't poor we would not work there. There was another son born. He was named Salvador. They say this younger one was very white, whiter and much prettier than his brother, and the people there in Tzajalemel who knew about the ladino wondered whose child Salvador was."

"What happened about the ladino?"

"Antun's mother and Rosha's sister carried him over across the way in the night to the little place where the old woman lived. She had sheep, not many I think, maybe only a pair. They buried the ladino in the sheep pen under all the dung. And they left him there to rot. The sheep wouldn't like it much, would they? Stepping where they had to step.

"My grandfather said that the mother kept just a few of the ladino's things. When he grew up Pedro Díaz Cuscat sometimes wore ladino boots with little silver spurs. His grandmother made the mistake of trying to keep the ladino's horse which is how they found her and why she could not pretend for very long that she didn't know anything about the missing man. The ladinos came looking. In those days the ladinos could come here to Chamula and take anything they pleased from us. They found their friend's horse and they were going to kill the woman.

"But then the president of our town came through the mountains in his black chamarra wearing his hat with the ribbons and behind came all of his officials, and maybe some of them even had guns for shooting rabbits, and they stopped the ladinos from killing the old woman and just asked her where she had hidden the body. And the old woman told the president how the ladino had forced Rosha and the president was sorry for her, even if the ladino's friends weren't.

"So they made her dig up the body. What they found was awful after so many months tramped down in the sheep dirt, and they made the old woman wrap up what was left of it, bones and clothing I think, and they went with her when she carried it all the way to San Cristóbal to give to the ladino's boss or his wife or whoever still wanted it. And maybe then they put the old woman in jail in the city to make the ladinos happy. But maybe they decided Pedro's grandmother had been punished enough and let her go home. I don't know.

"I *do* know that Pedro Díaz Cuscat was never baptized, at least not by a priest in our church. Here they charged ten pesos, which was too much, and even if people were afraid for the souls of their little ones they were more afraid of San Cristóbal and didn't go there if they could help it. So they baptized their babies in their own parajes, in Tzajalemel or wherever God had set them down. They had curers do it or men who had done their year's service for the saints, the *pasaros*, or men who had been sacristans for the priests and knew the priest language, which isn't even Spanish. And if the person who did the service knew the priest language, we thought that was better for the child's soul and we gave the man his gift, a bottle or even a chicken or money if we had any.

"But it was the same. The curer or the sacristan or the *pasaro* would call up all the devils and the other blackwing things which live in our mountains, and he would tell them. 'Look,' he would say, 'here I am pouring the true mother water over this child, so no matter if you played with him before he came to us, even if you held him close in your arms and loved him, from now on he doesn't belong to you. He is born over now to *us* and to *our* saints, and you may as well go away and leave him. You may as well forget *this* little one and the hopes you had for him.'

"And then three times the curer would spit rum on the baby's head and there would be a meal, the godparents would give the food, and then for a while, for a life, the little baby was ours and did not belong to them."

2

His neighbors knew Antun Díaz as a man without any calm. Some, still imagining him a boy and expecting some suffering still to come would nail him down and stop his ceaseless flapping, were troubled by his early death. He went too fast, they thought, nothing was settled about him when he sought to begin a grown man's duties to our saints, he hurried, bragging and believing himself, into the dangerous work.

Even in the moment he was first spotted by Rosha on the road up from San Cristóbal, he was excitedly bargaining with a stranger over renting a field, cajoling, promising a greater return than the red-scarred land would ever yield.

A boy left as little as he was needs to marry himself into a well-off family. But instead Antun Díaz had that girl from Larrainzar who had brought nothing with her. And he had the black bull. He spoke about his animal as though it were the secret key to tremendous good fortune. Some of his neighbors were taken in by his talk and believed him a hardworking, lucky young man. Only old men noticed that he came to banter with them when other young men were busy cleaning weeds from their corn, and were not beguiled by his explanations of how the land he rented was plagued with slugs and rabbits or mice when the plots near his somehow were not. If a man does not seem worried by his own failures, in innocence and unconcern his neighbors often accept the opinion he gives out of himself.

Only old unheeded women said the boy's wife never went to market because she had only that one skirt from San Andres and it had worn so thin you could see through it.

One day Antun Díaz was sitting hatless in a gentle summer rain on the side of a hill well above his own little house. Below him no one stirred, but smoke seeped out of the deep-canted roof and he knew his Rosha and his boys were safe inside listening to the rain drop at last from the ends of the thatch into the water pots, and he knew that he too was safe inside with them, though at the same time he was sitting on the mountain slope while the warmth of the sun winnowed the gray rain clouds. Everything was green and growing rich, the corn already haloed yellow by the touch of the saints, his bull tethered in its pen gathering force to itself, big-shelled tasty snails gliding effortlessly along in the slicks between the growing things. Below him also was a river, as wide and heavy-flowing as the Grijalva in real leagues far away. On the water large ships went by under sail, and around them like nursing puppies about their mother jostled small canoes maneuvered by Indians. The Indians serviced the bright golden ships and got rich from the trade. It was wonderful to see the steady, relentless vessels and how the men, paddling hard, could race up to them, latch on for long moments and do their business, then untie and drift away from the river's mainstream and the ships' progress.

Pedro's father heard noise in the underbrush, a struggle, and then a porcupine, all bristled large, came rolling out of the weeds. The animal looked at the young man, the young man fearlessly watched the animal and something in his soul had the power to quiet it. The needles settled precisely into place along its back so it became a sleek furry thing instead of a spiked one.

Pedro's father sighed and, when he looked again, the boats large and small were gone.

And there on the far side of the river stood a man in a new black robe with sleeves doubled back to his white wrists, waiting for the appearance of some easy way to get across. Even though it was raining hard the man wore a new broad flat straw hat with fresh colored ribbons. The rain will ruin that fine hat, the dreamer thought. But the man did not seem to care. A wrapped package of candles big around as a young tree was strapped to his back, and a basketful of delicate flowers, the parasitic plants men find dangling like hanged tropic birds from the highest, nearly inaccessible branches of oaks and bring to decorate the saints' places and to give life to bare wooden crosses. But, like a person who has worked all his life as a bearer, the man moved on the riverbank comfortably with his loads, they were no weight to him.

Where else in life had Pedro's father seen such newness? Men, beginning a year's devotion to a saint, come from their borrowed houses in the center wearing their costly, specially made clothes and, as they are lifted by the runners and carried, like dreamers they are amazed to find *their* bodies decked in such riches, and at the same time they are frightened because they are vulnerable to the envy of other men and to their saints for showing the wealth of their bodies before they have proved their worth.

Down by the river the sun momentarily broke through a worn place in the clouds, the water flashed silver for an instant like a mirror turned to light, and the river had changed into a road. Though the miracle happened right before him, the man in black was not surprised, he did not even test first with his foot, he just crossed the road and started up the hill. He climbed toward Antun Díaz by the easiest and most obvious path, one Pedro's father had not seen. At the level place by the rock, he stood a moment, and Antun saw how handsome he was, and how clean. His legs and the sandals with the high leather backs had no mud on them and his face was as hard to remember as a saint's. The porcupine came sidling like a cat and ran himself familiarly along the official's bare leg.

Setting a bottle down before Antun, he covered his mouth with his hand and said softly, 'I was looking for you, my little brother, to ask if maybe you could do me a great favor.'

Antun Díaz felt himself filling with the desire to do whatever the man wanted. Yet at the same time he was hurt because the official had found it necessary to ask, and he longed to throw all of his failings against the man, to test the strength of the other's love. The excuses came bubbling up. He had just returned from hot country and was too weak. He was poor, his wife had little babies. He saw it was an evil to own the black bull.

But he found himself asking the official what favor it was he wanted.

'Our Father came to me,' the man in the black said, 'and He asked would I carry his days, his flowers, forever. And because it was Our Father, of course I told him yes. And He, because He is Our Father, promised me that men would help me do my work when they could.'

'How long would you want me for then?'

'Little brother, could you go to the mountains for me and bring my flowers to me, and come see me in my church and carry me and help me dance and sing to me for a year? Could you do that much? A year is only a little while, even for a man.'

Antun Díaz thought of the debts, of the sickliness of the corn now standing in his rented field. 'I'm very poor,' he mumbled. And once he had said them, his words grew in meaning. The young official understood that he meant not only poor in land, but poor in the estimation of men too wise to fool, and rich only in tricks and inabilities and in sins of the body.

'You couldn't believe my work would diminish you, little brother,' said the man in black. 'When you stand here and look out on all this growing, and know it belongs to me and the others my brothers, when you see the water changes to solid ground where I want to walk, you must also know that working for me can only increase you. You must know I will make it good to you, that I can make it happen.'

Pedro's father nodding to the man's words, wanting to be serious about this most serious of matters, and to be taken seriously and trusted for once, but in the radiant man's presence unable to keep from grinning. He had seen the ocean. Forming in his head like waves far out from shore came thoughts. I am afraid. I won't do it right. I can't. And as these rushed toward his mouth the force of the saint came back soothing to meet them. Of course, fear is that quality of men we cannot stop, though we would, though if we had it our way we would not want men to grow old and die either, you must know.

And the doubts of the man then were dissipated by the force of the saint and softly Pedro's father said 'All right. I'll be glad to do it.'

The man in black offered the bottle to him. Antun tried to see under the brim of the hat what the man's face was like, because the first sight of its clean whiteness had so pleased and calmed him, and because he was already beginning to stir and be aware that it was the still middle of the rainy night and his babies were asleep in the hot cleft between his body and his wife's, and he was beginning to know which dream it was and how important and even as he shot up toward waking with nothing to cling to on the way he would have liked to bring with him the name or face of the saint he was going to serve. And he seemed about to achieve that single sight when the man in black put the bottle so hard into his outstretched hand and the touch of it became so real that he started awake.

Much later, in the 1860s, there was a period of several years when Pedro Díaz Cuscat must have lived at peace in Tzajale-mel, with his own growing sons and his wife and his Augustina nearby. In those years he often sat alone, or watching his boys, and pieced together what must have been the real events of his own childhood. But he found himself relying more on the dream memories than on the actualities, just as when he looked at the night horizon the earth as a flat thing held up by the kindness of four old dwarfs and the black sky as a wheel with candles fixed in it were more his possessions and his truth than the whole purposeless abstraction of systemed orbs, the grapefruits and oranges and lemons Padre Cresencio once rolled around the seminary courtyard for Pedro's particular enlighten-ment.

He remembered his father below him on the path, in the patio by the standing cross, ducking into the little house. Bring-ing from his net satchel raspberry-colored ribbons and green yarn for Rosha to weave into the borders of her blouse and into her hair. And then a thick round of tawdry copper, the first thing the boy coveted which he did not eventually get, coveted busily even long after it had grown to his mother's finger. Sweet leathery cooked maguey and rare little bananas from some hot country town to the north. His father had been to a fiesta.

A memory of waking in the dark, not as always before between them on the pole bed, but wrapped in a blanket on the floor. His mother crying, saying Pedro's father did not know the dangers, he did not know what people in Larrainzar thought about her. And Antun Díaz urging her to share the work with him, speaking as a man does to make a horse go through a fence or into a stream which has frightened the animal.

And then a memory flushed with daylight. A windy whipping morning, a Sunday or a fiesta because the church bells clattered, Pedro high on his father's bumping shoulders coming down into the center, the man running along, the boy hanging on to the man's hair for life and, as they came up the little rise to the open space marked out by two or three whitewashed ladino stores and watched over by the stone pile of the church, the boy gaily turned back to make sure his mother was right behind, and his little brother tied to her back and somehow, by the woman's lagging, he knew they should not be here on whatever business this was and he wanted to get down. Then inside the churchyard wall, still on his father's shoulders, he was above many straw-plaited circles, men's hats all bent together, there was jostling and then laughter, and the man who kept the lists cocked up his head and, smiling at the boy, asked his father which saint it was he wanted so badly to pay his time to. From between Pedro's legs came his father's voice saying *It doesn't matter, I can take any of the jobs*, which surprised and pleased everyone.

Then the old guardians said they were sorry, but they had nothing for even so rich and anxious a young fellow, though of course the man who wrote down the names of servers for future years would put the name 'Antun Díaz' on the paper. And the circle of hats turned down and Pedro could not see the bemused, bristled faces anymore.

And then there was another memory, similar except now the boy was not on his father's shoulders above the men, but standing in a grove of muddy, scaled legs with hardly any sunlight around him. One hand kept him tied to his father and the other was clutched by his brother, a Salvador so young he was wearing the beltless tunic a baby trips over when he is learning to walk. And the old men no longer laughed. They hesitated and droned together like horseflies, and then the moonfaced one who smiled, the one named Mesha with the fluttery hands climbing his face and digging at its various holes, said, 'Well, since you are the owner of a bull as you have so often told us, and since you want the work so much, we see it would not be an offense for you to take the place of the man who was going to be our *pasyon* in the new year.' And his father, reaching down and lifting Pedro, hugged him to his chest so tight the boy could hear the thump of the man's excited blood at its gates.

A recollection of being alone in the tiny house tucked up under the brow of the wind-constant hill in Tzajelemel with another boy named Ignacio Panchini? Pedro showing all of the new things his father owned and his mother for some reason hated, things the boys were warned against touching because they were holy. Big crocks of liquor fat in their net holders, and a red wooden box his father opened when he prayed before the candles, as he did now morning and evening, and Pedro had to stay quiet then, though his mother went on loudly slapping out her tortillas. When he and Panchini? finally succumbed and looked into the box, they found red cotton pants and shirts and a rattle which Pedro shook once or twice in the stillness.

He still spent most of his days with the women. His mother and his mother's thin unmarried sister sat on hillsides where the sheep grazed, sometimes with other women, pulling wool through wooden combs, spinning strands from revolving sticks clicking in cups set on the ground, turning reed baskets which grew magically in their hands as the sun ambled across the sky. Punctuations of You, Tesh, get me more of this grass. See the kind I want? and Pedro, watch, the lamb is going into the brambles. Hurry! run! and much laughter.

Once they saw a young man whistling as he clomped down into a valley on his way to San Cristóbal. Not saying anything,

Pedro's aunt got up and soon disappeared in the apple trees by the road. Then Pedro disappeared too, down through the red ravine he went, cutting diagonally through corn tall enough to hide him, he came to the stone wall with its hole where a blushing, desperate boy could see women, even his own mother, when they pulled up their skirts and eased down on their legs, and could hear them sigh and then, after a silence, the water hissing out of the haired places where Nacho Panchini? and the older boys claimed babies were let into the world. But his aunt was not there.

When he returned to the hill his mother laughed. Strange things concern women, things a man would not stir himself to find out. Rosha got up and went to sit with her neighbor, and Pedro heard her asking about the man who had gone by, whether it was true he had already asked for a girl.

There were day-long trips to the shrouded mountains with machetes and hatchets. Pedro's job was to gather sticks and to carry a load balanced on his back with a burning line across his forehead. As they walked his mother pointed out plants she might ask him to bring for her food, and likely muddied places to look for larvae to eat. Merely by running a stick under a dark ledge and speaking smoothly, Rosha could make a snake twine onto the stick and come sleepily riding into the light.

All at once she stopped on the path and, slowly raising a hand, pointed out the bright tawny back of a deer, half-hidden in the depths of the trees. Pedro heard a rattle which it seemed could come from no animal's throat, and seeing the deer crash away into the undergrowth, he thought of his father.

She told him why clouds so often swim about the mountains and how the gods inside sit at their table and tell the clouds what fields to go to and give the water.

He found a cleft in rocks which went into the heart of a mountain. Inside were tiny dying geraniums and good-sized, useful candle ends. But when he came running to her with the stubs, she told him to put them back in the cave where he had found them.

She said there was once a time, and she spoke of it with such longing Pedro decided she had lived then, a time when we all could speak plainly to our fathers in the mountains, without candles or other gifts. The people then were different from us, they were never unhappy or hungry and did not wonder today what would happen tomorrow. No one was murdered and there were no witches. Seeing and speaking to our fathers was no secret. But then the people forgot to tell their children, and the bad times came down as fast as night. So now, Rosha said, only the curers can tell us what to do, and even they speak to the gods as poorly as children and get our instructions mixed up, so we are told only enough to stay alive, and not enough to make us as happy as the people used to be.

Pedro also went to the mountains with his father. They brought back baskets of orange and purple flowers to place around the red box. He went when his father begged the house in the center where they could live while he was *pasyon*, and when Antun Díaz tried to borrow money from his neighbors and asked them would they hold him in his work. Some said they would not dare, it was bad luck to serve the replacement for a man who died. That's not true, Pedro's father told them. Our saints love us more when we take up the burden of people who have fallen in the road. In town you've seen the statue: even Jesus Christ carries his little son San Cristóbal on his shoulders, and they are smiling, both of them. Isn't that true, boy?

Pedro did not answer. He was learning what an odd man his father was. Other men did not scratch themselves so much in front of people just because they were itching. His father was drunk from all the rum he gave away, even to the men who said they were too poor or sick to help him. The boy carried the bottles in his own satchel, and learned how to mete out the liquor when his father called for it, first to the men and then the women, and then the sedimented last drops for himself. He did not believe he would ever come to love the burning as the men did.

He was no longer carried, and sometimes returning in the dark to the little house, Pedro could hardly push his legs after one another.

The morning Pedro had to go away with his father, he stood

watching his aunt on her knees grinding corn. She rocked above the stone metate, turning the roller with a backward twist of her wrist at the end of each stroke. The action he had seen thousands of times, memorizing it now finally, as though there would never again be women for him to watch working. His father saying the usual words, *I'm going*, and as though nothing was happening, his mother answering, *Go on then*.

By midday they were in the center. His father took an iron key from his belt and unlocked the door to the dank, decay-smelling borrowed house, though there were three or four places in the crumbled walls where Pedro could have gone in without needing any door. They gathered new thatch to tie into the roof where it leaked the most and brought sticks and mud to fill the biggest gaps in the walls. They slept there and the mice and lizards moved out.

In Tzajalemel it had been Rosha who stirred at dawn, but in the center Pedro had to get himself up and feel through the white ashes for eyes of coal and put what he found under new wood shreds and blow until he brought about a flame.

His father bought their tortillas, which had less taste than the ones Rosha made. He invited the old men who taught him the work to come and see his black bull, and to try the liquor he had gotten to see if it was powerful enough. When he asked them to stay and eat, they sat down and waited for the woman who would fix the meal to come.

At last the boy settled himself by the fire and rewarmed the tortillas, remembering what he could of his mother's actions. Since his father forgot other food, Pedro went every day to hillsides above the center and picked the whip-stemmed green onions Rosha had taught him to gather. When he had the meal ready he mixed boiling water with cold, tested it and then passed the bowl to his father. The men dipped their hands full and splashed their faces and Antun pushed the bowl back to his son.

After they had eaten, the old man named Mesha who taught his father the prayers looked for a long time at the boy kneeling uncomfortably on the floor. He belched softly and said, It's good you know how to take care of other people, for then you must know how to take care of yourself.

Though he had passed all the cargos and could have gone about in the special clothes, Mesha chose to wear old ragged things. His round hairless face was often dirty, and most people paid little attention to him. But the other past-officials listened when he decided to talk. They believed that because Mesha had devoted his whole life to the saints he had been rewarded with a childish purity of sight, the ability to receive every day with a balance of love and fresh excitement. It was said that he grinned so constantly because he might hurt himself if he laughed.

On Sundays Antun Díaz took his son and went to the great hollow church to pray to the saints standing against the walls swaddled in their clothes and their ribbons, and to peer at himself in the mirrors which hung from their bodies.

Once when they were going home toward the wet dusk and the big empty peaked house, Pedro said, My mother told me the church was built in the good time before people had to work.

What else did she tell you? Antun asked.

The god, San Juan, came from the mountain and saw this place, this valley, and decided to stay with us. So he clucked and the stones came to him like chickens when you have corn for them, and the church was made. And San Juan took the light away for three days so what he was doing would not scare the people.

At the stream which crossed the path, Antun said, Try not to believe everything she says to you. She is an outsider with odd ideas of how things happened here. Look—and Antun separated his chamarra under his arm and lifted his cotton shirt, revealing to his son a wrinkled line of scar crossing his back. Before this church, Antun said, there was an older, smaller one. When I was your age the priest came and called for the people and when we came he told us our saints were not happy to be living in a house so small, and we had to work to make the big place they have now. And when we wouldn't work, they kept us locked in the old church and beat us on the back with whips.

At dawn on the day his father took the cargo, Pedro was

up first and had a fire started. Going outside to urinate, he saw scurrying up through the valley's cotton bright mist two women, jostling pots and bundles. Water ran from their hair and one of them had a child. There was hardly a greeting, the women went inside and went to work, so when Antun Díaz turned over and opened his eyes at last, he found his Rosha by the fire warming food, her sister bending into the work of grinding corn on the metate, and his soot-faced smaller son set crosslegged and doleful in the path of the smoke.

Pedro watched his mother putting on the wool overdress with the bands of red at the neck and the red circles, the wife's costume Antun had commissioned for her even when he thought she would not come. She did what was expected, went behind the new *pasyon* and his helpers, kneeled in the spitting rain with the women she did not know at all the crosses where they prayed, a river of babble, for the strength and grace to serve their year without giving offense. In the pine sweet gloom of the church where the prickling harp music played and they passed the first night on their knees, Rosha was present. The other wives' hair was carefully washed and braided, and they lifted their new skirts when they crossed water or mud. Rosha marched through the days dead-eyed, unconcerned. She worked, she made the meals for Antun's disreputable and drunken helpers, but furtively, as though she was stealing, with the shamed look of a girl being married too young, and for money.

Antun, daily offering his life and his strength to the saints, being for them the best he could, and drunk all the time, was pleased just to have her here, because she was a necessary figure in the pattern, because the old men said the *pasyon* must have a wife to serve with him.

There is a kind of man who always buys the shiniest tool. He never thinks to test the world, or that a hoe blade might get special polish because it broke in the forge and was repaired. Men who do not judge the inside of things.

But the boy knew differently, Juan Tushim said. He knew it would have been better for all of them if his mother had stayed in Tzajalemel. He knew, even then, that it was wrong for her to be forced to worship saints she did not love.

Yet Pedro was also carried along by it. Twenty years later he told his own son, I thought the time of noise and joy for the whole world had by chance begun when I was seven and came to the center, and that it would continue forever. I knew then what butterflies know, and moths, when they come from sleep into life.

He himself slept in the day and then for whole nights bobbed along in the wake of his father in the bright red suit unlike what anyone else wore. They went always preceded by a drum and a shrill flute. In a stranger's house Antun told jokes and the people laughed, and then after a while they handed Pedro something to eat or drink, saying, We've filled ourselves, but there is so much we can give what's left away to the babies! He drank his first real coffee and ate his first bread, a sourdough roll with sugar glistening on it which came from San Cristóbal.

In February came a day when the plaza filled with more people than Pedro had ever seen before. Men dressed like ladino soldiers in black coats with red stripes and high-peaked hats covered with fur came dancing down through the crowd, clearing their way with small whips. They were called *maš*, these men, and children half-believed they were devils and ran yelling from them. The *maš* had with them, heavily tied with ropes, Antun Díaz's famous black bull.

Then the officials in their hats and ribbons came out of the church carefully bearing what looked at first to Pedro like a coffin. But when he wormed in closer, he saw it was a great polished log with a long slit. Two men sat down to it and when they hit it with round sticks the sound echoed around the valley deeper than a powder explosion. Pedro started and then laughed at himself because he knew of such a drum's existence, his father had told him there was a drum which spoke with the voice of the earth.

Its resonance silenced the crowd. The bull raised its head, eyes wide and white, and bellowed to the drum as it would to its own kind. It was set free by the *maš* and the officials moved toward it across the open space in a slowshuffling line. For all the excitement he felt, Pedro was also disappointed because he could not see his father's red in that wall of black-dressed men.

The animal seemed about to charge the approaching officials, but then it swung away toward the crowd. In the white clear light the bull was like a dark hole, a center, as the sun sometimes becomes in the sky. There was a hushing sound from the crowd and Pedro, turning, saw the bull racing toward the line and the men already falling away before it, and magically his father in the red waiting, laughing and drunk, and still. The bull ran for him alone then and the people gasped at their endangered *pasyon* and the bull, at his father's chest, barely pricked the cloth and then veered off to the left.

All through the afternoon, while the drum boomed beneath them, the men chased the bull and were pursued by it. One or two were scraped by its horns. The dust rose from the plaza so by the end of the day from the hills above the valley it looked as though a fire had burned in the center. Toward night the bull was brought down and held, its black mottled with white froth, and in the odd silence the people watched while their *pasyon* slit its throat. Still thrashing, the bull was bled and, in deep longing moans, it died. Great earthen pots had been set to boil in the yard outside the *pasyon's* house, and by morning there was a cup of meat and chile broth for all of the crowd which had waited out the freezing night to have it.

Sometime in the dark the *pasyon* came across his son sitting with his head in his arms crying. Antun asked him why, and Pedro said he had been afraid.

There was no need, his father said. We were only showing the saints our courage. When we are all right, the best men we can be, and honest to them, they will not let us be harmed, because then we are like favorite children. They spoke to me today.

He was surprised the next morning when Rosha told him he would be going to Tzajalemel with her. The great drum was already sounding across the valley and his father sleepily tangling himself into the red clothes. Go on, he said, she'll need a man with her.

They had traveled three long valleys away from the center before Pedro could no longer hear the liquid constant voice of the great drum. And even then, as they neared Tzajalemel, he thought he could still hear it from time to time, like the sudden single throbbing of the heart when something frightens us and the life inside us jumps up to join the life outside. The day had an endless light, the sun Our Father hovered above the thin clouds motionless, and Pedro saw himself and his little family as small animals in a milky opaque bottle, watched by great interested outside things.

They stopped near their house so Rosha could dig herself some of the red earth the women of Tzajalemel use to make their pots. At home she built a fire and formed a small clay figure of a man and baked it dry. Pedro took little Salvador into the patio and played with him while the women worked.

After his brother was asleep, Rosha set up a row of little black candles in the corner where her husband had kept his altar. She laid her dried clay figure on a bed of pine needles and then with her sister kneeling beside her, she began to recite.

Eyes tearing from the smoke hanging in the air Pedro sat in a low chair with his hands clasped between his legs. He had thought all day the sky was going to crack open and the sun finally appear, but now harsh wind was driving the rain around his house. He saw they were in currents of water, moving, but more slowly than the host of scabrous winged black things, horned *pukuh* and devils from the mountains which the wind curled and blew in circles and eddies about his house. His mother speaking sweetly to the owner of the earth, and Pedro saw a man fat and mustached and sweaty red like a ladino, pushing the devils at them on his foul wind. But when Rosha pleaded with him, he kept his flock moving so no harm came to the little people inside the house. His mother's voice coming and going, calling them to her and keeping them from entering. Rosha cajoled and begged from them what we, only poor human beings, need.

She gave Pedro a turtle shell with beans or pebbles inside and told him to sit beside her. He believed the little clay doll dressed in a tatter of wool was his father lying sick and in danger, ready for death and the black bull, and he added the merciless steady grind of the rattle to the attempt to pass the man through the danger. Antun Díaz standing between two great upraised things, one black all over and moving as water, the other also black but whitefaced and static, hard and unattainable as the calm above a sheer cliff.

They were outside kneeling in the mud by the little cross with the pine branches whipping about it, Pedro still thumping the rattle against his leg, rain hitting him and wind pulling him one way then back another and his mother pounding the wet earth with her fist, begging them to come and make the man want her little sister, and Our Mother oddly complacent in the black sky, her face turned full on them through the cold rain, when another figure in black, still in the middle of the ones which changed and came and went flapping by, appeared before them. Not speaking, it went past them into the little house. Pedro turned, waking, in time to see his father's face grow cold and to hear his aunt cry out as Antun's foot came down on the little clay man lying on the pine needles. Then his father went away in the dark.

At first it seemed there was no one home. But then Pedro saw the *pasyon* sitting in the darkest corner, alone, in only his white shirt and cotton drawers.

Can I come in?

There was no answer. Pedro hung in the doorway a while, and at last went up to his father slowly, as to a frightened animal and bowed, hair in his face, and waited for the hand to release him. One of the man's feet grasped the other, self containing self, like the feet of the saint in the church which hung from a cross nearly naked and unloved, though people said because of the cross he must be an Indian. Several times Pedro sensed his father's glowing hand rising, but it did not touch his forehead or come to hit him, and settled again in the man's lap.

You should do what you want, the boy said.

Antun Díaz took his boy's chin in his hand and raised his head. And what is that? he asked.

You were going to hit me. You should do that if you want.

His father's eyes glistened. Did she send you back?

I have been wanting to come a week now.

But she sent you finally?

Yes.

She knows how sick I am, Antun sighed. Of course she has her ways of knowing that.

Juan Tushim said that in later years the people in Tzajalemel told the tale differently.

One day when Pedro Díaz Cuscat was only five or six, his father came upon him at the red ravine where the women get their clay, and found the boy was playing with five little figures of saints. Antun Díaz was afraid of the saints his son had made and ordered him to break them. When Pedro did as he was told, the clay pieces turned into sparrows and flew away into the sky.

And Antun Díaz, who was *pasyon* that year, was so terrified his boy had to help him home to his bed.

But then, the people say, the son, who was still just a tiny boy, had the dream which told him he had the power to bring frightened souls back into the body. And he worked the cures on his father and returned him to life, he made his father strong enough to dance with the bull at Carnaval and do all the devotions a *pasyon* must.

But even his son could not help him when Antun Díaz had his wife again and again during fiestas and disobeyed all the laws. So, the people say, the guardians warned him and tried to beat his sins out of his poor body, and in the end the saints even came to him and told him to stop, but it was a sickness in him, it was like telling your dog to stay home when your neighbor's bitch is in heat. And it was for his errors, the people believe, that Antun Díaz died.

For a while, as though moving backward in time, the boy returned to the life he had shared with his father before. He cooked and the others came with the flute and the drum, and Pedro would dress the *pasyon* and stay with him in the processions. Antun Díaz still drank when he had to, but the liquor made him burn, his neck and ears grew red at once, and he sang and danced before the time was right, and threw himself on the ground and hit his chest calling out the Spanish name of God as priests do. His lips protruded and he ate the dirt off the floor until he vomited.

Thinking Díaz had gone deeper into his work than they

had, the others began to imitate him. They became so drunk on the first day of a fiesta that the rest of the time they lay about in the mud, singing and rolling like pigs. Then Mesha and the rest of the guardians had to clean them and carry them to the church to do their work, and tell them that the saints did not love these strange outbursts of the *pasyon.*

When he lost the strength to stand on his legs, Antun ordered Pedro to lock the doors and sit beside him in the dark, and they shivered together when the man thought he heard the music coming for him. At times it was only dreaming, and at times the others were really there calling to him, and he sang back to them, O San Juan my flower, San Sebastían and Santa Rosha my flowers, forgive me now, it was in your service I got drunk, in your work I lost my force, so forgive me now, and they would leave him alone.

Great pulpy growths appeared in his throat so he could not even swallow or speak. Pedro washed his father's thinning body in hot water with salt. Perhaps he felt in the crook of the man's arm to know what the blood said was missing, but Pedro did not have the skill to make his father well.

They came again for Antun and rattled the barred doors and would not take the son's excuses. Then they heard what sounded like the *pasyon's* voice, great and hollow, reciting the drunk's prayer, and they went away, not knowing it had been Pedro speaking into the mouth of one of the big pots his father had borrowed, but not believing quite that they had heard the man himself. And thinking some spirit had possessed the house, they went to their guardians to ask for ways to liberate the poor man.

Pedro hardly escaped the house. He had almost no desire to leave his father. But on a market day, it was in Holy Week although he did not know it, he thought he saw his mother going by on the road. So after he had fed his father he went down into the plaza to find her. The church bells rang and there was a crowd, yet no officials appeared. Everything was hot and burning to the boy's narrowed indoor eyes.

He went into the crush of people in the churchyard, but could not find Rosha. Then, pushed along forward to the wall, he came face to face with a white man in a black dress. He had thought only animals in the moment of dying could be so afraid and possessed, but as he stared at the priest, he saw what must have been in his own eyes when his father had crushed the clay figure on the pine bed. The man's black robe was dusty and frayed at the bottom and he smelled. Beside him, nailed to the church wall, was a gigantic cloth filled with colors and what Pedro finally saw were pictures.

Through an interpreter, the Dominican was explaining the canvas to the crowd. On a river floated two canoes filled with brown people, Indians like yourselves! the priest called out in Spanish. In one boat the people knelt, looking up and holding crosses which gleamed gold in the sunlight. Above them floated ladino women with white doves' wings. These people, the happy ones, are going to heaven! the Indian interpreter said, pointing to the whited sky. And Pedro knew it was true, their boat was rising from the green river into a blue mist where a very large and important ladino with arms outstretched and eyes flaming like the priest's waited for them. Pedro thought the man must be the owner of the earth and the people were going to be his slaves and pay for their sins. But the interpreter said this great man, this *one* god, loved the people who loved the church, the people who made themselves stones for the god to walk on.

Pedro could tell the people in the other boat were celebrating the saints, bottles were going around as busily as bottles travel in a fiesta. One man was so well drunk he was only held in the boat by a friend who had grabbed onto his foot. A man without any clothes was lying between a woman's legs, their red mouths were stretched together and their eyes were wide and happy. At first Pedro did not notice the creatures with the teeth and the scaly red wings dragging the second boat down to the bottom of the canvas. There a fire burned and huge beasts the boy had seen only in dreams devoured men.

These, the priest thundered, these are the unsaved who ignore the church, the animals who refuse the water of baptism, who anger the dear patron San Juan with drinking and dancing and copulation in Jesus Christ's sanctified temple!

Padre Cresencio was already an old man in 1845, but his vigor had not left him, and the interpreter could hardly keep up with him. Luckily, the priest just then paused and stared at the hungry, silent people. He pulled from inside his cassock a cloth bag, dipped into it and produced a handful of rosaries made of cheap black beads with thin gleaming crosses. But! he shouted, but God has eternal forgiveness for you, and for those who come now to be baptised, or if baptised once to cast out their latest sins, there will be these things!

As he was speaking, a force in the crowd, perhaps a longing for such simple keys to salvation, pushed the frontmost Indians at the priest, slammed him back against the wall and ripped the canvas he spread his arms to protect down onto his head. Seeing what they had done, the people pulled back and ran. And Cresencio, his satchel and rosaries stolen, got to his feet and began rolling up his torn canvas, almost as satisfied with the zeal which the savages had exhibited today as he would have been with another massive, disorderly and insincere baptism.

Running, Pedro found that when he had fallen he had reached out and grasped, and in his hand was a small shining cross with three black beads attached to it. He did not tell his father what he had seen, but he strung the cross on a cord which fit easily into the groove his umbilicus had cut permanently into the flesh of his neck.

The ladino month of May came and then June. Though Antun Díaz never went outside except after dark to relieve himself, and Pedro only for water and food at times of day when no one else was around, like mice who live in the bowels of human houses, they knew what a bad dry year it was turning out to be. In the night Pedro held his cross and prayed for his father and for the rain to come.

The officials no longer bothered to stop for the *pasyon*, the drum and flute approached the house and passed it and they forgot. Life shut down on them, man and boy. They had no concern for it, no interest. They felt the darkening madmen experience, and men who lose their wives too late to seek out others.

When it came during the fiesta of San Juan, the real arrival of the music and the sharp rapping at the door, Antun whispered Don't answer! Don't go!

But they beat the door and would not leave, calling *Pasyon* we know you're there! until the bar at last gave way and light flooded the room. The *maš* in their black uniforms and furred hats, their faces whitened with fireash and muskets in their arms, and women in wide shiny ladina skirts wearing masks with big red lips and gold teeth showing, came and found Antun Díaz. They dragged him out from where he had been hiding behind the huge pot and propped him up like a scarecrow in the light at his doorway.

Now what's been going on with our *pasyon*? they said.

Here, I'll show you, said one of the soldiers, and he grabbed a ladina around the waist and pulled her to him, his mouth open, and flattened himself against her mask, his body rocked against hers. The woman responded with deep pleased laughter. Doing *this* with his—what's her name? who's the wife?

Rosha, said a voice from the crowd.

Yes, with his Rosha, the one with the chilies in her hole, all the time they do this, until they're sick of it, burned out inside and hurting. And the saints are sad because—listen to me!—because this one made his promises to them, but all he knows how to do is *this*! And the *maš* pumped away again at the woman and knocked her mask so it lifted and Pedro could see at last she wasn't a ladina at all, but one of the *maš* his father had fed and given presents.

At last, having performed the mocking ritual with all the vehemence it could hold, their anger began to leave them. Perhaps they were cooled by the actual sight of the ruined man. After all, he was still their *pasyon* in name at least and had killed his bull for them, so even the angriest and drunkest of them were afraid to kick at him too much. They left him.

Pedro dragged his father back inside and found a way to close up the broken doors with rope. Through the rest of the day the house was besieged, rocks were thrown against it and people came to repeat the terrible things the *maš* had said.

He heard the knocking in the night and the gentle old voice, but Pedro did not move from where he lay beside his father. The door was tried. Then there was a light outside, a candle, and a knife or the blade of a machete forced through the slit and the rope slowly sawed in two.

The man who found them huddled in the corner was not a stranger, and not an enemy, and even a man so long in fevers that boneache had overtaken him had to believe that whatever Mesha was going to do to him, even if it was his own death which fluttered busily in the old man's mind, was for the best. Antun allowed the old guardian and the son who had been his comfort to pull him upright and dress his battered, disjunctive frame a last time in the red clothing. He let them lead him and carry him a last time down through his town. It was midnight, the change into San Juan's very day, and the valley smelled of burned powder from the blasts discharged in His honor. It smelled of the excrement of three thousand people and animals who had come to see, and of the dangerous dryness, and of the fires built by those who had found no place in the churchyard or on a ladino's porch to sleep.

Tiny deaths of fire and powder smells in a deep night when clouds which pass over us without giving water are edged in gold by the moon behind like priest's garments. Almost exactly twenty-four years later, Pedro Díaz Cuscat stood on a rock on a hill dividing two valleys, and gazed down at the white regular city of San Cristóbal in one and then turned back and for a while tried to count the fires he had allowed his soldiers to make for themselves against his lieutenants' advice, nearly a thousand fires and five or six thousand men, and Pedro then would remember the night Mesha took his father to shrive him.

They went out beyond the village to a great pile of gray rock in the middle of a pasture. Mesha searched until he found the spot, saying to Pedro, You understand, the holiest places are the ones that are never talked about and never dressed up as the churches are and only visited at the dangerous times. Together they set the *pasyon* on his knees, skinned off the red shirt and then, without any summoning such as his predecessor used or his successor would feel it necessary to introduce, Mesha told the saints the man would speak now. He prodded Antun.

What do I do? the man whispered.

Oh go ahead and confess! Mesha said happily. Tell them what brought you here, to this danger.

How?

As you have been taught to do it.

His voice silky and small, regular beating like the insistence of birds' wings, Antun Díaz began calling the names of the saints to carry him through it, confessing his pride and his poverty honestly now, the tricks he had played to make people help him, the promises and debts in his darkened heart he never meant to repay, the many days San Pedro, San Mateo, dear little Santa Rosha, in my prayers I was not speaking to you but so my neighbors would *hear* me speaking to you. As he proceeded, head bent to the ground so Pedro did not see the tears or the blackening of his father's face, but could only hear the words rattling out between the uncontrollable gates of his father's mouth, then Mesha took from under his old chamarra the supple strips of leather tipped with glinting shards of glass and nails and swept it easily over the hunched back, kindly urging *More!* Antun Díaz confessed that he *had,* on drunken nights, several of them, climbed on his wife when it was prohibited, Forgetting, not myself, asleep, devils taking me, he cried, and then *Yes* my fault too, knowing my little wife and what magic she owns but only good magic, San Pablo, San Pedro, magic to make some boy want her ugly sister, after all who *made* her ugly and skinny so no one would want her? and the guardian still urging *More* and allowing the scourge to curl around the man's chest, catch and, returning, tear strips of skin from his back and sides, and the boy could not see his father's face and found in Mesha's no anger, no fright. He was the first man Pedro had ever encountered who did not fear dying.

At dawn they dragged Antun Díaz back across the valley, taking hidden paths now with the *pasyon,* for in their excitement people at a fiesta are up earlier than even roosters and often have called each other awake and eaten and washed themselves and readied for the great day before Our Father has seen fit to throw light on the valley's western heights.

In the late afternoon Mesha was standing by one of the pole platforms where the officials sat drunkenly waving their flower-print flags and pulling each other back when they seemed in danger of falling out. The old man, grinning as though this were his first fiesta, worked away at a tiny green ear of corn someone had given him. Even so soft a piece gave him trouble, for his few remaining teeth wobbled like ducks. A small boy tugged at his chamarra and Mesha looked down.

He's dead now, the boy said.

Is he? Mesha could not quite remember who the child was. Where are you from, boy? he asked.

Tzajalemel.

Mesha sighed. Oh. So far away. He tried to hand the half-gnawed sweet corn to the boy. Do you want this? But Pedro would not take it.

They watched the officials' perilous descent from the platform with their jugs and flags and flowers. When they were all safely down, Mesha said, Now we can go, and with arms tight to his chest, he gently pushed his way out of the crowd. The boy stayed close behind him.

Pedro waited in the yard while Mesha went into his own house. There was a girl in a new, heavily embroidered wool blouse and skirt sitting weaving, her loom strapped to her back. She was perhaps fourteen and her face was long, her nose thin. On her head was a shawl neatly folded to shade her eyes. It had bright orange and red tassels which hung before her face like flowers or candles. She knew she was pretty. Calmly she reached into a basket beside her and pulled out a piece of ladino bread with sugar on it, and when she handed it to Pedro and he had put it to his mouth, he began to cry.

Mesha came to the door carrying a white sack which he gave to the boy. Cocked on his head was a very old official's hat, half the brim broken and hanging down over his nose, the ribbons blanched nearly colorless and frayed. Tzajalemel? Mesha asked. So far! He started for the slope behind the house, adding But so pretty there by the river. When he clucked softly, an old swaybacked gray mule came up to him from across the yard and he took the tiny gnawed corn from under his chamarra to feed the animal. Then without a word to the pretty girl or a rope for the mule, Mesha set off for the *pasyon's* house.

He listened carefully at Antun's mouth and held his limp arm, fingers pressed in the crook of the elbow, then he stripped off the red pants and, using the man's blanket to cover him, he bound the body with rope. He called Pedro and they carried the man outside and draped him over the back of the mule. Moving in the darkened house surely as if he lived there, Mesha collected some of Antun Díaz's things and wrapped them in a bundle. This he strung on one side of the mule, and his own sack on the far side for balance. It was near twilight when they started north and the road was filled with howling men going home from the fiesta, their light wives toddling along behind with the tired children. Mesha ordered his animal to go on ahead and told Pedro to stay well back. For all its age and blindness the mule picked a careful way through the families right in the path beside their fallen men, settled to wait for them to wake up and be able to go on. They sailed like honesty through the quick world. When they passed puffing over the ridge and entered pine woods and the blue of the evening, time of the first strong stars, Mesha whistled to the mule and told it to slow down, and then said to the boy, Stay by me and give me your shoulder, because these parts you know and I have forgotten. And they went on, Mesha leaning heavily on Pedro with his eyes sometimes shut and his mind resting or asleep.

The time to Tzajalemel for a man traveling alone is three hours, but it was well after midnight when Mesha and the boy and the gray mule reached the closed, black house under the brow of the hill. There were not even dogs to wake those inside. Mesha sent Pedro over the stile. The boy hesitated and the old man said Go on! go on! and before Pedro could knock the old man heard the wood bar being pulled back. Mesha considered any time appropriate for a lesson, so he said You see, my boy? and Rosha opened up for them.

Since there were no other mourners or helpers, Mesha ordered the dead man's little family through the night, allowing nothing or at least no time for their sadness. Pedro was sent to gather laurel. Mesha took salt from his own bag, tested the water with his finger and tasted it before he sat down to wash the dead man. When he saw the stripes of red in the sallow skin he shook his head and his eyes watered. Once the body was laid out, he took the *pasyon's* red suit and his ribbons and necklaces and dressed him in them and, kneeling beside him, began the prayers to release Antun Díaz from his office.

A moment later he stopped and got up. You! he said to Rosha, who was crying, her head to the floor beside the body, are you going to let him starve at last? get his food ready woman! and burn it well because that's how they like it there, though I don't know why. And put something sweet in for him, a piece of sugar or whatever there is. Do you have a small comb of honey? that would be good.

Rosha and her sister had never heard of putting out sweets for the dead to eat. Then the old man in the patched clothing decided he must dress to pray the *pasyon* from his work and pulled from his sack a black cloak which even in the near dark they could tell was the finest, thickest dyed wool. Mesha put his battered hat back on his head and returned to reciting.

Toward dawn he had spent both bottles he had in his sack, so he gave Pedro money to go and bring more. When the boy came back, Mesha was gone and Rosha and his aunt were asleep where they had been sitting. Pedro stared at the familiar face lying before him and in the light of the remaining candle he saw his father not gray and dead, but as he had been, laughing, one day when they were at the river and a fish escaped through his hands.

Pedro clenched his hands and apologized to his father because, though he felt the pull, somewhere on the mountain path stumbling down rocks after Mesha, his own heart had decided that he would not go along.

They woke just an hour before sunset to find the old man still missing, and Rosha felt they were now as they should be, two poor abandoned women and two useless boys with a man to bury and no help.

Then they heard him at the foot of the hill. Woman! you'll have to come down here now! Rosha went running out to find Mesha standing proudly beside a new pine coffin. They carried it up to the house and hurried to get the body inside. Mesha put the packages of Antun's things in beside him. Pedro got the blackened, burnt tortillas and the bowls for his father's journey and placed them in the box.

Then standing in the patio were two strong young men, strangers to Tzajalemel. They were telling Mesha, Now look, old fellow, where is this work you want us to do? And he was

saying to them it was only an hour away and they would have
to dig quickly. Then they noticed the raw box and backed off a
little and said, Now look, we are just passing through here, and
our wives are waiting for us in Peteh and maybe you had better
get some of his friends to do it, because this is going to take a
lot of our time. But Mesha said, Whose time? Our time, they
said, backing up a little more. And Mesha said, Who gave it to
you? And the men didn't get a chance to answer because Mesha
was saying, Even a year you know, just one year in seven. Or
what about every year? Even every year, as some of us decided
to serve, and every day of every year, isn't too much, you know.
After all that's what *they* are carrying without a complaint, as
you know. And then he was asking them where the musicians
were and the young man said they hadn't heard about musicians
and Mesha, now guiding them out of the little house with the
closed box and clucking to them and leading them down the
hill with Pedro and Rosha behind and then her sister and little
Salvador last since his soul had the greatest longing to go with
his father's and must be shielded, and then the blind gray mule,
on down the hill they went, Mesha saying sensibly, But since I
have given them the money and the liquor they must be coming,
for after all he was our *pasyon* and did the work in our service
as well as he could, slowly, go slowly now, here's a gully, so
the musicians must know there has to be music for him, such a
jolly man, he loved music and before he got sick he could
dance! the best!

Going along talking until they reached a milky silent waterhole with a grove of trees buoyed by lightning bugs in the
sunset where Mesha insisted they stop and pray and, opening
the coffin, took a crumpled geranium leaf from the bottom of
his sack and dipped it full of water which he poured into the
dead man's mouth to quench his thirst, and there the musicians,
three squat brothers none larger than the homemade harp one
carried banging along with him, caught up with the little party
and accepted some drinks to prime them and then they began
sprinkling the air with their sweet biting sounds. But by now
Mesha was all hurry again and helping the strong young
men to shoulder their burden once more as though whoever

called this wasteful halt wasn't himself and saying how they *must* get the *pasyon* in the ground quickly now, for it is one thing to go this first time into the new world as innocent and defenseless as a soft baby riding the gold path the sun lays for you across the new country, and something very different to wake up there when the day is well along and Our Father has withdrawn himself high into the depths of his sky to contemplate his work and all the people there, strangers to the new one, are up and about their business and perhaps not so eager to take some new baby in their arms, so hurry, please, if it won't be too much for you, he said to his little pack of people.

The field, in grass as small and smooth as moss, sloped to a ridge, to what from the distance looked like a stand of spindly pines, some barely green and clinging to life, the others dry and dead. The dry ones were crosses, three or four times a man's height and grayed by weather, and the others were trees with the bottom boughs shorn off. Mesha chose the spot and the young men went straight to work digging a hole. The liquor and the music, and perhaps the soothing voice of the old man who said only what we all know but may forget from time to time, had changed the men from Peteh too, they cried as they dug and wiped dirt onto their shining faces and recognized themselves in the dead *pasyon*. For a while in all the world they cared only that he be put on the road with the speed and good wishes and small helps the living can give the dead, they applied themselves to the work as we sometimes can, in the hope that some last day some stranger will return us the favor. And Mesha prayed with his eyes open to the quickly departing sun.

The hole was ready, the coffin settled in with the *pasyon* facing the west and his new road. The men from Peteh and the musicians had taken their handfuls of dirt to throw in, when Pedro stopped them. Even the old man was surprised, for the children had been made to sit well back for their own safety, and Mesha had forgotten them. Pedro jumped down into the hole and, standing on the box, gently called to his little brother.

Mesha whispered, Hurry, hurry, the sun is going, but Pedro waited while Salvador scrambled to his feet and came to the hole, and then lifted him down in and said, Now stamp on it.

The little boy did, once. Harder! Jump! There was a cracking in the wood and a hollow sound. Rosha reached out to snatch her baby away, but Mesha stopped her. He was grinning, and spit was running from his mouth. No, let him go, the old man said. What the boy does is right, of course.

3

"Why jumping up and down on the coffin?"

"For the good of the baby himself. His soul had to make it clear to his father's not to come back to the house the next day to pester him and promise him sweet things."

It was the grandson, sitting with a little bottle held upright between his feet, who answered me. We were looking down on the dry yellow valley and the center, recuperating from being drunk in the night by having a few small drinks in the early morning.

"That man Mesha lived in that house down there," Juan Tushim pointed. "You see where the road dips?"

To me all of the houses looked the same.

As though he heard my mind, Juan added, "Well, not the same if you want, because every piece of straw and lump of clay and, after all this time, even the beams have been replaced. But they tell my grandson in the school the same is true of your body every seven years, yet you call yourself the same person you were, don't you?"

The night before, drunk and lost in the caves the old man created by his talk, I had fixed myself on his grandson's face, I had seen him as the boy speaking from behind the jars, and I had known that, whatever the story of Cuscat could ever come to mean to me, it would still mean more to the boy. When Juan spoke of little Pedro pouring drinks the first time for the men, I might picture it, but the experience itself could not be replayed in my mind, or yours, as it would be in the boy's.

And as we traveled farther on, Juan became to my mind all

of the story's old men, and I was somewhere aside, the ladinos fat and thin, evil and good.

"The boy came from Tzajalemel to see Mesha whenever he liked," Juan said. "The pretty girl's name was Augustina, and no one believed she was Mesha's daughter."

Pedro would find them under the blanket together, and the old man would sit on the side of the bed in his much-patched cotton drawers and pull the skirt down over her thighs with the distracted concern a man may give to burrs in his dog's coat while he is talking to you.

Sometimes he stayed at Mesha's house. In the dark lying on the floor, he told how he had cleared and planted his father's hillside, but only half of the corn had appeared above the ground, and what did was stunted. His aunt and his little brother tried to help him, but they got nothing in return for their work.

And your mother, Mesha asked, where is she?

Pedro took a long time to answer, and when he spoke his voice was very low. She goes away into Larrainzar.

What does she do?

I think she cures the people there.

And does she bring back money?

A little. Or sometimes things to eat.

I see.

Mesha was about to say more when they heard noise outside in the night, men and women calling to him and a guitar playing. Pedro got up and peered out through the slit in the door. There were pine torches and the boy could see thirty or more dark figures waiting. Mesha was telling Augustina to hurry and dress and make a fire, and himself stashing debris and clothes away under the pole bed. The people outside pleaded that they were cold and over his shoulder Mesha suggested that they go home then. But at last he let them in, two other *pasaros* in black, the suitor's family, the suitor himself and his friends carrying gifts, loads of bananas and oranges, cloth sacks of coffee and chocolate beans, and big crocks of liquor.

Mesha gave what chairs he had to the elder and honored men, he refused their drinks and looked as angry as a man who

ys smiled could. When they complimented his girl he said
ow sorry he was to tell them they were badly deceived. Worth-
less, Mesha said. Bad. She's too young. She speaks to any man
who looks at her. Your son couldn't keep her at home with a
rope. And she can't weave. Look at this! He showed them the
bottom of his chamarra, a garment obviously as old as Augustina
was.

Mesha did very badly. He cried as he was supposed to and
begged them not to take a sick old man's only help from him,
but when the officials explained the boy would be his son and
make his corn for him, when they mentioned he was strong,
Mesha touched the boy's rock brown calf and would not stop
stroking it, and accepted the big glass of rum they held out
to him.

The girl hardly did any better. When it came time for her to
say she was stupid and could not leave Mesha because she was
devoted to him, she looked at her potential husband as though
she was going to devour him and laughed so hard she had to
cover her face with her shawl.

And Pedro, seeing all this, thought of kittens who scrap and
hiss all day and then at twilight curl up so you cannot tell where
one ends and the other begins, and lick each other's fur. The
long haggling and the speechmaking were only ways for Mesha
and the boy's family to say how pleased they were, what a
beautiful and obedient treasure the girl and how honorable and
fine the husband-to-be.

Many other times the boy came, together with the couple who
spoke for him and more gifts. And Pedro saw Augustina growing more lovely the more she heard it said, for the one time in
life she would hear the words themselves, how valued she was,
and as the time approached when the boy would come to live
with her and work for Mesha.

"Often when he came now he had his little brother with him,"
Juan Tushim said, "for there was no one in Tzajalemel to look
after the smaller child. And they would be told Mesha was here
or there on his business. People knew Pedro by then, when they
saw him on the path in some far part of our town, they thought
of him as the old man's dog or his shadow hurrying to catch up
with Mesha and would give him directions before he asked.

He had learned the old man's smile, and some people believed he was Mesha's child, because Mesha was pleased by him as a man who was thought himself dried up will be with a late son.

"Looking for Mesha, this Pedro learned all of Chamula, not only the roads, but the shortcuts a boy will find for himself because boys are in a hurry and have less time than men for the pleasures of meeting and passing on the way. He came to know where people would gather, about the market in Katishtik on Thursdays, and where at the river in Mitontic they met on a Friday in May to bless their crosses. You know," Juan said, "in that time all the ladinos traveled through our land on horses, and they thought we were slow because we went on foot. But a man on horseback on the road who has to stop to light his cigar would be surprised if he knew the Indian who kissed his hand in Chenalhó in the morning may be the same Indian who leads his horse into the stable in San Cristóbal that night."

According to Juan Tushim, in his old age Mesha no longer made the distinctions most of us draw between our nights and days. He slept when he was tired and traveled when his dreams dictated a journey. And so it was that after a period of a month or more when Pedro had not come to see him, at dawn one day he suddenly appeared in Tzajalemel accompanied only by his feeble gray mule.

Pedro came to the door yawning and rubbing at his eyes and invited Mesha to sit in the disordered little house. Salvador was still asleep. After getting the fire started, Pedro said, She has gone for water. But if you would wait, she will come back soon and then we will eat.

Mesha said he would not stay. He was bound for a place in Chenalhó where they kept an image of the Mother and now (it was toward the end of the white month of December) the women there had been dancing with the Saint and keeping Her company so She would not be lonely, and today She was going to give birth to the Child. I am going, even though I don't know what help a man can be, Mesha said. Will you come?

Pedro was knocking his leg against the bed to wake up Salvador. He told Mesha he had to take his brother outside and carefully, as though Salvador was sick, he helped him pull on a too-small chamarra. After a while Pedro came back in alone and said, Excuse me, but I can't go with you today. My mother told me to stay.

Where is she?

She is working with her neighbor, but she will send us food when it is ready.

And you don't want to help the Baby to be born in Chenalhó?

I can't.

All right. I'm going then, Mesha said.

In the yard, Salvador was just coming back over the fence with a basket in his hand. She can't give us anything, he told Pedro.

Who can't? Mesha asked.

The woman.

Your mother?

No, another woman.

Mesha understood at last. From the bag strapped to his mule he brought out tortillas, two hard-cooked eggs wrapped in a handkerchief and some mottled yellow and black mangoes. Salvador began to eat at once, but Pedro would not touch the food. Mesha watched him for a while, himself sucking from a mango whatever he could get without teeth. A desultory flock of black birds limped through the clear sky, going northward along the path of the river valley.

If you wanted to surprise people and make them believe in you, Mesha said, you could tell them it might rain a little, not tomorrow, but the day after.

I don't want to learn tricks, Pedro said.

You know enough already, is that it? Mesha asked. What were you going to do when your mother didn't come at last?

I was praying that you would go away soon, that's all.

Tricks which will only come out right if you pray are not very good tricks, Mesha said. Now what has made you afraid?

At that moment, not much was left. Mesha had found out what was for Pedro the great remaining secret, how his mother had surrendered her boys and had given in to the pull of the magic life which increasingly drew her back to her own place. Pedro was free then to tell his old friend what had happened when he had gone with Rosha to Larrainzar. Though the pictures he saw as he spoke remained terrible, the story itself no longer hurt him. It was becoming just a story because, with all a ten-year-old's strength, he had closed his mind on it and had willed himself never to see such things again.

She had taken him deep into hotter country where bananas and coffee trees grew, to the place where her uncle lived as a tenant on a ladino's ranch. The house they were led to smelled, and even Pedro was made uneasy by the filth there. Rosha's uncle and his whole family, even the children, sat in chairs with sad, hanging faces. The neighbors who had brought Rosha said that for days none of them had moved, and they could not be made to take food or even water. Fearing for him, the neighbors had finally taken the baby from his mother and given him to a nursing woman. But he was affected too, they said, and had chewed at the woman's breast until it bled. When Rosha was led into the house, the sick people began to shiver and their eyes moved in their heads. She told Pedro that was because whoever had made them sick had done it to get even with her, and because the spirits inside them knew she was the one who was capable of drawing them out of the bodies.

Mesha nodded and smiled while Pedro was telling what he could recall of the prayers Rosha had said and the order of colored candles she lit. Though what curing the old man did was of a different kind, he could admire not only Rosha's knowledge, but her boy's precision in remembering. Then, Pedro said, after a night of it, came the time his mother stood by the bed where she had made her uncle lie, and she named the woman whose jealousy had struck them down and the animal the woman had sent to infect them. Rosha's uncle sat up and his wife and children came awake, alive again, and the man howled and flung himself on the floor, moving blind, nosing into the dirt and eating it. Rosha held onto his trembling body until he became calmer, but it seemed not even all her power could contain the power she had recognized and when her uncle's voice stopped his children's voices began. They howled and tore at their clothes, even the wife, and the pretty daughter climbed on her mother's back and tore into the flesh with her teeth. They crawled outside and rooted in circles, and then one by one they escaped screaming into the early morning and disappeared. The neighbors found them later lying exhausted in muddy riverbottoms and other places pigs go. They were roped and driven still on four legs to the hacienda chapel and the priest.

And you? Mesha asked.

The neighbors told us to run away.

Mesha took Pedro's hands and held them lightly in his own. And for you, he said, the worst of it was that they stopped looking like people. Is that true?

Yes.

You know, Mesha said, God sees all of us as clear glass. We are His bottles and whatever force we are given is pure and true when He puts it inside us. To some, like your mother, He gives more than to others. There is no reason for you to be afraid of the strength, since it is always a gift. But some, and I don't understand why because they are God's children too, turn their force against others. When she takes money for her work, her power turns against herself, and I have never seen anyone able to turn it back.

She only takes money so she can buy us our food.

Mesha sighed, but he knew not to answer people when they spoke to him of necessities. Even Pedro would not yet understand the differences between desires and needs.

That year the Saint had to give birth to Her little Baby without Mesha there to dance and make jokes to ease Her pain, for he was off climbing a mountain somewhere, leaning heavily on Pedro's shoulder for the help which Juan Tushim said Mesha only needed when his boy was with him. They took Salvador along part of the way, until Mesha found a woman with a good face and plump children, and convinced her to take care of the younger one and the gray mule until they came back. Mesha begged her to be especially good to his mule.

Finally, at the top of the mountain, he found a blunt little cave he said would do. They had no candles and Mesha would not light the stubs Pedro found on the ground, but in his leather bag were a few brown sticks of the resin-coated pinehearts used to begin fires and a flintstone and a steel spike. They kneeled together at the cool cavern mouth, Pedro was told to watch the little flames and after a while Mesha began to sing:

We are at the gates, we have come to the mouth and we can, with your help, see across the flames between us and into your land.

Today, just poor men of meat and bones, we will not ask the special favor of coming inside.

Today, only men and afraid, if it pleases you we will just peer inside and look around.

For today we are thinking about ourselves, our arms and legs, and about food for our own bodies.

But another day, if you are pleased to remember us your children and to make us unafraid and to take us by the hand, we would like to come inside.

For we have heard that when you lead us there your land is all real and good. For ourselves alone we would not come, we are not thieves.

If you would carry us and show us our fathers and mothers, how they are doing with you, we would be glad.

If you made us see how we could help our little ones, your flowers, then we would be glad.

We know men who can get across alone, men who take themselves across without your help. But they are thieves in your land and we are not.

We are just poor people who care, not thieves in our land or yours.

If you would bear us, and give us sight, and carry us through, our work will be to make our land here as much like yours as poor men can.

So when you come to visit us you would be happy here, for a day, for a while, and stay again with us.

Afterward Mesha took Pedro to a stream pouring from the mountain and washed his hands and feet in water so cold it woke the boy.

Nearly eight years later, after first Pedro and then Salvador had become students at the seminary of the Merced and dressed as ladinos, one day as they were walking through the streets of San Cristóbal, the older brother suddenly asked the younger if he remembered anything about his father. They were speaking Spanish together for practice.

Once, after you were gone, I came home from some place and my mother showed me a thick-furred dog, Salvador said. She told me a man had brought it as a gift for me, and at first I thought it was my father she meant, because I believed then my father had not died, but only had gone away from me. Then my mother told me the man had said that when I had bad dreams I must hold on to the dog's coat because animals are closer to the heart of things and will carry our fears back into the earth for us, and then I knew the dog came from Mesha. But of my real father I remember only this: I stand holding two things which go up into the air like tree trunks. They are my father's legs. I look up, but I cannot see his face. Then I cry and I want him to pick me up and embrace me, but he does not hear me. You are there and holding my hand and many other people, and he lifts you away from me and I am lost.

Do you have dreams about him? Pedro asked.

Yes. Do you?

I dream about him often and I see his ghost.

And then Pedro thought, But never Mesha's. Why was that? After being swept away into the life at the seminary, he had gone back to Chamula several times. But he had never even passed by to find out if the old man was alive or dead. It did not matter so much. Mesha was one of those who, each time they leave you, go away as though they may well see you tomorrow or perhaps never again in this place.

4

Even though he was sick, Juan Tushim had new cargoholders coming to learn their prayers, and then new mayordomos were taking the clothes of a saint from the ones finishing their year and all the vestments and ribbons and the necklaces of old coins had to be counted in front of him. His house was crowded with people all the time, most days we were drunk, and at last a little sadly he admitted that he would not be able to go on with the story for a while.

So I took a truck to San Cristóbal, to have a bath and satisfy my white man's hunger for red meat, and to wait for Juan Tushim to drift back into calmer waters.

I sat reading at a stone desk under a pine tree in the garden at Na Balom, wondering if at that moment I was the only person alive in the world thinking about Pedro Díaz Cuscat. I was afraid to touch his life, because in no way did it seem to belong to me, and sometimes I was ashamed of my willingness to make up what I did not know. But then maybe tales are not permanent possessions of anyone. For whatever the reason, a story comes to have particular weight for us, its equations are, for a time, our equations. We dream it. And so we bear the story a while, until its burden becomes less.

From the written sources it appeared that Cuscat himself, his life and his character, were of very little importance to the ladino historians of the nineteenth century. Though he led a religious movement which became an insurrection and threatened to destroy them and a society which had endured for over three hundred years, they could only report that Cuscat was an Indian who could write and that he was a fiscál, a town tax collector, in the paraje of Tzajalemel. His motive? he was a charlatan. The cause of the War of the Castes? In their darkness savages become filled with hatred against the light which civilization casts on them, just as owls hate the sun because it blinds them. About the lives of these savages, the color of their clothing, there is almost nothing.

The ladino historians, conservative amateurs probably beset with teaching schedules and children yelling in the courtyard while they wrote, were hardly more illuminating about their own leaders in the War of the Castes. Without comment they transcribed to their books the events as reported in the official state newspapers of the day. I looked for diaries and accounts of ordinary life in San Cristóbal in the period while Pedro was growing up, but found none. Seemingly, if they had any interest in chronicles at all, these people preferred the delicious business of tracing their knightly lineages back before the discovery of this second-class continent. A sense of the value of our own history grows strong only when we feel that something is slipping away. And in the isolated mountains of Chiapas very little had changed since the sons of the conquerors and their religious brothers had consolidated the territory in the sixteenth century and began building the great adobe fortresses which were their houses and churches.

Their belief that time was not passing made the nineteenth-century historians unhelpful to me. But when I allowed the same sensation to work on me, then the last hundred years of San Cristóbal began to lift off fairly easily, like a painting which covered another, more durable painting. The paved road up from the hot country brought the plenty of automobiles and trucked goods only in 1948. In the 1840s San Cristóbal was the capital and major city of Chiapas. There were over ten thousand inhabitants and eighteen churches. The state government has been moved down country now, the revolution has come and gone, the churches have been closed several times but they are open again. Until very recently, trade with the Indians in the mountains was the sole important business. One senses that much of the power in the town still resides in the bishop's quarters next to the cathedral on the parque, and inside a few huge old houses where Spanish coat-of-arms are painted on raised plaster in the entryhalls.

Sitting in the still garden, I could hear the creaking of wooden saddles on Chamula horses going by on the road outside with loads of charcoal or pine kindling for ladinos' cooking fires. Beside me grew a velvet maroon dahlia with a hundred or more pointed petals. The old formula: see far enough into anything and come to know everything.

What I dreamed last night. There were four Indian mayordomos, either dead or being put to death. In all their black wool clothes, their round straw hats and their bunched necklaces of tangled red and green ribbons, they lay in sleek, beveled black-lacquered coffins. We were told to make sure everything was tucked inside and the thin board lids nailed down. We began. Then old Juan Tushim stirred in his box. I asked, Aren't you dead yet, father? He said, No, but go ahead and nail me down anyway, and I woke up.

In some ways with the Indians everything had been easier

for me to see, because it was all so strange and new. For a long time I had worked at learning the forms of their cargo system (and had achieved very little). Then, away from them, speculating, I came to what I believe now. Through the rituals and practice of any coherent religion we express our amazement in the face of two great opposing mysteries. Not only our ignorant fear of death and the cause of suffering, but the mystery of continuance, rebirth in nature, and grace. The work of religion is the attempt to reconcile: we must learn that we belong to life itself, which is all-enduring; then we must learn that what endures is not ourselves, but the life in us. It was not so hard for me to make up an Indian boy who, by the age of ten or eleven, had been washed almost clean by the contradictions of a natural religion which explained his father's death and his mother's strangeness as punishment for failures of constancy and intent in their devotion, but which also produced a mystic like Mesha, who could make the boy believe that we, like plants, are tended every day by gentle protective hands.

A cold, north-born Protestant like myself finds it more difficult to perceive the life-promise in Mexican or Spanish Catholicism. Like the Indians, I am more interested in the tortured figures bleeding their eternal dark blood in regular rows along waxy hands and feet and ribs. Often in a church I forget to pay attention to the infant Christs and the Virgins with great topply gold crowns and plump adolescent faces, the statues set on theatrical plaster clouds and supported by cherubs whose legs would be a credit to any gang of piano-movers.

When Thomas Gage, an English priest, came to Chiapas in the 1600s, he fell in with hospitable friars who loved games and tricks and good things to eat. From his descriptions it seems likely these men were loved in return by their congregations, Indians who somehow recognized the sacrifices their priests had made to bring from Spain news of an Incarnation which the Indians had known of, but not in the form the priests told it. I have tried to imagine that vestiges of that same affirmation and joy still existed in San Cristóbal for Pedro to discover.

Doña Laura Figueroa de Estrada had assumed mourning after her only child died in infancy. The sharpest-tongued gossips of

San Cristóbal said Laura recognized her only beauty lay in the whiteness of her face and she was clever to show it off by wearing black. Her stark, flat eyes were accusing even in laughter and people instinctively shied away from her on the cobble streets. Wife and daughter of nobles, lateral descendant of the chronicler Bernal Díaz who had been given all of the Indian town of Chamula and more beside by his master Cortés, Laura had black for all occasions, and it was told in the town she changed these garments, similar in cut and differing only in material, ten times or more a day, like a feverish girl deciding what to wear to a ball. Foul servant girls hinted that an unpleasant smell came from Doña Laura's blade body and the multiple changes of costume kept her secret hidden.

Laura knew she was a subject of constant speculation. Without the talk she would have been as lonely as an orchard tree without insects or birds, for she had been raised to believe her life was de facto interesting to the lower classes of men.

Her home, the family mansion of her husband Hector Estrada, occupied an entire block on the main plaza in the city. Begun in the sixteenth century, it had a now-worn Moorish gate and, at the four corners, the mermaids from the Estrada family seal primitively carved in yellow stone by Indian sculptors. Though cooks did most of the buying for the great establishment, Laura herself often stepped the few blocks to the market to pick out the fruits for her own lace-covered dinner table. Kind people thought she went to market because, for all her greatness, the señora was a humble woman. The others said she liked her rivals to see the three servants following her, since even the women nearest Laura in station had but a single maid to carry their baskets. The kind gossips said the extraordinary number of servants in the Estrada household were proof of the señora's great charity, the others said it was just another of her multitudinous ostentations, exasperating because they were so impossible to imitate successfully.

The truth of the matter was that Laura loved to bathe in the slow-moving currents of the town, her Jerusalem, and best she loved the market with the Indians squatting on the ground under the full trees. It gave her a lush sensation of walking into the

Bible, like the angel looking for Jacob in a desert encampment of unbelieving women.

The Indians knew Laura's slender black shadow. Having no way of knowing the pain bargaining cost her, they believed she came to the market herself because she was mean and cheap.

That morning there was only one Chanula woman with decent apples. When Laura said a price though, the woman simply closed her shawl over the fruit and looked away. Laura bent down, her eye caught by the small gold cross the fierce woman's son wore. Thinking of a new offer, the lady told the boy to hold the cross up to her. She was afraid to touch him. Not real gold, she saw, just brass or copper. It had turned green on the back. Wear your cross always, Laura said, and the boy laughed, probably not understanding her Spanish.

There were eighteen churches. Now, at noon, a bell clanged somewhere and the others, as though they had been waiting, picked up the signal. Men took off their hats and women bowed their heads. When the brave sound died there was startled silence all over the city. Then the people sitting under the market's calm canopy of trees heard something else, far off down the road, the ring of horses' hooves on cobble, and they looked out to see what this sudden change would be. Laura shielded her eyes with her hand, and immediately saw it was nothing really wonderful. Two men, tired and bored after eight or so hours slow climbing up through the mountains, on reaching the paved street and finding a ready-made audience had, for the fun of it, decided to race into town. Clearly now Laura could see them, even the buckles on their saddles, and she recognized the excited face of one of them, her husband's cousin, an adolescent licking his first thin mustache as he came. They looked very fine and free. My spirit, Laura thought, represented allegorically, an independence nurtured in bondage and adversity like a child for a childless woman. She saw the Indian boy whose thin cross she had been holding a moment ago at the front of the crowd, saw him forced into the street by their jostling, she saw the moving horse's head cock sideways, not in great alarm because it was too late and too near accomplishment for the animal to fear it, the horse's eye on the boy saying, it seemed, Is it going to be you then? as a girl seems to ask her foreordained husband before he proposes or later at the moment of the rending she has never truly believed will take place, and then the horse's forward plunge, hooves not touching earth in the pause, the boy's head turned toward Laura just before it was struck by the blackened chest, the face pushed out of shape by the impact, then the body down and lost between the delicate legs like a body tangled in vines, and the horse tripped and stuttered sideways, its main movement through the thick air swelling against gravity, the hooves sliding on the cobbles, the man her husband's blood leaning against the line of fall so horse and rider formed for an instant a perfect drawn bow, then the righting and the continuance beginning, the direction surer and faster and both horsemen receded toward the mouth of the channeled street, yelling and laughing at their own good luck.

A way spread for her as Laura came through the crowd, her black-gloved hand anchored to the substantial silver crucifix which was her only ornament. The lady felt their parting and her servants filling her wake, and she was aware of the blood and the boy's startled face and knew, as she stooped and felt the rough street stones under it, that he was too heavy for her slight strength, and must be left to her little porter Adáno. But as she lifted, the expected weight of the child was not there, he was lightboned as a bird and, running, Laura could support him in her arms, and so she carried him, pressed against her, his fluid bleeding through her dress to her own cold body, up the vacuum middle of the street almost to the shaded plaza. There the boy became too much for her and she had to pass him off to Adáno's big hands. Laura ran ahead, the black blotch shining on her dress, and pulled open the great oak doors into her own becalmed courtyard.

By chance it was the day of the month the doctor came to treat the ills of servants. From the tiny lavendered cell where her maid slept next to Laura's own bedroom, messengers were sent into the bowels of the house for him. The doctor was extracting teeth and did not understand Laura's intended urgency, transformed by the girl asking diffidently would he come. Accustomed to such adumbrations of whatever she willed, the mistress sent Adáno.

She had Dolores lift the boy while she herself picked off the chamarra and ripped away the dirty pieces of cotton shirt adhering to the small body. Noticing the cruel chainlike indention around the neck, Laura wondered that a string with a little cross could have dug such a deep channel in the flesh, as we marvel at the record of power and time when we see the shard of stone left in the bottom of a granite sink.

He breathed still, hoarsely, with difficulty. Each time his chest puffed, broken ribs showed yellow like tight knuckles under the brown skin. Laura composed him, arms straight and soldierly at the sides, feet together. When the porcelain basin and the linen towel finally arrived, she herself soaked the blood away, tasting sweat on her own pulsing lip. Longing, she thought, for the doctor to come. The mistress stooped to pour more water, and her Dolores threw a piece of the soaked linen over the child's exposed genitals. Laura picked the linen off and the boy's hand moved, as though to protect himself, then fell back. Even so ruined, one side of his face flayed raw, the open-eyed Indian boy was very pretty.

The doctor cleaned the open wounds and applied a sulfrous paste to them. Then he dosed the boy with laudanum and had him tied to a board. We will have to see, he said. The external damage is unimportant and he is breathing well, a good sign. The lungs may not be punctured.

When he came downstairs, the doctor encountered the master of the house and his brother the priest in the entryhall. A whimpering Indian woman had her face pressed into the slit the porter had cracked in the gates. The doctor explained to Don Hector about the accident. Tell her her son is being cared for and she can come back in a week or so to get him, Hector said to the porter.

And that should have been the end of it. But the woman remained, her fist wedged in the crack below her defiant face, silent, and the gates would not close. Hector sighed and dug into his fitted linen trousers pocket for a coin. The woman took it and withdrew her hand and the door boomed shut.

The doctor said the mistress would not appear for dinner, and was honored by an invitation to stay himself. At table, while the brothers talked, he maintained an appropriate silence and quietly ate as much as he dared. Unfortunately, his mouth was full of custard when Hector at last turned to him. Doctor, wouldn't it be better if that boy had been left on the street? The doctor tried to force the lump of custard down his throat. I mean, Hector said, if you notice such things, lately our city has been turned into an asylum for the maimed, white and Indians both. The classic politicians wrote that an army of useless beggars or helots was a credit to a state's humaneness but a positive danger to the *civis* itself.

The doctor finally managed to say, I wouldn't myself want to be the one to have to deny Doña Laura's impulse for goodness.

Hector pushed back his chair, lit a paper-wrapped cigar infused with camphor, and smiled. Not goodness really, Doctor. Not in our Laura. Not a moral sentiment but a religious one, if you will allow the distinction. Laura is incapable of emotion concerning human beings unless they are crippled or, better, bleeding. A fault of our Church, I believe. It proselytizes our females by thrilling them with agony. Don't you think, Dio?

The priest, Hector's older brother, turned his faceted blue eyes up at them and refused the bait. Yes, I think so, he said, smiling. He selected a second pear from the bowl before him. Light struck the crystal and was refracted on the priest's smooth round chin. Yes indeed, he said, we have too many crucifixions and not nearly enough nativities.

Pedro, bring a pot of charcoal for us now. My sister and I are going to dress for supper.

Laura was aware that stumping downstairs from the gallery clinging to the iron bannister, the long voyage to the kitchen and the return with the smoky jar would exhaust her staved-in little boy, but she was working her own method on him. The doctor had decided he was doomed to be crippled and, since Laura insisted on keeping him, said Pedro must remain in a chair or lying down, locked in the rigid circle of cedar stays the household carpenter had carved for him. Instead, from the first Laura had demanded little things of Pedro, such as journeys across the room to get her stationery or her embroidery. And the Indian had improved. The doctor then grumbled, He will always limp. Laura knew differently.

When he returned, Pedro stayed to watch the señora and her younger sister. It was Elva's first visit to the capital. Repeatedly she went to the clay brazier of charcoal and came back to the candlelit mirror, hands cupped as though she could carry a little warmth in them. Laura sympathized with her, remembering her own endless chill when she first came from Acala in hot country to live in this inhospitable mountain outpost.

Again she thanked Elva for bringing the honey and the sunny loaves decorated with rolled dough flowers. The bread here is, like the life, sour, Laura said.

Elva pressed her slight hands against her dress and asked if Laura recalled the man who came to their hacienda every year to gather the honey. Laura remembered him, a crusty, near-blind beggar. Well you know, Elva was saying, Mama doesn't mind the honey, but she dreads having to go down to the well to wash him when his work is through. Yet the servants and the field people are so insistent that we observe the silly custom. So last week when he came Mama put Serafina—you know, the cook?—into a dress of her own and earrings and powdered her face with flour and sent *her* to wash the old man. And he is so blind by now he was completely fooled by Mama's trick and kissed Serafina's hand when she was finished!

Elva glared at a curl dangling in front of her ear. She pulled it out through her fingers and it returned, still a good deal longer than the curl on the other side.

Here, let me. Laura took some small gold scissors and prepared to even off the limp curl, but Elva jerked her head away, saying, Don't! I would rather look funny.

Elva, what is wrong?

Nothing, nothing I tell you, Elva sang, and danced away to her trunk, which stood open in the far corner of the room. I'm free to look as odd here as I like, aren't I? it's my protection!

Laura pursued her sister across the parquet floor and took her arm. Now you explain to me what in the world you are talking about, she said. Who do you need protection from?

No one, dear. But to sit at table and have a priest from Father's generation put his hands on your arms and your cheeks, and even tug at your skirt under the table and breathe on you and ply you with *unbelievable* questions—

What questions did Dio ask?

Because it was a secret, Elva leaned close to Laura. But she spoke loud enough so both Pedro and Dolores could hear. Surrounded by servants at all times, the sisters gave no more thought to hiding things from them than other people would to keeping the furniture from overhearing. Last night, Elva said, he put his face right up to mine and asked had I ever felt the dear little Jesus inside me!

Laura laughed. That is what he is asking everyone these days. What did you tell him?

I said that at Mass and in my prayers at night I have experienced the Lord drawing *near* to me. And your brother-in-law wanted to know what it felt like. I said I had no idea what it *felt* like, and *he* asked me 'Wasn't it like music and waterfalls and flowers bursting open and like being a deer with an arrow in your heart?'

And you told him?

That I had no opinion.

Which disappointed Dio and made him wrinkle down his eyebrows.

Yes. And if he is coming again tonight, I will take supper upstairs, thank you.

Of course you won't. That would be sinful, Elva. Everything in the house would be upset. I cherish Dio deeply and I know that he is harmless. Come now, Laura said, leading the way to the door and waiting there for her Pedro to stump forward and open it, as it is you've made us late.

At the top of the broad tiled stairway Laura said, Dio was considered a great charmer at one time, and even now you can't be angry at him for staying in practice, can you? As they say, a boy need not stop sharpening his pencils just because he has left school.

At last Elva's face lost its pinch and she laughed her laugh, which came from unfortunately deep inside of her and sounded like a man's. And is it true about Dio's cat? she asked.

Not a word of it, Laura said. Dio will tell you himself. A fabrication of the credulous and nothing more.

That particular story had so irritated Laura that she had

gone to her bishop to discuss it. As the simple people retailed it, when Dio was a seminarian in Michoacán he had kept a tiger cat. Seeing the bad bread and inadequate food his master received in his cell, the cat had taken it upon himself to go out every day to the fields and woods in order to catch Dio a nice rabbit or pheasant or a plump pair of quail. Laura confessed to the bishop her suspicion that her brother-in-law did not work as hard as he might have to stamp out the belief in the tale among the poor. Also, when they came to the gate of the seminary at the Merced where Dio lived and wept for him, he allowed them to kiss his soft hands and hold their sick children up for him to touch. Laura had seen him do it.

Outside the rain pounded, inside the men discussed politics, Elva blushed and twisted her napkin whenever Dio turned to her with a kind question and so, even though she had a glass of champagne for her spirits, Laura found supper especially sad that night. Elva had raised her old longing for family and home. At least her own people in Acala were not odd and did not need to be apologized for.

As a clan the Estradas had of necessity claimed eccentricity as one of their virtues, and through generations they had developed their strain of it to a fineness. The surviving brothers were odd even in not looking at all alike. Dio was squat and muscular as a peasant, rosy of face, blue-eyed and already nearly bald, while Laura's husband, honed away to bone and tightly trussed by his skin, had a brittle black-eyed beauty and a grand aristocrat's languor. To avoid imputing their saintly mother, one had to assume that God may at times love contraries and, in the creation of Dio and Hector, took a single piece of clay, stretched it to natural limits, halved it and called the two pieces brothers. Their father, now dead, had said that he had a son who disliked no one and another who needed only one friend in the world but luckily had that one as a brother. In his youth Dio had admired Hidalgo, and told his amazed family that the old priest had recanted the revolution he began only after being tortured by the Inquisition. When Dio took up with the town's few dreary and meddlesome liberals, his father had decided that the aberration was a proof by inversion of the boy's nobility.

Less mystifying of course were the stories of his son's generosity and stamina with disreputable young women. In any lesser family Dio would have caused a scandal. But since his father treated him as a charming eccentric, when the seminary was suggested to him it was with no hint of punishment and Dio went off to Michoacán willingly enough. Of course, he does everything broached to him with good will, his father had remarked. Should you want to get rid of my Dio, you need only suggest to him that it would make you laugh to see him climb to the top of the cathedral tower and jump from it.

At his ordination in Michoacán, the heathen name Dionisio had been taken away and he was blessed with the more ordinary Juan and Lorenzo. But when he returned to San Cristóbal, he was again called Dio by everyone.

Expecting the younger brother to be the greater hellion, the family had braced itself against the day Hector should show his colors. Then he too surprised them by becoming a callow, sanguine snob, as complete an aristocrat not as his father, who maintained that one must live in his own time whether he is comfortable there or not, but as his grandfather long deceased. Hector's extreme devotion to the past was boring, but it made him the obvious heir to the management of the house and the plantations in hot country. The boys' father died feeling contented but tricked, as a man will feel at the end of a long chess game which he wins by a fortuitous mistake on his opponent's part and not by his own elaborate strategy.

While Elva mangled her napkin, the brothers discussed the news from the north. Laura had never been to Mexico City and whether the generals there wanted to make war on the United States or the United States on them made no difference to her. Perched on her mountain, she did not care to see out into the world.

They are doing it everywhere, Hector was saying. In their foolishness they did it in Yucatán, where they are as outnumbered as we are here.

Did what?

Hector was stretched long in his chair with his thin black hair falling over his big eyes so to his wife he looked like a nasty boy sulking in his bed because someone has made him be sick. To provide troops for their political wars they arm the Indians my dear, he said. And now, having decided things between themselves, they are surprised that the Indians aren't also neatly concluded. The Indian remembers who his eternal enemy is. Those people in Valladolid were amazed when they were dragged from their beds and had their throats slit or—

Hector stopped, noticing his sister-in-law had turned white. He raised his shapely black eyebrows and said, Or worse. The savages tell their history from father to son rather than writing it down in order to forget it, as we do. The Indian watching us squabble about liberal and conservative is like a lion, bewildered that children should fight over a toy when he is about to gobble them up.

Dio gave them his mischievous child's smile and the full beauty of his eyes and said, Terrible for those who died in Valladolid.

Yet edifying for us to consider, Hector said.

Edifying?

Yes. Because we may be forced to prove our superiority to them again, to make yet another demonstration. It will be good for the Church, Brother. Again we will need you and you will need us. The liberals will have to stop eating away at your property and so forth and good men will be sent into the priesthood again.

Dio looked disappointed. Wouldn't it be better for the Indian to take over the Church and make it his own?

You mean because the savage soul stands closer to God? Hector asked.

Yes, 'the least of these my brethren.' Myself, I would gladly worship in an Indian's church, Dio said.

Where they carry the Blessed Virgin about in their arms, drunk, falling down and making water against the walls if they feel like it?

Laura's bishop said there were men in the north, some of them clerics themselves, who meant to destroy the Church. She knew her husband was only saying these things to upset her, but to hear Dio himself— It gave her pains in her chest.

Yes, Dio said, I would like that.

It was her heart which was affected, she knew. Tears came to her eyes and Laura got up so abruptly the table shivered. She said she and Elva would leave them now, and nearly ran from the room.

After they had repaired and calmed themselves upstairs, the ladies returned. Passing the library, Laura saw Dio speaking to her Indian boy, Hector lolling in his chair breathing into his handkerchief and examining the lines of his hands. One of his camphor cigars curled smoke toward the lamp. The library was the room in the ancient, damp house Laura disliked most. Hector's leather antique books, although in glass cases, mildewed and smelled. If he cared so much about his line, why after the first failure had he not even tried to get himself a successor? Of course she was glad that he did not force her to anything, but why didn't he bring one of his young cousins into the household and adopt him? Even illegitimate children could be recognized. Other people did it. It would not have caused Laura any anguish.

In the sitting room Laura worked at her embroidery, rapidly jabbing bright emerald stitches into the linen. Elva talked of an army officer, older but quite dashing, whom Father had brought to visit in Acala, but Laura was thinking bitterly to herself, Twenty-seven. You are condemned, my girl. Fate written, and not an army of army officers can rescue you from it now.

Dio came limping in, his hand on the shoulder of the stooped Indian boy who was carrying a large book for him. Dio announced that Hector chose to remain in the library and, settling himself on the plush sofa next to Elva, he took the book from the boy. Once Dio was involved in his reading, Elva shrank as far away from him as she could.

Coming to a print in the book called 'On the Road to Tlaxcala' Dio asked the boy what he thought it was a picture of.

O Dio, he doesn't know ten words of Spanish! Laura said.

But he understands me, my dear.

The print showed a small contingent of the Conquistadors on their spiny horses and a couple of monks following along on foot through the jungle. The boy stared at the figures and then pointed at two men, heads on their chests, hanging from crosses in the background of the drawing. Dio hadn't even noticed them. Those aren't Christs, the boy said.

True, Dio replied, his parchmenty face crinkling into a smile. How do you know?

Because they don't have God in their faces. And they don't go *up* to heaven.

Pedro, you can leave us now. Go on, Laura said.

Let him stay, Dio said. He frowned, his lovely eyes on the little Indian. Where *are* they going then?

To die. They die and they go in the earth. That's all. Maybe they go down, the boy said seriously, and pointed to the floor.

Who are they then?

They are only Indians.

All true, the priest said, reaching out to hug the boy. He handed the great book into Elva's lap so she could see the print. How old is he? the priest asked.

Eleven or twelve, Laura said.

And are you baptized, my boy?

The Indian shook his head, no.

Dio rubbed his chin. Can I have him Laura?

What?

I mean do you have a purpose for him?

In the first place I'm going to make him walk right. And then—She faltered. And then we will see, she said.

It would be a terrible loss if you merely turned this one out. Or had him join your regiment of floormoppers.

Why would that be a loss? Laura was standing, embroidery in her hand, irresolute, under her black skirts rocking forward, about to go and snatch the little thing from Dio, and in the next instant rocking back, restraining herself. I saved his life when no one else would have cared to, she said. The nuns would have turned away an Indian woman with a boy so badly hurt. How many nights, sleepless, had she gone into Dolores's room and found the maid snoring and the boy awake, immobile, staring at the ceiling, how many times had she brought him water with her own hands? She felt the tightness of her lace collar, and all the constraints which bound her, and her white face flushed again and the crystal rock tears were hurting her, so she said Yes, that's exactly what I had planned for you to want, my dear Dio. Please take him away with you. Tonight. He is ready to go just as he is. He has no things. And I hope he proves to be as full of the Holy Spirit as you seem to think and that you make him into a nice brown priest in your own image!

And turning, she again fled from Dio, made blindly through the rainy dark for the stairway, pursued at first by both of them and then, she knew when she reached the gallery, only by her fast-pattering younger sister.

From the top of the stairs, not caring if even Hector heard, she called back, Just do not force me to look at him again! and she propelled herself on into her own great dark bedroom.

5

High on the blank facing wall was a gray slit. The boy not yet really awake could feel it growing, sweltering more and more toward the purity of light, until finally a narrow lathe of sun broke through, sweet yellow it touched the ear and shoulder of the man kneeling on the stone floor and then, teeming with dust, fell into a thin line well behind him.

Like someone stepping into chill water, the priest paused and then the rumble of his prayers continued. Pedro thought of the bull, his father's animal long forgotten. The pure white living thing, light on its soft hair, light curving over the bunched shoulders, light not finding the dark concave or the broad round of the backside or the gathered weight of the legs, one slightly thinner than the other. The boy's own prisoned body pushed against the stays and bindings and the pain it had come to live with. Having slept the strange night through next to what kneeled now erect in the sunlight swatch unaware of it being anything other than himself, belonging to him as he be-

longed to it, surprise welled in him. Then discomfort and confusion, the desire to get free of the wood bed, a rapid search
for a way out of the deep narrow cell began, well before the
knocking and the voice beyond the door calling Father? Dionisio?
are you in there? Outside a bar was lifted and the door swung
open.

A tiger cat, like a flame more intense than the early sunlight,
got up and darted out the door.

Pedro had rolled himself into the brown tick and had covered
himself with Dio's black robe. There in his hiding he heard his
own heart clearly and rediscovered the thick sweat and the dirty
smell of the night past. He heard the other priest's impatient
coughing as Dio finished his prayers, and then the confident
words, Dio saying he knew it was late but he had been loiter-
ing at his brother's house and drinking too much wine. And,
he added, I brought you a holy gift Cresencio.

What?

A new child. He's there hidden somewhere in my bed. I
came in so late I decided to keep him rather than wake up the
dormitory.

And then all at once Pedro was pulled from his covering into
the light by the thin arms of a man he had seen before, a face
as outraged as it had been the day he had explicated the painting of Heaven and Hell to the infidels before the Chamula
church. And the boy was dragged away by Cresencio to the beginning of a life he would lead for eight years.

The Dominican House at the Merced, only a long block away
from the place where Pedro had been struck down by the
courier's horse, was still called a seminary, although as an
educational institution it was much reduced. In the old building
with its multiples of courtyards there remained only five or-
dained priests, one of them senile, an Indian donado or lay
brother also of great age and little use, and forty or so Indian
boys.

The notion of educating Indians had never been popular in
Chiapas. Most laymen thought it a frivolity. So in the years
since the War of Liberation with the Church under general
attack, the Dominican effort had received less and less support.

But the seminary still struggled on, the quizzical brown children were led to their Latin six days a week without prior knowledge of how to read even Spanish, and it was in fact the only school in Chiapas at the time where Indians were taught to read or write anything. In other states, such as Oaxaca, the liberals of the thirties had worked hard to invent an education for themselves and their sons which was not devoted to the study of archaic moral argument and the thinking of scholastic saints, but though the idea was discussed in Chiapas, no reformation had yet occured.

The priests at the Merced were hardly deviled with illusions about their work or their effectiveness. They ran the school because it provided a choir for daily Mass and evening Vespers at the church across the way and because it was one of their labors, a given, and because they had a sense of the history of themselves. In the early days Dominicans had been great missionaries and educators. And even if we live in unheroic times, we must still carry out the plans of our heroes, is that not true? The fathers treated the Indian boys as Indians, without any liberal fuddlements concerning the aborigine's natural equality with the white man. A new student like Pedro had his head shaved the day he arrived and every six months thereafter. Each morning the students were inspected for lice. Pedro was given a uniform, white cotton pants and shirt, and the remnant of his wool chamarra, which he had worn even at the Estrada house, was burned. Taking his Indian clothes away from him was considered the necessary first step in extricating a boy from his primitive longings. The priests were pleased to think that their students were indistinguishable from the children of any humble but decent ladino farmer. But since they were still Indians underneath and Indians were known to be able to endure great extremes of temperature, the Dominicans did not bother to give them any extra clothing in the cold times of the year, and their students were often sick.

Pedro came to sleep in a huge room with forty other boys on a mat on the floor. He was nearly the youngest, and of course the elders were the leaders, though there was none of the cruelty and testing which white boys in the same miserable condition would have inflicted on him for the sin of being new.

In the dark mice skittered across him and he woke praying. Not for Rosha. She had not come for him at the señora's house and never would find him here. He dreamed he ate a whole chicken in a church, and when he turned around, there was Salvador trying to pick meat off the bones Pedro had discarded. Everything was broken or sick. He had rope and longed to bind up his brother and save him as he himself was bound. Then, fully wakened, he would run his hands over his body, looking for disruptions in the smooth shell.

At first because of his stays he wasn't called to penitencia and beaten as the others were. But when the casing was removed, he had to learn to punish himself like the rest and he found the action a release. The marks he made on himself objectified his fears.

He dreaded the classes, which he could not understand, and Padre Cresencio's hand, so fleshless that when it hit it gave not a sting but an ache. All of the boys suffered from lack of sleep. They sang Mass and then had classes before they ate in the morning, worked through the afternoon, sang again and then had more classes. In the middle of the night they were usually roused for Cresencio's saying of the Vespers of Our Lady.

Dio protected him as far as possible, removed him from gardening to teach him his first catechism and the beginning of his letters. It was a disappointment to the amiable priest to find the boy did not learn singing easily and had an unclean, deep voice. But Dio put him in the choir anyway and told him to sing only the three notes he was surest of. Besides, he said, I will teach you to dance, which is the celebration of God which is beyond singing and near only the Mass as a holy performance. The boy was looking at the thinner left leg under the cassock. Well, Dio said, you think because *I* can't dance that I couldn't know about dancing. But you will see. The little Jesus loved lambs and you must recall, my little Chamula, how lambs dance and make His fun. Dancing is all of you, mind and body, given over to Him. You will see.

Only with Dio did he ever escape the seminary. The priest took him along to his brother's house where Pedro would be given a meal of leftovers from the master's table by the cook.

Dio remembered his sister-in-law's wishes and maneuvered it so well that Laura only once or twice caught sight of Pedro and then, wrapped in her own concerns, she did not recognize him.

When he was finished eating Pedro would sneak through the darkened corridors, stopping to wash his mouth and face at the well, and then slip into the library. He sat on a footstool next to the priest, who faced his sprawled unhappy younger brother. The talk of the two men ran slowly, with long gaps between the utterances, and an apparent discontinuity of ideas. Only later did Pedro see that Dio and Hector worked together on a huge tapestry, Dio pulling threads through to the front, Hector knotting and tying them behind, or vice versa, and that it did not matter if one of them spoke of a different section of the design than the other, since they both knew by heart the intricacies of all the parts.

It is most difficult, said Dio, patting Pedro's close-cropped head, to plant Jesus Christ in a patch of ground such as this one. I tell him about the angels of glory and the Virgin, or even about the Resurrection, and he sits before me with his hands crossed and his face a rock, waiting for me to beat him. But let Cresencio or one of the others gather them together to explain some minor martyr, to tell them how even after being stoned in a pit San Malcriado smiled and called the name of God, and immediately these boys come to life. They think because they are Indians that all of their emotions are hidden from us. But I see them, covering their mouths to hide their pleasure, like crows storing the precious little details. Their eyes light like candles over their brown fingers. The pitiful miracles astound them, the great miracles of love are beyond them. Dio sighed.

Silence. Hector reached into a glass humidor for one of his cigars and Dio placed the end of his black sash on Pedro's head so the fringe hung down over the boy's eyes. Dio went on, For the same reason I think the Jews didn't accept Christ as the gentiles did. Though it may seem so, Christianity is not a faith for the downtrodden. The saints are for the pantheists among us, which of course include the Indians. Those who divide and parse experience, Dio said, smiling. On a napkin beside him sat five sugared green figs. He selected the plumpest and gave it to Pedro. God is an alien to them, he said.

Oh they know God, Hector said, God as we have given Him to them, His triumphs over them, and they pay their homage to His success. But as conquered people, they find nothing of *their* lives in the life of God triumphant. Only on the road to Calvary do they recall themselves, and in the Agony on the Cross.

And in the strange love for the Santa Cruz, Dio said. They take that barren wood and decorate it with the flowers, thinking they are making the wood come alive, and then they worship it.

Because the flowers are themselves, Brother. Insubstantial and lovely and passing. Not like our permanent hard figures. Hector was agitated by his idea. If you want to make them love your dear Jesus, what you need to do is to take an Indian and crucify him, and let your savages play with the enormity and human responsibility of *that* act, as we have done for eighteen hundred and some years.

Dio laughing and patting Pedro's head in time to some tune heard only by himself. A nice idea, Hector, considering that they are so near to idolatry already. And what particular Indian would you suggest I use?

Hector's eyes widened as though he were regarding Pedro for the first time. Why not him? he asked. Again silence, and then Hector continuing, Of course they're no more idolatrous than you are or I am. The religious fear of idolatry among the Indians is the fear of a mother who thinks she has given her baby the cholic by pressing the teat at the brat too much. Here, let me read something to you. Hector searched through his glassed-in bookcases and came back with a volume only loosely holding together. 'Ornamentation and pomp in the churches are very necessary to uplift the souls of the Indians and bring them to the things of God, for by nature they are indifferent to internal things and forgetful of them, so they must be helped by means of external appearances.'

I will believe that, Dio said.

Even though a Franciscan wrote it?

Yes.

And you boy, are you indifferent to internal things?

Barely understanding what Don Hector was saying, Pedro looked to the priest for an answer. But Dio would not help him.

Hector pulled a coin from his pocket and held it up with both hands like the Host turned to silver. Now, would you rather have this or would you like the baby Jesus to love you?

I would take care of the baby Jesus, señor, Pedro replied seriously.

Both brothers laughed, and Pedro was given the coin. Hector and Dio agreed, not that Pedro was sanctified, but that he was an exceptional child, one of those with a natural understanding of how to perform for adults and to ferret out their wishes.

Juan Tushim made me hold the chair steady for him while he got up on it and felt around in the thatch where the roof joined the mud wall. He handed down the leather cylinder saying, "It is time for you to see this." Outside the serene moon had arrived to watch the work. The mayordomos continued counting the coins on the saints' necklaces, not noticing that the old man had stopped watching them. If they came out ahead of the known number everyone was happy and had a drink. When they were short, they had a drink to hide their worry and started in again. Time, I was thinking, is the necklaces and the silver cinco-veintes are days. We go round and round the same ones until the count seems right in a way we, in our exhaustion, could not explain.

Juan and I crept off to a place in the moonlight where the tinkle of the coins sounded like rain coming on gusts of wind. After wiping his hands on his chamarra, he unstopped the cylinder and pulled from it a roll of browned papers. I thought of a film of Blood Indians in Canada opening medicine bundles, the fresh delight of the old men, as though they did not know the contents by heart. Juan handed me the top paper and told me to read. The writing, covering only half the page, was ornate but not easy, the embellishments shaky, the hand cramped and unsure. The ink had faded to tan and yet the words were clear except in three places where water had obliterated whatever was written there.

I see. I see in the mountain to the other land. There is light in the other place. I see in the mountain my father. He works in his field. I go without fear always ————— the man in black with his hat. I have none. To the river, to the other side we go. We have our flowers to carry, we have our food and our dog. From the road I see my father working his ripe corn. I see he wants me. I see he wants to come with us. He does not ————. In the road there I see my younger brother, I see the man in black with his black bull there in the road at night. We have no fear in the other land. The wide road ———— narrow road. My younger brother is a flower. There is light. He goes to the right and I carry him there, there on the narrow road. With my cross in my arms I carry, I go below happy. My younger brother goes happy with the children, the flowers and my father, where there is no work for good people.

While I read, Juan nodded, and when I finished and began puzzling it out, the old man gently removed it from my hand.

The time of Christmas nearly a year and a half after Pedro came to the seminary. Dio had been teaching them the dance of the Seville choirboys with the tambourines for the midnight mass—veinticinco de diciembre, zum zum zum—and as a reward had given them little glasses of wine and then sent them to bed. As they went in the dormitory, the old donado counted the boys off before locking them up for the night. He stopped Pedro. The priest wants to see you.

Pedro went along under the cloister in the silence, his breath clouding in the frosty night air. From behind a pillar Dio sprang on him and swept his thin body up in his heavy arms. Zum zum zum and Padre, let me down! whispered.

But Dio only held him harder, not letting the boy's feet touch the square stones as they passed wheeling crazily along. Pedro's heart going, what if they were seen? and over and over begging to be let down. Zum zum zum.

And at last Dio slamming into a wall and resting there, his chest heaving, and Pedro believing it would be sinful to struggle, as sinful as submitting.

I know what it is you want, Dio sang in his ear.
Padre?

It's a puppy, isn't it? praying to Jesus for a dog at Christmas, yes?

Pedro nodded. How did you know?

Prayers boy, the intercession of prayers. You pray aloud in your sleep. Dio's tight grip on him seemed to loosen a moment, and then tightened again. Pedro?

Padre?

I am your puppy. The priest's chest sighed, collapsing. Dio's tongue pointed from his mouth and licked once, a tentative swipe, across Pedro's chin. When the boy did not resist, Dio licked him again, wet stripes up the cheeks to the eyes. For certain the man heard his own heart, less certainly the boy's.

In the third year of his education Pedro obtained permission to go away for a while during the summer rainy season. With a bowlegged yellow dog named Primavera, a gift from Dio, he took to the roads and then the slick paths and passed through the sad empty village of Chamula and then into the mountain forests. At last he came to the barranca of Tzajalemel, the great red wound in the earth. He stood at the foot of the hill below the house where he was born and, instead of joy, a bitter indifference came over him. When he called at the fence, they did not at first recognize him, because of his shaved head and his ladino clothes, and because it had been so long since, at the Estrada gate, old Adáno had told Rosha her boy was dead.

And they in turn were not the people he remembered. His mother's face had lost all of its youth and shine and her hair had turned precipitantly to gray. Salvador was stolid and light and unlike Pedro who, at fourteen, had grown thin and tall for an Indian.

He stayed with them, three days, maybe a week, and ate their food and, in long idle times while the woman worked and his brother plucked at the first sparse hairs growing on his face, Pedro told them what had happened to him.

The way Indians there talk, the river of their speech. He says a sentence, Salvador repeats most of it, Rosha perhaps a phrase, then Pedro goes on a little. Narrative a slow-turning whirlpool for them, never a line.

Much of what he wanted to tell them was outside their experience. Dio forgetting, assuming he was baptized, allowing his confession and Communion, the dryness in Pedro's mouth all that first day following his mortal sin. The smell of his own short hair on fire once, twice, when he leaned too intent over a candle he carried in procession.

Beyond a point they could not be interested, and as the days went by Pedro found he had more and more time to spend by himself. Rosha had to go away to Larrainzar. Pedro would take his book from the cleft between beam and wall where he hid it and go sit on the hillside to read.

Salvador came to him and asked him what the book said.

Nothing, Pedro replied.

The next day the book disappeared, as he had hoped it would. In the night it was back, and Salvador asked him again to tell what it said. Pedro was already half mindful that in such deviousness he was imitating his confessor.

The 'book', which Juan Tushim once showed me, was made of cheap paper folded in half and sewn with thread to bind it, then covered with oil cloth for protection. Not all of the sheets were written on, the ink and handwriting changes, and the sayings from Dio are numbered.

1. God admires me when I work.
2. God loves me when I dance.
3. What we do ourselves is done in darkness. What God does for us happens in the light.
4. Blessings come, joy comes, mysteries take place in the light.
5. Be ready to play at any hour.
6. Do not be surprised or feel honored if God calls on you to amuse Him when He is lonely.
7. We were made a little less than the angels and with more variety than the animals only to make Him laugh.
8. The Hebrews were correct to maintain a distaste for pigs.
9. Do not try to tell people who will not understand that God is always playful.
10. Because He plays tricks on you, do not think you can trick Him.

11. Now you are young and dress yourself and walk where you want to walk. Soon you will put out your hands and someone will put your coat on, and take you where you would not go.
12. Jesus says different things. God made us the animals who carry more than one thought at a time. And more than one thing.
13. Men are the animals who die for their children.
14. Jesus is everywhere and has no home.
15. Whisper when you tell me about God, for He is a secret.

It was a month before Salvador sounded the bell at the seminary gate and asked for his brother and was admitted also into Dio's keeping.

The younger one refused to have his hair cut and to give up his white wool chamarra. Dio did not care, none of the other priests were as fanatical as Cresencio and he, the mad one, got the notion lodged in his head that Salvador was the natural child of the old woman who helped in the kitchen. The boy was obviously too stupid ever to learn anything, but he could do no harm crouched in the vacant benches to the rear of the classroom. Cresencio got the habit of rapping Salvador on the crown with his knuckles whenever he came upon the boy, on the chance that some sense could be instantly knocked into him. Amused by Salvador's wild, matted hair and filth, and later by the un-Indian stubbled face, Dio would ask him, And where have you been? to the wilderness? Or, And how are the locusts this year Salvador? tasty? questions the younger brother did not understand.

When Pedro could read and write well enough, Dio removed him from all the classes the other boys took. From the beginning he had suffered the special difficulty of being known as the priest's favorite: the other boys knew he sometimes spent the night in Dio's cell, though they could not know how he hardly slept those nights, his own body pressed away from the priest's, hot itself and waking when even inadvertently Dio's touched it. But in the daylight there was not such a distance between them and, while Dio worked, Pedro sat on his own little stool by a lamp and read the Gospels over and over. They made him dream of a river, like the Grijalva, flowing broad and placid at times, and then through quickening narrow channels, unfathomable and tricky for men. He read Augustine, both the *City* and the *Confessions*, and the lives of various saints. He was fed so much sacred biography that he began, in his dreams, to confuse the events of his own life with those in the saints' and even in the life of Christ Himself, which was Dio's purpose.

Pedro still could not escape Padre Cresencio's acts of faith. The need for an act became apparent to the old priest at unpredictable moments, although there seemed to be some faded reference in his brain to the calendar of the Church. The acts came most often during Lent, which made a certain sense, but then one of the most memorable occurred nearly unannounced in the middle of the chill Night of the Kings.

The priests were in their cells snoring when suddenly they were woken by screaming. Dio refused to get up, but the others, feeling they must guard Cresencio against irreparably damaging himself, pulled on their robes and came running to the main courtyard where they found the old scarecrow naked and surrounded by sleepy boys. The youngest was crying. And Cresencio, his face warped with pain, implored them to spit on him and revile him. Some of the older boys complied with a good deal of vehemence. The priests clucked together and, though they wondered why the screams, were about to return to their rooms when Cresencio snatched up tongs and carefully selected a coal from the pot beside him and laid it on his arm. He gulped for breath and then hoarsely, rapidly, croaked at the boys, If *I*, if I a priest can't stand a little fire, what is Hell going to be like for *you*? you with such small hopes for Heaven? And the screaming erupted from him again, and continued until the coal on his arm had burned itself out. The sequence, the boys spitting on him and begged to kick him, the coal applied each time to a different surface of his body and the sermon and the smell of flesh burning, continued until Cresencio lost consciousness and the other priests could take him away to bandage him.

After his acts of faith, when Padre Cresencio reappeared he was surrounded by a deep, contented spirituality. Not even Dio, who so disapproved of the demonstrations, dared contradict him.

At this time Pedro was writing out his vision for Dio. The large page which Juan showed me was dated 'the 1st day of January 1851,' the words by then were surely and beautifully formed with delicate rounding serifs and tails, so one line seemed to entangle the next.

Pedro Díaz an Indian of Chamula writes this. When I was young among unknowing souls I often dreamed idly. Even in the day I saw visions not belonging to the true God and His Son Jesus Christ, but to my people, who stand ignorant of God and enraptured by spirits.

In the company of a god they worship I often saw myself cross a river and enter the land of the dead my people believe in. My intentions were not sinful because I did not yet know God, but I was possessed by sin, allowing myself to believe my visions raised me above even those older and wiser than myself. I would not allow them to touch me.

The distant land of the dead I visited with the saint was not like Heaven as it is promised to the faithful. It was like the fields and mountains of my place of birth at the time of the harvest. With my guide I walked there only on the roads and paths, because I at least was a traveler there and could not remain, though in waking I often longed to. But from the road we could see into the fields, we could see how everything there grew perfectly. Not a meter of land was wasted by the workers, not a plant lived without yielding its goodness to the people. And though they worked, the people were always happy.

I could also see into the depths of things there, into the well-ordered houses where the women made jokes together as they worked, where babies slept without hunger or devilry. In the trees there were swarms of bees and honey. Because there was plenty, in the land of the dead men did not fight. Men and animals knew they were the same as the earth and the sky. No one needed to speak because thoughts ran through the sharp air and all wishes were heard. If a woman wanted wool to spin, a sheep would come and stand calmly beside her to be sheared.

My guide was honored in that country, and not only because people feared his power. As we passed, men looked up from their work and called to him. He was as welcome to them as a cloud or the sun. The children there, who looked like flowers, ran to him because they could see the handkerchief full of sweets inside his black coat. Because I was with the saint, carrying his things, I was not afraid there, although my body was very thin, the smoke from fires and the mists there were more corporate than I.

The people understood what was being told them by animals and even by the earth itself, which spoke openly. Everything was ordered by a plan, and no thing sought to be more or less than it was. Only in this aspect does the land of the damned resemble God's Kingdom on Earth as promised by His Son.

Often I would see my father in his cornfield, and although the work made his hands bloody, he was perfectly happy there. He would call to me and ask me to help him, but my guide told me I could not stay until I had left fear behind, as these people had done.

At times I would carry my younger brother in my arms instead of the saint's flowers. At other times I carried a cross and met my brother at a fork in the road where he would offer me a wide, lighted path and one which went into the forest narrow and darkly. If I chose the winding small path my brother would lead me by the hand and soon we would again be in the sunlight in corn tasseled with halos over our heads, and there would be people around us singing and joking. On this path my brother and I carried the cross between us.

If I chose instead the wide road, the saint would accompany me. The darkness would come more quickly than it comes with a storm. Then I heard crying and when I could see again, it was all in smoke and flame, as though the mountains and the earth itself were on fire. Without any clothing, the women there attempted to put out fires in their sinful parts by pushing things up between their legs, but they only brought about worse suffering. Men climbed over each other to escape, but the devils standing by the pit or floating over it threw the people back in, or took them entire into their great mouths and ate them and then disgorged them. Always when we visited this place, the saint would read my horror and smile on me and point, saying, This is *our* path, the one for you and me, and without understanding I would look up and for just an instant through the smoke I would see white light, at times as big as the face of a baby and at times no larger than a star. The light was far off beyond the inferno of the damned.

Handing the paper back to Pedro, Dio said, Now, just in case we should find ourself one day in a moment of historical repetition, write this at the end: I record these dreams not for my own edification, but at the request of my confessors, so they may know what beliefs about the life after death the Indians still hold, and will maintain until such time as they come to God's Church.

When he returned to the boy's table, the priest noticed Pedro was silently crying. He asked, Does it give you pain to recall all of this?

No Padre

What is wrong then?

Nothing. And then, a minute later, Do you think Padre Cresencio is close to God?

I can't know that, Dio said. For all of us who are less than saints, unity with God comes and goes. It is like the phases of the moon.

When are you closest to Him, Padre?

I can't say. But when we have gotten ready and you open the door for me into the chapel, I am like a bride going to meet her husband and I feel I know how a wise man will go toward his death.

His death? why?

Because this world is a womb, only a preparation for the next.

And ecstasies, Padre, like the saints had?

Have. I myself have had them, but I no longer seek them.

Why?

They take our energies and spend them too fast. They are like eating chilies—the heat is fine for the time, but afterwards the discomfort in the back field is too great. Not worth the pain. And if God is in all things at all times, why rush toward Him and suffer the disappointment of being refused because you are not prepared? Now why do you ask about Cresencio?

Last night he got the little boys out of the dormitory and took them to the kitchen and showed them the torments of Hell by putting my Primavera in the bread oven.

And yet, a few days later, when Pedro came on the old man lying on the chapel floor with a scourge beside him and several boys silently watching while like a turtle Cresencio tried to get his feet under himself and crawl away, Pedro picked him up and carried him to his cell. There, in front of the tagalong children, Cresencio grudgingly said, You are good. And Pedro replied, No, Padre, none are good except God. The news of the encounter ran through the seminary and the other priests smiled at it.

Saturday afternoons the priest and his boy went walking through the meadows in the shadow of the abrupt mountains which shut off the valley of San Cristóbal from the Indian towns around. Once with Hector the antiquarian as guide they went to stand beneath the chalky overhanging cliffs where the Chamulas had, in 1523, defended themselves against the conquerors. Where your ancestors tried to throw ours, Hector told Pedro, describing an arc from the heights to some rocks below with the silver point of his cane. Usually, though, they were alone, and they walked east toward the separate little village of Kushtitali. Chamulas going home from market, seeing the black dress, would run after Dio and grab his hands to kiss them and even, if they were drunk or especially careful of their souls, fall to their knees and remain until long after Dio and his boy had passed on.

In spite of such interruptions Dio worked on, demanding his opinions and recitations from Pedro. But on those Saturday walks the student could not concentrate, because nearly every week after confession as they were about to leave the seminary, no matter how casual or quick Dio was about it, Pedro noticed the hand taking the soap and disappearing it into the cassock pocket. Then he would stumble and be unable to think the simplest thought. When they got to their place on the treeless riverbank, Dio would gather his black skirts about him and sit on a large rock, and say Now get yourself into the water.

I washed yesterday, Padre. I am clean.

No you are not, Dio would say, and hand him the soap.

Then, turning his back, Pedro would have to shuck his cotton shirt and drawers and would race into the milky cold flowing water. His body shrunk in on itself and he had to gasp and push out his chest to draw breath. To his thighs in the stream, he pulled water up over him with his cupped hands and ran the soap over his body, putting off as long as he could the moment he would have to dunk his head and hobble up over the sharp rocks onto the bank. There he would hand back whatever soft dab of soap was left, Dio would wrap it into a leaf and it would disappear back into the soutane pocket. Then playfully Pedro would grab for his clothes, but the priest would not allow that.

He used the shirt to dry the boy's back, working without haste. When he was done, he slapped Pedro's rump and held the damp shirt out for the boy to put on. And Pedro then had to turn around, humiliated and dreading because, no matter how cold he was and how he tried to keep his thoughts away, between his legs it began to loosen and grow heavy and painful.

Where is your mind, boy? the question asked him so often, in the cell while he was reading, in the anteroom while they were dressing for Mass, that he opened his mouth to speak automatically. Clean first what is within the cup and platter then the outside of them will be clean also, Pedro said.

A monk's answer. In spite of all I have tried to do to save you from it, Padre Cresencio has done a good job on your mind. Dio had Pedro's pants bunched in his hand. Like a servant finishing dusting, he dabbed at a line of water on the inside of the boy's thigh, and contemplated the penis standing out toward him beneath the shirt, and the tightened scrotum. Above the intent priest, the equally intent Indian staring at the perfectly round pate and the rich silver hair. Separate small shudders passing through them.

Someone walking on your grave, we would say, or perhaps the great mind's recollection that this is exactly, with the same hunger, how the ladino fifteen years ago stared at the perfect baby in the firelight.

The pressure of Dio's fingers became distinct one by one and he slid the skin off its head. Pedro thinking of the pate as a marbletop table in Doña Laura's salon which he, in the weakness of his knees like an old man, might just have to lean against, and Dio, thinking of the prisoner and truth as his ransom, said Now tell me again what you are thinking.

How it may happen, and I will get you wet and make us both sin and— Pedro talking now all in a jumble.

Dio let go of the penis and, standing up, saw Pedro was crying. He turned him around and began to dig his fingers into the boy's shoulders. It makes me very sad, he said.

His legs shivering with cold, Pedro watched the cows on the other side of the river, wondering how they could be so calm. All day the sky had been empty except for the sun and some heckling birds, but now the sun had lowered itself beyond the church of San Cristóbal on its hill and behind the stately mass of the great Indian mountain called Older Brother which blocked the western extent of the ladinos' place, and lit up one by one great clouds which had come from the east and passed like pictured travelers above the north line of the ridge. A deep swirl of the kind artists like to paint around the Virgin all at once began to fill with pale yellow light. Its rim went red. Pedro saw Her there, half-hidden, a woman who steps back when men come laughing to the waterside. But in spite of this, he achieved no new calm. The worst moments of the week were done now, but the fear would not go away.

What is it that makes you sad, Padre?

Your little thing is poking out of you, your face is all flushed, and when I ask you what you are thinking you quote San Mateo. That denies me, Pedro, denies the recognition you have always made.

What recognition, Padre?

You've never been fooled into thinking I wasn't a man. You've never tried to fool me on human matters. You know that I know. And when a man's penis is swollen, when some other man is playing with it or it's softly inside a girl or about to be, how could you be thinking of anything else?

But you tell me a good man can think of God at any moment.

Dio sighed. Only because he sees God in everything, Pedro. Who made that penis of yours?

Knowing he was stepping into a trap even as he did it, Pedro said, The Devil.

Dio very close up behind him, pressing him back against his own body, breathed against Pedro's ear. No no no. Cresencio's easy heresies, Pedro. Dio released him, stepped back and added, more to himself, Growing now, the body's confusion in growth, not knowing where arms and legs are going to end up when you stretch them out, mind and body and self betraying themselves separately and one the other. You are susceptible now, I suppose. Here, put on your pants. We are late.

Dio handed him his drawers and sat down again on his rock, watching the boy's misery as he pulled on the clothes, tucked in the too-short shirt and tied the strings in a tight bow. But don't think I'm going to give up on you so easily, Dio said. I shall still fight for you.

The sky had turned lighter, that moment when the sun throws back a few seconds of its strength not directly on us, but reflected off the belly of the clouds. Pedro kneeled and kissed the priest's palms.

Now tell me this, Dio said rapidly, what happened to our Christ at the very moment the soldiers pierced His side?

He gave up the Spirit.

And what more?

The earth grew dark and the curtain in the great temple in Jerusalem split open of its own will.

And?

Pedro's mouth opened and closed. He did not remember any more.

And, Dio said, even though He had lost blood, in that moment there was a swelling like the ones you have between His legs.

Pedro shook his head. It does not say that.

No, but even an ignorant boy like you can deduce it.

Pedro was still, staring at Dio. The last moment of the sun had passed and the priest, though no longer angry, looked gray and old. How?

Because when men die there is a rush of blood to the sexual organ. And He was a man.

I did not know that, about the blood.

Well you have learned something, then. Let us go, we are late and you will not eat if we don't hurry, Dio said.

6

He would knock and then, pressing his hands and ear flat against the wood, listen, wait and knock again. The girl sat on the pavement against the wall cracking peanuts the old man had bought her and popping them into her mouth. She might have stayed there forever, watching the parade of city life and the white people in numbers she had never seen before. Mesha had thought to make her fresh, only half calculating deception, and half preparing a gift concocted from his memory of what it was that he had seen once, fifty years ago, that made him summon his courage and speak to a girl. They had stopped at a stream on the way to town so she could wash her hair and make a straight white line of part down the middle of her narrow head. He had put a light copper ring on her finger.

After a while a ladino woman showed him where the bell cord was and a bald child appeared to take him inside. Augustina got to her feet to follow, but the child pushed the door closed against her.

Mesha was led into a small courtyard where ten or so students were seated on the ground intent on an older boy wearing a cassock which came to only slightly below his knees, who was lecturing them while he moved various green figs, onions and lemons in patterns around a grapefruit. Half-hidden by a squat column, Mesha observed the lesson for a long time and overheard a tall priest and a short one commenting in Spanish which Mesha did not understand, on the student's demonstration. Then, as though he knew the Indian, the shorter of the priests came over to him and whispered, My brother says that, in terms of salvaging their souls, it might have been more opportune to stick with the Ptolemaic universe. This one does make the earth seem so friendless.

Though Mesha did not understand the words, he could tell a joke on loneliness had been made, and since he knew the secret as well as Dio did he grinned, toothlessly.

How can we help you? the priest asked.

I want to talk to *that* one, Mesha pointed to the boy giving the lesson. He is my son.

Is he?

Pedro stood before them, not knowing what to do. But Dio half-raised a hand and Pedro thought it was a dispensation, and he bowed to have Mesha touch him on the forehead.

They walked together through the seminary, mostly in silence. Pedro told his old friend what they grew in the gardens, he showed him the windowless bathing cell the priests of another era had constructed, and the long downsloping trough above their heads through which a servant standing in the next room had poured the buckets of hot water when the priests called for them. Mesha peered down the grated drain and said, Not much used, is it? No, Pedro admitted. And while they were standing there they heard howling, and Pedro tried to find something to say to blot out the noise, but he could not think of anything.

They have not changed, have they? Mesha said.

How?

We always knew they were crazy. They do not seek women or drink or a good time, they look for misery and give pain to their bodies so freely. We used to believe they hid their women from us in their Hell, and in the night they snuck off to sleep with them. I came to see if it was true.

And what do you see?

It is worse than we believed. Well, will you show me how to get out of here now?

At the gate Mesha held Pedro's hand tightly and put his other thumb on the inside of the boy's elbow, and said he was going. Then he nodded to the girl sitting against the wall. It did not work out with her man, he said, he was good but he died. So I will leave her here with you.

Pedro pulled free of Mesha's hold. But I have no place to put her.

She is for your keeping, the old man said. Find a place. If I kept her now people would talk. And besides, in a year I will be dead and buried in the place where I can hear the churchbells and the skyrockets and all the fiestas.

I live *here*, Pedro said.

I know. You chose this life, but you still have to do what you have left to do from your other life. Did you think I buried your father the *pasyon* for free?

Yes I did.

Well, you were wrong. There is a price. But there is a pleasure too, you know. And you are not to be one of those men who won't trouble themselves with the hardshelled sweet fruits.

Standing in the noon sun and hearing the persistent bell at his back summoning him, Pedro found himself not angry but tired. Mesha was saying again he was leaving the girl, and Pedro said he did not care, he could not help her, and backed himself through the small gate and barred it inside.

In the afternoon it rained steadily and hard. Pedro sat in his confessor's room trying to study. By chance Dio set as that day's text the difficult admonitions to the disciples. His face red and his hands wet and unquiet, Pedro stuck on "I send you to be sheep among wolves, then be wise as serpents and as gentle as doves. And when they seize you, do not think how you will talk, for you will be given what to speak at that time. For you do not speak, but the Spirit of Your Father speaks in you. And a brother will surrender his brother to be killed, and fathers their children: and the children will rise up against their parents and kill them. And all men will hate you for being Mine. But he that endures will be saved in the end. When they persecute you here, flee to another city. . . ."

All seeming so easy, so given, and impossible to act upon.

She had hardly changed. There must have been no babies, for she had not thickened, her breasts remained small. Mesha had dressed her in the necklaces and ribbons of a girl, not a woman. Pedro's throat felt small, his breath pressed out against his chest as though he had been forced back into the stays they had made him wear once.

Come, Dio said, we'll go to Hector's and discover what the hedonists and the godless eat for their supper.

I have not learned this text, Padre. I should stay and study it.

You weren't a scholar yesterday. What makes you suddenly one today?

Nothing.

Against the seminary's outside wall, turned gray in the rainy twilight, there was a heavy smudge of blackness. What's this? Dio asked, pulling the soaked woolen shawl back from Augustina's head. It was a not infrequent occurrence for the various religious houses in San Cristóbal to find sick Indians and babies abandoned against their gates. Pedro was going to let that be the explanation when the shivering girl smiled up directly and shyly at him and he saw the miserable hollows of her eyes. She stirred to get to her feet meaning to follow, as a dog trying to attach himself to you will pretend the relationship is already long established. His anger at Mesha turned itself into hatred for the girl. He thought how in her condition he himself would have known where he was not wanted and, in spite of Mesha, gone away alone to find his own life. Dio was helping Augustina up.

The old man left her for me to find a place, Pedro blurted.

Is she your family?

Yes Padre, she is.

Well let's have a look at her then, Dio said.

And they took her along to the Estrada household, where yet another Indian girl to pluck chickens and sleep somewhere on the straw made no noticeable difference in anything. The work did her no harm as she was used to work, and the higher servants, Indians themselves once or the children of Indians, beat her for her stupidity and yelled at her as they were or had been beaten and yelled at themselves, and she answered them with soft helpless laughter as they too answered their betters. For months the secrets of the household were enough pleasure for her, the upright many-pedaled loom which made linen and the master's china through which light could be seen, since in her grief for her husband she had determined that she was the evil one, the cause, and though she lived she was not worthy of desiring anything again (this in the year she was twenty-one or -two). And then for a while her happiness was fed by the moments when gates and shutters flew open and she was allowed a glimpse of the colors and the movement outside the Estrada walls.

For half a year what was bound to happen to her was postponed by her own darkness, not the dark of her skin but of her moving, the slowness and the lack of care for anything. The male servants of the household hardly saw her, because her loveliness was drained away from her. Men seek among women not only for bodies and faces which please, but also for lamps they think they might be able to light.

Then one night there was a man from a ranch of Hector's near the town of Chiapa staying at the house. He was telling the group of people drinking their coffee in the big kitchen how, as they had heard, Chiapa people were more cagey than any others. Just today, he said, my old jenny got tired of life and lay down to die in the middle of that road in to the market. I couldn't get her up even with the wagoners helping me kick at her, as I say, she had decided to end it there in the middle of the road. Then the commandant of the San Cristóbal garrison came and he warned me if I didn't get my mule out of the way I was going to jail sure enough. So finally I leaned down and whispered something in her ear, and that mule got up damned quickly. Well, the commandant was amazed. He asked me what I had whispered to the old girl. And I told him it was a secret, and on my life I couldn't explain it to him. But the commandant wanted to know very badly by then, so he said 'If you don't tell me you'll go to jail and think about it until you come to want to.' So I told him the secret.

The man stopped and looked around. He had all of the servants expectant. Even Augustina was smiling. Somebody said, Well what was it, the secret? The man turned smartly on his heel to the Indian girl and asked her in Tzotzil, Do you want to know? Yes, she said. Will you pay for it? Augustina nodded, and the man swung back to the crowd and went on, Well, I finally had to tell him I leaned down to my jenny and I whispered in her ear, 'If you don't get up out of the road now, they are going to make you commandant of the garrison here!' which did the trick.

All the next day Augustina smelled of horses, and she could not tell whether it came from the stable where she had slept, or from the sweat of the man himself. He was good to her, and left her a coin when he went on his way. In a while she was given a castoff long skirt to wear and, looking more like a ladina, she became more attractive to the men in the house and several of them had times with her. She did not conceive, and began to imagine it was impossible for her.

Though Pedro would not speak to her, he regularly had his supper in the kitchen where Augustina was free to watch him. It pleased her when the other servants talked jealously about the special treatment he received, and spread the information that he was Padre Dio's 'little pet.' Why Don Hector liked him they did not know, but since the master had become incapable of spending the evening alone or with his equals, when his brother could not come he often had the Indian boy sit up with him to talk or read aloud. Then Pedro would spend the night in the store room where the sugar brought from the Estrada hot country fincas was kept.

She noticed everything she could about him, how he cultivated the few hairs on his upper lip and stroked them as though they were a real mustache, how he used a fork if it was put before him unlike most Indians who were uncomfortable with them, and how he liked to wash his hands before he ate, so she took it on herself to bring him the warm water.

One night she met Pedro in the hall and stopped him. Yesterday a woman came and asked for you, Augustina told him. She said you were to come to Tzajalemel tomorrow.

I can't, Pedro said.

Augustina pulled from behind her a small round loaf of bread and handed it to him.

What's that for?

I saw you like their bread better than tortillas, so I stole it for you. Here, take it.

Thank you, he said, and stuffing the bread into his shirt, he went back to Hector's library. Deeply wrapped up in himself, as most young men are, Pedro assumed the girl meant more than she did by the simple gift, that she, Mesha's spy, knew all about his mother, and that she was saying to him that he was presumptuous and vain to have such ladino tastes as the one for white bread.

Hector asked him, And what's to become of you, young man? will you be a priest, or will you go home to Chamula and have a wife and children and live in ignorance molested by the knowledge they've forced down your gullet?

I will do whatever Dio wants me to.

Hector's face soured. And Dio is always telling me how proud he is that he raised you to be open in your feelings. Certainly not the best training for an Indian.

After a long silence Hector asked, How old are you now?

Nineteen.

When I was your age, I was very insane. On even-numbered days I believed that I was the Second Appearance of Christ Jesus, a delusion which filled me with an excitement and anticipation for my own death I could taste in my throat. But on the odd-numbered days I knew that I was mortal and, in spite of my line and titled forebearers, not an especially important mortal, certainly not different from others in type. Hector sighed. Just another fellow bound to apply a pistol to the side of his head because a particular young woman—a frivolous girl who wore white then and today has ten brats and not a line left to her body—could not love me or at least did not love me enough to marry me and save me.

I don't see that your two beliefs were fighting against each other, Pedro said.

Hector nodded. I knew you wouldn't. He tapped a leather-covered box on the table. What's in here is proof that you too are one of those who can hold opposites comfortably in his head. Hector opened the box and pulled out Pedro's second version of his dream. It would be perfectly clear to anyone who has read that, except my dear brother, that you don't believe anything is wrong with what your people there do or how they conceive of God. You don't, do you?

No sir.

And you shouldn't. What do we live for, Pedro? experiences? not just those to tell others, but for our own, to possess them alone? if so, there is no education, no learning, no teaching. What do you want? a woman? a man? a god? There, Hector said, indicating his bookshelves, are people who have had them all. Why not just read the books?

Pedro did not answer, and again there was silence. Finally Hector said, We are born to places, my boy, all of us, and into societies and systems. We may get joggled, or addled, or removed from the compartment we were born into and placed in another, as you were, or struggle through a lifetime to lift ourselves out of one box and into the next higher one, as the bourgoise do. But I doubt anyone is ever happy until he knows that the box in which he was first placed by whatever hand is as comfortable, as complete and as various as any of the others. My place in the world seems enviable to many—though I doubt *you* are deluded about that—and you will probably disbelieve me when I tell you that I sit here many nights and long to have been born a person who could make something with his hands, a chair say, or a field. But that is the case. I admire men who can. And moreover, I sincerely hate the people of my class. Nothing remains in us of the qualities which made us the masters of this supposed new world. We are fat and ugly and proud of our ignorance or, like myself, lost in the dreary land where we live with our nostrums. I think the true nobleman never believed in the nobility. Look at the history of the Marquis himself: all that he won by trickery and vast military cleverness and ability and by sheer daring, his inept son, supposed possessor of the same qualities of blood, managed to let slip through his fingers. But still, the nobility is the box that I came from, the one I understand, and I do not think we can do anything but damage to ourselves and to our happiness by presuming to be anything more than we were meant to be by God or by chance. So if you go home when your education is done you will disappoint my brother, but for whatever it's worth, remember there is someone who approves of what you are doing, even if he can't imagine your life.

As he grew up with men who could often read his thoughts, first Mesha and then Dio, Pedro had never been able to gather to himself many secrets. Now he had the one he had not even told Salvador, the secret of how she was trying to draw him back, the rare things his mother was asking him to help her do, and he came close to telling it all to Hector, but at the last minute he held himself back.

He had been to Tzajalemel again, irregularly, for a day here and there which they would allow him, or when Dio was away baptizing during a village fiesta and the other priests thought Pedro had gone along to act as server.

There was a man in the house with Rosha. They slept together in the bed, but the man was so wizened and creaky, whatever his age, and his mother lived in such a frenzy of continuous praying that Pedro could not believe they had time or energy left over for the simple action a man and woman perform in the darkness. When he came, they assumed he was there to help them. Petitioners arrived at all hours, bringing the sick with them, sleeping sprawled under the eaves when there was no more room inside the little house.

There was a child lying senseless on the bed, surrounded by a border of red flowers. Rosha's man had been gone since soon after nightfall, and she was very drunk, bent over the boy, Pedro kneeling at her side beating a rattle against his hand. See our tears, see us crying, I beg your holy pardon, she prayed, I beg your holy forgiveness. We cannot beg if there is no pardon, we cannot beg if there is no forgiveness. If we have repeated an action, Pedro thought, we have not repented it. And then, to calm himself, he made himself say what Dio had said, This too is an access, this standing in the anteroom waiting for the free gift of being allowed to come briefly into the light.

His mother paused and got ready to rise. You do it, she whispered.

I can't.

She stood and covered his head with her hand. You are only afraid, she said, and pushed her way through the child's wondering family to the door. He got up, dropping the rattle, and went after her.

The night was chilly and there was the moon, so what he saw he saw clearly: the strange man's clothes, his chamarra and pants and shirt, hung on the waisthigh cross in the corner of the yard. His mother was at the stile, slowly climbing over. Go back, she called, go back and make it happen.

And you?

I'm going with him.

She fled down the hill toward the river valley, hair streaming behind her, running crazily and limping, going too fast and unsure for a woman her age. Pedro started for the cross, meaning to take the clothes from its arms so the people inside would not see them, but he hesitated and stopped, caught in a crosscurrent of thoughts. A witch hangs his clothing on his cross and turns into a goat when he goes to do whatever evil it is he has contracted for with his own heart or his spirit. Pedro didn't know whether he believed it, but he knew it. He also knew that the clothes hung there were surety, the means of return, and by taking them from the cross he could condemn the man. He went back inside and prayed until the child's family was satisfied, sometime near dawn. Later, when they woke, the child seemed better and the clothes were gone from the cross. But his mother had not returned, and Pedro had to leave for San Cristóbal knowing nothing, he felt, certainly not whether it was his own intercession which had caused the child to get better.

The next time he came she was all fire. When I die, she told him, see that I am buried not here where they will find me, but within the sound of the bell.

What Mesha had said. But for Mesha it was the place he

deserved to be buried, the one he had paid for. And Rosha wanted it only to protect herself, her body. Pedro wanted to tell her, In our town, here, each ringing of the bell drives a nail into the body of a witch, but he could not bring himself to say the words to her.

On a Saturday morning in May he was sent to market to buy onions for the cook. There he met Augustina who told him an hour ago a man had come with a message. They wanted Pedro in Tzajalemel that night.

You know everything about this, don't you? Pedro asked.

No.

Shall I tell you?

If you want to.

All right. He nodded, mouth fixed. I will—if I come back this time.

In trying to be kind to him, Augustina had made Pedro think she was smug and all-knowing. When he returned from Tzajalemel he meant to tell her about his mother and even about what Dio forced him to do on the riverbank.

He asked for a free Sunday and Dio said No, I will need you tomorrow to assist me at Mass.

What about your Francisco or one of the other boys?

None of them are you, the priest said.

In the pearl-clouded afternoon they went for their usual walk to the river. The yellow green of the meadow throbbed. Dio sat on his rock and, contemplating Pedro's sullen face, said, When you cannot go home to what is difficult, turn aside into the easy road.

Nothing which is easy gives me pleasure, Padre.

Then you are not living a good life, and not celebrating Him, Dio said. He pulled the inevitable shard of yellowish soap from his pocket and handed it to Pedro.

When he came out of the gray water and saw Dio once more holding his shirt out to him, Pedro rebelled. Arms folded at his shaking chest, he said, No Padre, I cannot allow you.

You don't have such choices. Come here. And then, a few moments later while he was still drying Pedro's back, Dio said to himself, So Godgiven.

What?

So perfect, I said. You cry too much for a man. What is it this time?

I love you Padre.

I know you do. But there's no reason to cry over that. What more? Pedro did not say anything, so Dio went on, You mentioned Francisco earlier. Is it about him?

My brother claims Francisco is your little fellow.

Are you jealous of him? Dio handed Pedro back his clothes and told him to put them on and to sit next to him on the rock. When Pedro was dressed, Dio said, Well, I will tell you then. For three years or so now I've done with little Francisco all the things the priests and the boys assumed I did with you. For your sake, I think I have ruined Francisco for women. I always thought of forcing you into it, every time we came here, but I didn't. I preserved you from any anguish in your love for me, and now little Pancho will hang on your neck as he hangs on mine.

But you told me any love, even a sin of the body, was good, an act of devotion.

That is still true. But what you don't understand, my boy, is that every act, even an act of devotion, has its price or its consequence. I've kept that news from you, because I wanted to see you develop freedom of thought first, as most men never do. Would you roll on the ground with me now, here?

Yes Padre, I would.

Well it's too late for that. You tempted me once, as much as a man would be tempted if he could seize Jesus Christ and take Him away from the rest of humanity, keep God all for himself locked in a room. But I overcame that temptation. Do I, my body, tempt you now?

Yes, Padre. You do.

Dio took Pedro's red face in his hands. Shall I tell you how you may make love to me as I want to be loved?

Yes.

Some time be my dancer. Be my only one.

The next week Dio allowed Pedro a night and a day to go to Tzajalemel. Returning Sunday evening he did not even stop at the seminary to tell his brother the news. He would not eat the food the Estrada cook set before him. Augustina was working and only after nearly everyone else in that early rising household had gone to bed was she free.

Had they been in the place they came from, Pedro would not have taken Augustina's rough hand and kissed all over it, he would not have pressed his body to hers against the wall and dug at the top of her blouse until he could find her breast and hold it. Everything he knew of the gestures of love he had learned peering at ladinos, maids and their swains in those public intimacies on stoops and in entryhalls which poor lovers must make do with as the places for the delicate business of discovering one another.

As he had seen it done, he forced his mouth on hers, not knowing until she taught him that he must form his lips somehow against hers. Augustina had not thought of what to expect from him and did not understand his hunger except as newness, her husband had been as forceful as this at first, but she held his head to her and absorbed what she could of the strange energy in him. There was a wordless sweet sound in her throat when he stroked her, which soothed him because he knew it would happen to him now, and they sat facing on the ground while he told her what he had seen.

To an observer on the balcony quietly smoking his paper-wrapped cigar and unable to hear them, Pedro telling of going and discovering her not only dead but already locked in the earth, and the man who had been with her missing and the little house picked clean of its few things, and Augustina nodding seriously and lightly touching his arms, to an observer on the balcony they looked like two children planning a game.

When he was through with his tale, she said, We can find a place in the stable.

No. Not where animals go, Pedro said.

But there was no problem, since the world sometimes seems to honor haste for its own startling energy, as though haste were a virtue. Only a few minutes before Pedro came to tap at the library door Hector had returned there from his sleepless wanderings. When Pedro explained it was too late for him to go back to the seminary, even over the back wall, Hector gave him the key to the sugar room.

Pedro had a candle end which lasted only long enough for

Augustina to glimpse the great white towers of sugar in sacks around them and the place on the stone floor where they would lie. Like a gallant, he took off his shirt and spread it for her, but then when she hesitated he misunderstood and forced her to the floor so her back was not on the shirt at all. For a long time he lay on top of her holding her tightly pressed against him, nothing moving except his mouth which worked in a clumsy way against her cheek, and Augustina was for the first time afraid. Her arms were bound under his and she could not get free. She moved her head against his until, by feeling, she found his tight-closed mouth, a slit she worked her lips to until, at length, the spell or whatever it was broke and he sighed and responded to her kiss with a soft one of his own.

I want only to be good to you, to serve you, he whispered, wanting his words to be true and knowing they were not if he was willing to subject her to this act on lifeless cold stone.

But his body loosened then and she, with her experience, found the way to get his penis out of his drawers, and after pulling up her skirt with her other hand, she put it into herself. For a long while then again he was silent and rigid and then he shivered and little jerky floods ran into her. When they woke in the morning, they saw sparkling sugar all around them on the sunlit floor. It was sticky in their hair, and small stingless bees swam around them until they moved to rise.

On the evening of that day, a Monday, she was waiting for him outside the Church of the Merced when the students came from chanting their service. There was no priest with them, and Pedro saw the choir back into the seminary and closed the gate before coming to her. She told him Doña Laura knew he was the man in it, and she had been beaten by the master's steward and then sent away. Pedro, not yet suspecting the map which had been designed for them to travel, told Augustina to stay by the gate and went directly to his friend.

Dio gave him another key and told him of course they would have to wait until after everyone was asleep. He also gave Pedro an oil lamp, and a warning about the donado getting up to start his fire an hour before dawn. And so a second night they had a place, this time the priests' bathing room.

Dio got himself a chair and carried it to the opening on his side, softly so the children would not hear him, carefully so the chair would not scrape. He stood watching for an hour, head wedged well into the smooth-bottomed trough, hands cupped at the edge. He could feel his heart beat against the stone wall. Unfortunately he could not see everything, but there was enough. The girl's hand touched the back of Pedro's head, moving tentatively along the straight hairline Dio himself had formed there with his scissors seventy hours ago. The boy's buttocks moved, the line there tightened into a grimace and again the seemingly bodyless hand of the girl came and stroked there once rising and then holding, bodies for the smallest time so balanced, the smallest pressure from one can stay or move the other. Dio remembered that. The lamp flickered, oil ran out, and the wick, hissing, gutted itself. Dio remained at his opening and heard them in the dark beginning again, Pedro more violent and insistent, Growing to like it, Dio thought, and beginning to know what to expect. The priest had his own quivering response to the sounds of growing urgency and reaching inside his robe touched himself. In the dark he heard the moment come, Pedro speaking and then subsiding. Dio dislodged himself and sat in the chair. He prayed against himself and then time, he did not know how long, had passed, and the sounds came again. They would not sleep, which pleased him and disgusted him and confirmed him. They, being young, would not sleep when they could.

He heard a rooster crow once and went to the door. The rooster, it seemed, had been dreaming of dawn, for it was still the darkest part of the night. But not too early to begin. He went along the corridor, knocked on a door, knocked again until he heard the man inside stir and said Father, it's Dio. I think you had better come along and see what's going on in the bathing room.

Not staying to see it happen, Dio went into the back garden and sat down on a bench, suddenly very tired. Beside him grew a flower he had planted himself and was very proud of. It had now reached its full singular beauty, a burst of soft maroon points which in the night looked a gentle brown. He could tell lights were being lit and could hear calling and shouting, Cresencio's outraged, womanish voice rising above the others. The gate opened quietly, and Pedro came in, closed the gate, and slipped the bolt into its hole. He stood before Dio, breathing.

Well?

They've taken her.

Who has?

The soldiers.

Soldiers? Well. That's a serious approach. And what will they do with you?

In the confusion I got away.

Then you had better hurry.

You were never my friend, were you?

How can you say that Pedro?

You would not cross borders with me.

True, but not the ones you think.

You would not tell me.

Not what the miseries of manhood were going to be, the disappointments waiting for you, I did not warn you that, no matter how much you believe, a time would come when you are bound to see yourself a lone, broken old man on a road which goes only toward death, which itself is nothing. And then you will wonder why any man has the sheer stupidity to go on putting foot after foot—

The stout wood seemed to belly toward them as bodies were flung against the other side of the gate.

All that I kept from you. If you're going, you had better go now, Dio said, waving Pedro away from him.

When he was over the wall, Dio went and unbolted the door and Cresencio and the soldiers with their lights and rifles poured in around him, not even stopping to ask him, assuming that he was willing to betray the honor of the seminary for the sake of his little Indian fellow. They streamed to the wall, the smallest of the soldiers was hoisted to the top and from there, straddled on the adobe, he announced that he could see nothing. Pedro had disappeared.

When I first told Juan Tushim I had to return to the States

for a while, he seemed disappointed. Although he did not say it, I felt sure he was asking himself if he hadn't made a mistake and wasted his time with me. Hadn't I promised to hear him out? and was I, the owner of magical tape recorders and Coleman lanterns, manipulated by great worldly powers beyond my control? And if so, what use was it to tell me the story of Pedro Díaz Cuscat? I would lose it or be forced to corrupt it too.

He was drunk again in the line of duty, and I was drunk with him for comfort and reading too much into his old sad face, feeling guilty for having pretended to him that I ruled my own life, and for not having told him about the workings of the great world.

"My mother is sick too," I added.

"Is she? I am sorry to hear it," he said, and getting up he went into the house.

After a while, I went to his doorway and, peering into the darkness, said "Uncle? I will be back in August."

Juan came out, the leather tube under his arm and papers in his hand. "August is late," he said.

When I first looked at the new document, I thought he meant to bribe me into staying and hearing him out. Later I decided he was safeguarding the story, giving me an important part of the ending in case he was not around anymore when I came back or since, as they cheerfully say there, a man is very likely to die on the road.

The writing was in pencil and smudged, though luckily the old real graphite seems to hold better than our modern stuff does. The paper was a cheap grade, and at first I thought the hand the most childish of the examples I had seen. But then I realized this last was Pedro's own way, writing done in a hurry for himself and not for a teacher. The date was June, 1870.

My whole life has belonged to visions dreamed first by a boy ten years of age. I have loved the vision given me as a man loves and cares for his children. All my troubles have come from it and all my happinesses. I go to it now as to a place where I have always prayed and kneel there not in wonder anymore but in contentment. I know it all by heart, each thing.

At times I have felt what I was promised by the saint has not happened yet and I was pained inside and believed I must cut the vision out of me before it took my body along with it into the place of desolation. At those times I was set apart from my own by myself.

But that feeling comes less and less. More often the dreams have been a light or warmth for me on dark cold roads. The vision is myself. My life was given me to protect Her vision in this world for a little while, and for no other reason. The death of my body does not trouble me, since I know the vision did not come only with me and will not die when I die.

In the other land, the real one, it is hard for mere people to see all for everything is visible and always moving. When the shadow of a cloud crosses a field, there are two fields, one yellow in the sun and diminishing, the other blue and growing. A woman there eats an apple in secret. But when we meet her, we see she is a woman who has eaten an apple. A road is not a road, it is a way many men have chosen to travel, and we know them all and where they have been and where they are going. We know everything. We know who will come after. It is blinding for mere people in the real land, because everything shimmers and is every moment all it is. When we go there we see the spirit of things and are frightened and shy away as horses do when they see their shadows.

From the beginning I was led to pass through the glittering mirror candles into that world by Santa Rosha or the blessed little Christ calling to me from the other side. From the beginning I went in great chords of wind which sucked me down and spoke to me as I flew through their tunnels, and from the beginning I saw my dear father there, working his corn. His hands bled and he had callouses because in life he had not worked hard enough. But there he is content. He would smile on me, bless me, and then turn back to his work. It happened again and again. From the road where I stood I would call to him. I knew he wanted to help me because he would grip his hoe until his knuckles turned white, but he would not come. I began to cry and the vision began to flee from me. From sadness I would begin backing out through the gates of my dream, and I would return to the river and the candles. When I learned to stay I learned not to have sadnesses and fears while I was visiting there. I learned there was nothing my father could do for me. I knew that we people are greater than the total of our fears.

Once I had learned, I began to have the vision of my father sitting at evening in the doorway of our house in Tzajalemel. There, standing between his knees, just learning to hold himself up and protected by the man, is myself. Then I see the boy is my brother Salvador also, and you my children. He laughs and looks so happy to me that I become happy too, knowing that not only is Salvador saved and preserved by God, but I am too, and everyone.

The people are happy in that land because no one does another man's work, and so there is no hunger and no envy, and there is no death beyond them.

I live there more and more now, and I come back only to tell you. When I saw her the last time in this life my Augustina cried for you. I told her she must work harder to stay in the other land, she must not think you will remain here long after both of us have gone. We see you, we watch over you, and we are joyful always.

PART II
THE HONEY MAN
1856-1860

Also on the road another. Following. Meaning harm.

His own shuffle footfalls the old man heard sound ordinary to him as heart beats, constant as that other barrage to his ears, fum of bees, bullets in a distant battle. Ears, ragged and cavernous like conches and filled with sweet waxy grit, stretched back to pick out over or above his humming what manner of evil was behind him coming on. Another man at least, human at least. Tired and probably old too, the follower loped, bare feet flapping, stopped to heave and wheeze, fell back, then came running again to catch up.

But chooses not to overtake me. Not used to traveling long distances, not regular like horses and women. A mule not yet beaten enough. Could be young, old man. But if so, more tired out than we first thought, my angel.

As the old man puzzled, he began plucking absently at strings and frays of cloth. And still he worked away at the flat road through the arid, burned country where there was no shelter, no tree, only the grim wall of the mountains to one side and the plain to the other. Inside the old man's purblinded eyes appeared a demonstration, like a proof in geometry, ultimately reassuring. He saw this other man as life-and-death pursued, propelled forward, and himself a weaker force keeping the other from passing. A balance of long and short, weak and strong. And proof the other man was marked in some way, or else he would overtake—

And passing see I am marked too so *I* cannot see what mark it is he carries, and could not betray him to his special pursuers. Laughter and sneezing added to the mumblings and cogitations.

Endangered, the old traveler knew two foils. With warning, he could feel his way to the ditch, sit, pull his sticky pots clattering from around him, then reach into his shirt and, hungry or not, take out whatever it was and fumble for his water gourd. Even thieves who would steal a wallet off the backside of a man riding his wife will hesitate at robbing a fellow at his lunch. But other times they came on him so silently he felt their hands on him before he could hear them, and then he simply stopped dead on the road, knees locked and arms extended in surrender. Becoming, he wildly believed, a bare dry desert tree dogs might like to lift their legs at. Usually then the other travelers, startled, merely laughed or pulled a whip across his shoulder in passing, or swiped at a vulnerable ear as they went by. Once in the days when he still had his sight, a horseback ladino paused, reached down and snatched a tuft of fur from his head, and then remarked to the lady riding beside him, I will be damned, Maria, it *is* real! and blew the hair up into the air where it hung dancing like a milkweed fluff, suspended in the dry afternoon sky. When the ladinos had gone by and the pain receded the old man had found it miraculous too and had picked his head nearly bald before he had placed in the sky what he deemed the right beautiful number of moths.

For many years, being beneath envy, he had been invulnerable to robbery. Though there were unfortunates below him, in his world he was the least of those who were, who had a part and were counted. He himself could not have plotted how to gather more things to him, and it was in the tradition of the work for him to have only what he carried now. A water gourd, three tin pots held to him on a piece of bad rope and a filthy covering made from manta, white once in the beginning of time, odds and ends sewn to him in the doorways of shacks by pitying and devout hacienda women concerned with keeping their old man decent on his road, so many pieces sewn over so many times that no one except himself could tell what, if anything, belonged to the original garment. But he knew it as well as most of us know our skins. The women at the haciendas sometimes drew things, arms and legs and radiant hearts, on the offerings they sewed to him, as we pin reminders to the figures of saints, in the hope the honey man's goodness might protect them or bring about cures. He could keep no money. Small coins or bits given him dropped through his fingers like water. No sandals, no blanket to roll in at night, no friends or family or dog. The apparent memory of a woman, though now in his age it became questionable whether his starved brain had the capacity for memory as we have it.

Before, in spite of his ruses, which he thought wonderfully clever, he was sometimes beaten up. But only by drunks who had half done with him before they realized who he was. And certainly they were not murderous, these hot country people with flairing, quickspending childish angers the honey man, a stranger to them, could admire.

Now though they told him there was fighting again in the north and hard times all around, and he knew it was true that people were suffering. Other homeless itinerants plodded the roads he worked along and now from time to time he was robbed of even his pots by women. And snatches of his clothing were ripped from him by children not meaning fun.

With this change a new worry had invaded the honey man. A reason for someone to put an end to him. One man only, another honey gatherer wanting his place. Happily, he thought, there was no such person. The plan allowed for only one. But still, in his walking sleep, he now dreamed of the likeness's coming, in the same way a savage could conceive of a mirror without being able to picture it. And the notion of the likeness sometimes brought him, not terrors, but an enervation and sighing relief.

And this one, my angel, hanging back, breathing, plotting, could be the man. Children too amuse themselves with unlikely demons.

But reason enough for the honey man to step on a little faster.

A new burst of running and the hot wind turned a bit as it came across the plain and, through the muffling sweetness which enclosed him like a second blindness, the honey man smelled new information about his pursuer. He had been running a long time, the sweat was thick on him. And drunk, he had recently been wonderfully drunk. That smell in a man is unmistakable, stronger than the smells ladino women take from bottles.

Sssh—old man!

The honey man stopped. Two arms shot out, perpendicular to the thin stump. The other man called him again, but he did not answer. Slowly the other circled him, urgently whispering You must hide me, not tell them anything.

The honey man shivered. He has been around pigs, my angel.

In their dark his eyes rolled like floundering animals, in the outer world his eyelids fluttered and fought against the ghee which held them. He sensed some whiteness and clarity, and a shadow before him. Darknesses against light and lights against darkness were the most he could discern now.

The other one whistled in his teeth and laughed shortly, a bark. And the honey man thought, Now he will begin to kill me, and then many questions, what are we? are where today? be-cause the boy begged and his urgency was like a disease the old man, mind galloping along barely touching ground, had caught.

He must work hard at thinking. His life was such that, though information about space and time were still retained, they were stored in neglected piles in back corners of his mind. His annual course was east to west, then back, the mountains traveling by him on his right now, the sun overhead so it was midday. But what day? two from one hacienda and one before the next. But which? along this part of his road there were three equidistant places he stopped. Did you sleep in a hammock two night ago? I don't remember. The old man smiled at himself as a school-boy does when pushed too far, out beyond the limits of what he is expected to know. It was on cornhusks, he thought. And alone. Are you sure? No, I think.

Come on, quick! the criminal breathing hot and close against the honey man's face. I see them!

And the honey man did too. Saw where they were, and grew sad. A sorry spot in this brown world where there was no ditch or barranca for the fugitive to hide in.

Say something.

Young. Younger than we thought by his voice, Angelita. And a corn eater too, his Spanish learned.

How many after you?

Three.

With horses?

No, guns.

Are they Indians?

Yes Indians. Said with disgust.

Do they know your face?

No.

Your age?

They might.

How long have they seen us?

Just when I stopped you they came over that last ridge. Now they're into the valley, coming faster.

Then stand close to me boy. Right against me, the honey man said.

Are you crazy?

Are you going to die then? the honey man asked, indifferent.

The boy, it seemed, did not choose to die then, for he stood as exact as a man's shadow when he leans to a wall against the old fellow's body. And, fighting with his rope, pulling the noisy pots off himself, the honey man discovered what marked the boy: no clothes on his huffing body. Stumble-fingered, the old man picked at his rags, gently severed bindings grown weak with age and washing, his mind turned to the cumbersome task of undressing and dressing the dead, an act he himself had performed many times.

Now get into these. He held up the tatters, to his half vision a jiggling ghost. How close are they now?

In sight but still small, the boy told him.

If they ask you where you were bound, tell them Don Jorge's place.

The honey man let himself down and gingerly stretched out on the burning road. He moved on elbows and knees like a scorpion adjusting himself, then slowly his knees drew up, his body rolled half on its side and the hands, palms down, curled into themselves. To the watching boy like the dreadful agony of paper consumed in fire.

Next to the sound of his heart, the honey man heard the pounding of the men coming. He began to draw breath, the first deep, a rock into an endless well, the next a little shorter. Giddy thoughts swelled him, and perhaps recollections began, and the near-useless eyes pulsed. When he heard, far away, the men's voices calling out, he drew a last saving piece of the scalding air into himself and began.

He suffered in his own created darkness, hearing the four talk as voices soft in another room, they a stable element, he an animal safely hidden who hears men without dogs as they come, purposeless, chattering through the forest. He was, perhaps, as the stars are to our earth, amazed at that frantic single point of consternation in the vast still.

Pain became his concern. In his haste they kicked him with blunt toes, forced open the eyes to see the milky things inside, pressed fingers at his chest to find a heartbeat. But more the pain of something inside swelling, wanting escape. His soul, he thought. And then he went beyond, into the hardly remembered region of ice. There, as he came into it, the voices from the other room returned, one he knew particularly well which pleased him, as a father is pleased when he discovers a child without his watching has learned to speak. The bitter, sad voice of a boy he knew once whining I was wrong forcing him into coming with me this time, he looked capable of it this morning, but the heat and his age— Who can know? And what happens now? who carries him on to a decent burying place? and where is that?

Even in their own exhaustion, the three men were not without a moment's pity for the boy. The youngest looked one-eyed down the dirty barrel of his old gun. They shuffled, stared at the bones showing through the hide which was not delicate like the skin of an aged person, but calloused and scaly like a lizard's, waited for the boy to close off. But he continued, tears streaking his face, and at last they could not stand it anymore and simply turned from him and set off, loping, down the road in flagging pursuit of the man who had dishonored them.

A whistle began, first high above the range of the human ear where dogs might hear it, then slowly descending. The old man quivered and his mouth opened and a great rush of air poured out. He stopped, it seemed as if he was making the hard decision whether to begin again, and then wheezed and took in air. The old man laughed and the boy, tears in lines on his cheeks, got caught in a bout of noisy little hiccups.

Inevitably it was a child who first saw him coming, toward the gentle close of the locustsung day when a boy has run through all the tricks he knows to speed the passage of time, has carried water and been especially good to his mother, has been forced outside for tormenting the baby or knocking something over, has been off with his friends and an ember to create interesting catastrophes in the world of ants, and has even tired of his own cruelty. Sometimes the child was of such bare memory it would watch him come in confusion, right words not available, then run for its mother to tell and be told, that strange combination. The man is coming. Which man? The one with the pots. You saw the honey man? That's what I said. And the mother then might smile, doubtfully, as once not long ago she had smiled at a young man offering her a comb or some ribbons in a time when she knew she did not know everything such a gift would mean in the end.

But if he was old enough to recall well, the child would set up the cry and come running, and other children would crowd around the old creature, digging their fingers into pots which in their imaginations always contained honey, and were surprised, tricked, to discover the pots dry and caked inside only with dirt from the road. (A moment which, in the coming night, would yield dreams of a man who arrives with nothing, makes something good and leaves again with nothing, in other words fixing in the minds of these children the basis for belief in the true magician's existence.) Buzzing and piping the news in all registers, the children led the blind man past the walled main house of the hacienda—hearing the break in the stillness the master's children would peer out between shutter slats, and be disappointed when they saw no good thing had come to disturb the drone of *their* days, passed reading romances and playing cards or fitfully plucking at guitars or mandolins or imported rosewood spinets—led him with dancing down the ordered street to the square of the 'village' where the life-indentured lived, and to the well where they were permitted by custom to dip the old man a single welcome cup of coolish water. At the places where he was best received, and these were not always the most prosperous of the ranches, a boy would go and report to the steward, or the priest if there was one, and might be told to climb to the top of the village's church and hit the bell. And then, if it was late enough, the foremen in the fields might call their workers from the perfumed coffee bushes or the corn and set them trudging home.

Of course the women were less obvious than the children, finishing whatever they were at or pretending to before they came to lean in their doorways and smile their satisfaction at the sight of him. Even then they brought work with them, suckling babies or a lump of masa to slap back and forth in their incessant hands as they gazed at him. Unlike the children, they remembered the almost unbearable waiting which came between his arrival and the fiesta itself. One or two, older women, would splash water in their faces, tie up their ribbon-woven braids and set off for the master's to help with stoking the ovens and beating out the bread.

What is this? You've come in two, honey man.

Sitting on the edge of the well with the slight cool drifting up his back, he had been resting, almost asleep with the children around him, their buzzing a salve, their laughter his music. It was a woman calling him. What?

We can't let our girls come down to the well, honey man.

Who is this boy?

Another woman, rough-voiced, saying, He's not a 'boy' at all, from the look of it.

And in the undercurrent of laughter, Only you, my dear, would have looked *so* carefully *so* soon, and farther away, softer,

Well if that one's still a boy I'll be glad to wait for him. And all the children were laughing, those still in shirts, too young to know why, catching it from the faces of the older ones.

This is *my* worker, he said. Ha, even the honey man when he gets old deserves a slave of his own!

The women murmured, agreeing that was fair. But one voice insisted, Then you had better dress him in something, honey man, or Don Jorge will have you both beaten. What if his wife should see?

It's not as if the señora hasn't *ever* seen one, you know.

Your old man says the mistress has a hard look at *his* every week.

Yes, she bought those eyeglasses just so she could see it.

Before daybreak he had again torn his single garment, keeping to himself only what might pass for pants, and giving his fugitive the top, which was the better part, more thickly secured with patches. Dividing it and dressing the boy in the cold of the desert dawn he had felt a special rightness in his action. But now the careless women made him cry.

The boy was slumped next to him, hunching, tugging at the tail of his new shirt. Angrily the honey man ordered him to get up and himself reached out for the shirt, pulled at it, heard it rip. A piece of fraying came off in his hand.

A woman tapping his shoulder. Don't, patrón. Let me run and get a little piece I have which will cover him nicely for you. I'll make it right.

No! The honey man kicked at the boy, hardly doing harm because his balance was slight and he could not take either foot far off the ground, but in his mind he was a still-strong fellow of only fifty or so with a round chest, and he was beating the best dog of all his life with dogs, an animal so loyal it would not shy away even when its flanks quivered with pain. He had killed it in fact, during the rage and terrible drinking which had followed on his Angelita's death.

Dumb now with hunger and insensible to any more changes in his condition, and perhaps even awed and humbled by the honey man, the boy did not move to defend himself.

His new master rubbed his foot against the boy's ankle, then stepped back, aimed a final awful kick at him and missed.

And then the honey man subsided. He felt for the stone edge of the well and sat there breathing. The women waited, eyeing the boy suspiciously now, thinking perhaps something unnatural had happened. They were like people who have made a fiesta to celebrate the great dark cloud-covering which marks the coming of the rainy season, and wake to hear no regular drumming on the tiles overhead, and look out to see the sky singularly blue and dry. The honey man, bringer of brief joys, had never before been subject to such ancient and silly rages. They could not decide what changes were brought by the matter of this grown young man dressed as a child in a shirt which hardly hid his navel. They returned to their single-room houses to wait for the men, and one of the women who had made jokes about the boy remembered the time her friend got her silly on drink at the fiesta in Acala and she had danced in the line with the men who embraced the saint in their arms. What she recalled most clearly was going the next morning to look for her husband and how she was hopeful then of not finding him even while she was searching the bars and alleys.

Warned by their wives, the men of Jorge Gamboa y Vasco's famous hacienda La Golondrina joined that night to make precisely, canonically, the fiesta of the honey man. To make it exactly as it should be. Usually the old scarecrow himself breathed the event and its pleasures into the sluggish people. Tonight at sunset when the world he could no longer see was darkening and the world he was beginning to learn opened its gates to those daily few prepared to go inside, not the honey man, not yet he pleaded, and they woke him and fussily strapped his pots to him, he felt them leading him, pulling him along into it. They guided him to Don Jorge's orchard where plums and big-pitted cherries were already ripening, his new slave following at a distance, and there to a small fire they had prepared in advance. Delicate, girlish in their concern for him, they handed him the bundles of pineheart sticks, thick with gluey resins.

At the edge of the intent little crowd his servant noticed how the honey man made up for his blindness with patience and listening. He waited for them to hand him the next piece of equipment without knowing exactly what it would be, the honey man shifting easily among limited changes as a good reaper easily shifts his swing in an uneven or rocky field. Just waiting, and listening, knowing that the people remember their rituals more doggedly than their priests do.

One of the men gave him a clay bowl. He sniffed at it. To their surprise, the honey man simply inverted the bowl and let the contents splash on the ground. Thinking to appease him for what their women had done, they had nearly caused him to drink rum before the work began, thereby endangering him and the whole business. But he could forgive this impiety easily. The ignorant often think they can improve on things by increasing whatever gives pleasure or by joggling natural orders.

They moved him closer to the little fire. Crouching, he put the resinous sticks into the flame and they began pouring out smoke and crackling. Boy! he called, and Pedro pressed through the crowd to him. Take me to them. On their way to the gate where they could watch in safety, the men pointed out to Pedro the hives, lengths of hollowed log closed at either end by doors and set on top of piles of stones. Approaching the first one, the honey man told Pedro to open one of the doors. When Pedro put his hand on the log, he found it was alive, already humming with excitement; he did as he had been told and the honey man waved the torch across the opening once, twice, efficient, a practiced accolyte incensing the Gospels. Pedro opened the other door and the process was repeated, though now he could not see it; at first he thought the cloud was the smoke from the torch, then he saw it was living and even in the terrible ocean-like roar and the pain of the attack, most awful to his legs but most frightening when they stung his face, his lips, stung his eyes shut, through it, even that first time when the onslaught was the greatest he managed to see the honey man dancing, the torch waving back and forth above his head like a ladina's yellow scarf, and to hear him croon as his other hand deftly scooped honey into the pots, pulling it off his fingers against the edge, So many voyages, so many flowers, visits, and you thought the honey was all for yourselves, my poor friends. So you thought. In the smoke no one ever got to hear or see it, except the boy standing dumb, holding open the doors, not protected by the torch or the freedom of movement as the old man was.

So many flowers, so much work, over and over he taunted them.

The men waited for him at the far side of the orchard, and when he came blindly running between the trees they got him away and back to the village street as fast as they could, not escaping a few of the more earnest bees themselves. Sometimes he was swollen and delirious, always he was covered with the tar dirt of his work and the torches. Yet the villagers did nothing for him except take his pots from him and seat him by the well where he waited until the owner came. Usually it was not long.

There were not many other times in a year that the master descended from the house to them, so like the honey man's his coming was inevitably like another visit from still another world. The indentured dressed up and bowed to him. And some of the masters recognized that the honey man was their own mirror, a reminder to them of themselves from the far end of the corridor as though best and least had a day each year when they paid respects, honored one another over the vast distance.

The master himself drew the buckets from the well, and at the places where the women were shunted inside, the master also took his ragged clothes from him and washed his body all over with cool water and abrasive maguey fibers separated and wadded. This once a year none of the servants leaped forward to help him. When the honey man was clean, the master applied the ointments which reduced swelling, even to his hands and feet, and then lifted him up and, if he followed the oldest notion of the tradition would, in thanking him, kiss the honey man's hands.

The washing was one of those things the owners clung to longest. Even after they have surrendered the day-to-day powers, our rulers often keep to themselves the performance of the charities, knowing it is their largess which keeps us fooled about their hearts. Only when the master grew too sick to walk would he send a son or wife, and even stewards or overseers who ran plantations by themselves were not permitted to do the service to the honey man.

Chairs would then be brought for the family and lanterns lit everywhere in the square. Tables were set up and the white biscuit made in the main house kitchen laid out, and some part of the new honey. The people filled themselves quickly and dancing began to concertinas and guitars, at first tentative and away from the eyes of the master, but then, as the fiesta grew, closer where they could see. Liquor they had saved was brought out by the tenants, and sometimes by the lord himself if he was in a good mood, and the fun lasted into the night. The master's sons and daughters would quickly grow bored and return to the house. That single fiesta the poor know how to make, which varies in size and length and intensity but never in elements, made them sad, although they did not know why. Young, they thought life and fiestas should include changes, new things never seen before. The master and his lady were more likely to remain, placid and observant. The village children fell asleep on the ground not meaning to, and young men sometimes saw something new in girls they had grown up with and had not noticed before. Or an old anger was stirred and it might all end with knives drawn from boots and a scream and a sudden dousing of lanterns and a woman's crying.

Sightless as he was and used to it, the honey man could hardly stay awake after he had been fed. They would come to him where he sat, again on the edge of the well, nearly forgotten, and thank him and bring him a drink or perhaps venture a question about what was happening out beyond their world, but they had to shake him to get a response, and usually he made no sense to them. At last it would be someone taking his hand and leading him to a bed she and her husband had decided only a moment ago they could give up for a night, or some humbler place on straw in a corner, and all accomplished through a continuing sleep which the honey man dreamt of.

In the morning, before dawn, there would be sweet coffee and a satchel of food ready for him at the big house. Always they put some of the white bread in the bag, but often the sleepy girl who served him seemed already to have forgotten who he was, and to remember only he was someone who must be fed.

Fifteen, really fifteen? the old man kept asking, munching at his gums and cackling. Like someone with a tear in his pants he could not stop fingering at that number Pedro had given him. His brows came down and his cheeks up until his useless eyes became slits. All young, I suppose, to be so stupid and taken in.

No, Pedro said, some brought their mothers to make a novena.

New delight. So there was some old experience for you too. Older than mine.

Fifteen! the honey man clapped his palms together. Not sixteen?

No, fifteen.

Well why *not* sixteen?

One of the husbands came to beg the saint to cure a boil on his ass.

Well that's sixteen then! and the honey man was off again, newly pleased with his own little joke and his eyes' great sacrilege. But Pedro was growing very tired of it, and they had not eaten since before it was light, so he asked the old man to bring out the satchel. The honey man got it from under his shirt and weighed it in his hand saying, Many things tonight. Three. He passed the bag across the little fire to Pedro.

Pedro untied the knot. Inside he found a large hunk of the white bread, an equally large piece of cheese still in its cloth and covered with wax, and a small packet wrapped in banana leaves.

Saliva running a little from the ragged edge of his mouth, the honey man asked what they had been given this time.

Two chunks of bread, Pedro said.

And the third?

Pedro unwrapped the banana leaf carefully. Honey, he said, and they laughed together. They hated honey. Pedro tossed the packet aside.

Throw it far out, the honey man barked. No reason to hang a lamp out for ants in this godforsaken place. And get some more wood for the fire before you settle in to fill yourself with my food. I'm not going to die in the cold tonight for your laziness.

Pedro wandered out beyond the spare circle of their light, picking sticks of wood as he moved under the great delicate network of the stars. As the guide to a blind man, he was called 'Eyes' by everyone, yet often he would sit at night and stare at the old honey man and try to determine if it wasn't a great trick, if those opaque round objects didn't work perfectly well, since the honey man knew everything, how big a supply of wood he would gather now, where there was water to be found in this dry world. After they had been pacing a whole morning in silence, all at once he would wave a bony finger at some faroff point on the horizon and say sweetly, A beautiful blood color those trees have. Then Pedro would see them a first time and, in the transitory madness brought on by so many days in the blank sun, he would believe the honey man had created the trees to amaze him. Then he learned to say, I am sorry, padrecito, but those are yellow. Pretty, but yellow, though the trees burned with redness.

Since in the day he believed the honey man God, when they were working with the bees Pedro knew he was Satan. (Not remembering it was Dio's admonition which made him think this. The priest had said, Wait for the man you think is a god to reveal himself: odds on he will turn out to be a devil of some sort or another.) The honey man would approach a hive from behind, and suddenly bow to it. Not afraid of idolatry, Pedro would bow too, as many times as the old man did. And then the honey man would catch a bee and, holding it to his huge ear, say, Is that true? well! Pedro tried the same thing, but he heard nothing from the captive bees except how angry they were. And he continued to be stung mercilessly, and the honey man only casually. In the quiet of the evening when the old man was asleep, then, Pedro would wait for the furry white hair to part and the nubs of the horns to show.

When Pedro asked to be taught the secrets, the old man became furious. What I know I have bought, and when you come to me with money or something valuable, *then* maybe I will teach you, he said. After a while he softened and said, I will tell you one thing: don't horde, and don't try to gain anything for yourself from this business. They will kill you for that.

The only thing the old man seemed to want from him was the tale of where he had come from. If I tell you, Pedro said, will you teach me so I won't get hurt?

It depends on how good your story is.

Pedro invented nothing, though he left out the information about being educated at the seminary, because it seemed safer that way. He told the old man about coming down the mountains and how late one night he had found the shed of a house a little apart from a tiny village poised on the edge of the last steep descent into the plains. In the shed, which harbored hogs, he had discovered great jars of homemade rum. He had tasted, he had in his thirst tasted a good deal, so in the morning when a young girl pushed open the door letting in a shred of light, and prepared to sling slops to the expectant swine, Pedro was still drunk. But instead of giving himself up as he had been planning to, from behind the jar where he was sprawled, he said That will not be good enough! and was nearly as surprised as the girl at the deep booming of his own voice. She dropped her tin slop pan and ran then, and he thought the game was ending, but he fell asleep again anyway for he didn't know how long, and when he woke it was because the girl was pushing back into the shed on her hands and knees, now bringing a decent plate of beans with her. Speaking again over the mouth of the jar, he told her to stop where she was and bow her head. He found out from the terrified girl that her parents had gone to town, and he decided she must be a little stupid since she kept her head down in the hog turds because he told her to, so he went on a little, eating the beans she had brought and the tortillas, and letting her wait. When he told her finally he was San Mateo, she struck her head into the mud over and over and cried and though he was not wise enough yet to know that true evidence of the gods terrifies all men, he reasoned this child must think herself in some state of awful sin (how quickly he had moved from a belief to a knowledge that others believe), and so he crept around behind her and, lifting up her skirt, in the darkness allowed his hands the fun of playing all over her round backside, perfectly drunk lucid then, not knowing exactly where to find what he was looking for, not knowing how it would deepen a little under her buttocks, but figuring it out fairly quickly when his hand grazed the soft hair and came to the flesh which he had learned now and would not be astonished by whenever he came across it. He played there, let it suck his fingers while the head-down girl wept, waiting really for them to come and discover him and capture him. (Poor Pedro, now deeply lodged in his skin was the understanding that when he believed it possible he might do anything, he would soon be destroyed, an understanding it would take time to extricate from him.) And then, rampant for the soft thing, he put himself into the channel, which proved a little turned down, at a different angle from the other one he had been into, he thought then girls differed in body. He reached around and pressed her belly to him and found she was fat, about to give out with a child and he understood the ease of it all. After a while he sent her away, still not having seen her face clearly, promising her that her sin, although not gone, was much relieved. In the evening she brought her friend and they wanted to light candles to him, but he thought that was not a good way for them to show their devotion and insisted on food instead.

It had ended as he had told the honey man. A woman's husband was in such pain over a huge puss-whitened welt that she, one of sincerest adherents of the cult of San Mateo, brought him to be healed. Pedro felt the boil, promised the man it would soon go away, and himself honestly prayed that it would. But Pedro somehow lacked the ability to convince the husband of his divinity which he had so abundantly with the women, and in the middle of the night the husband started up in his bed and said 'That was a man's hand on me!' and his outrage over the dishonor to himself was as great as the anger about his wife and his two girls, and he got a light and a machete and the other men, and started for the pig shed. San Mateo had no time to find his clothes before he ducked into the little escape tunnel he had fortuitously dug himself in the shed's back wall.

The first time he heard the tale the honey man laughed so hard he urinated all over himself. But when Pedro asked would he teach him, the honey man said Of course not. That is a bad story. Evil triumphs and we learn nothing about how to lead our lives from it. Besides, it is full of lies. Even an idiot girl would not put her head down in hog turds, though if you had said she was crazy, then maybe.

With an armful of branches pressed against him, Pedro stood staring at the wall of the mountains. Through the dry season they had been darkly omnipresent but now, wrapped with clouds, they seemed to move closer, like giant friends striding through fields toward him, with their hands separating the wet white as they came. And of course they never arrived, just as here in hot country it never rained enough for Pedro to get wet through, something he longed to feel again.

When he came back the fire was nearly out and the honey man was curled around what remained, sleeping. You took too long, he said, so I ate my part. Not bad. Going stale, so eat up. Pedro took the satchel and found in it only the large chunk of bread. Later, when the old one was snoring busily away, he searched the ground for any bits of the cheese which might have fallen from the honey man's mouth. The snoring stopped. Does a mouse leave crumbs behind, Eyes? does he? And the snoring began again on the same breath where it had left off.

Together they made the circuit once through and a little more. Thus from the time of the honey man's saving Pedro's life to Pedro's standing a little way off to watch the honey man die was the span of about a year.

Like any two people who travel together and depend on each other, they developed a particular range of fondnesses and suspicions which was all they truly possessed in common. The older man forgot he had first thought Pedro was himself and meant to kill him. He remembered it one night when he was curled up against the boy like a baby and in his sleep licking salt off Pedro's shirt, but then it was too late to be afraid. When Pedro stopped thinking the honey man was either god or devil, he also shed his loyalty to the man who had preserved his body and given him a life which, in spite of its hardships, caused him to eat only white bread and never tortillas. His skin developed a toughness like the old man's and gradually he learned how not to make the bees angry, how to hear them coming from behind and duck out of the path of their flight, how to hold one cupped to his ear and from its humming to tell the mood of the hive. He learned to sing to them and dance with the torch, and knew he was better at it finally than the old man, though no one else saw him through the smoke, or thought of rewarding him with cool water and salves afterward.

He learned to cheat as the cheating old man did. He once saved back in his gourd some rum the people at a hacienda gave him. Then, a month later, after the honey man had been attacked on the nose and could not smell or taste, when they had their torches ready the honey man called for water, and Pedro gave him the rum. Then he waited to see if the honey man suffered that night, which he did.

What did that teach you?

That your law against drinking before you go out to them is a good law, Pedro said. And what did it teach you?

Nothing. I have always known I was a fool not to give you to those men, not to go on alone, to rely on you for senses.

But what would you do without me?

Ha. I would find a cave and stay there until my nose got good again and it was safe to go on.

Finally one afternoon they were walking toward the town of Chiapa near the Grijalva, Pedro looking at the coffee beans spread to dry on lengths of cloth down both sides of the road, thinking how strange that coffee drying had no smell.

Unlike *you*, they truly speak, the old man said.

I don't know what you are talking about.

Of course you don't. To the south of here, in the mountains, lived some people who found they could make real money growing coffee on their land. 'So we can buy our corn and have plenty besides,' these wise people told themselves. Then their god appeared to them, some say he came dressed in the feathers of the quetzal and some say he spoke through the ears of the corn itself hung up in the rafters of their houses, but either way he told them clearly 'If you forget who you are and who you belong to, if you spend yourselves growing coffee for white people all you will get is hunger and unhappiness.' And some of them listened and some of them didn't.

The old honey man, whose walking pace had slowed a great deal in a year, and with it the pace of his talk, came to a complete halt. His eyes waited. Asleep again. Pedro took his arm and started to pull him forward, but the honey man balked, his feet would not move.

There were other people on the road, and they looked foolish standing there in the middle of the twilight. Come on! Pedro whispered.

Yes, the honey man said. And so then the revolution came to

Guatemala and the white people had their good times shooting each other and when it was over they had to suck in their stomachs a bit and drink dog piss for a while, as is their custom, and coffee wasn't as much used because there was no pastry to dunk in it, and the Indians who had listened to what their god said went on as they had before eating those plump tortillas they like down there and the others—

Again he stopped and again his eyes urged him on.

—ha ha, the others died!

All right, they died. Good. Let's move, Pedro said.

We turn off here.

Pedro couldn't see where, but he didn't doubt at all that a path must in fact exist. Starting at the place where the old man's grappling toes dug in the dirt, he searched beside the road and then in the gully among the weeds picked out a tiny hard tracing. Soon, Eyes in the lead and blind man holding to the back of his shirt, they were lost in a maze of tall bushes, where moths were shaken free from their homes by the human passage, and snakes waited, and lizards reared to expose their red gullets and then disappeared. The path had not been used by men for many years and Pedro was once again thinking how, by attaching himself to the man who had lost his sight, he had somehow committed himself to an innumerable past, before history and, sometimes it seemed, even before men. *In the days before there were people,* Mesha's tales had begun. And now Pedro was living in that time.

They came out into a clearing of sorts where a hill rose above the chapparel, and the honey man stopped. Pedro found a nearly level place to settle, but the old man said, No, tonight I am going to sleep with a roof over my head, and ordered Pedro to lead the way on to the top of the mound. Climbing, Pedro noticed the large cut stones standing out of the dirt in broken rows liked aged, encrusted teeth. And on the other side of the hilltop facing east there was a cave, or rather a finished small room with a flat space before it.

As Pedro was getting a fire together, the old man said You, of course, are prohibited from going in there, unclean boy.

He waited alone in the cloudless twilight, watching the arc of violet follow the sun down toward the horizon and Venus beginning. The honey man had stumbled off somewhere, to relieve himself or to pray, Pedro thought. Which mattered to him as much as to God, he imagined. He lit a fast-burning branch in his fire and crawled to the doorway of the room. It was larger inside than he had thought, the ceiling was deep-canted and he could stand. Bats hung in their little sacks above his head and on the floor were the remnants of the kind of feast curers made in caves when he was a child—dried flowers, a little pot where incense had burned, sweetening the room with its pinelike smell, and pools of wax. His branch flared and went out, and Pedro was disappointed. There had been no image, though the back wall, whiter and less aged than the others, seemed once to have had something standing against it.

You are not to be here.

The voice was deep, it filled the room, and for a moment its shivering resonance terrified him. He turned, ducked, hit his forehead on the low lintel, and crawled on his belly out into the still warm night. No one. But then, as he lay breathing, expecting it to come again, he heard laughter far off and realized the god's voice was only a deeper version of the one it was his penance to have to listen to all day.

The honey man was on the ground on the back side of the hill, lying next to a hole he had scraped the dirt away from. His newest trick on his boy had so pleased him that he had again lost control of himself and smelled awfully of urine.

Leaving him to roll around and have his convulsions of laughter, Pedro got another burning stick and searched as far as he could into the small square tunnel. It went back a way and then turned. When Pedro approached with his light, there was a scurrying inside, blind little animals living now in the throat of what had once been the people's god.

After he recovered from his fit, the honey man asked him, Well, what do you think of that?

A trick, Pedro grunted, just another priest trick like the others I've seen.

So wise, the honey man said, reaching up and softly touching Pedro's face with his sticky hand. Then, hard, he slapped the boy's ear. Thick-headed, he screeched, you *remain* thick-headed and obstinate! By now you *know* the difference between a trick and a show, but you will not accept it. Yes, the man who stayed back here was a priest, always. *He* knew. *He* had no trouble hearing the gods speak to him, but also he remembered what difficulty the people had hearing. That is all a show is, a way for the faithful to get under the skins of the faltering.

Pedro's ear reddened and began to ache and buzz strangely. But you don't know what they told the people, he said. Not even you were around to hear that. 'Leave the fattest girls here for us,' the gods said, 'and some meat, in fact all the meat you have, the deer and the iguana and the pheasants, please.'

Do you think so? the honey man raised his child's face to the light of the moon. He was willing to consider Pedro's notion possible. His smile spread, his eyelids fluttered. What a good idea. What a smart, thinking boy you are.

When Pedro woke before dawn, his ear still hummed. The old honey man was gone. He waited and then grew hungry, so he went down from the temple toward the lightening east. Off the path in a thick swirl of bushes, he found on the ground two hives made of logs with their doors open and only the home guards, questioning and uncertain, remaining with the queens. At first he did not know whose hives they could be, hidden here in the tangled brush. Forgetting his search for the honey man, he followed a track of broken branches and spills and then the low hum of the insects.

They had attacked with that vehemence which for undiscernible reasons they sometimes had. The old man had not, for once, had the smoke to fend them off or his eyes to help him escape when he fell. His face and his body were not even recognizable, covered with the tiny animals, those still alive busily cleaning sweetness from him, and the many thousand dead lying with their feet curled up in victory.

If he had been able to speak, Pedro might have softened and risked going to try to help him. But in the absence of even a word, the prohibition against what the old man had done struck Pedro, and in youth's myopic purity he saw only the death of an evil thief, not the death of anything which could ever have been connected to himself. So he withdrew and waited and prayed to that hard cold nothing which had become his god until, soon after the creamy dawn, the old honey man's thrashing ceased forever and the remaining bees, wobbly with victory, were led by tame messengers back to the hives.

Then Pedro went and took the cord from around the old robber's neck and put it in the groove of his own. He found the nearest good water and sand and spent the day washing the pots over and over until they tasted freshly of the tin. Then as meticulously he bathed himself in the shallow stream.

In the midday when no one in his senses traveled so close beneath the fire, he walked the empty roads, mouth parched, lips cracked and white as limestone, tongue so bloated he could not get it out between his teeth. The work had infected the bone above his eyes and made it thicken early. He appeared very old and his eyes were like black animals restlessly waiting out a storm in the caverns under a rock shelf.

Now in loneliness he talked sometimes to himself and sometimes to the tiger cat riding his shoulder any other crazy wanderer on those roads would not have seen. The mind, which had been bound to earth by the presence of the other, was free, and if he missed the old honey man it was only when he woke and was afraid for where his thoughts had gone.

Whole pages from the lives of saints he had once read, ornately lettered, would fill his vision. He could no longer tell which episodes went with which biographies or why they should be nailed to themselves so. They are all the same, these lives, he shouted in disgust. Except, said the more calm voice, unlike us, they are allowed to know how many years are given, allowed to pace their music and make it come out right. But we are left, dead before the last part where we meant to make a whole song out of the snatches of melody we had perfected.

They experience 'always' what we, trembling, will allow for only brief 'moments.' For us doors open, sights are revealed, doors slam shut, and we are left, knowing we are unclean and yet feeling wronged by God. They continue with Him.

He woke up one morning, began picking burrs from his hair,

and knew that he knew how it was all going to go, what day of the month he would die, and where, and in what box made from what tree be put away. The tree, a pine, growing now in the shade of greater trees in the forest in Ik'alumtik near his home. This knowledge put him into a terrible hurry to get on to the finca of La Golondrina where, as he had forgotten, this life had begun for him. He was strapped by distance only and must run. For a week then he made curious wheels and epicycles across the map of his course, as though he were trying to deface it, trying to protect his pitiful route from some greater, keen-smelling animal. One day he lagged, he dawdled on the road to the Figueroa place at Acala, like a suitor on his way to the hour his love has given him knowing that if he arrives early he will encounter the other one leaving.

He found himself in the town of Flores, which had never been on the honey man's schedule because there was no work for him in a town. But he begged a place to stay at a widow's house there. It was a jolly inn, there were many children underfoot, and the honey man felt calm and breathed and rested from his madness. Only men took rooms at the señora's and all of her female cousins tittered about half-dressed. In the evening Pedro watched as the servants of the men who visited there set about to trap the señora's kitchen girls. Like snaring pheasants, it was a tedious process and hardly worth the effort or the slight expenditure of skill. One familiar girl fell to a man who made her smoke at his black cigars until she began to weave. And only then did the honey man realize what kind of house it was and he ran, his pots clattering around him, afraid that there was some prohibition the old man had kept from him as a last, posthumous trick.

He walked all night to get far enough away to be safe and his voice, the soothing one, began to repeat over and over, The life of the saint is the life of us all written in blood and joy. And the gruffer one said, This Jesus Christ of yours did or said nothing new, nothing which wasn't said or done elsewhere at some earlier or later time.

And instead of being tempted as he stumbled blindly along, Pedro was consoled by this. In every time, he thought reasonably, they tell us we are God's children, and we nod and believe it and wonder when food will be coming, or night, and then Jesus Christ stands up and says it out loud, *I am the Son of God,* and they, who have said the same thing to themselves many times, they kill him.

You are late honey man, the women at the well in the afternoon complained to him. No, the honey man is early, one said wisely. And when he did not answer, they stood about, eyes questioning the air, each of them looking as a woman does in the moment when she weighs her breasts, not remembering which is full.

As he always did now, the honey man described a girl to them, not in the hope of ever finding her, since for all he knew her disgrace had propelled her back into the mountains and not, as his had done, down into this hot world, but in the hope of finding here a body and face and manner, or any of these, so like hers that he would be willing to lie next to it and fool himself. Like all the others, the hacienda women here were shocked, or played at it, and said, Surely not for yourself honey man. You don't have 'desires' as we have, do you? Oh not for me, he said, as shocked as they were. This girl was the old fellow's daughter and I inherited the care of her and now she's lost.

In spite of his clear sight, the people at the ranches still called him the blind man. When he heard that, he asked them why and they laughed and said, You're the only one who can get away with looking the master in the face, so you must be blind.

The only one not tied to a single master or bound by obligations, he alone was free also to see how heavy the workers and their women were. Knowing no other, they could not feel how tired they were of their lives. He imagined that if he left them they, without a single remnant of consciousness, would somehow be lost and die. And wrongly, for a time, he imagined that the little respite he provided gave them hope, while in fact he only brought them comfort.

After he had collected the honey, he sat at the well hearing the water gurgling below him. The women had warned him earlier. Their master was off fighting for the president against the infidels, and the mistress suffered from awful faintings and fever and a rash, they said, clucking and shaking their heads, like all servants oddly more pitying of their betters than of themselves.

Yellow glowed in the upper windows of the main house, and from time to time a dark figure would come and stand a moment, faceless before the light. He knew he was being watched, and they were hoping he would just go away. The children, skittery as dragonflies in the hot evening, approached and shyly offered him the first of the bread, smeared with honey milky and thick with sugared wax. Kindly refusing them, Pedro wondered when he had last eaten, what day.

At last she came, supported by her thin priest. One side heavier than the other, the wishbone couple arched imperfectly, black against the last blue of the sky. Behind them stalked the señora's tall spinster daughter. The honey man could hear the mistress complaining as she came, And why *this* to suffer now? and he had a sudden lifting hope the priest would say *You were never promised an end to suffering in this world just as you were never promised tomorrow*, but in fact the priest said under his breath, You must observe the forms in order to keep them under control while Don Oscar is gone.

Her face hidden from him by the darkness, the mistress took the bowl the steward offered her, dabbed the towel in the water and held it out to Pedro's face. Then she stopped and said, What *is* it you want?

The honey man looked up at her. Tell them to go off a way, he whispered.

They did not at first want to leave her with him, but she hissed at them and stamped her foot and they withdrew a little.

Sit next to me, he said, taking the bowl from her and putting it on the edge of the well between them. As she settled he could hear her bones, and for the first time see her face, sad to look at because obviously it had once been delicate. But now it was pocked with red marks which showed through the heavy powder. And though she held her head erect and tried to keep her mouth in a tight line, something jerked it on one side into a smile and made her eyes start and flutter.

How long have you felt this shame?

I don't feel shame. It is an ungodly disease put on me for no reason at all. I am a faithful woman and wife, and when my husband comes back from Señor Comonfort's war, if he does—

But it hasn't been only since Don Oscar went away. You managed to keep it hidden for—how long? eleven years? twelve?

The woman noticed for the first time how young this honey man was, and thought, Well, it doesn't matter to him, he goes tomorrow, and nodding she said, Yes, twelve is correct.

And you thought because he was blind you could fool him, never believing that some day he was bound to come back with sight.

The señora inadvertently drew in breath and touched the bone stays at her waist. She tried to laugh, but her face was somehow very active now and betraying her. Why would I want to fool the honey man?

I can't know your reasons, señora. You were tired and it seemed a game to dress your Serafina in your own clothes and powder her face with flour and send her to do your work. Hopefully you didn't mean to fool all of your people. We do such things, all of us, because our lives are boring and hard to lead and we fall down, that's all.

You are guessing all this! she said.

Yes I am. I was only a boy when it happened, and I was far off in cold country. And I will go away now, if you like. You don't have to wash me this time. But you know it will be a year before I can come back, and all that time you will be in pain, and Don Oscar will return and not even recognize your face. The honey man stood up.

The señora touched his patched shirt. What will it cost me? she asked.

In money?

Yes.

Nothing. You can get rid of your shame as anyone else can.

She looked at his face again and said, Come to the house with me, then. Come quickly.

The honey man hesitated. Then he said, I'm sorry for you, señora, and I would not humiliate you for anything. I would like it to be in secret too, but since you played out your trick here the cure must take place here also.

She had already committed herself to it. She got up from

the well and called her steward and told him she wanted a bottle of brandy brought from the house and the village people sent inside for a little while.

No, the honey man said, they have to watch. And the Señorita Elva should stay. But your priest goes into his hutch and closes the door on himself.

The steward stood a moment, waiting for the mistress to counter the honey man's order. She turned on him. Go on! hurry!

When the man returned with the brandy, in the darkness Laura's mother unbuttoned the collar of her dress. Bowing her head and pulling the cloth away, she revealed to the honey man the soft white freckled back of her neck. He took a mouthful of brandy and spit it on her there. When she turned around to hand him the towel, he saw she was crying, and he spread the linen and gently wiped the liquor away.

A second time he sprayed her neck and used the towel, and a third. When it was over, she raised her head and smiled directly at him. You must do my face also.

Pedro was not thinking of her, he was staring at all the crowd of servants and laborers, and wondering why they should be humiliated as he was and hiding their children against themselves. It was as though the señora's unsupportable shame had been conducted from her by his action, and given out, a little, a bearable portion, to each of them.

She, though, was radiant. You weren't listening to me, she said.

What?

You must also do my face.

No, señora. That is beyond what was called for.

But it is my face which is afflicted!

Not any longer.

And you do forgive me?

What? oh yes, I did a long while ago.

She washed him then, as she was supposed to, and the fiesta went on. In the morning when Pedro went to the big kitchen to get his food, she was alone there, waiting for him to tell him she had slept well. He knew that, he said.

He got up and retied his drawers and scratched dirt all over
the little hill he had made, and smoothed it with his hand. He
put the pots back around his neck and started off. The black
dot was still there, the same distance behind him it had been
when he stopped. He returned, trotting, and sniffed all around
the place for the odor of himself. But great heat is like great
cold, so he could smell nothing. He walked until the stars had
done half their turning for the night, then left the road and,
frightened, doubled back on himself until he picked up a
trail which led to a string of villages and then into Flores.

He sold one of his pots in the market, which he was not allowed to do, and then for a half hour, with his great new
cunning, he completely disappeared from sight. When he came
up again, he was back at the widow's gay house, begging posada
for the night. Again he felt relief at being there, listening to the
girls laugh and watching them press the cousins' bright dresses
with irons heated on the charcoal.

In the evening they fed him. He clumsily grabbed the girl
who served him his coffee around the waist and said, If you
bring me water to wash in, I will pay you for the favor.

With what? she asked the beggar.

Bring the water and you'll see.

So she went and drew the water and hurried back to him.
Now what have you got for me? she asked.

The honey man reached into a tear in his ragged pants. This!
he said, and forced a huge, badly wrapped cigar out of the hole.

I don't want that, the girl laughed.

The honey man, holding the cigar out to her, was confused.
You seemed to like them, he said.

When?

It hurt him, now that he understood that the one thing he
knew about her was ordinary, unmemorable in her new life. He
dropped the cigar on the ground. It had cost him a tin pot he
needed and had no way of replacing. He picked open his shirt.

The girl put her hands to her cheeks.

Well don't pretend now you've never seen a man before,
Pedro said, and the girl ran into the house.

He got more water and, as he was washing she came creeping

back, and he saw she was in tears. She came to him and ran her finger into the natural collar at his neck. There was a new cord in the groove, and hanging from it a small closed bag. What do you keep in here? your money? she asked.

No money, he said, but my hair and my fingernails when they break off.

Why?

Because they want to kill me. They have sent someone, and I don't want to die in hot country.

Is it your soul they want?

He trusted her. I don't know if I have one.

She laughed, her hand still at his neck. It must be a tiny new baby's soul to need such protection, she said.

For a long time then before they could begin speaking of what had happened to themselves, they sat in the dirt, forehead to forehead, and cried. Augustina would not believe at first that Pedro would forgive her, and he did not know what she needed to be forgiven. Her face had yellowed, and she was unhealthy. He could only promise her that there would be a time, not now but soon, when he would take her away.

But, as with all the stages of his life, this one was coming to a conclusion before he was ready for it.

He left Flores that time happily, and began to hurry, to push himself as though he could accomplish the period of his servitude in distance instead of days. But it was no good. The hives were not full, and the hacienda people complained that he came too early.

It was at least a month before he was convinced that the animal still followed him. He knew it was an animal because it was too quick for a man, it knew to approach only when Pedro was worn out, and knew not to follow him into the haciendas where it might be trapped. When the man was sleeping on the road, in the depth of the night he would dream or half-sense the cur being drawn to the light and warmth of his fire. It seemed to know he was beginning to at least tolerate its presence, and waking one night Pedro saw it well at last, a boy with wild, matted hair, his nose and lips thick in sleep.

Then Pedro left bread out for him, a little closer every night, and when, in a week, the boy was willing to sit within shouting distance, Pedro tried to ask him questions. But nothing worked, nothing seemed to be worth answering, except that when Pedro called, Do you believe in God? on the second evening, the boy opened his mouth and sang in a high crooning voice, which Pedro realized was a form of laughter.

Through the hottest months they continued in this way. Then one night Pedro dreamed he had been kissed and in the dawn woke to find his clothes damp and all the gray stakes of bush and tree around him thriving, coated with a soft impermanent green. After the next hacienda he did not leave out any food. He pretended sleep and waited. And finally the boy came, crouching, moving, crouching again, and stationed himself at a distance from the man. He opened his mouth and, pointing at it, grunted. Pedro rolled over and pulled from under himself a large chunk of the bread. Do you have a right to it? he called. This made the boy very angry, he shook and began to howl and pull himself toward the bread. When he got near enough, Pedro leaped up and grabbed him and wrestled him to the ground. He pushed in on the cheeks and forced the mouth open. Inside was a stump of flesh standing forward like a dwarf in a cave, quivering as though seeing light and the cause of its pain for the first time.

From the beginning the tongueless boy was deft at the work. He danced back and forth in front of the hives and taunted the bees with a perfect imitation of their own humming.

It gave Pedro a new pleasure to teach the boy all of the rules the old man had made him learn on his own. But he did not think of leaving the job to the boy, because he had come to believe that being the honey man was holy work, like being a clown or a juggler.

When the route brought them near to Flores again, they turned off and went to the widow's. Augustina had a male child to show Pedro. He was disappointed that it had not even a small tracing of the collar on its neck, but it had a pretty head and clutched Pedro's fingers and he chose to believe her when she promised him it was his. Augustina could not tell him the sacrifices of her body and the tricks she had learned to make this be true, and Pedro slept the night peacefully beside her. In the morning he offered the baby his own breast to suck, which soon made it cry and Pedro laugh. He had dreamed again. The world, all of its people, had come to him. They asked him, they begged him for things he knew he could give. But he could not hear them for the buzzing deafness in his ears. It was a sad dream, except at the very end Laura's mother came to him wearing jewels like a queen or the Virgin, and asked him for pretty things, rings and mirrors, and he could understand her.

They planned an escape. Pedro took the dumb child out to the road and showed him how to go. It will be fine, he said. The honey man always has one of three faults, and you were lucky to be born with yours. I have faith in what I have done and I believe in what you are going to do, but now I can no longer believe it is my own job to make these hot country people brighten and sing. I don't know what songs I could give them. Go on now.

There were soldiers on the roads at that time. The battle to save the Church from dismemberment by the Indian who had set up his government of high-born republicans in Veracruz had its strange small echoes even in Chiapas, so Pedro and Augustina with her well-wrapped and silent baby traveled by night.

The second evening Pedro heard a familiar clanging behind him. He turned and there in the moonlight with the glowing pots strung from his neck stood the boy. Pedro went back to him and hugged him, already he missed the boy's silent company, and begged him not to follow them. The boy cried and Pedro said, Please don't do that. You know I am always with you. I haven't run away from you, you know. And he gave a tug to the tail of hair growing down at the boy's neck.

Unlike his father, Pedro would now never see the Pacific. But watching the boy picking his way down the steep path, he looked back on the pale seething lowlands, and he was lonely and exhilarated at once as people often become when they gaze at the ocean and think, It changes so, and there will never be a tracing left of my passage through it.

PART III
GOD'S PLAY
1867-1870

1

We were in the high-vaulted or perhaps reachless place where, in a day, in a year, arcs of tracery mantled much of the pine-boughed floor and like spiders' webbing helped close the wounds of many of our startled dreading saints. A giant network through time nearly all filled with light.

Yet there were corners and godspaces which, to my thin knowledge, the sticky strands never touched.

In the near right corner of the church, in a shaft of dark from ground to ceiling which we hardly worshipped (except once I recall, one tipsy cold night in the little evil month when we ringed it with candles and strummed and prayed to it along with the others) stood the great thick cross leaning, a man waiting for a man, against the wall. Between Carnaval and Easter this more than four times man-sized brute and smooth cross was wrapped in white manta and tied off tight with ropes, like a crazy or unrepentant thing. But most of the year in the place of adornment and elaboration it stood singularly naked, and I had missed seeing it dressed.

Only the saints and one sobbing family were with us in the church. Simply joined, two thick beams, the cross had no hand- or footholds. It appeared some wood I knew only from bureaus and desk tops, a hardwood like walnut, not gnarled like the highland oak or soft and fleshy as the pine in Chiapas is. A man tied to this cross would be a dwarf. My fingers searched along as high as I could reach for old stains of blood, but though I felt them, in the milky half light I could not see them.

"They used ropes, not nails."

I turned, exposed in my dark purpose. We speak of God, they speak to Him. The church was Juan Tushim's domain. Even in his blindness he moved there without faltering, feet coming to a stop short of the lines of candles people had planted before the figures of the saints.

When I came back at the end of August to find the land all magically greened and wet, Juan was not angry at me. He didn't have time to be. The fiesta of Santa Rosha was beginning and, although it was not one of the biggest anymore, Juan did not care. He had reached the point where fiestas were all he still loved. They consumed him. He went wherever the officials were, prodded them, got drunk, sang with them when their voices didn't seem to him loud enough to reach up to heaven; on the second day he got himself a terrible cough from standing too long praying in the rain. And I was brought along, someone fortuitously sent to help him down the hill in the morning, and someone to tell the rest of the Cuscat story in the odd tatters of time the fiesta left him free.

In the soft pine forest it grew as dark as coming night and Pedro's four-year-old reached up for his father's hand. By chance they uncovered a group of women, all of them small, bent over picking dead branches or hacking out hardwood saplings with machetes. Pedro did not know them but because of his brother or because they had seen him ring the church bell, they knew who he was and, straightening, some called *peeskal!* and the others *sakristan!* to him, voices forced high and coming shrill through their noses. *Peeskal!* again and then long laughter, as some birds will jape away on a fence well after the cause of their excitement has passed, these tiny women unmindful of the approaching rain, not knowing this man would not answer them, and not caring when he didn't.

Once Pedro and his son were out of the forest, the illusion of night did not hold. From the pass at the top of the next hill the underbelly of the clouds pursuing them was blue going toward purple, and far off to the west and north where the natural white battlements above the Grijalva stood, there was a welter of rich sunlight.

Bare feet thumping hard, they strode down a lane and at the bottom, in the paraje of Mahomut now, they came into an arcade of apple trees. The trees were planted inside low-huddled stone walls, their branches reached out and met over the path. The fruit was still green and hard on the trees, but there were a few on the ground and Manvel went to work scouting the gullies and collecting what there was. Pedro laughed. His Primavera too had known which days you brought her along to scour the bushes and which days she was free to follow her own snuffling great-wheeling circles.

He sorted what Manvel brought him, putting the apples with any flesh left away in the pouch his chamarra made at the belt. So involved, they did not notice the old man who appeared and leaned on the inside of the stone wall, watching them and chewing at nothing in his mouth. At last the old man said, Fiscál, and Pedro nodded to him. Together they scanned the sky. The old man hawked and let the phlegm dribble onto the ground. He rubbed it into the dirt with his toe.

He would not expect Pedro to speak to him. They knew him in that part of the world, Juan Tushim said, as the man who spoke casually only to children, and as the one who had two wives. When they asked him what two women were like, all he said was 'Hard work.'

Reaching into his chamarra, Pedro suddenly announced, We've been stealing from you, uncle, and held the apples out to the old man.

The farmer pushed Pedro's full hands away and, going to the nearest tree, shook a big branch which hung out over the path. New apples fell to the ground. There, said the old man, and Manvel went off to gather them.

Have you been to the center?

Yes, Pedro said, I was there.

And what does your little brother have to say?

He says the people are wrong to talk against him. He says he did nothing but try to help them. He still tells them that selling was the only way for them.

And what do you say?

Pedro considered the sky. The low clouds had overtaken him, passed him. I don't know.

What they used to say is still true.

What is that?

Only people with bad sense ever come to the place where it looks as though giving up their land is the only road. Because giving up your land is no road at all. Your little brother must be a rich person now.

Pedro did not know the old man, but at last he admitted his brother did well.

The rain began, a few hard drops loud on the leaves. The old man went and gave another full bough a good shake. He was much stronger than his age would make you believe. He told Pedro he was going, and the younger man then saw the branched-over little shelter against the inner wall of the stone fence where the old man had so suddenly appeared from.

They walked up out of the little valley where the tree shaded the path, Pedro's chamarra fat with apples. He made Manvel laugh by imitating the ladino secretary of the town with his great belly like an independent thing preparing a way before him through the world. At the top of the rise, Pedro pointed out their tiny house on a hill across several valleys, but Manvel could not see it. Or at least his boy's knowledge of how things fit together, so much closer to the ground than a man's understanding, would not let him be deluded by his father. And there the full rain hit them. Manvel ran on ahead and Pedro came sauntering along behind, mouth raised to catch the cold water.

Their way then left the road and they ducked into corn standing high, ears already forming in the rolled green near the stalks, where first it seemed the rain had stopped. Instead there was a thunder all around them so that, even though they moved carefully, touching no stalks and both man and boy brushing aside all the soft-undersided green knives which hung wet in their way, they seemed to be crashing along, foundering in the thick shivering turbulence. Boy in front, they traveled in a glowing green cave of noise where Pedro felt well-being. At his feet the tiny becoming red flowers of the beans were curled womanlike around the hilled stalks and the new tendrils blindly sought their way up. He stayed, remained a moment there hunched over, himself a worm or any little animal in this place which was, for its season, for creatures such as himself, more important than any other place on earth. Though this milpa didn't belong to Pedro, he was at home in it and, squatting, he drew some small hands of weed out of the red earth and folded them into his palm.

Manvel went on down the hill toward the little river, and there he stopped and waited for his father. Pedro scooped him up and, riding his father's hip with his arms around his neck, the boy became heavy and will-less.

It grew chillier as the rain poured out, and the air lightened. They were in Tzajalemel by now, and though the rain continued, Pedro met people on the path again. In the fields were men waiting where they had been when the storm began, like the plants themselves profiting from the watering. Pedro's own corn on the gentle slope of his hill was wider spaced than any of the level milpa and less high. With luck it would come along later. Also he had the field his wife's father had given them, so he could hope there would be enough.

When Pedro first returned from hot country, he had found his mother's house deserted and ruined, lolling back against the hill like a drunkard. By custom half the land should belong to him and the other half and the house to his younger brother. He had gone to see Salvador, who had left the seminary and had become a sacristan at the church in the center. He did not look so much older as more complete, his face like a dream face which conveys at once, in concentration, the entire substance of the person. Salvador was wearing ladino clothes and he told Pedro, You can have the house. And the land too if you work it for five years or so and give me some of whatever comes out.

For the first years it had been very hard. Pedro delivered the larger part of the corn to his brother, and he hired himself out to others at the wages a young boy would take. At one place he worked in Mahomut, a man named Joconot liked him, and eventually he offered Pedro his oldest daughter. This Joconot must have known about the woman and child Pedro kept in Tzajalemel, but he had no sons of his own and his girl was plain and shy and nearly beyond the age to find any husband. And Pedro made her smile. People in Tzajalemel said it was for the land he was given that Pedro married her. But then, the people also said he slept in the bed with both of them at once, and did not know he had built Augustina her own house at the top of the ridge.

In the time since his return, while Pedro stayed in Tzajalemel and led an ordinary life, his brother was becoming well-known. After being sacristan for several years, Salvador became a field foreman on a ranch in Mitontic, and some of the men who had worked for him told Pedro his brother was very good at giving orders, which meant they had not liked working for him.

In 1865 Salvador was named judge of Chamula, which gave him power above any Indian in the town except the president. It was claimed that so young a man got the job because he could read and write Spanish, but Salvador told his brother the ladinos had wanted him. While he was judge, he made Pedro collector of taxes for fiestas in Tzajalemel and got him the work of sacristan. Pedro wanted neither of these things. He saw how people increasingly distrusted his brother. They did not like his sarcastic way or his disrespect to older men, and would not come to the court the days he judged cases.

After his year was up, Salvador had become an agent for ladinos buying land in Chamula. The King of Spain could no longer protect the Indians' property through the Church, and the Juárez laws, intended to enable peasants to obtain individual title to their old common lands, had in fact made it possible for the white men who knew lawyers to step in and dispute their claims. Forced to decide, the Indians preferred to become tenants rather than to sell out everything, and Salvador got paid each time he convinced the people to do what they knew they did not want to do.

And now the men who had made their marks were angry over what they must have known from the beginning. On Sunday they were going to the president to claim the documents they had signed were not legal because this Díaz Cuscat was paid money by the ladinos buying their land.

The rain clouds had passed on and the weakened sun was out. Three boys, friends of Pedro's older son, were waiting for him at the foot of his hill. All the children in Tzajalemel had learned to watch for Pedro, since he never seemed to forget to bring them something, hunks of coarse brown sugar knotted into his red handkerchief where other men carried their money or, as this time, the green apples he pulled from under his chamarra for them.

When this strange new thing had begun, Pedro had brought Augustina's boy down to stay in his wife's house. But Pash was not there now, nor Maria. She had probably gone to get her water. Pedro put Manvel down on the pole bed and pulled the thin brown blanket up without waking him. He unbelted his own good chamarra, took it off over his head and left it hanging from the low rafters to dry. Taking a little chair with him he scrambled up the mud embankment behind the house and settled himself among the bushes lining the ridge.

Drowsing, Pedro could feel the cotton shirt and drawers steaming and shrinking back to his body. It was like the first year after his return when night on night in sleep he had sensed his skin contracting, tightening onto his frame as the poison swelling of four years subsided. His hide became again the shape it had been, but he remained leathery and oddly tender and sensate, his skin like the paws of cats.

The old official came to him, tumpline squaring off his forehead and the tremendous heavy burden bending him over. Ashamed, Pedro turned away so he wouldn't have to look at the by now too-familiar face. And so they were for a long time, Pedro wanting to dream something else but unable to think of anything except the importunate old man. Pedro divided himself and was left with nothing. He knew what fathers with no money feel when their sons complain of hunger and they are waiting by the road. All at once he missed his hat, wished most in the world simply to be wearing his hat.

Finally, not daring to look, he said, Well old fellow, what are you carrying today?

Sometimes the official would say his load was flowers, sometimes years, once he had said, You know I carry souls. And once Pedro had recognized him as the venerable Christ in the Church of San Cristóbal with his jolly baby son on his shoulder. Today for a long while the old man did not say anything. And then, You know what I carry.

No.

As long as you refuse, I carry you too.

Pedro got up on the seat of his tottery little chair, spread his arms and flapped them, as though he might be able to take off from this hillside and fly away forever from the old man's unpredictable, insistent visits. And as he flapped, became chained into the action of flapping, he shouted shrilly, he cursed God and all the saints he could name, he yelled to the west that he wasn't going to, he said the little gods had never given *him* anything he needed to be grateful for, but only miseries on misery, and miseries weren't going to make *him* go jump about or sing or get drunk with other fearful idiots who—

The official was still standing before the little chair, still bent forward against the weight the tumpline threw to his forehead, still as patient and submissive as an old horse. He reached up for Pedro's hand and helped him down from the chair and softly, his voice as gentle as Mesha's had been and, if you cared to stop and confuse yourself with the memories, as Dio's could be and even the honey man's at times, softly the old man said, No such thing is being asked of you.

Well I'm glad, Pedro said weakly, because it would not have happened. And he sank back into his chair.

He was waking. A cloud was just finishing its passage across the sun and light wind came running up the narrowing red arroyo toward him and spouted at the top by the bushes. There, barely above the hill, stood a black bird holding its place, its own, against the tide, and the golden light made the feathers of its outstretched wings go green. In its stasis the bird looked down on the man and called to him in Spanish or Latin *More! more!* until the wind swept it back and it climbed above the

invisible thrust and darted off surely into the valley lying below
Pedro.

The soft wool of his black chamarra brushing Pedro's shaking
arm, the old one stood now just outside the man's vision. Not
idiots or fools of course, he went on, simply men with a different
obligation than yours. Since you have been allowed to visit our
green world, since you have been allowed to see and touch
the body of Our Lord Jesus Christ and since you stand saved—

And since you see how impoverished they live, another voice
said, and how the land falls apart, and since you know what
to do for them—

I don't know what to do, Pedro said.

Then, as a kind of hardly hoping afterthought or appeasement,
he asked would they stay and tell him.

But they would not. He was alone again. Or not alone, because he was in a garden he had seen once in a book in Hector
Estrada's library, and now he knew this courtyard was of their
construction, for not even the best of men could have conceived
it. The flowers were hard glowing, faceted in their colors, the
leaves gold-rimmed enamel. Here Pedro was less than a breeze
in substance, his tentative feet, soundless on the ordered cobbles, hurt as though he were walking on burning bones. Peering
down the well he could see to the onyx surface of the water,
and for a second, in heartcrushing excitement, even into the
depths where paled carp looked questions up at him from their
solitude. On a single looped rope were a pair of buckets, one
empty along the side, the other heavy like an overladen ship
half submerged in the water below. Though he longed to drink,
Pedro felt sure by himself he could not pull the partially full
bucket to the top. But he knew the empty silver pail was not
for him, was not him as the mossy darkwood one was. When
he touched the rope, the light bucket fell and fell and the heavy
bucket rose with greater and greater ease and speed and a kind
of gay joggling, and Pedro too rose, scene changing, above the
garden, seeing last the silver or tin bucket inconsequentially
thud against the black skin in the chasm far below him and then
he was rising farther, with no effort of his own, like the bell he
had seen once in childhood when it was hoisted into place above

the Chamula church, ringing softly by itself, kissing lip as it went and he himself turning to gold and, coming awake, he shivered and hugged himself.

He went walking upward toward the crest of his own hill. At the top on another man's land he passed for a few moments through a cool stand of pines, and then down into a field only half planted in strips of corn, half left to weeds and rocks. He stopped. Tricked once today when he believed the bird was a character in the waking world, he remained still quite a while, peering calmly through the tiny space in the tight leafing of a bush beside him.

He knew the woman there, knew these particular movements by heart. She set down her jug. She must have already been to the river for her water. Looking out over the valley and then around her, making sure she was alone. A tall woman for an Indian, with a long yellowish face and a thin-bridged nose. Her breasts were larger of course and hung now. Her hips slanted out. Thinking no one could see her, she hiked her skirt to her belly and squatted down. There came a sweet single noise from her throat, the burbling Pedro could remember from the first time he ever had a woman, her surprise and pleasure.

Silence. Pedro spread the leaves a little to see better. His Augustina hunched over, black skirt bunched at her waist, her spreading round buttocks facing him, the dark underneath. The water began slow, a finger of it on the ground between her legs, exploring toward him. She pressed with her hand and the water hissed and spat, receded and died. Again she paused, still squatting, then she picked up a large squash leaf and wiped herself.

Doesn't that leaf prickle you?

Her back tensed. Then she laughed and, straightening up so her skirt fell to her ankles, she held the big leaf out to him. No, she said, I only pull it one way and the prickles don't rub me.

Come through here, he whispered, separating the branches so she could step between them. Pedro was sitting on a rock and Augustina stood with her hand buried in his thick hair. Pedro touched her ankle, stroked along the back of her leg and then pulled up the skirt and held the warm damp inside of her thigh, feeling hard muscle beneath the thin flesh, thinking how odd it was. Meat. Meat and nothing more.

How was it?

My brother claims now that he makes nothing for the ladinos.

Then he shouldn't spend time with them. The people see him drinking with ladinos and then they think things about him.

He wants me to speak for him on Sunday.

No one knows you except as his older brother.

I told him that.

Will you go?

I don't know yet. He stroked there again, exploring with his fingers the fringe of hair and the edges of her hot place. Thoughts of the still bird calling in Spanish or Latin. Augustina's thighs came together like gates, trapping him and holding him.

It talked.

His heart chilled, but he laughed and asked, What did it have to say?

It gave me its name. Just now. I was coming to tell you when I stopped here.

He thought to ask if its name was Augustina, but seeing the face which never hid from him hidden now, he could not make the joke.

You don't have to believe me. Come and see for yourself.

A trick to get him to her house. More. Do you think it will speak to me?

Yes, it will.

He let her go. Tomorrow, in the morning. He stood up and, touching the soft cleft in her back as he pulled her near, kissed her. It excited him as always, the way she had learned so long ago to kiss as ladino women do. He released her and said, I'm going.

As he came down through the dark pine wood he was thinking of what Dio had said about the beginning of the Gospels. Why didn't more people believe at first? Through many generations we seek manifestations from Our Lord God and centuries of men die in longing and hunger. But when they come, they come as a feast, and many will be dazzled and lost simply by the plenty of the signs.

Augustina's news and his own dreaming now made Pedro buzz as though he had begun a day drinking without first putting food in himself. She had shown him the figure, a woman of the red clay of Tzajalemel dressed in a mud-crusted mantle and wrapped like a cornstalk doll. It was no larger than a man's hand and forearm. At first Pedro had thought Augustina must have made it herself. But the doll had an age to it, and the joke he expected to break at last from Augustina did not come. From the careful way she took it out of the box hidden under the bed in her house and the gentle, almost frightened way she had first plucked the cloth away to show him the Indian face, it had been clear she loved the thing.

Near his own house was a sandy gully, land claimed by no one since it was useless for growing anything. There, Pedro saw, his older boy had decided to plant corn.

The last of the sun had been cut off by new clouds and it was getting chilly, but Pedro sat down on the grass and watched his son work. He had cleared away what weeds there were in the sand and then, instead of borrowing his father's planting stick, had gone and gotten his own and sharpened the end himself. Whatever seed it was he was using Pash had in a coarse fiber bag at his side. He stood surveying his little plot and then, when his mind was made up how the rows should go, he went to the first place he had chosen, raised his stick with both hands and drove it down into the sandy earth between his feet. Turning the stick with his wrist, he pulled it free, bent his left knee and at the same time picked four or five corn kernels from the pouch hanging at his side and dropped them in the hole. Still bent, he covered the hole with dirt, and laid the stick along the ground, measuring the distance to where he would gouge the next hole. Then he stood and moved, his eye already on the new spot; he stood over it and again plunged his stick into the earth.

Not quite as quick as a man, but not much slower either, his father decided, and surprisingly the eight-year-old had a man's patience for the work, proceeding to the end of the first row, not wasting his force or varying his pace until he was finished and stood to look at what he had done. Only then did he notice his father watching him. The boy nodded and Pedro nodded back. They looked at each other a moment, Pash catching his breath and wiping his forehead, then he turned and went down the finished row to begin the second.

Perhaps he was embarrassed to be caught playing at such a serious game, knowing as he must nearly as well as his father did that it was too late in the season to expect anything, and that in the sandy gully bottom his corn would probably not even sprout. But he worked on. Earlier, in March, he had helped Pedro with the real planting, and Pedro had been surprised by how much the boy knew without ever having done it. During the weedings, Pedro had inspected his son's work and had been pleased to see how careful Pash was with his broken hoe. There had been no cuts on the vines and stalks, but the weeds were sheered off within a finger of them.

It also pleased Pedro to know that, no matter what else happened, he would have at least one son who was a good farmer, in the end probably better than he was. Discreet and careful, given Augustina's patience by God, the kind of man whose little domain gives any visitor a good feeling merely because of its order. Not a man who would desire power. To marry some serious woman and spawn many children. Not a server of cargos, but a man you would make godfather of your children, knowing that if you died they might not be loved as much as you would want, but at least they would be cared for and never beaten.

In the last of the dusk Pedro sat in the patio with his other boy standing between his knees. Behind them smoke from Maria's fire poured from both doors and seeped from the thatch. They could hear her rapidly patting out tortillas. Then from the dark east came a fastmoving black cloud which turned into a flock of small birds and wheeled over them, fluid and symmetrical at the same time, and chattering together as they changed direction.

Where will they go now? Pedro asked.

Up toward Grandfather's, Manvel said.

How do you know?

They did yesterday. Birds like the morning and the evening.

Yes, Pedro said, and not the heat of the day. And where did they go last week?

Maria called them from inside the house. There were enough tortillas ready to begin. Manvel made a move to go, but his father held him, hands alone nearly surrounding the boy's chest. I don't know Papa, he said. I don't remember.

Are we nearly through with the rain?

No. The boy's eyes half closed. Are we?

Pedro stood up. Try to remember where you saw the birds coming from last week, he said, and then you will know for sure.

There were no guests, but Pedro brought the tiny table inside the smoky house anyway, and set it for himself. Maria, on her knees by her fire, put a gray clay bowl by Pedro's feet and he scooped up warm water for his face and then washed his hands and wrung the water from his fingers. She gave him a gourd dish of cold water. He rinsed out his mouth and handed the dish to Pash beside him on the floor, and the boy drank. Maria counted the pile of soft tortillas she had ready with her finger and stuffed seven or eight into a big round gourd with a smallish opening. This she reached across the fire to set on her husband's table.

You Pash, get the other chair and sit up to eat with me, Pedro said.

Maria pulled handfuls of squash leaves from a pot into another bowl, then tipped the pot to add some of the juice before handing the food to her husband. Pash brought a chair. Pedro, very hungry, had already taken a tortilla—it was the last of his black corn and the tortillas were the gray-green color of young peapods—but when Pash drew his chair up to the table, his father stopped and said, Will you eat?

Thank you, the boy said.

They began, using pieces of tortilla to dip out the leaves. Pedro asked for salt, but Maria said there was none. She handed him three more tortillas and gave one to Manvel who was sitting beside her, eyes on his half-brother who had suddenly been separated from him and allowed to sit up like a man at the table. He could not understand why.

The squash leaves had little taste, but their texture, their smoothness in the mouth was like something. Pedro closed his eyes. He saw the maid's room next to Doña Laura's bedroom. He heard the lady coming in the dark, the rattle or rasping of her sharp petticoats under—that was it, under smooth black velvet.

While she was feeding Manvel and herself, Maria let her fire begin to die. Pedro dozed in his chair, tired out from his trip. When he opened his eyes his wife was standing with Manvel in her arms, in the dark nudging him and telling him to come sleep lying down. Pash had already snuck off to the pile of old blankets on the floor which was his new bed. Maria climbed onto the pole platform and settled Manvel between them and Pedro pulled up the cover.

Outside the hens woke, talked briefly, and then there was silence.

Sometime in the night Maria woke up. She had dreamed that she had gone to the forest alone for wood and the *pukuh*, a man and a woman with bat wings, had come on her there and by running their sharp claws into her made her pregnant. She was all alone, so heavy with so many awful creatures inside her she could not move from the black mountain path. But then Pedro came with a machete and helped her to her feet and she thanked him because she was light again, but he went away. Waking, she remembered he was there, asleep on the far side of her Manvel, and she leaned over and kissed the man's arm before turning back to her own sleep. A moment later Pedro blurted *What?* in Spanish. Silence again, then the man sitting up, taking the sleeping boy, lifting him out and putting him down beside his brother. Still more-or-less asleep Pedro got back onto the bed and rolled to his wife. He pulled at her skirt, raising it to her knees, and moved himself over between her legs. There was a pause, Pedro still asleep perhaps wondering what was wrong. He fumbled at his pants, drew himself out and eased down on her, finding her place, his hand like a dull knife. Maria spread her knees and lifted off the bed so her skirt would move up out of the way, and he came into her, his whole body straight and taut down the length of hers. His mouth closed on Maria's, though there was still no sign that he was awake, and his movement inside her began. It went quickly, Maria still as always, waiting until his thick water came flowing into her. Pedro sighed and rolled off and returned to his wooden sleep.

Maria lay there in the dark, smiling at the storm she had made by a gentle impulse and then at all the things she only half-understood. She knew the other woman, they had gone to the river together today and had stopped at her mother's to pick squash leaves on the way back. She knew somehow Pedro had spoken to Augustina when he came home. He had told her about the saint when he asked her would it be all right if his older boy came to live with her. Maria did not mind. He was kind to her as his wife, and she believed the hold the other woman had on him came from secrets Augustina knew about what to do with him in the night, secrets Maria would never be able to learn. She herself was not made to handle the dark and perhaps wonderful things Pedro and Augustina played with, but she was only afraid for them, not jealous.

2

Waiting for their priest and for eight o'clock, the sacristans noticed Padre Miguel had a visitor, another cleric in black skirts who came stumping across the yard with him and into the church. Excited, Pedro followed them into the darkness. Their white linen surplices glowing, Padre Miguel floated and his fellow bobbed, tilting down on every other step, toward the altar, and as they went ladinos grew up around them. It was the day of the glass-guarded saint who had chosen to love the white people of Chamula, or at least who had been chosen as the object of their adoration, so there were fifty or more good-spirited ladinos present for Mass. Except for the servers, there were no Indians in the church.

Pedro crouched and went through a low door in the back wall. Above him he could see a round of daylight. The spiral was only about as wide as a man, and his shoulders brushed both sides of the well as he climbed. He came out suddenly high in the air over the center's humble buildings and the tiny people buying and selling below him, and seemingly on a level with the enclosing ridges of the mountains with their great crosses.

Only when he had scrambled up the tiles to the arches where the three bells hung and had, with a hammer, broken the morning open with his clatterings, did he realize what it was that had excited him. Together with a company of the dead, Dio had become so persistently a figure of his dreams that Pedro had not first recognized him in life.

He sat waiting and the time came and a voice calling up the well, Now Cuscat! And again, now! And once more! And Pedro rang the news of the Elevation into the world and was free to come down. The other sacristans had said a boy could be sent up the tower to do the bells, but Pedro kept the job for himself, since it allowed him to stay away from Don Miguel.

After his meal, the visiting priest strolled over to the cabildo to see what had caused the gathering of so many Indians there. The people made way for him and he came to a post where he leaned, arm touching a man's arm. Soon he recognized Salvador Díaz, who had been his student, sitting on the bench with the president and the other officials. He waved to the boy and Salvador waved back to him. He seemed to have been drinking and he played with his eyes and scratched himself and made jokes with the ladinos standing there while the Indian men were reeling out their long complaints.

Several times Dio asked the man next to him what they were all laughing about.

And Pedro, his face averted and his body aching, thought, Good beef and wine, what the resident feeds him, the fruits of the earth and the goodness— Yet what cause for anger now merely because he does not know you? You did not know him. And then Pedro thought of importances, orders. With the bulk of his old confessor pressed against him he could not concentrate on his brother's case. Finally Pedro said in bad Spanish, These men are telling how this fellow forced them to sell their land, and he is saying they were so drunk when they did it he had to help them make their mark, and refuse the offer of their wives and daughters.

The crowd, a swelling of perhaps a hundred, laughed at Salvador's remarks. The president grew dour and irritated at the interruptions, but Salvador went on, throwing himself at them like a bug at a lamp globe, arrogantly disregarding himself and their trouble, as though perhaps with laughter he could mitigate the unhappiness of people who had lost everything.

Like the other ladinos, Dio lost interest in the long, complicated proceedings and went away. Then the president, the officials and the ladino secretary retired into the cabildo and shut the wooden doors behind them.

Pedro found his brother squatting behind the building with two ladinos who were still his friends. Salvador offered a bottle, Pedro took barely a swallow, and then Salvador said, Well, you wouldn't speak for me. I expected that. What do you think?

Pedro answered in Spanish. I think you are making a mistake.

What's that?

You think because what becomes of these people doesn't matter to you it must also be a small concern to them.

Salvador did not answer him.

A thunderous rain had long been coming from the east. Now it darkened the sky and inundated the plaza. In the sudden cold the petitioners huddled on the cabildo porch, men stooped together and women seated on the stone. Everyone took succor, babies from their mothers, men from the bottles which went around while they repeated everything which had been said through the afternoon. Watching, not a part of them, Pedro saw how they were in a ship together, going to some new and not easier land. But, he thought, at least for the moment they have themselves, and their fears for what comes next belong to them all, not like your own visions so solitary.

By the time the president returned, the rain had ended and the plaza turned into an ankle-deep lake. The music of an accordian and violin and laughter from the ladinos' fiesta across the way came clearly to the Indians as they waited for the *mayoletik* to find Salvador and bring him back. Now there was no place for him on the officials' bench. It took a good while to explain the judgment. The secretary referred regularly to the paper in his hand and prompted the president, and the people made interjections, their mood lighter now the business was at last over.

Then they began gathering themselves for their long marches to— To what? Pedro wondered. Not to a home if they had sold out. Did they stay with relatives now? or sleep in gullies and caves? Suddenly he was more interested in their faces, as we grow concerned to see images of our fathers only after we decide that we too will die.

He went through them to speak to his brother, but Salvador was surrounded by officials and had to go into the cabildo with the secretary, probably to confront the details of the impressive and powerful paper they had drawn up.

Dio was guiding a brown mule between the people leaving the plaza. The mule picked its way through the cold water like a lady. Dio wore a black cape which hung to the animal's belly, but his head was bare and his remaining hair silver in the color-drained luminance which was all the light left to the day.

Friend? what did they decide?

The priest had reined in the mule right before him. But luckily Pedro had his hat on this time to hide his face, so he pretended it was another man nearby Dio was speaking to.

You talk Spanish don't you?

Dio's voice had the master in it, the command which came out only in haste. It was a disused ability, like his knowledge of cards. What did they decide about that fellow? he insisted.

They decided, Padre, that we do not need white priests anymore. They decided you stand before our own saints and block our sight of them. They say you absorb our prayers into yourselves and that it is your fault we live in the dark as we do. They decided now to look beyond you for their own.

It came. It happened. And when it passed Pedro looked down at his feet enlarged and pale under the water and he shivered.

Is that you, Pedro?

As though he had heard his servant come into the house

from an errand. No surprise. Dio bent over in the saddle to see under the hat brim. It doesn't look much like you.

But it doesn't look like anyone else either, does it, Padre?

Dio swung himself down easily from the mule and held Pedro's arms a moment, staring at him.

The only difference Pedro could see was a crop where the second chin had been. The eyes had lost none of their color. If it was possible, they seemed even brighter than ever. Dio embraced him and he felt the heat of the priest's body and he thought, Nothing changed, nothing. He held himself upright, denying Dio's pressure on him to soften, aware of the people stopped to watch them.

Releasing him, Dio said, Well even after years you don't forgive, do you?

I don't know, Padre.

And I don't know why you should, except— Well, you remember what I say about living side by side with us.

No, Padre, I forget.

Living with us the Indian is blessed with more opportunities to practice Christian charity and forgiveness than we are.

Pedro did not like to think how well he actually remembered the saying. Like Dio's body against his, it had the potential to weaken him.

And though he said he had to start home, Dio gently insisted they must talk and led him to the house of a ladino woman and into a small room which gave onto the lighted courtyard where the accordion played and the violin whined and the dancing went on. The woman brought them a homemade liquer with tiny plums moving in it. Dio closed the door on the damp gaiety outside and they sat facing one another with a candle, the bottle and two glasses on the table between them.

Go ahead and pour for yourself, since you are an Indian and we all know drinking is the only thing an Indian enjoys.

I'm not ashamed of being an Indian, Padre.

No reason you should be. Dio uncorked the bottle, carelessly filled both glasses to the brim and drank from one. It's a pity, he said.

What is?

You don't have any feeling left for a joke, do you?

No, that was beaten out of me.

Dio searched Pedro's face, as though he might find marks there. Then he took Pedro's hand and held it on the table. I am sorry my boy. I always planned to say that to you first of all.

Don't be, Pedro said, moving to withdraw his pinned hand from under Dio's, then deciding to leave it. You taught me to believe that the great design exists for every man, and if you were the particular scourge meant for me, or one of them, then you have no reason to be sorry.

The priest looked away.

Is there something wrong in what I say, Padre?

Oh no. You are right. You appropriately catch me with my own arguments as you were trained to do. But, you see, anyone who instructs cannot help longing to affect certain students only in the ways we would all agree are good. You were one of those for me, one of the few, God forgive me. Dio's blue eyes were wet. He squeezed Pedro's hand and then relinquished it and drew himself back, saying, All right. Now tell me about this trouble our little Salvador's got himself into. Miguel says they want the money he made from them back. Did they have a decision today?

It's twenty percent. That's the commission the ladinos claim they gave him.

So much? but of course the people don't understand commissions and percentages, do they?

Well enough, Padre.

I'm sorry. Of course they do. And yourself, Pedro? where have you been?

Flatly, to preserve himself, Pedro told Dio he had been a field worker in a hacienda, and named a place near the little town of Tuxtla. After a while, he said, he grew homesick for the mountains, so he came back and married and had children and now worked a little piece of land.

Dio finished his glass and set it on the table. The candle flickered in the breeze his arm had stirred. I dreamed you dead, I imagined you far way, and so never looked for you here. I woke some nights knowing you were in trouble, but I never thought of this end for you.

Why is it so bad, Padre?

No one said that it is.

You don't look happy for me.

Well, the education you were given— I mean how many Indians here have Greek tucked away somewhere in their heads?

One less than you think. I have forgotten everything.

Don't return to denying me so easily. You remember. I know. Where's the girl? are you married to her?

No. She lives nearby.

And you—?

Yes, Pedro smiled. My first was by her.

A boy?

Yes, I have two boys.

Hector will be pleased also. It's all we wanted of you finally, to make many images of yourself for the future good of the world.

They talk, Padre.

What talk? your boys?

But then they were interrupted by shouting which came from the courtyard. There was a knock and the ladino woman came in, her shiny dark skirt flashing about her. Quick, Padre, I want you out of here. There's been a fight, and there's going to be a scandal. She took Dio's hand, leaned over to blow out the candle, and hurried him out to the porch. Pedro rose, feeling the liquor running in his body, and stumbled after them.

Young women who had been dancing in the yard had re-treated to the safety of their mothers on the porch. The two musicians were with them, cradling their instruments to their bodies to protect them. In the yard a lamp had overturned and spilled oil burned around it. One group of men held back a man with a pistol still clutched in both hands, another a very drunk young fellow in a torn shirt. He sagged against the man holding him, then righted himself and let out a long owlish cry. But I love her, he whined, I love her. All around the courtyard in dark corners Indians stood watching.

He insisted on dancing, the ladino woman explained. That's all. My nephew didn't like it.

Pedro went out into the mud and said to the men holding

Salvador, I will take him now, señores, thank you very much. He grabbed Salvador around the chest and dragged him across the courtyard, through the cobbled entryway and out into the empty moonlit plaza. There he stopped and shifted his brother onto his shoulder. The accordian had begun once more at the ladinos' fiesta. Salvador began to babble again I love her, I love her, and Pedro whispered, No you don't, you're not capable of that, and then liquid came flowing from Salvador's mouth and down Pedro's back.

He was nearly across the plaza when he heard someone following. First be reconciled with your brother, and then come to offer your gift.

Pedro did not say anything.

You can come to the church, if you like. I'll have Padre Miguel find you both a place to sleep tonight.

My brother has a house, Padre, thank you. Good night.

Oh my boy is so changed. A man now who disposes of people. Will you at least come see me in San Cristóbal?

Pedro said he would, knowing he would not, and again told Dio good night.

After he had roused Salvador's wife and they had shucked off his smelly clothes and laid him down to sleep, Pedro went and looked out at the night, the mist like stirring lakes of milk in the hollows. Dio on his mule mounted the road toward the great cross of San Sebastián, going slowly away in a halo of wet white moonlight. Go and lead him on the steep descent to the city, Pedro thought. Tell him it is not safe for a white man to travel alone through our land in the late watches of the night. Of course it was untrue. Dio, fearing no evil, was perfectly safe. But Pedro was made sad by the imbalance. The priest had led him through dangers of body and mind for so many years, but now there seemed no land in which Pedro could be host and guardian.

He dreamed he was walking to market in San Cristóbal to sell some pearly pigeon eggs he carried safe and warm wrapped in a bandana in his hat. But when he got there he went immediately to the Dominican house and confessed. He could only speak to Dio by pulling himself up with his hands to a tiny boxlike opening in a vast oak door and, quivering, hanging there, he could not see anything in the darkness except, oddly, the priest's black cloak.

Father, I have sinned.

How, my son?

But She speaks to me. She does. In a tiny voice. And I love Her. It is good to be near Her.

What does She tell you, my son?

That I have the power, if I will use it.

What language, my son, what language does She speak?

It is *like* Latin, Padre, but not.

And if She has promised you the power, why then won't you make use of it?

The strength in Pedro's hands had run out. He found it necessary to let himself slide down the smooth plane of the door. He crouched there on the stones where he could still speak and be heard. Many answers floated by. It was clear now She meant Pedro to act, and not Augustina as they had first thought. But the work She demanded had not yet been set out, not even the form of praise which would please Her. The voice unsettled him because he heard his mother in it, and sometimes his father. And when he concentrated hardest on the words the saint emitted, he heard also again the voice of a child, himself, in total simplicity saying a single thing: *I am afraid.*

He cried openly and confessed more. Hobbling, I ran before Doña Laura and threw doors open in her path. I walked before you with the thurible smoking into the cold chapel every morning. I led a blind man. I do not speak well for myself.

But, said the voice in the cell, you still have not told me why you do not act.

I could act, Padre, if only there were someone to walk before *me* now, to shield me. I would not mind being my brother's sacrifice. But he will not be mine.

The confessor said, You are well along in the sin of demanding a perfection and balance in the outer world which you have not achieved inside yourself, my son.

Pedro got to his feet and with taloned fingers again clawed his way up the smooth door to the tiny window. The man inside turned questioning toward the light and Pedro saw it was Hector Estrada, not Dio, and he woke, his body hot between the bodies of his two women.

Though it was the middle of the night, his wife was awake. Pedro whispered to her, In the morning send Pash down to the people who came and tell them the saint will take care of their children later on. Then Pedro got up.

It was still dark when he reached the center, and Salvador and his wife were packing their things by lamplight.

They spoke in Spanish. Pedro begged Salvador not to go, and his brother said he had no possible way of getting together so much money, and they would take him and kill him if he didn't get it. But if I run away, lock up my house, they will be satisfied with me.

Stay, Pedro said.

Why should I?

I need you.

Well there were times I needed you too, Brother, Salvador said.

And I was there.

In court last week? speaking in my favor? I didn't hear you.

Long ago, in a time you were too young even to remember now, I fed you. I was your mother and your father. I kept you from burning up in the fire. Times I lost my friends on the road because I had you along and couldn't keep up with them. I took care of you. I gave you food I needed for myself.

But it wasn't enough, Salvador said. And I was too young then to make a contract with you. All I can remember is how hungry I was.

They bid each other a sullen goodbye. Half way out of the valley, Pedro heard someone coming up behind him running. Salvador stopped and held out a small bottle of rum. I thought you should have this, he said. Pedro took the cornhusk stopper from the bottle and offered it back to his brother, but Salvador shook his head. No, take it with you and drink it at home, and then a second time, friendly at least, they parted.

When he got to Tzajalemel, Pedro found his wife just plucking at the ashes for coals to begin her morning fire. Maria had agreed to Augustina's coming to live with them so the saint could have Her own house, but the changed condition made Maria slow and wary in her movements. Pedro bent over her and kissed the top of her head and both his sons laughed at him.

He called to Augustina, who was still sleeping, and then went out. It was barely dawn. She caught up with him in the grove of trees at her own place, pulling her fingers through her hair as she came. Pedro unlocked the door with the big iron key and they went inside.

He prostrated himself, his face against the hard dirt of the floor, and waited. Augustina was behind him. In the dark he could smell the incense with which they had adorned Her, could hear his own breathing and the woman's and the first of the morning's breeze in the trees outside. But the saint said nothing. After a while, Pedro dared look up at the table and the wooden box with the door closed, its tiny catch glinting silver. He had made the box himself only a week ago, but already it did not belong to him and when, still on his knees, he crept forward to open it, his hands shook. The lady inside smiled in the darkness. He told Augustina to light a candle.

There are none left.

You should have gotten them. I told you that.

Yes.

Hastily he began an Our Father in Latin. He said the prayer several times, his eyes fixed on the saint, but it was no use and he fell silent. She spoke at odd moments, not when addressed. A week ago, the day before he made the box, and while Augustina was still sleeping in the house with the image, in the dark, after nearly an entire night of prayer, he had fallen asleep on the floor and then had been awake, up on her, when they had heard the voice together a first time, distant and exploratory, like a child teaching itself to speak, saying half words which could be understood and half nonsense.

An hour went by and the house was lighter and still She did not speak. Finally Pedro got up and stretched himself. Each new time he came to the saint with awe, and it ebbed away. He told Augustina to bring a basket.

In this wet season of the year, the mountaintop was nearly always covered by clouds. Pedro collected the various kinds of pine, long- and short-needled, and the geraniums and laurel which all curers use. Augustina worked with him, silent because he was silent, only once breaking it to ask what he was thinking. Maybe the flowers will please Her and She will tell us what She wants from us. What services. I hate this, he added in Spanish.

Why?

My mother brought me here, to this very place, when she was about her business. I don't like this. I imagined that when it came at last everything would be different, and it is not and I dread it. I promised myself once, when I was a boy, I would never come back to this place, and here I am.

When they came down, they stopped at a waterhole and Pedro filled his hat. The water dribbled out through the straw and he did not offer her any, so Augustina got down on her knees to drink.

I hate sick people, even the smell of them. And weakness. I hate it in myself, he said.

She looked up at him and he realized she was more fearful than he was. So he smiled and said, But maybe we can make it all good for them.

At the house they unfolded a rose-printed length of cheap cotton Pedro had picked out in San Cristóbal and covered the table with it to make a fitting altar. They laid the pine and laurel alternately around the table's rim and placed the geraniums.

In the afternoon of that hollow gray day, Pedro went to try to beg a few candles and a handful of copal from a man in the paraje of Ik'alumtik who sold such things. On the path She stopped him and told him in Latin that he should not worry. Worry would only block his heart. You and the woman I have chosen as my people in the world. I have adopted you, you are the glass through which the others will see themselves clear and therefore will see me. Any way you worship me will be pleasing to me if it seems right to you. The father of the sick baby is buying his candles now.

When She spoke to him, Pedro saw there was nothing at all to trouble himself about. When She was gone again, the dread returned more heavily. But he went back, and on his own land he found himself pulling up cornstalks. At first he was unsure and took the ones which had no growing ears folded in them; then what he was doing began feeling more and more right and he dropped those he had taken first and filled his arms with the stalks which had the most mature ears and ran all the way back to Augustina's, where he decorated the little house's rafters with the green corn.

It rained and the wind came up and thunder prowled the sky and lightning puffed clouds to sight a moment and the night caught the people coming on the road and turned them around and back, frightening them into the kind of terror a bird exhibits caught between a cat's quick paws. When they arrived, wet through, there were many more of them than the family of the sick child. They crowded the decorated house, silent, taken in by the beauty of the altar and the little locked box, and watchful, some suspicious, of the man they knew who sat in a chair beside it, and of the thin woman kneeling beside him. Pedro called for lights and the candles were taken from satchels, unwrapped and lit. He called for liquor in the saint's honor and the people brought that out too, and a boy was sent around with the bottles to pour for all of them.

And Pedro, who many of them had known when he was a child believed to have many skills from his mother and from a man who lived in the heart of the village by the church, the boy of such seriousness who had gone away and then reappeared one day fourteen years later different and the same, a man who gave sweet things to children and hardly spoke to other men, who never laughed and seemed always to be thinking, although maybe not unhappy at it, this same Pedro began to laugh with them now and made jokes before the box which held the very saint he claimed to have heard speaking, and he took the little girl who was sick and, laying her across his knees, undid her clothing and felt all over her hot body and thumped her belly as though she were a melon he was seriously considering choosing. And when they were all laughing over that and preparing a new round of drinks he got to his knees and touched some of the candles in the pinch of his thumb and softly began to pray the Santo Dios in Latin, a language strange to them. They had never heard it spoken outside of the confines of the church where the priest, a richer and more powerful man than all of them together, used it as the tongue to address their white saints. The room grew silent.

As he spoke, intoned what he had never set out to learn and had only from another time always known, Pedro too began traveling and looking. He knew then that it was right to make the sad laugh and only to purge the content with storms and thunderings, knew that practicing at being men is the only practice given to prepare us to enter the mountain homes where the gods sit, black in their robes, waiting for us. Pedro, praying, whispered a plea for pardon to Her. He begged Her not to punish him for it, then, hands trembling, he slipped the box's simple catch and swung the door open. Only to show You Your people, he repeated several times. Not that we would disturb You in the silence of Your eternal happy calm and well-being just so we could have a reassuring look at Your face, but because we know You care for us, not that we could know why, the bird of all the birds he stuns with his stones a boy takes home to heal, who knows why? but that You have taken our hearts into Yours and in our moments of happiness we know it might please You to see us, our smiles and our laughter. And even saying these things he had not thought before to say, Pedro himself was feeling the weight of them behind him, the load of all of them drawing tight across his forehead, making his temples throb and his head pull back, and the nervous thrill of that weight all down over his shoulders and down spearlike through his knees and into the very ground, rooting him at the time he must move most swiftly, pursue Her and find Her face and turn it to him and make its sheep round eyes move and its wide mouth open and speak. And not merely to find Her, but to have Her come of Her own good will and speak to him and through him to them.

At some point he turned to the baby's mother and told her what to bathe the little body with, water and laurel and salt. For a long while his praying continued, some in Latin and some in Tzotzil so low his voice became the same as the breathing in the room. The candles gutted and burned out and they, believing that he still prayed though the sound was their own, remained, changed by the sight they had seen, the brown woman as simple as any clay thing they could make themselves and yet magic too, desirable, and hoping together for the light to return and bring Her back to them.

Outside, pressed against the damp wall to keep away from the water pouring off the thatch, Pedro shivered in the cold, and Augustina covered him with what warmth of hers she could.

Don't do that, she said.

She has spoken before to both of us. She is and She speaks, and they have to believe that.

Augustina shaking her head and in the dark trying to see his eyes. My father knew a man who had one and it talked for him. But when he showed it to other people the saint didn't want to speak. So the man got inside the box instead, and the people believed it was the voice of the saint, but when they went away his wife went to open the box and all she found inside was a lizard.

If I am a lizard in God's eyes, then let me be one. A cold skin and a close careful view of the ground. He explained to Augustina what she would do once he had gotten under the table. And if you become a lizard too then we will be together as lizards, he said. Do it.

When they were allowed by Augustina to light more candles they found, through the thick contained smoke of the copal, that the saint was still among them. And in a while, when Augustina had prayed to it in a high-voiced mixture of the Spanish prayers she had learned as a servant in a religious household, it answered her in that same voice. Through Augustina She told them she was Santa Rosha and that She had come for them, for all the people were now to return to their own, and were to believe in the true saints and not in the ones the priests set out for them, unless they wanted to merely die and never live across in the green land.

In the dark under the table the man lying, hands splayed on the dirt, traveled elsewhere, to a desert plain which had never been green, where the only motion was his own rising and falling when he drew breath to speak, or reared up to see if he could further divide the line, scorched light above, darkness scorched beneath it, the thin band which was his hope and his danger for anything which would crush him he would know coming only as a widening space on that band and nothing more.

3

On the hilltop that morning it was very quiet. Clouds were clinging to the mountains all around the valley and there were many small gray swallows. They cleared Juan Tushim's hill with a single chop of their long wings and floated off down into the valley. In the pine trees I saw many hidden, questioning faces, moth-wings as big as my hand, each with a circle eye on it. It was noon on the second day of the Santa Rosha fiesta and down in the plaza white puffs of smoke appeared in the air, followed soon by the explosions of the rockets and the music of the cheery band and all the church bells. The smoke turned blue as it rose and spread, and the echoes, trapped, bounced back and forth across the valley until they came to sound like deep waves rolling onshore. The quiet returned and I felt the rain coming before it actually began, a gathering cold in the air which then thickened into water. When it started finally, an old white mule stopped cropping, raised its head, ears back, and stood waiting for it to pass. I went inside.

Because the old man was so ill, his family had not gone down to the fiesta. They seemed upset or ashamed by my appearance, since I had been with Juan all yesterday and had helped carry him home after he passed out in the mud.

He called me to the bed. There was a pregnant white and black cat curled up comfortably against him. I bowed and he released me and said, "I thought you had packed up and gone back to your country again."

"Not since yesterday, uncle."

"But haven't you been thinking about it? imagining you could get the rest of it from books? Because there *are* books, I've heard, which tell *their* side of it, how Cuscat was a liar and a thief." He reached over and spat on the floor. "How is the fiesta?"

"I don't know. I slept and came here to see you."

"That little girl at least got well."

"Did she?"

"Yes. And so others began coming to the saint and they made their offerings to her and waited like sheep until Santa Rosha spoke to them, and then they were pleased, happier than they had been, because She cured them and promised them a new life was coming.

"This went on for a long time, the saint gained more and more power among the people there. They came to Her not only for the herbs to cure their bodies. Boys would come and ask if a certain girl was the one to get married to, and if it was right the saint would tell them 'Yes, you may have her because I say it.' Then the girl would be sent for and Santa Rosha would tell her the news and it would be settled. In the same way the saint settled things between men who were having a fight. And the people went to Her and not to the president of the town because She was from heaven and loved them and they didn't know the officials. The saint told them not to go to the priests to baptize their babies. 'You have seen they have no women here on earth,' She said. 'But in Hell where they go at night, they have many.'

"Then the people made their fiestas for their own saint at the little river which runs down through Tzajalemel. There they baptized their children, with Cuscat and his two wives showing them how it should be done. The people came from all around, from other towns too, and at first they went to the river at night so the ladinos would not know what they were doing. They took along music, guitars and harps to play on the riverbank, and rockets to set off, and carrying Santa Rosha in their arms they danced in the water."

The old man's daughter came to the bed and told him to be

quiet for a while now. He let himself down slowly and lay on his side, mouth tight, watering opaque eyes intent on the fire, angry I decided at the young people of his own who were listening but not believing, or not listening well enough to satisfy him.

"Where's your grandson?"

"I had to send *someone* to see how they are doing down there, didn't I?"

"And Pedro Díaz Cuscat, what did he do?"

"Him? he had the people there build a new house for him and his women so his saint wouldn't have to listen to him grunting in the dark *twice* every night. And you know"—Juan reached for my sleeve and pulled me up close to his mouth—"that Checheb woman, Augustina, was said to have a vagina as big as a glass you drink beer from! My grandfather told me she kept her tortillas in there so they came to the table still as hot as they came off the fire." Juan cackled and juices came from his mouth and nose. He didn't bother to wipe them away.

"But you told me Cuscat only ate white bread."

"When he could. But he ate tortillas too, you know. He was an Indian, and Indians eat tortillas. Besides, do you think a woman like that Checheb cooks for only one man? bread for Cuscat and tortillas for the rest!"

Again he wheezed and laughed.

His sons and daughters were convinced their father was dying. In low voices they discussed whether they should go against his orders and send for the curer. Only the daughter who served him found her father's crudeness funny and the others got angry with her too, so she covered her mouth and her eyes grew sad and appropriately worried.

Juan Tushim rested and then turned onto his back and stared up at the grime-hung rafters and the deep black overhead. He said, "When he knew it was going to happen he went around to all the towns here in the mountains and to the places he knew people would be—at Yochib where they have market on Wednesdays, and Larrainzar on Friday—and he would tell them about the saint. Sometimes he would send my grandfather or Nacho Panchini?, his friend, or one of his wife's brothers.

"On the evening before the day, Cuscat never ate. He went

into the sweat bath they had built him next to his new house and made himself clean beating his body with palms, as old people do and women after they give birth. My grandfather, who was only a boy when he began serving Cuscat, said sometimes he would beat himself until his back was bloody and torn and they would have to carry him out of there and work on him with medicine to get him ready for the next day."

Why had that detail been preserved through time? I wondered. Whenever I thought I knew who Cuscat was, I was fooled. What in the loneliness of that hot little cave provoked him to hurt himself? The only reassurance for the naked man about to face the crowd already camped on the hill above the river the words of the padre in the anteroom. *Remember the Mass is a birth too.* And the birth of children the proof He still loves us and has not yet turned away His face. Then Dio's gentle shove would hurry the boy with the censer out into the blue light.

But Pedro would no longer want those particular promises and might instead seek the pain Cresencio used as his transmission into the other place.

Whatever you do here is only a shadow of what They are doing so brightly in the sky. Whatever you see is only half seen.

Then he would recoil once again, burned, and beat himself, the strokes the rhythm he would use, even if he didn't yet know what words would come bobbing on them. With practice nothing right became easier. He grew afraid of repeating himself, of going back, as much as he was afraid of continuing. Yet there seemed to be a place inside which he could reach, or at least had reached before, where nothing could harm him. If he prayed to get inside, even if he thought about it, there was no chance that he could go there. And because he had been there, and because he sought it, there was no escape from limbo that he could manage himself.

Except through one set of small doors.

And then they would come looking for him at the sweat bath and find him gone and only his clothes left hung on the arms of the cross. Those who were closest, his women and his sons, would set out in the night to look for him, afraid to call out his name because the believers were sleeping all around in the hills. Then toward dawn they would find him crouched naked at the riverbank, staring at the reflection of himself which only he could see, since the river there flowed white and steadily in the rainy season. He would come home willingly, without being held. Other times they did not find him, but around sunrise he would reappear at the gate on his own, grinning between yawns.

His wife said, But what if they should see you? and he said kindly, *You* have seen me and that has done little harm to you.

The morning after such a night had no terrors left to offer. He would not tell even Augustina where he had been. But perhaps, if only his brother had been with him, he could have explained it. Her face, he would have said, you would recognize it too. She is wise and trusting and Her head tilts up like a horse's does when some news comes to it on the wind. She tells me not to make the mistake of growing old. She tells me that when I was little, very little, toward morning our mother would put me over against our father's back so she could sleep a little more and then I would wet and our father would wake up and say, It's all cold and wet in here! and not know who had caused that. And another time, my brother, I was walking through a field of reeds and I saw Her coming toward me. She was very beautiful, very light. I got down on my knees and put my head on the ground. I heard Her move, but then the whole world became very still and nothing happened, so I got my courage back and there before me on Her knees with Her head to the ground was the saint. We laughed and laughed together.

Without Salvador, Pedro felt like the man who has been away and not burned or cleared his field does when he sees the other men jabbing the fat soft earth with their poles and bending at the waist to drop in their seed. Dio had said once a man might become a prophet, but at times even a prophet longs to have his prophets.

Waiting through the long morning and into the afternoon, the people could not help doing what they always did with a Sunday. After they had first lit candles and said prayers to Her closed box in the little house or, on good days, in the courtyard, it did not seem wrong to go to the hillside above the river and exchange things, to show off a nicely embroidered blouse you had made and would be willing to part with, or to have a round of drinks with your husband's family from Ya?alinch'en. Sometime in the afternoon the saint's box would be moved down to the river, and the music would be played and the baptisms and marriages performed while everyone watched.

Augustina Checheb would come, the people made way for her and the other women with incense bowls who surrounded her. Over her black skirt she wore a white robe. Some said it was satin. She opened the box and they could see the saint and she got to her knees and prayed before it, and the people prayed. Those with petitions or questions would be led forward and if you were close enough you could hear, above the sound of the crowd and the river, the saint's small voice answering the Checheb woman. The people kept well back and Pedro was nowhere to be found.

All at once the music would stop, the great drum go quiet, and somewhere toward the front of the crowd a small clearing was made by men who stood motionless, their eyes at rest and steady, among people who shifted and swayed.

There is a moment before true sunset when the light seems to stretch long and to be losing its power. Watching, we see he is an old man lying down on a bed he doesn't plan to get up from. Just then a man, freshly washed, hair flattened to his square head, and wearing a new white chamarra, would be there in the middle of the empty circle, standing between them and the sun so they could not see his face. He began speaking in a low voice and half the crowd, wheeling to find this sound, would be hit by the sunlight, and sigh. It was warming, at least to the mind, to turn into the sun so suddenly. The crowd pressed forward to hear. He waited and watched the valley fill, the density increase until the mass was like a cloud ready to open. The readable faces closest to him began to push forward under the weight of the bodies behind.

Then he raised his head and threw out his arms as though to embrace them all, opened his mouth to speak and took a single step forward. The people nearest him leaned back on the importunate living thing behind them and, balanced, the little circle in which he stood was maintained.

Speaking, he grew hot. The words came from his mouth like water from an underground river coming clear and powerful and unending from the side of a mountain. He told them everything he knew. He felt their hushing breath pushing back against him. It was like the first wind of the planting season which beguiles us into going out well after dark to be with the fresh land. He could have made his life in that wind, leaning into it, all his strength gone to hold him upright against it. His mouth only a funnel for precious metal, his report dictated in the real world of the sun, himself only showing in this insubstantial place truths we have always known but, bound as we are by clouds and shadows and stone, have forgot.

Our Holy Mother loves all living things. She will love us when we are again alive, when in darkness like seeds we struggle to come into the light and in the light complete ourselves and prepare ourselves for death and our children for life as it was meant to be, when we shake ourselves free of the devils who have trapped us now.

The end would come on him. He would drive toward the people another step, arms raised, stop, seeing the sun now gone reflected in their thousand faces, a glow, a longing which remained in them a moment after but was already passing from him.

His own body existed again, whatever acrid juices had collected in his stomach were about to spew forth, but still he would not let them go. Having spoken of what is fated, the only other thing he could give them was a momentary hope that for once it would not happen, the sun not die. And once more he would fill his lungs with their breath, and they did not know what he was taking from them, the food and strength. What they could see was how much of himself he expended. When at last the yellow light did go and his hands sank to his sides, he lost the sense of where he was and, like a wounded animal, lumbered away into the crowd, thrashing through them until his helpers got to him and lifted him away.

Then a long silence. They could hear the wind and water again and perhaps a baby here or there cried out. The drum began, heavy, and the people swayed to it and cried themselves for something lost, or laughed, or didn't know which they were doing, and grabbed strangers and held them to see reflected in each other's faces mirrors of the wonderful thing happening to them. People fell and were not trampled, and on the ground they repeated in the high whistlelike voice of the saint what the saint's man had told them. They too saw the other world clearly. And sometimes Pedro himself would still be among them, dancing, just a person again like any other, and his women were with him then too. It continued into the night, sometimes until dawn. But he would always be gone before it ended.

They put him to bed and several hours passed before he woke at all, hours of chill and fever punctuated with brief intervals when he spoke to the air rapidly, urgently, in Santa Rosha's voice. They were not frightened for him, though. His face appeared tranquil and his body was relaxed. Slowly he came awake to things around him. He would sigh and smile. Once he said, I am the man who has eaten the whole chicken. In the night he would take a little broth, giving profuse thanks to whoever stayed awake to serve him, and maybe a piece of the white bread the people had offered the saint.

This time he came hurtling up from the depths of it, fleeing along passages and trembling as he came, because they were calling him. A voice he knew far away saying in Spanish, A very impressive show, my boy, very impressive. I'm glad we stopped to see it.

Pedro got his eyes open at last, and there, seated by his bed, uncomfortable on the tiny chairs given them, were the two brothers. To the side of the squat one was a glowing oil lamp, and to the side of the one with the flopping bow spilling from his throat was another ladino. He was darker than the brothers and his lean face was irregular, like a piece of land an earthquake had divided down the middle and put back together with one part slightly below the other.

Nacho Panchini? whispered to him, We tried to keep them out.

Pedro said, It is all right. He struggled to prop himself up in the bed.

Pedro, this is my friend Ignacio Fernández de Galindo, who has just arrived from Mexico City. He is going to found a technical school in San Cristóbal and your work interests him greatly, Hector said.

The Indian bowed his head and then looked up to see more of the face of this man Hector was claiming for a friend. The ladino gave out only a brief, formal little smile, and continued staring at Pedro. He had large eyes. The lashes, as long as a woman's, were the only softening thing about him. He has a wolf's soul, Pedro thought.

Dio stirred in his little chair. Are you planning to have us all murdered?

What? Pedro strained forward.

The man who translated for us this afternoon said that you spoke against ladinos, or rather that your Santa Rosha did, and the people who come seem to enjoy that part of your sermon best.

Your translator was lying to you, Padre. Through the saint I only try to bring their own real life back to them. I try only to make them happy for what exists, which they have lost the power to see.

And not to excite them to blood?

Doesn't Holy Week excite white people to blood, Padre? You told me the sins of word and thought were as bad as the sins of action, and sometimes worse. So don't you kill your Christ each year?

Dio smiled. But we resurrect Him also, my son.

Hector liked that, and Pedro too grinned. Don't be afraid, Padre. If I led those people out against the ladinos they would certainly be killed, and their deaths would be on me. As you know, I have done enough to keep me from getting into heaven without having that too.

My fellow Miguel here doesn't like your meetings.

Does it make his own audience smaller? Hector asked.

For one thing, yes.

Hector leaned closer to the bed. You must be careful, Pedro. Anyone who is afraid of another man stealing his joy has good reason. As you had ample opportunity to learn, we are a race of thieves. Not knowing how to manufacture the ineffable things ourselves, we have always had to make do with seeing to it none of the other races enjoyed them either. Hence, for example, the story of Señor Cortés is not only history, but also mythology.

Pedro said, You keep a sapling covered through the cold season, but there comes a time, a moment when your green stem is not yet ready for it, that you must risk exposing it to the world. That moment is fearful, when more of your carefulness can only cause the tree to wither away and die.

At last the stranger, Galindo, spoke. And aren't you afraid for your immortal soul?

No. My confessor will take care of that for me.

Dio asked, Who is this confessor? I would like to meet him. I have not changed, Padre.

Well, And I haven't heard your tiny voice through the grill in many years now.

Haven't you? I confess every night and put my mind in order.

In your dreams? Dio didn't wait for an answer. He pulled himself up out of the little Indian chair and told the others it was time to be going.

Pedro threw back the cover and sat on the side of the bed. It was chilly, and his cotton clothes were still pressed to him with sweat. Isn't it late, señores? isn't it dark? wouldn't it be better for you to stay in this humble house tonight?

Dio stared at him, not amused by his sudden ladino servility. Hector, who did not notice it, got to his feet and said no, they were going on to his cousin's ranch in Chenalhó, which was not too far on horseback. Pedro tried to stand, but his legs were weak under him. The brothers bade him good night and ducked out through the low doorway.

The man named Fernández de Galindo leaned over to him and said, You are doing well. You know your people have an imitative temperment and only when you change that will you be able to free them. As long as they continue to want only what we keep from them, they will be slaves of one sort or another. But don't try anything until after they next plant their damned crops or you too will find them melting away at your back.

Pedro said, I don't know what you mean, señor.

But you do, young man. You do not fool me at all. *You* see that God has set them on a pinnacle here just to tempt us into casting them down.

The ladino laughed quickly, put on his worn felt hat, survivor with him of many battles, and followed the Estrada brothers out into the brittle January night.

Miguel Martínez, who had the church in Chamula, saw his personal situation as primarily 'triste.' To escape, he went visiting his family in San Cristóbal in the middle of most weeks. Chamula was sad for him because, as he saw it, he served two congregations, neither of which he could really speak to openly. The Indians he could not understand and they could not understand him. Yet he recognized that there was a religious impulse in them, the piety simple people seem to have in such abundance. He learned to pronounce the name of God and the word for heaven in their language from his native sacristans. They said the people blamed him for the holy objects being gone from the church. So he applied to his friend the bishop for the return of the vessels and crucifixes. But the bishop still had the persecutions of the early years of the decade in mind, and had decided the sacred things from all the temples would be safer staying in Guatemala at least until the military liberals were ousted and Chiapas again had a government which would assure the safety of the churches.

Padre Miguel felt even more removed from the ladinos he served than from the Indians, and the fact they presumed he was one of them made him uncomfortable. By and large a despicable class of people, indolent men and hawklike women who had no skills to keep them alive in civilization and so camped in the hinterlands methodically cheating savages out of their precious centavos. They fawned on Martínez as though he personally kept the keys to heaven. When they first came to him to complain of the meetings in Tzajalemel, they could barely hide their fear of someone else stealing the illegal trade in rum from under their sharp noses. Martínez calmed them with the story of a man with a talking saint who had appeared in the village where he had worked in Guatemala, telling how the saint quickly made the mistake of asking for the young girls and in short order the people there ran the charletan and his doll out of town. For several months Padre Miguel assured the ladinos this Cuscat fellow was bound to foul his own nest sooner or later.

Then his bishop sent for him and said the shopkeepers in San Cristóbal had noticed Chamulas were buying large supplies of gunpowder. They have begun making their own rockets and bombs to honor Santa Rosha, Martínez explained. But the bishop was not satisfied. He wanted a full report.

So after Mass and his meal on the second Sunday in February Padre Miguel went to the president and three or four officials were assigned to him. They set out for Tzajalemel, the priest on his little mare and the officials in their pretty regalia carrying their staffs.

It was the time of year when the nights still have frost but the sun at midday is hot, the sky clear, and the corn is dry and bent over. Martínez had eaten well and it was pleasant to get out and ride. He did not have to slow his pace for the men with him afoot, because they left the road and took the paths and would reappear a quarter hour later a bit ahead of him, like dogs panting and eager for him to catch up. As they neared Tzajalemel the priest did notice the people he passed were not bowing to him and twice before they found the river and the meeting they were given directions which got them lost.

The numbers of people on the slope with the westward view Cuscat had chosen struck Martínez, and the fact that it was not only Chamulas in their white and black wool who came but Indians from the even less 'civilized' Tzotzil towns to the north. He had expected the drinking, but not the openness of it. Near him on the ground was a couple, along into middle age, and though the woman fought it, the man had nearly succeeded in getting her skirts up and was astride her before their children stopped them. The priest had seen such things actually accomplished at fiestas in Guatemala, but the Indians here were not usually given to such lascivities.

The Checheb woman appeared in white, women all around her providing a blue cloud of incense. She went to the river to begin the baptisms. Then the box was opened, the saint revealed, and a mighty sigh escaped from the crowd.

Padre Miguel went striding down the hill through the people to get a closer look at the image. Men, perhaps Cuscat's assistants, put out their arms to stop him, but he pushed them out of the way and came to the box on the table and took it up in his arms. Inside was only a clay doll surrounded by brownish cotton wadding he supposed was meant to represent clouds.

Augustina Checheb had come out of the water and stood watching him.

The priest turned to the crowd and held the box out before them. He boomed out in Spanish, Where is your saint? In the silence the words bounced back from the hillside. What is she if she can't protect herself from me? And where is the man who speaks for her? afraid to come out and face a solitary priest of the true God?

As he looked out on all the faces, tears filled his eyes. He had no fear of these people, he was only terribly sorry for their ignorance. He had expected the sacrilege, but not the tawdriness of the trick being played on them. *There* is your God, he cried out, pointing to the sky with his free hand. There is San Juan, the patron for you, waiting in *my* church. Make your prayers to Him. He was the god of your ancestors and He is your God. Not this! Padre Miguel shook his head at the box. *I* am your priest, he said, tapping his chest. *I* give you the word from God. And I protect you from the bad spirits and from Hell! Martínez pointed to the ground. Again he demanded, Where is your Cuscat? where is your saint?

In the silence a tiny muffled voice answered him in Spanish, Here Padre. For a moment the priest imagined the voice came from the box. What's that? he said.

One of the officials the president had sent along stood grinning, frightened, beside him. It came from here, Señor Padre, he said, indicating the cloth-covered table where the saint had been.

Of course it did, Martínez said. Lift that up.

But the man did not seem to understand.

So the priest himself ripped aside the cotton nailed to the

table-leg. Here, hold this, he said, giving the saint to the official. Under the cloth was a man Martínez thought he recognized even though he was very drunk and his face pale and dirty. There was not even a decent wool garment on his back. The priest pulled him out by the arm and held him up. Do you see? he shouted. *Here* is the voice of your saint! When I take him away, *then* see if she talks to you!

Oh, the man said, shaking his head back and forth wisely, then I don't think she will, Padre.

Martínez had not meant all this when he came, but he had been trained for drama as priests are, and when he saw his opportunity, he took it. Hugging Cuscat to him in one arm and carrying the saint in the other, he made his way through the crowd up the hill to the place his horse was tethered. The suddenness of his attack must have helped him, for the saint's followers did not even move to come after him until he had bound the Cuscat man with his rope and lashed the box up behind his saddle. He was gathering his skirts to him and had his foot in the stirrup before they reached him. He swung up and his mare skittered and turned, pushing the men away from him. Climbing the path he paid out the rope so his prisoner seemed a moment left behind. But then the mare stepped into a trot and Cuscat was jerked away from his followers and came running blindly behind the priest, swinging wildly from side to side and calling for help.

In twenty minutes they were out of Tzajalemel and on the road. Padre Miguel looked back and saw the Indians had stopped. He realized then that in his anger he had forsaken his dignity. So he reined the mare to a walk and proceeded for an unnerving half hour through the deepening afternoon alone with his captive running along behind and every once in a while pulling back and letting out a deep prolonged yell. At last, ascending to a ridge, Martínez saw a group of men standing against the sky. He took out his pistol and cocked it, and then saw they were the officials the president had sent waiting for him.

They had taken off their ribbon-decked hats and had hidden them under their black chamarras.

Come this way, Dio said, busily leading Pedro and his woman down the hall, indicating the corner they would turn with his hand, guiding them and in his nervousness forgetting that Pedro and Augustina knew the passages of this house nearly as well as he did.

When the seminary was closed in 1861, Dio had been asked by the bishop to stay in San Cristóbal, and had moved back into the home of his childhood. In those years he had worn non-clerical clothes, but he had insisted on taking a tiny servant's cell at the back of the house and had kept priestly rules for himself.

He got them into his room, carefully closed the doors and latched it and only then noticed there were no chairs. He went to get them. When he returned, out of breath, with a ladderback in each hand, he announced Dolores would be coming with refreshment in a moment. She remembers you dearly, Pedro, and won't give our little secret away to Laura.

Does she remember me? the Indian said.

Dio sat on his small bed and Pedro, after much prodding, sat in one of the chairs. Augustina settled onto her knees beside him, so there was a free chair for the tray with the pot of steaming chocolate which Dolores brought. Dio poured three cups and handed them around. Then he looked a long time at Pedro and finally said, As the priest for so many thousands you do not wear very fancy clothes.

The Indian always wears what is oldest when he comes to town, Padre. It does not please the people here to see us dressed.

Dio finished his own cup and brought the china pot over to Pedro. But the Indians were not ready, so he poured himself more and drank it.

Pedro's eyes were sunken, sleepless. We drink chocolate to celebrate a marriage, Padre. I have noticed how many cups a day priests drink. Does it reaffirm your marriage to God?

No reason to be so angry with me, my son. It wasn't I who stole your little saint from you.

I'm not angry, Padre.

Then what *is* going through your head?

Without Her we are alone. When She is with us everything is

bright and happy. We don't come here to tell you how to worship your gods. Why should you come and take ours away?

How exactly does she make you feel?

I have told you. Like a bird I rise above the world, and then I can see where we are going.

Aren't you suspicious of a mere image which can do that to you? don't you doubt? ever?

No.

And she doesn't ask anything of you in return?

She asks everything.

But no restraints? Dio's eyes flickered on Augustina. No celibacy such as our God demands of us?

Does He get it?

Dio snorted, but then did not seem pleased. You must be furious with your brother.

Why should I be?

For hiding out under your saint's altar.

Padre, maybe you do not understand. My brother went to hot country to get work and found none. He is very sick with the hot country illnesses which we do not know how to cure, and he came back to me. And when he got to me he was afraid, and so instead of coming to see me, he got drunk and managed somehow to crawl under the altar, which is where Padre Miguel found him.

Have they released him?

This morning. I sent my men to get him and take him home.

And your people won't now grow suspicious of you and decide you also get under the table to make Santa Rosha talk?

Now there is no saint. Unless you can get Her back for us.

And that I cannot do. Why don't you simply fashion more?

There was a knock and Dolores came in for her tray and to announce that Laura had gone to visit a sick woman. She smiled on Pedro and asked if he had children. Dio showed her to the door and Pedro could hear them talking in the hallway. Are they married, Padre? Yes, in the way goats marry.

But when he returned, Dio was all smiles. He clapped his hands together and said, Well my son, I'm sorry I can't help you. I would if I could, but now you are in the world of men

and must find your own way, and in spite of your recent con-
verse with saints, you must expect that men will act as they
always have acted.

Thank you, Padre, Pedro said. He grabbed Dio's thick hand
and kissed it.

It was not until a month later that new information began
to come down from the mountains into San Cristóbal. Hector
and Dio had an account from their fat cousin who, since he
lived nearby, seemed truly reliable. Since Martínez had 'arrested'
the first saint and the wrong Cuscat brother, the number of
saints had proliferated. Like the first, they were clay-faced, and
more or less were dressed and put in wooden boxes as she had
been. But now there was one in each paraje and a man ap-
pointed to provide the nightly services and to collect money
from the believers for candles and incense and so forth.

I don't know whether the secondary deities talk during the
week, said the cousin, but on Sunday they are all carted off to
Tzajalemel and there they jabber away together like hornets, or
so I'm told. And the drinking is terrible. Any man in Chenalhó
who has a horse and a barrel to his name goes there to sell,
since there's not an Indian in town on Sunday. It is dangerous
after nightfall, people drunk and hooting along. Last week my
foreman's horse trampled a man lying there in the road. Did
not even see him. And do you know who is the cause of it all?

Pedro is, I suppose, Dio said.

Not precisely. You see, they now believe that the Checheb
woman gave birth to this whole litter of saints. Consequently
they have decided she is the 'Mother of God.' She sits in her
own box and converses with her little 'children' in their boxes.

That is very sweet, Hector said.

Wait, there is more. Although Laura had already gone upstairs, the cousin leaned forward and spoke in a low voice. Since
she is the Mother of God, they have women who follow her
about all day and all night, and they perfume her with incense,
even when she goes to urinate or to void. Now what do you
think of that? the cousin said, sitting back.

Hector yawned and said, Were I the Mother of God, I would
insist on it myself.

4

Pedro often tried to get away unseen, to be by himself so he could calm his trembling body and order what he now knew must come next. But there was a contingent of young men who assumed the duty of following him and protecting him from dangers he could not see, and hardly would he be down the hill when at least a few of them, tying their machetes to their belts, would come running after him.

That morning traveling up into the pine mountains through mist sparkling in the first light, he hardly spoke. The boys were surprised by the pace he set. They had assumed that it was a search for Pedro's brother they were going on. Salvador, drunk once more, had not appeared for two or three days.

Pedro stopped and turned around. His followers clattered to a halt around him. You, he said, pointing out one of them, what are you doing here? The others pulled a little away from the boy who had offended their master. He was a stranger to them anyway, they had seen him around the saints' houses in the last few days, a boy of indeterminate age with a silly smile set in a meaty, bloated face, and no sandals or extra covering for warmth. His wild hair crept down his neck like an animal's tail.

The boy looked down a long time and, though his thick lips moved, no sound came from him. At last he cocked his head up and smiled. I came to be with you, he said in a soft, tongueless Spanish only Pedro could understand.

And your work? what about that?

I found a man.

Does he believe in God?

I asked him.

What did he say?

He laughed.

Then Pedro kissed him and hugged him hard, pulling on the tail of hair at the boy's neck and, arm around him, led the way on through the trees.

They came to a fallen-down house in a ravine. His followers stayed at the gate, but Pedro went to the door and rapped on it and then, turned sideways, said softly, Do you have him, father?

There was no answer from inside.

Even more softly, Pedro said, If you have killed him, father, I am not angry with you. But if you have him and will not give him up, then I will be angry.

The door swung open. Inside stood a man with a broad nose and a fixed mouth. The skin folding down over his eyes made him dubious. Beside him was a younger man with a dirt-caked flintlock gun. The older man asked what Pedro wanted.

I've told you, father, I want my brother. I know the wrong you feel he did. I think you are just. And he is near dying anyway. Yet he still means something to me he cannot mean to you. And I do not want the sin of killing him to be on you.

The men in the doorway said nothing.

Look, I am going to pay you for him. Pedro took a red handkerchief from under his chamarra, picked the knot open with his teeth and showed them a pile of coins, mostly silver, and a few dirty pieces of sugar. There is more than he owes you. If you want you can pay some of the others back too. Or just keep it all for yourselves. It doesn't matter which to me.

So they decided to give him back his younger brother, apologizing as they let him into the house, saying that they hadn't stolen him, they had merely come across him lying drunk in the road and had seen who it was and then had felt the injury he had done them all over again, and had brought him here.

Pedro did not listen. Moving quickly, he scooped up the wasted, near-weightless body of his Salvador, not even pausing to loosen the ropes and rags which bound him, and carried the bundle out in his own arms. On the way back, Salvador came to life several times and tried to speak. Pedro leaned close to hear, nodding and murmuring to soothe him.

In Tzajalemel he went into the house where the women were grinding corn and put his brother up on the table. In Spanish he told Augustina, I want him washed, first with hot water, salt and laurel, then in rum. I will be in the saint's house. Bring him to me there.

Several large houses had now been built on Augustina's hill-top, and the court in the middle was pounded bare and hard by the feet of believers coming and going. But the small place where the first Santa Rosha had lived was kept as it had been before, the rafters decorated with airplants and cornhusks in honor of Her new image. The room was always warm with the deep smell of the copal and flowers and candles.

Pedro took the dumb boy inside and locked the door. He lit more candles and unlatched the box so the boy could see the saint. Then they sat before Her, waiting, side by side, Pedro with his old Bible open in his lap. He wondered if there were more instructions coming, but in the silence he heard nothing. So they talked, the boy with some words but more with gestures, about the various haciendas and fincas, about certain hives which had swarmed and where the boy had decided to move a queen or terminate a hive because it was old.

Do you understand about the Christ?

The boy nodded emphatically, yes.

Is that why you came? Pedro asked.

No.

Do you know how the first Christ came to be?

No, the boy did not.

A long time ago, Pedro said, the ladinos lived in darkness, like animals, the way they say we live now. And they are right. Each person going his own way, being born and taking what he can and dying with no thought for the others. Each man living in fear of his own death, as though that were a matter of any importance at all.

But among the ladinos then were a few who were smart or blessed and could look beyond their own little circles and paths and they saw that it was not worth it, being alive as they were alive. Just living. If they sang a song other men would not laugh or sing with them. If one of theirs died, the others would pass the box on the road and not even take off their hats or cry a tear for the dead man. 'Not me,' the people laughed, 'not this time.' And the wise men knew this was not the way for men to live.

So they took one of their own, the best, the one they loved most to be with, and they said 'Look everyone. Here is the prettiest.' And they put him up on a cross and killed him that way, and he knew why they had to do it and he forgave them. 'My own life is not so important,' he said, 'but the life of the people together is.' And then they had their god to worship and they became strong.

But after a while, being people, they forgot what they had done, and they did not love the Jesus as they had before. They told us to love him, and we tried to. Yet the ladinos themselves don't love him, and he was a ladino, so how could we even begin to love him?

There was nothing that Pedro told the boy which he hadn't, in the last weeks, been telling his followers when they came on Sunday. But he could explain it more easily to the boy. He did not need the preparation the mass of the people did.

The other part of it, his sadness, he told no one. When all of this had first been delivered to him, Pedro had believed it was his own crucifixion and immortality which had been revealed. Only slowly did he come to the understanding that once again he was only to be the person who announced the arrival of another.

Going outside to allow Augustina and the women carrying Salvador to pass, Pedro saw on the black outline of the hills all around torches, little processions of families descending, each led by a man with a guitar. By the river cooking fires sent smoke up into the sky.

Salvador lay strapped to a board, his hands bound to his sides. He slept and woke and did not see Pedro and the tongueless boy kneeling, contemplating him. He shook, some bad dream or spirit they could see passing through him. Pedro put a bottle to his lips and filled his mouth. Salvador choked and Pedro said, Swallow! When he did, he opened his eyes wide as a baby does when he has gulped down something he hadn't known would be sweet.

The skin was smooth and clean, the body smelled of the laurel and the rum. Even the nails of his hands and feet were soft from the salt. The flesh was so much less than it once had been, and briefly the older brother was ashamed. But still it was a living human body and it would satisfy. In small ways, in the thickness of the wrist and the slight bowing of the legs, it was Pedro's own.

I know everything, Salvador said suddenly, loud.

What do you know?

There's a cross. I saw it.

That's true.

But they won't use nails, will they?

If you don't want them.

No, they would hurt. How long will I be there?

I do not know yet. All day.

But I will survive it.

When Salvador smiled, even as weakly as he did now, he was still the prettier of the two. His nose was finer, sharper. Pedro touched his cheek. Of course. You will survive it easily and then this sickness will pass.

They made a covering by wrapping around him from waist to thigh a piece of the printed cotton the saints wore. Throughout the night the groups arrived with their precious cargos on their shoulders. Skyrockets went off each time a saint was brought into the little house and the explosions made Salvador start in his sleep. The boxes were set in a circle around him and their doors opened so the pretty ones could peer out at him and remember him. Men had been sent out into all parts of the world in the days before and had brought back baskets full of flowers. The roses were pulled apart by women and the petals spread around on the floor and over the sleeping man's head and body.

It pleased these poor anxious people, the ones allowed inside were closest to the various saints, because in spite of the proliferation of fiestas over the last months, they had never seen before an expenditure of themselves as great as this was becoming.

They did not have gold or precious stones or clever artists who could repeat or exaggerate reality on cloth as the ladinos had, and none of them could figure out how to arch a great wall and create the suspensions of stone which white men had once been able to make. They knew who they were, only farmers at best, connected with the potential of God only through the means He had given them, the ability to grow with their hands the best of what could come of the land He lent them, and the eyes to see in nature what of His creation was freshest and must please Him most. They were His servants, His children placed a while in this world to delight Him by pointing out the mysteries He had set for them to see. Their priests were only those they trusted most to know His mind and His pleasure.

Dawn that Holy Friday held off far a long time and it was cold and windy in Tzajalemel. When the light came at last it broke suddenly, just a band of cream under the dark banked clouds. Then the people at their fires on the hillside could make out two great pines, round and perfect with long stretching needles, trees still fresh-smelling, set up a little distance apart near the river. Smoke settled in the valley and made the air hazy.

Some time before the saints appeared there was a disturbance, and many men went running up toward the road. The ladinos had found out the people of the talking saints were going to hold some great fiesta that day and had come on horseback and in wagons with their barrels and goods. But Pedro had men posted at the road with guns, and the ladinos were not allowed to come down. Afraid, some returned to San Cristóbal. Those from Chenalhó, who lived side by side with Indians and so had to convince themselves regularly that they didn't fear them, stayed. They set up their little stands along the road and waited, knowing the Indian's nature as they did, knowing he was chained to rum as flies are bound to sugar, figuring that later on their paganish event, whatever it might be, would not hold their attention any more and they would surely come to drink.

Even for the bravest of those ladinos, men who had killed Indians with knives over small debts, it was an unnerving day. The saints' guards remained and they could make out nothing of what was happening in the valley beyond the woods. They heard the hollow drum and the explosions of gunpowder, and the people moaning and crying. By mid-morning some of the women, though they were nearly as fierce as their men, made up a party for mutual protection and, carrying their small children, started home on foot.

By the river there were no great events. The clouds in the east broke open, separated, and for a while there was some thin sunlight. The saints were brought and set up so they could watch and the Mother of God came in her white like a wedding dress, and Cuscat himself, also in a white robe, and they stood easily among the little saints in their boxes.

A company of men followed by their wives with bowls of incense brought the great cross down the hill with the man already lashed to it. The wood was still soft green in places and bled fluid from its smooth planes. Salvador looked small in the join of its huge arms. They raised the cross in the space between the two pine trees, its foot fitted into a board-lined shaft they had made. Coming upright the cross wavered forward and back, and poor Salvador's strapped body slumped away from the cross and then, falling back, hit it.

The people waited for Cuscat to speak, but there was only the drum and the crying. Though they had known this was to happen, because he had prepared them for it, the sight of the man so far above them, it was impossible to reach him or help him in any way, his body stretched out from the cross and held by strands of himself pulling his chest, his only movement or freedom the head rolling from side to side, and the eyes opening wide and closing, all this made the people feel abandoned themselves. They cried and, crying, held each other, or kneeled and put their faces in the dirt.

They heard his voice, high and like the sound of a rabbit frantic in a snare, but no words.

Pedro, beyond them, did not take his eyes away. He cried too and prayed directly to Salvador, asking him to forgive and to bless the people. It is not after all your own death, but mine and all of ours you face, the death of the friend you call your body. But not the death of life, not that.

Salvador from that great height staring down at him, mouthed words it took Pedro a long while to understand. His brother was cold. Pedro called softly for his silent boy to come to him.

People smiled inadvertantly when they saw the child clammering up the cross and, hanging over the arm from behind, forcing the mouth of a bottle at the suffering man's lips.

The clouds had broken up and moved over the sky like dark frightened animals. The sun stayed largely behind them, and shadows chased one another across the fields and the mountains.

Having hidden themselves and covered their faces with dirt in shame and having waited for so long with nothing but the man on the cross's misery and fear to reflect them, the people had grown restless. They began to wonder why they should cry if this new god was still alive enough to fill himself with whatever the monkey boy had taken up the cross to him. Then the various attendants and assistants appeared among them with bottles and clay bowls. The liquor went around and people began to feel that doubtful energy we feel when we wake up from being sick. Tentative, afraid still of sacrilege, they began to move about, or to say a gentle word to someone near them on the ground still honestly wrapped in the misery of it. The men and boys came again with bowls of cooked corn sweetened with honey and brown sugar, and halfway down the hill an old woman, a grandmother who had been given rum several times, stood up with a baby in her arms and began to thump the ground in time to the drum and to sing to quiet the child. Old women are hard to deal with when they have drunk a little. They seem to believe in a kind of holiness all their own, and it doesn't matter to them that others are crying when they want to shake their little grandchildren out of their sadness, or to sing foul songs to the saints about their hot vaginas. People nearby tried to quiet the old lady, but with no success. And Cuscat, hearing her, turned his back on the cross and raised his arms to her. Then other women who had been hiding their babies all through the morning with the little faces pressed against the teats to keep them quiet, knew what they had been thinking all along—that though this was sad, it was certainly not the end of everything. The sun is only hidden, they thought, but not gone, so they took the chance also to stand up and give the babies a shaking and an opportunity to look out on the singular gathering of people and gods.

At first Pedro had thought of how to avoid this, how at least for one day of their lives to keep the people fixed on their sadness. But then, while he was giving orders to the mayordomos of the various saints, the thing had been lifted away from him. For the others even a ceremony which would begin a new life and bring them a coherence they had never felt before, was still to be a fiesta, and must have what fiestas always have. And Pedro knew they were right. He was the one who had been away, his fever the immigrant's. So he doubted himself and did not allow himself to doubt them.

He went away. He sat on the hill where his father had waited for the man who carried the years to come up to him, and watched. His heart beat loud, echoing inside his body as the drum sound volleyed around the hills. Not his own heart, but his brother's. He tried to hear Her speaking to him, but She did not. Then he began to think again of Dio, not the tricky man of these days, but the one of long ago. Part of Dio would understand the crucifixion and those hours of fear and moaning now gone for good. But none of the priest's mind would ever be able to share with Pedro what was happening to them now. Only blasphemous drunken Indians to his eyes. Pressed body to body in the valley bottom, swaying together and stumbling together, drowning people going toward a core which doesn't even have a name, certainly it is not called any god's name, just the place where everything comes from, life and death. At a fiesta the people pull toward that place, going the crucial action, not arriving. A ladino priest would not understand. Having lived as a white man, Pedro knew the sensation of being himself, of being a person in the world under God's golden watching eye, and how a white man comes closest to his God when he is least humble. These people were very different. Self was a burden to them, ordinary desire put them away from the core, from the sight of the saints. They loved giving away to children whatever they owned. They loved rum because it made them all alike. Their music was regular and insistent, like the pole rungs of a ladder which descended into the dark of the earth where everything which was real existed. The dance happened to them and passed away. Tomorrow they would wake up lost as children again, with their sorry bodies strapped to them again, and only the most elusive of memories to maintain them until the strength and courage came back to go again to seek the heart.

In mid-afternoon, wind came up. Dust blew into the valley and women had to clutch their shawls to keep them from flapping away. Harsh rain followed, but caught up in it, the people went on deeper and deeper.

Pedro stood at the foot of the cross. The ropes had cut into Salvador's wrists and blood ran down his arms, washed thin by the rain. From time to time his mouth would open and Pedro would try to hear what he was saying. But Salvador was only gasping for breath or trying to wet his lips and at last even that stopped. Pedro called for his men, and they lifted the cross out of the ground and lowered it. He went and put his head on the chest and listened for the heart, but there was none. The others were crying and crowding the body, forcing Pedro against it. He stroked the wet hair away from the face and then pulled back the cotton binding at the waist. The penis was shriveled and gray. He told the men to make a cut along the ribs with a machete, and they drained away what blood they could.

By nightfall the rain had stopped and the people sat in the mud in the courtyard. Candles were lit wherever there was cover from the wind and the door to the saint's house stood open, light coming from inside. The body had been laid out and washed a second time, and only his brother and Augustina stayed with poor Salvador and spoke to him. Drunk grief blocked Pedro's throat. Only happy little tales of their childhood could get past. The weeping outside was the part of him which was allowed to cry, and from time to time he would go to the doorway, appearing as only a black shadow in the light, and he would try to count the number of people sitting there.

He got into bed at last near dawn. Augustina touched his belly. Pedro stopped her hand and said, No, tonight I am all alone. Then when he closed his eyes he and Salvador went walking together on a road which went on and on through gray country.

5

In the town of San Cristóbal opinion divided over the reports of the latest events in Tzajalemel. Dionisio Estrada held with those who believed that the 'new Jews,' as someone called them, had drunk the blood of their martyr. Surprisingly, his brother Hector thought the blood drinking was a detail added by the Chenalhó people who were afraid not so much for their lives but for their trade. In the council, Hector was heard to murmur, They wouldn't mind the blood if only the dark beasts would cut it with rum.

Why do you say such preposterous things in public? Dio asked.

Because the council is so endlessly boring. Today Don Silvestre Gutiérrez begged permission to speak, kept us waiting a good ten minutes while he settled his buttocks so he wouldn't strangulate his hemorrhoids and then announced 'The Indian learns only through his back, not his head.' I applauded Silvestre for not being afraid to make use of an occasional piece of ancient ordinary philosophy when the seriousness of the occasion calls for it.

But just because one man is along in life and perhaps softened a bit in the brain, there's no reason for you to side with the radicals.

Don't worry, Hector said, the radicals are fully equal to our friends. This lawyer Culebro Álba explained how the land reform code of Señor Juárez and Señor Lerda, although a beautiful and just piece of legislation, has not worked properly for the small propertyholder, in our case the indigenous population of Chiapas at large and the Chamulas in particular. In the second hour of his discourse Señor Álba concluded that the Indians are upset. He made the telling point that the man they crucified had, in fact, been an employee of those ruthless ladinos who have been, in effect, using the new laws to appropriate the communal property of the Chamulas' Aztec forefathers.

Did you explain that the only common property the ancient Chamulas ever had was the land they farmed to support their priestly royalty?

No, but I woke up at that point and told Señor Álba that the Chamulas' grandpapas were Mayans and not Aztecs. He thought me frivolous. Yet in spite of the boredom hammering in on me from both directions, I did manage to come up with my own theory of all this enthusiasm in our placid mountains.

What is that?

Hector settled himself, stroked the white cat sleeping on his lap so the fur rose up electrically to touch his fingers, and lit a new cigar. The cat woke, sneezed, smelled the tobacco and saw the smoke, and jumped down from Hector's small lap. I have concluded, Brother, that we invented Pedro Cuscat.

How did we do that?

By a series of errors too systematic to be called chance. There must be a mentality of some sort behind this business. Remember it was Laura who brought Pedro to this house. Then you, once a reader of Rousseau, took him off to be educated just in case his savage background hadn't cooked him up to the proper degree of nobility. Now *I* sit in the council and between naps get to legislate his fate, allow him to continue or put him in jail for ever and ever.

Dio said, I think that *you*, Hector, are making the classic error of trying to comprehend the antithesis of everything you believe in by claiming you created it.

As God claims to have created the Prince of Darkness?

Dio laughed. He had had wine with his supper and could not at the moment remember what the various commentators had to say about the possible existence of evil before the creation of the Universe. He did, though, recall a school argument long ago with his younger brother in which he had the first intimation that Hector's mind was much more supple than his own. Hector had asked if God was everywhere, and Dio had said of course. Then Hector had asked if God was everything, and less sure Dio had said He was. Then God must be bad as well as good, since there is good and bad in the world! Hector had trumpeted. And Dio then had cried and repeated, No, God is good, over and over until long after Hector had left the schoolroom.

He asked Hector, Why do you invite this Galindo fellow into your house? To my mind there is a clear example of a devil walking around with his tail tucked into his pants.

Hector set his lips and blew out a narrow code of smoke blooms. How things have changed, he said. My once-liberal brother cannot tolerate the first true democrat to set foot in Chiapas.

Merely because Galindo says we in our minority have no right to rule here, he isn't a democrat. Given his way, he would create no Indian Athens. If he could arrange it, he would have the dictatorship of Ignacio Fernández de Galindo in a minute.

Hector said, I would like him to know Pedro. He was impressed by the boy's oratory that day.

You like meddling, Hector.

But not without a purpose. I like play, Brother. Though because of my physique I could never engage in them, I still admire the blood sports.

The whites against the savages?

Well, as I've told you, from time to time history demands a reckoning. If we lack the vitality today to withstand the Indians, then the books of the future should contain that fact. And I think we might as well know it ourselves, whatever the truth of the matter is.

You don't believe that civilization is good, but vulnerable, and ignorance evil but powerful?

No. I think it highly likely we are all evil, both sides. And if that is so, I could point out to you in Scripture the place where our fate is forecast. You know what I'm referring to.

Dio nodded wearily, and without much pleasure repeated the words: 'If Satan rises up against himself and is divided, he cannot stand.' But isn't that passage simply a warning against dissension?

Oh I don't think so. Remember it is Satan who is referred to. I imagine God gave us those words as the formula for the fall of His eternal enemy.

In the year 1868, the liberal and conservative factions in Chiapas had reached a detente. The Juárez forces had regained Mexico City and control of the nation from the French and Austrian adventurers, and as was usually true during that era, the state government reflected the national. The Governor was a soldier who had fought the conservatives named José Pantaleón Dominguez.

Because San Cristóbal was dominated by the Church and the reactionary 'nobles,' as the aristocrats still fashioned themselves, the liberals had removed the government to the little town of Chiapa, down the mountains on the Grijalva River. Chiapa had been the capital at the very beginning when the Spanish conquerors established their first outpost in Chiapas, but the city people of San Cristóbal now considered it a dreary, inenviable backwater of life.

The state in fact would be two states. The liberals could swelter and be bitten by mosquitoes and die in hot country and promulgate the progressive measures of the broad-faced Indian from Oaxaca to their hearts' content. After all, San Cristóbal was the metropolis, and there culture would flourish again, the Church return to its previous glory, and the offensive new laws could be systematically overlooked. Of course the separation would leave the city without full military protection, but the members of the council Hector Estrada sat on took pride in their ancestry and inherited ability at arms. And there was always a small contingent of soldiers in the city since it was still the seat of the largest and most populous of the state's ten departments.

José Maria Robles, the administrator of the Department of the Center, was a son of one of the city's oldest families and, though technically he took orders from the Governor, in fact he understood the Indian problem as only those who were brought up to deal with it could. He was a pleasing man of thirty with a child to show for each year of his marriage and an eye open for all possibilities. Silver spurs on his boots jingled sweetly to announce him, and he kept a servant his father had trained whose only duty was to shave his master smooth each morning and razor cut his hair. When Robles came to the council his face glowed softly and he smelled slightly of the cocoa butter his man rubbed into his red skin.

He claimed that the twenty troops of Captain Benito Solis, together with any of the gentlemen who would like to come along, could arrest Cuscat and his woman accomplice, smash the images, fire the cult's village and be back in San Cristóbal before the majority of the Indians knew what had happened.

No one objected to arresting the Indian on charges of murder, since that was certainly the crime, but Señor Álba pointed out that breaking the images and setting fire to houses of worship, no matter if they were pagan, would not be permissible under the new law of the freedom of sects.

(Many of those present had heard the bishop himself announce the preceding Sunday that this particular law was the most outrageous of the prices they paid for having allowed Freemasons to seize control of their destinies. It would not be unlikely, the bishop had said, that Jews would now overrun Mexico as they had once overrun Spain.)

So it was decided to arrest Cuscat and his woman in relative secrecy, and the gentlemen of the council would not call on the potential of the nobles, since they did not want to alarm the coletos, as people in San Cristóbal were called.

With eighteen mounted men, Robles and Solis trotted out of San Cristóbal on a rainy Friday evening. They were accompanied by a guide from Chenalhó who had sold rum in the saint's village. By one they were dismounting in a pine woods above the path into Tzajalemel. Robles had expected the Indians would have posted a guard but, probably because of the weather, there was none. They took the opportunity to dry out a bit under the cover of the trees and warm themselves with a drink, and one man was left to keep the horses. About two o'clock they made their way across to the open valley where the fiestas were held and, pistols ready, went up the hill to the houses. Dogs came out to meet them and set up a warning, but the people who served the saint had grown used to worshippers arriving in the middle of the night and did not look out to see. The ladino from Chenalhó took Robles and Captain Solis to the saint's house, which was not locked, and Robles was impressed with how pretty the decorations looked in the candlelight. The ladino showed him the boards in the back wall which Cuscat could remove when he snuck under the altar to provide the saint's voice. They forced open the latch on the box with a knife and Robles laughed and said not even his littlest daughter would be taken in by such a crude doll. They debated whether they shouldn't break the image anyway, since it was heathenish, but they settled for leaving it on the floor with the saint's clothes stinking of their urine.

Cuscat was not in the house where the ladino thought he lived, so they stationed two soldiers with rifles held on the frightened, half-dressed people there and ran on to the next. It was difficult, the one dark lantern they had brought with them had gone out in the rain and they had to line the men up and walk them in front of the nearly dead fire to see their faces. Still no Cuscat. Then Robles heard a rifle shot outside and something in him said what causes panic in even the best soldier: he knew he was over-extended. Taking a stick from the fire, he put it to the thatch above his head. But the grass was saturated with rain and did not catch. So with his boot Robles swept the fire under the nearest pole bed and used the wool blanket to fan it. There were too many people in the house and he repeatedly yelled to the lieutenant to keep a rifle on them.

The bed began to smoke and the people were herded outside into the rain. Robles had his men surround them and ordered one boy to kick a hole in the wall of the house. The fire spread quickly and at last there was light.

Robles told Solis and his men to shoot once into the air, which made his captives quiet. In the silence he called for Díaz, but there was no answer. Robles called again, I have your people, Díaz, and I will shoot them one by one until I see you. Robles nodded to Benito Solis, who picked the Indian nearest him from the group, forced him to kneel and shot him through the head. If it became necessary, Robles could claim there had been resistance to arrest.

When the Indians saw what had happened, as though they wanted to follow their friend, most of them sank to their knees and whined or prayed. Robles went around the circle until he found the guide from Chenalhó, the only one who could speak in their language, and told him to make them quiet.

Then as Robles turned, he noticed a powerful, shirtless, square-faced man crouched beside the one who had been shot, cupping the blownout piece of skull back to the ruined head. Saying something, the man lifted the dead face a bit and kissed it. Then he stood and held his hands out to Robles, wrists together and palms down, and said in polite Spanish, I am Cuscat, señor. Go ahead now and bind me.

None of Solis's men had remembered even a rope, much less handcuffs, so Robles pulled off his own studded belt and looped it around the soft-faced Indian's bloody hands.

Well at least Don Panta got himself dressed in a uniform in order to impress the savage, Robles said, and threw out the women and half his hangers-on for the moment. And he gave forth his famous enemy-reducing glower, but then he asked your friend to have a seat and left the rest of us standing and thereby lost the whole effect. He talked to Cuscat as he would to a five-year-old.

They were at table having a late supper, Robles still in his uniform and sweaty from the road, the dear Estradas and Hector's brother the priest, an engineer and schoolmaster named Galindo and his wife, who Robles did not know. The soldier did not mention to any of them how dreamlike the last few days had been for him, the abrupt translations, the Indians in the light the burning house cast, and now the jeweled brightnesses touching the glasses and the women's powdered cheeks.

What was done? Señor Galindo asked.

The Governor threatened him. 'Another instance of this fanaticism,' he said, 'and you will be taken to the great father of the nation in the capital.' And Díaz said, 'There is no father at all who stand between me and Our Father in Heaven. Not even another Indian.'

Hector raised his black eyebrows to his brother, but Dio was staring sadly at his plate and did not see. I like that, Hector said. And then the Governor let him go?

Well, Robles laughed, he asked him first if he had any more brothers, and Díaz told him no, so then Panta went in the next room with me and told me I was to release him once we got back to San Cristóbal. I asked him on what grounds he saw fit to release a murderer and he said we must be very careful for a while about the liberty of the sects. So I asked him, in case I should have to make a rapid decision, whether all Indians were now free to murder whomever they liked under this new law. Or to practice cannibalism, which is, after all, also a religion. And Panta said, 'As long as it is only the brown meat they consume, do not overtrouble yourself.' He means simply to make us, who must live with them, frightened.

Hector's wife Laura, thinner after years and with pure white hair dyed and clinging lifeless as a wig to her head, asked where Cuscat was now.

He is here, señora. I happened to meet your husband on my way to the jail, so I brought him along. He's under guard and chained. Would you like to have a look at him?

Laura shook her head. No, I have seen all of him I care to see. She picked up her glass. And on the road back, she said, was there no opportunity for one of your assistant soldiers to untie him and give him a chance to escape?

Would you want that, señora?

Yes. Because then you could have shot him under the law of fugitives.

Several people at the table stared at their serenely smiling hostess.

My dear, that trick is too old to play on anyone anymore, Hector said. Certainly you know our Pedro is too smart to fall prey to it.

On the contrary, Robles said, I still use it all the time. And with great success. But you are correct in assuming that Díaz would not be one to fall for it. When I told him I was going to release him tonight, he asked if I was going to give him a paper. He said he would not go until he had a paper in his hand.

Dio sighed, He has no shame at all. None.

After the ladies had retired, Robles went to his office to draw up the release, and Pedro was brought in by the two guards and the handcuffs were taken off him. His wrists were burned red from the rubbing of the metal. Hector invited him to sit down.

I am not clean, patrón, Pedro said, showing his hands and pointing to his face, which had the yellow lines of bad sleep on it.

Do you want to wash or to castigate us, my boy?

Pedro smiled. If I had wanted to castigate you, patrón, I would have done that.

Hector went with him and drew water for him, and got him something to eat from the kitchen.

When they returned, Hector said, Now, Señor Galindo would like to put a question or so to you.

Yes? what question?

Galindo sat forward, elbows on his knees. It's the land you care about, isn't it? land for your people?

You think so.

But I am right, am I not?

Pedro watched this ladino. Though Galindo tilted his head back to finish the brandy in his glass, his eyes did not leave Pedro. No. I do not think about land. I know, though, that any man who saves land another man could work will burn for it.

Galindo's eyes brightened. Ha, there we are! he said and touched something square in his coat pocket, perhaps a thin book. Tell more.

Anything we are forced to do for another person takes away from us the time and force we were given by God to do what He meant us to do.

And what is that?

Raise and feed our children.

That's a woman's notion of how the world works, Hector said. What about servants? would you have there be no servants?

We must serve one another, but only one master.

Why?

Because it is happiness and fullness we all look for.

Dio too had been watching Pedro's face. Now suddenly he spoke. Do you remember what a heresy is, my son?

Pedro said, The willful inversion of the good, the inversion of the good masked as truth.

And how do you feel, then, sitting here condemning *us* when you put your own brother out to be killed?

I feel well, Padre, thank you.

You are turned upside down.

My brother does more good to the world today than he did a month ago.

How can you know that? how can you set yourself up to judge life that way, knowing only God can judge us? Dio's voice was soft, and he seemed to shake as he spoke.

Priests do it, Pedro said. Every day. If what I did came only from myself, then I will be judged later. But if God spoke to me, I cannot do wrong, and you cannot stop me, for you cannot fight against God.

From heresy to blasphemy—a short road, Dio said.

When Robles returned with the order, Hector offered to let Pedro stay in the house for the night. But the Indian preferred to go. He tucked the paper away inside his chamarra and shook the hands held out to him, and then left the city alone.

Juan Tushim told me they carried along all the little saints from the parajes when they went to bury the man killed by the soldiers, so the little saints could see him a last time. There was talk then of taking what guns they had and going to San Cristóbal to get Pedro back, but Santa Rosha spoke to them through Augustina Checheb, and told them they must mourn and wait for his return.

Through the next five nights and days those who could stand it took turns praying. The rest carried their little saints home to stand watching them in the fields while the men started burning and clearing their land.

The new people coming with candles to begin their recitation on the sixth morning saw him sitting in the Mother's doorway drinking from a steaming cup. Startled and then pleased as we are by the sight of those we secretly believed dead, they forgot the saint for a moment and ran to kiss Pedro's hand, which for once he allowed them to do.

So, Juan said, the people of the saints learned two things. They knew the man in Chiapa who controlled the soldiers approved of what Pedro did. And they knew this man must also believe in Pedro's strength, or he would not have bothered to have him arrested.

Augustina told him the dream she had had each night in the time the ladinos had him. They come to me in the dark wearing rich clothing and bringing me gifts, she said. My father and mother have gone somewhere, I am all alone, and I do not know what to do. I do not want to keep them out because they are saints and they mean me well, but I am afraid. I do not know where my Pash has gone. I wait too long then and when at last I throw open my door, they have turned into ladinas, and they grab me and pull my hair. They force open my mouth like a horse's to steal my teeth, and their hands go up between my legs and they tear me.

Pedro would not comfort her. He said she was right to be afraid. In the night he waited until the last visitors had left the house and the boys had gone to sleep. Augustina and Maria were putting away food and covering the pots. We will have a while now, he said. I don't know how long. In San Cristóbal it will take them time to reason out what they can do to us, and then they will do it, and we will reenter the world where men act as men always act.

Then he described to Maria the house in Flores where Augustina had worked as a servant. Augustina said the widow was kind, and even generous in the way of people who live for each day's enjoyments and do not expect tomorrow will ever come.

Both of you may go along with the boys if you like, Pedro said. There you'll be safe.

Maria said, Manvel is so small. Couldn't he stay with my mother and father?

No. They live too close.

In the dark, he knew Maria was awake. Don't be afraid of

their being raised by bad women, he whispered. And he told her the story of the woman who washed Our Father's feet and dried them with her hair.

Nacho Panchini? and the tongueless boy were sent to deliver the children to Flores, and Panchini? left money with the widow.

It was not until a warm Sunday in June, when the corn was up and the first weeding about to begin, that the ladinos came back. From his hill Pedro saw three black-dressed priests following Robles and his soldiers to the river. They inspected the great cross still standing between the two browned pines and then withdrew.

When the time came for him to speak, Pedro said, It is strange to see the white priests here on a Sunday, and not in their own temples saying Mass. Why do they have to come to see how we have chosen to do it? And why do they have soldiers for their protection? for we do not go to them and kill *their* men and do godless things to *their* saints. But we know why. We understand. They have nothing, the actions they perform in their white churches are not pleasing to God. So of course they come to see how God's children do it. They need to learn all over again how to love Christ. But they will not learn, they only know how to take what we have away. And the time will come when we will have to protect ourselves from them.

Pedro himself baptized the babies that day. When he came up wet on the riverbank, the ladinos were there to meet him. He smiled and bowed to them and asked them to bless him, but they would not. What harm then do you see in what my people do? he asked.

Enrique Mijangos, who was the priest in Chenalhó said, It is idolatry.

We pray to God through these saints, Padre, just as you attempt to do through yours, said Pedro. There is no difference.

You set that Checheb woman up as a deity when you call her the 'Mother of God.'

But we do not *worship* her, Padre. We praise God for making women able to give birth to us, for allowing even poor people like ourselves to come into the light and live a while and continue ourselves through children.

The faces of the three priests were pale and blotchy. The idea of fecund women, unlike their own Virgin who produced her child through a clean miracle and no animal act, disgusted them.

Pedro said, I do not think you like our being happy with ourselves and with the way we have done it through the centuries.

You will not speak to the priests this way, Robles said. I thought you had learned your lesson, Cuscat.

I learned that there is a law in this nation which will protect me, señor.

Suárez, from Tenejapa, asked, But who will protect you from God's wrath when you die, my son?

And who will protect *you* from the anger of God's children while you live, Padre?

Look, Robles said, freedom of sects or not, I have responsibility for public order in this place. We set up towns and markets for your benefit, and churches where you can say your prayers and get drunk, since that seems to be the vice God has given you the disposition for. But I won't have your people doing it here where I cannot control it. It is my unfortunate duty to watch over you.

And make sure your friends can feed on our vices, Pedro said.

Robles turned and walked away. Suárez preached to the people and blessed a cross for them. But as he was speaking, the believers saw smoke coming from the hill and the soldiers there. When they got to the houses, many of them had their machetes out. Pedro calmed them, promising that all the saints were safely hidden. Then, after the ladinos had gone and the fire was doused, he took the cross Suárez had brought and hung it upside down from a tree with a chicken dangling on a cord from it, wings still flapping.

Ignacio Fernández de Galindo had his technical academy in San Cristóbal, with about thirty young men as students. But he arranged for the courses not to meet on Saturday so he would be free to ride out to Tzajalemel. In company with his follower Benigno Trejo and sometimes his wife Luisa Quevada, Galindo arrived in the morning and was gone by nightfall. When Robles came to see the fiesta, as he did nearly every Sunday in the latter half of 1868, he had no idea that the ladino teacher had been there the day before.

You are aware, of course, that the others have succeeded in their revolts. They will always succeed in the end, Galindo said.

What others? Pedro asked.

In Yucatán they have driven all the whites out of their territory and killed those who tried to stay. And in the north the Apaches—

Do they die?

Who?

When they fight the ladinos do many of the people die?

Galindo was unable to sit still for long while they were talking. He smoked cigars and reminded Pedro of a famous actor who had given a performance in San Cristóbal while he was at the seminary. The boy had not been allowed to go, but he had watched the famous man getting drunk on Hector Estrada's Spanish brandy afterward. When he was talking the actor was all fire and life, but when he thought no one was looking his face fell and his body slumped. This Galindo too had great energy, but it was not owned by him.

What do you think? the ladino said at last.

I think the people die too. Many of them. Do you believe that I could pray to my saint and even out the two sides of your face?

Do not bother, Galindo said. God made me for a special purpose, and not to be loved by people for my beauty. Understand also that I could not remove that collar printed into your neck.

How do you know about that?

I have found out everything I could about you, Galindo said.

The white man had fought with the French soldiers who came to prepare the way for the empire of the Austrian prince Maximilian. He had stayed a professional soldier, he said, even after he understood that the high aims of the prince were never to be realized, and he had surrendered along with the others at Cerro de la Campana.

What were those aims? Pedro asked.

For me it was the fight against injustice. Against the rich who control and for the poor who deserve to lead the lives they want, Galindo said. Nothing more or less. His eyes half-closed when he spoke.

Together they went through the military manual with the

diagrams which Galindo carried in his coat pocket. Pedro spent many hours learning formations and displacements and lines of fire. Then he said, It would not do for us—though it is good to know how the ladinos do it.

But you cannot have a mere mob descend on San Cristóbal.

Why San Cristóbal? the Indian asked. We only want to be left alone here.

In the end the ladinos won't allow you to do what you want. It goes against their plan for you. But if we take the city then we will be free, and will have all the arms we need to free the hot country people.

Although Pedro remained polite, when Galindo talked about extending the movement to the fincas, he saw the Indian's eyes were filmed and uninterested. They were bound to be limited, Galindo knew that. When the time came, he would have to find himself another leader for the enlargement of the war. So he concentrated on teaching Pedro about the ways of keeping a siege on an enclosed area like the valley of San Cristóbal.

Pedro gave Galindo a heavy black chamarra with sleeves very much like the one he wore himself in the cold.

Through the rainy season, alone or with a few of his closest men, Pedro made journeys to the parajes. Away from the watchful soldiers, in the middle of the week the little saints spoke to small gatherings of people. After the harvest Pedro sent men who could write to the mayordomos of each saint and they made up lists of the men who were faithful, and inventories of the guns. The men of one family formed the smallest unit, those of related families the next larger, and all the men of a paraje were told to choose together who would be their leader.

Many of them had seen battles between ladinos in the past ten years, and some of those who had worked in fincas had been part of the militia each plantation kept against bandits and marauders. When Pedro came to see them, they wanted to show him how they could form lines and march and he was pleased with them. Then very gently he would talk about hiding and about how much they knew about the land and getting from place to place without being seen on the road. They talked about machetes and axes, and even about whether they should carry their luques, long poles with question marks of sharpened metal used for weeding.

One day while he was coming home alone, Santa Rosha stopped Pedro and told him what Augustina's dream had meant, and what he was to do for her. So on the second of December, 1868, a great meeting was called and before the saints set in a half-circle around them, Pedro and Augustina were married. After nightfall a meal with beef and liquor and bread was provided for all. Sitting in a chair between his two wives in their white, Pedro watched Augustina's warm eyes.

While they were making the wedding feast, Robles arrived with Captain Solis and a contingent of soldiers. Solis had his troops form a cordon and, firing into the scattered crowd, they forced their way down the hill, arrested the Checheb woman and seized all of the clay saints in their boxes. In the confusion, Cuscat escaped.

Fifteen or so kilometers from the town of Chiapa, there was a village called Ixtapa. They spoke Tzotzil there and their saints paid visits to the saints in the mountains, but the people did not wear any of the upland Indians' strange clothes. On the eighteenth of December the president of the little settlement sent a message to Robles, saying Díaz Cuscat had appeared there with about twenty armed men, and that he was staying the night and then going to talk to the Governor.

Robles moved quickly. By dawn he and Solis had arrested Cuscat, and by ten o'clock in the morning they had him in jail in Chiapa. Robles would have liked to take the troublemaker to San Cristóbal, but since Ixtapa was not in his jurisdiction, he had to leave Cuscat and wait for the Governor's return from the capital after the new year.

Like a cardplayer who avoids looking at his hand because what he has may be reflected in his face, Robles tried to keep his mind off the Indian. During the Christmas season he danced with a young lady who was purportedly bound for the convent, and by the Day of the Kings he had made his conquest.

At the beginning of February, Robles brought a whole sheaf of papers to Chiapa for Pantaleón Dominguez to sign. Buried deep in the pile was the one which would remand Cuscat to San Cristóbal. Unfortunately the Governor noticed it and asked abruptly, What do you have him for now?

Disobedience to authority, Robles said, which is an honest charge.

What if I don't let you take him?

Then, Don Panta, I will feel I am not being given the power necessary to keep order in my department, and I shall be forced to resign.

José Maria Robles was not of the Governor's party. But then it would be difficult to find anyone of a liberal way of thinking who could manage the disorderly Department of the Center. And in his way Pantaleón Dominguez sympathized with Robles's problems, so he sighed and signed the order, and said, Well, now I hope you won't need to leave your post.

I doubt that I will, Robles said. For the moment he was happy. What a joy life can be if one only knows how to deal it properly, he thought.

6

Maria Joconot waited in the line at the gates with the other Indian women and the ladinas with their heavy baskets of food, but when it came time for her to give the name of her husband to the guard, he told her no such man was imprisoned there. She tried to ask him for Augustina, but he shook his head. Then, as Maria was turning to go, on the far side of the courtyard she thought she saw Pedro, sitting quietly against the wall, eyes closed and head tilted up to the sun. So another day she returned and gave the guard another name and was allowed inside, but Pedro was not there. Maria had to wait. Sitting on the ground beside a young couple, she watched the boy touch the girl's pretty round face, and then he gave her earrings he had fashioned from a piece of wire he had found, and they cried together. When the time was over, Maria was the first to rattle the iron gates and ask to be let out. The guard laughed at her.

When people came to pray at the place where their saints had been, Maria recited for them what she could remember of what Pedro had said. But then, as her emptiness continued, she got ready to go back to her father's. With her went the boy without a tongue who Pedro called Primavera. Though her family was glad to care for her, she felt as though she had left her husband, and the failure somehow lay with her.

One night in March they were awakened by the sound of horses coming along their path and voices talking Spanish. Maria's father got out his old musket, and her mother wedged aside a bag of corn in the corner and put Maria behind it with an empty sack over her head.

But they recognized the voice of Nacho Panchini? calling in, I have news from him! and so they opened the door. With Panchini? were about thirty of Pedro's followers, the ladino Ignacio Fernández de Galindo in the black chamarra which had been given him, and his man Trejo and his wife, whose hair was braided like an Indian woman's. The ladinos had ridden out on horseback after nightfall and were wet from the rain.

The people crowded into the house and the fire was rebuilt. Galindo asked for Maria Díaz de Cuscat and when she came forward, he got to his knees and kissed her hand.

Your husband sends me! Galindo said. He is well. By his order I am going to work to set him free. I do it because he is my friend and because I am God's sacrifice and He has commanded me. Galindo's voice became soft and deep so not even all the people who understood Spanish could hear him. For we are all God's sacrifices, he said, sent by God to rectify, to make the hungry full and the powerful come down from their high places.

As he went on, Maria watched the man's wife. And she thought how she had been wrong to leave Tzajalemel. Pedro had said the soul of the saint lived there no matter where Her figure went. And now there was no one to light the candles and keep Her company, and change Her flowers when they shriveled.

The ladino woman's eyes reflected her husband's. She believed every dark word he spoke.

Maria did not see Galindo reaching for her face and when his hand touched her, she started. Don't be afraid, the man said. His own long fingers trembled. We will fight your cause as our own. And you will trust us, won't you?

Yes, Maria said.

Your husband has promised me we are saints too, even as Augustina Checheb is a saint, we are creators of what is good. And soon we will go and bring back our man and the saint they have imprisoned, for otherwise the white people would kill what belongs to God.

Benigno Trejo carried an ember from the fire outside and soon there was a great shushing sound and another and far off above them rockets began exploding the silence of Mahomut. The people there, most of whom were strong believers in Santa Rosha, came to Maria's father's house. Some, thinking that the fight with the soldiers had finally begun, brought their guns. Others imagined they were being called to celebrate the return of Pedro and Augustina.

What they found in the barely colored dawn were three new saints set out in chairs in Joconot's patio and surrounded with pots of incense. All three looked like ladinos, faces blank, but they wore Indian clothes. They were told the man who spoke to them in Spanish was to be called *Htotik* San Mateo, and the young one in white San Bartolomo. The lady saint was *Hč̌ulmeʔtik* Santa Maria.

Two hundred or more people came to see. The sun began to rise through a pool of cloud, the burning wheel briefly became all visible like the moon in the haze and the broken-faced one with the goatee, *Htotik* San Mateo, put out the cigar he had been smoking and addressed them. I am no magician, he said, but God has given me certain powers to use to help the poor people who will believe in me. I have stolen the souls of many ladinos before and now I will steal many more for you. *This!* he said, and snapping his fingers he opened his hand and revealed to them a small dried lizard in his palm, this once resided in the body of Don Pablo Moreno. And *this,* he said, opening his other hand and showing them a sadly worn butterfly with wings that still struggled in the soft air, is Don Pablo's poor señora.

Galindo had done his preparations well. All the people there knew the wealthy rancher in Larrainzar had recently died, and many knew that his wife was now so desperately ill that doctors had been sent out from San Cristóbal to attend her.

The new San Mateo continued. The people of the saints, Cuscat's men, even when they go into battle against cannon, will not die or even be hurt, because I will heal them.

Turning to Maria Joconot, Galindo asked for children to be brought. Pedro's dumb boy was pushed forward. Galindo put his hands on the boy's shoulders and spoke to him, eyes fixing on the boy's canted eyes, and the child slumped forward. Galindo caught him and held him out to the crowd limp in his arms. He is dead, you see, Galindo said, and slapped the boy's face to prove it. The ladino laid the body on the ground and then slowly put one foot on the small chest and the other and stood there. Unfolding a penknife, he stooped and cut a cross in the boy's arm. He showed them how, though the blood came to the surface, it would not flow out.

Maria was terrified. Pedro had loved this child.

But then Galindo clucked softly and Primavera sat up. Sleepily he peered at the cross in his arm. It began to bleed and the pain was sharp, and he talked in his tortured, incomprehensible way, afraid and trying to ask them what had happened to him.

San Mateo promised, If you are wounded or killed in the saint's war, on the third day after I will mend you or bring you back to life.

Galindo ordered a new Santa Rosha made, exactly like the others, and had it sent ahead to the house in Tzajalemel. The following day he and his wife and Trejo were led in procession on horseback to visit Her. Coming into the chapel, *Htotik* San Mateo lifted Her from Her new coffer, kissed Her small face and held Her far above his head as a father would do with a baby. He frightened the people, for not even their own Pedro or the Mother of God had dared touch the saint except to dress Her, and then only after long prayers begging pardon for the offense. But nothing happened to the new white-faced saint when he held Her or when his lady took Her in her arms and danced in great dizzy circles around the room.

A house was made ready for the new saints. People were sent to serve them and a guard of a hundred men was established to protect their holy bodies day and night. Like most ladinos, they could consume large quantities of meat.

At once Galindo called a meeting of Pedro's commanders from the various parajes, in order to warn them the time for a fight was near. He hardly slept. By night the people prayed to him and by day he rode out on horseback with his cigar in his mouth and his scuffed felt hat on his head. The leaders used wooden drums to call their men to him from the fields, drums pitched so low a ladino going by might think the sound his own stirred heart and nothing more. In Chamula itself Galindo found Cuscat had done very well. There were more men than the soldier would have expected, though fewer serviceable guns than he had hoped for. But he knew enough to respect their ability with tools. Machetes and luques were, for them, mere extensions of their arms and hands.

When they gathered, he spoke to them through a translator. It makes us, your saints, very sad. It makes us think you do not love us when you let the whites with their small strength take us away to prison and make fun of our holy bodies, he said.

Disguised as an Indian, Galindo went deeper into the Tzotzil towns to the north. There he found fewer people devoted to Santa Rosha, but when he met with the men, he discovered he could stir them with the promise of revenge against the ladinos on the ranches where they were forced to live.

Galindo knew that in the Indian struggle in Yucatán the True Cross sent letters out to its people. So with the help of Panchini? and the others, he drafted an appeal of his own which was circulated to the native leaders of Larrainzar, Chenalhó, Santa Marta and San Pablo. 'Three times before the world has been destroyed,' the letter began, 'once by raging fire, a second time when the earth separated and fell away under men's feet and swallowed them up, and a third time by water, a great flood. Now, in only five years the world will be destroyed again, this time by a fiery star out of the sky, unless you believe in

Santa Rosha and the little saints the Mother of God has given birth to, and unless you follow me when I go to free them and end the rule of the priests who ride our backs and the landlords who steal the land from you and all the whites who have made your saints so unhappy with you.' The letter was signed by *Htotik* San Mateo.

By the tenth of June, 1869, only two months after he came to live there, Galindo felt ready. Many Chamulas and people from the other towns had brought their families and were camped in tiny lean-tos they built on the hillside overlooking the great cross and the river.

Early the next morning Galindo was seen in the wet streets of San Cristóbal in white pantaloons and a short jacket. By chance, he happened to meet Dio Estrada at the great crownlike fountain in the Zócalo. The priest said he had not seen Galindo for quite some time. I have been quite busy, Galindo replied. Dio mentioned that his sister-in-law had gone on a pilgrimage of some sort, but that no doubt Hector would welcome the schoolmaster at the usual dinner hour. Although they did not mean to, the Estradas condescended to him, and Ignacio Fernández de Galindo was deeply conscious of their slights.

He walked the long block to the Plaza de Armas and the military barracks where he counted the number of horses stabled, and then he went into the prison. He was conducted to a heavy wooden door, and when it was thrown open for him, the smell of molding straw and human excrement in the dark cell made Galindo draw out a handkerchief to cover his nose. The bodies of ten or a dozen men were against the walls or lying curled on the floor. Galindo called Pedro's name, but got no answer. He waited until the guard grew tired of holding open the door and said, If you aren't afraid, señor, I will lock you in for a while. Do that, Galindo replied.

But the guard's face remained at the small square peephole. Galindo said softly in Greek, 'I come not to bring peace on earth,' and far off in a corner a voice replied in Greek, 'But a sword.'

When he sat down in the straw next to him it was so dark the ladino could not see the Indian's face. Galindo's Greek was not adequate, so they spoke Latin. Are you well? Yes. Do you have the strength to travel? I have grown accustomed to dark places.

Pedro nodded to what Galindo told him had been done in his cause, but he did not ask questions. Deciding he was down-hearted, the ladino lied, saying he thought he could get Robles to release the Mother of God.

That does not matter, Pedro said. She and I have no need. The commandant of this place comes to me regularly. Your woman is sick, he tells me. She is near death. Then he tells me if I would agree to be taken away to—oh, many places I have never been, sometimes he talks about Veracruz—then they will get a doctor and make her well, and set her free. I say nothing. I have no ties. I made a mistake, yes. They took her and through her they trapped me. But now we are fine. She can live in prison as I do. And if she dies before I do, she will go into the other land to do the spinning and weaving to get my clothes ready for me when I come.

Galindo was silent.

Pedro asked, What about my boy? the one with no tongue. Primavera?

Who calls him that?

Your wife does.

Does she? Pedro's voice suddenly had energy and he laughed. That's good. But you have done something to him. You have made him dream for the first time.

Of what?

I think he dreams of gold. And of green. You have shown him a heaven without white people, which is good. But you have made him think it is gold there. And you have strengthened him for killing.

Galindo arched a bit, uncomfortable where he was sitting. Is that so bad?

No. I would not have done it, but it is not wrong. The ones who die will be waiting there for me.

Why are you so convinced you are going to die? Galindo asked.

But Pedro did not answer him.

Well, be ready then, Galindo went on. Your release will come quickly.

I will not mind that, Pedro said.

On his way back to Chamula in the early afternoon, Galindo recalled that Cuscat had not thanked him for all he had accomplished so far.

He stopped short of Tzajalemel and went into the pine woods to change back into his Indian clothes. His horse heard something, and Galindo went to see. Along the road came Miguel Martínez and the ladino schoolteacher from the center with two other men. The priest wore a well-cut frock coat and boots, and behind his saddle was strapped the box which contained the newest Santa Rosha figure. The men talked easily, though Galindo was not close enough to catch what they were saying.

He waited until they had passed well out of sight and then galloped in to Tzajalemel. By the river the women were bent on their knees before the cross. The wooden stands on which the little saints rode were toppled. *Htotik* San Mateo rode into the crowd and, his horse wheeling under him, told them where he had seen the white thieves. The saint called out to me for Her people to come and save Her! he cried out.

Galindo convinced the Indian leaders to send only the best-armed and quickest to kill the priest and to get back Santa Rosha. The rest he ordered to start for the other towns, and to find the followers of the saints there and tell them the war had begun.

The men went by the back paths with Galindo and found the priest and his friends in a place called Tzintik. Galindo was pleased. They did not even have to fire a gun. The surprise and the number of men and their unpredictable fierceness made it easy enough to accomplish the whole business with machetes. Two of the horses were lost, which was a pity, and the Indians wanted to bury the ladinos right away so they would not be found. They turned the faces up so the dead couldn't speak the names of their murderers into the earth. But Galindo, holding the saint in his arms and speaking in Her high voice, convinced them to throw their victims into a deep arroyo and start north

with him, to the places he said where the real work would
begin.

Laura Figueroa de Estrada had grown less and less dependent
on the world. Though once her husband's indifference had been
a mainspring of her righteousness, now she did not care what
he did. She had become so tolerant that young people seeing
them banter at table imagined them that rarity, a complaisant
older couple. Because she remained a loyal Catholic, Laura had
hidden those sacred objects and paintings which the bishop
asked her to guard when he closed his churches, and she had
arranged for several Dominican friars to be outfitted and
passed off as muleteers on a pack train going through the
mountains to Guatemala to rejoin the See of Chiapas. Then, with
most of the clerics gone, Laura had discovered what a tiny
part of her had always suspected: that alone she was stronger
in her faith than she was with the help of spiritual advisors.
In direct relations she could love Him better, and a new peace
and energy convinced her that He watched her more closely and
loved her more than He had before.

So she had high expectations of accomplishing the miracle she
came to ask for at her in-laws' ranch in Chenalhó. At that remote
establishment in the blue mountains, they met her and her
newest charge with the ample grace of all country people who
do not get many visitors. Even Hector's fat cousin came rolling
out, pulling on his coat as he came, to greet her black-covered
cart. They had prepared two rooms, not knowing the girl she
brought was a servant and would sleep on a tick at the side
of her mistress's bed. Hot water for washing came immediately,
and then the steward to ask would the señora like the chapel
unlocked so she could visit it before supper. Laura said she
would wait until morning to begin her vigil, and the evening
meal then followed almost at once. They told her how brave
she was to come to such an out-of-the-way place as theirs during
times of such trouble, and asked whether on the road there had
been bothersome Indians. Not particularly unfriendly looking
to my eye, Laura said. You passed exactly by the place where
they have been practicing their barbarities you know, the cousin
said. Well I didn't see any of it myself, Laura replied.

Quite early the following morning, when the sunlight was still soft and the ranch just dawdling toward life, Laura washed in cold water and took the little girl into the chapel, a small building, perfect in its way, clean and ordered and simple as a doll's house. There were no benches. Chairs were usually brought for the family when a priest visited, and the servants prayed kneeling on the earthen floor. Light came from glassless slit windows so high on the white walls that only sky was visible through them. Behind the altar in a glass case was an Infant Christ dressed in a white satin gown so stiff it stood out far before His perfectly shined little leather slippers. His tiny hands barely peeped from the lace bunched at His wrists. They set their candles out on the floor and lit them. Laura spoke to the little Savior, recounting to Him what He must have known, the list of the miracles she believed He had performed, especially those for children, and then, with her arm around the little girl so she could feel beneath the cloth the knives of the child's shoulders, without even a touch of recrimination in her voice, Laura began to tell Him about the fits which had come at first at great intervals, and how now they came regularly and shook the little body so it would not mature, as a tree will not grow if planted where great winds batter it.

The untainted little figure's arms reached for them as though He were setting out on his first great toddling expedition and needed them to catch Him. The light changed, clouds roaming the face of the sun, and in the silence Laura heard the noises of the ranch, men yelling to each other and the tinkle of harnesses, and then farther away through the rasping trees inconsiderate women loudly calling to their children. Maybe a cow was being butchered, for the shouts grew and there was moaning, but Laura fixed her attention on opening the little Christ's heart.

The chapel doors opened and people came in. They spoke in low, reverent voices. Accustomed to the eternal babble of servants and intent on continuing her devotions, Laura put these people out of her mind. She would not have understood anyway, the Indians with their machetes in hand asking each other if it was wrong to kill them here in the sight of the saint.

Laura may have tried to tell herself the clear echoing of the rifles came from hunters, but by then the dread had entered her and she and the little servant girl had begun to turn their attention from the Christ. Laura's laced black shawl was taken from her head and her hair fell free, and she saw the pack of dogfaced drunken men, and felt the sharp pain as her hair was caught up and nearly pulled from her scalp. They lifted her and dragged her, shoes making tracks in the dirt floor, out into the clear air. She could not see what was done to the girl, though she heard cries. And outside she saw dead people, and the heavy furniture of the main house spilled out in the mud like the contents of a box, and the fires lit. She saw how many of the savages there were and she began to kick the dirt and scream as they approached her, her whole body welling up in great thrusts of terror, such terror as we all experience for moments in dreams, but this continued and continued. She fought against their tearing her clothes from her.

In the afternoon as they filtered down though the hills, joining other groups coming from other ranches, some with goods they had taken, some driving animals before them and some only bloodstained and exalted by liquor and singing, the men who had killed Laura told about the ferocious woman they had found, and how the coloring of her hair had come off black in their hands.

Even the shadowy blue arcade under the officers' rooms was bright enough to blind a man who had been kept in darkness for nearly six months. The light amazed Pedro, it made him dizzy and he asked the guard please to wait and let him hold to the back of his uniform and then they moved along more slowly, with his eyes shut Pedro seeing red and counting the lefts and rights and the flights of stairs they climbed and descended. Memorizing even the steps, the smooth indentations at their centers where so many feet had worn them.

The various others who shared his cell had told him the prison so well that, set free of the chains on his wrists and ankles, he could have scuttled into the daylight street free. He knew what times the men and horses came and went, and the officers, whose decorated bodies jangled when they moved. And the history. The Tzeltals he lived with told how in the time *their* saint appeared they rose against the bishop and the poor people who were captured were thrown from the gallery onto the soldiers' bayonets below.

Shoved again into darkness he stood still until the door thundered shut behind him and then waited to hear if they would open the peephole. They did not. He was in a smaller cell and only one other person was there. Pedro squatted and waited until he heard the rats begin to stir again. The other inmate must have been in darkness a long time too, for he did not try to speak.

Pedro settled himself against the cold wall and, unafraid, fell into the half-sleep of those who have slept all they can and have nothing left to do but remember. He worked a while on fixing what he had learned on the great journey to this place. He was deeper in the prison than his own cell was, it cost more to breathe and to move here.

Crawling so the chains made no sound, the other inmate came and lay next to him, then tentatively reached out and touched his chest near the heart. Pedro in turn felt the other's forehead, then the high-bridged nose and her long hair.

Augustina?

Her body moved next to his, conformed with it, beating. There was noise, a yes in her throat, but no words. He tried to run his fingers into her wide mouth, but she held her teeth clenched.

Side by side they lay listening to each other's hearts. Augustina's familiar hand ran on Pedro's hip, curled on itself and the back pressed against the skin where a while ago there had been some flesh. Pedro drew it away, not knowing for sure there wasn't some secret way they could be seen, imagining to test their bestiality would be the only reason the officials might have now for putting them together.

Feeling her tears he wiped her face with his filthy hand. But we have our words, he whispered, because they are too lazy and crude to learn them and take them away from us. And so, mouth pressed to her ear, he told her what he knew. In the long darkness daylight knowledges and dreams had lost their distinction for him.

This Galindo is going to get us out. For three days those who have the permission to sit in the sun have not been allowed. The horses come and go at night even. I was in Chiapa for a time. In Flores, I saw into the widow's courtyard from the air. They were playing with tops. Hot country has reddened the boys' faces and I think all those women feed them too much.

And the other one, Pedro went on, by now he has killed someone, a white man who ran across a field toward a pole fence. That was also the first day he ever got drunk. They broke into the rum first, so when he was running after the white man he saw the sun drop low over him and it filled him with its power, so he brought the ladino down with his rope like a bull hard on the ground. Then with God watching him and his voice going all at once, he broke into the man and saw, on his belly and his chest, yellow fat good enough to eat. But in the quiet our boy could hear what he thought was the man's heart still going like a machine in his pocket. Full of fear our boy pulled out a great gold watch which ticked. First he thought it was a devil and he was going to break it, but then he remembered me, so he took the ladino's bloody silk cravat and tied the watch around his own neck. And that marks him for dying, and I am happy for I have many things to learn from him and now there will be time.

And time, he said, in the other world, to come into your body another first time, in another sweet place, and to have you again lift my evil from me. In the next world that much will be the same, except there only God will watch over us and not pitiful human beings. And you will be knowing as you were before, and I will be fresh, and your knowledge a halter to me so wild and crazy and young.

In the corridor there were voices he knew. Dio's saying, *I ordered it, José.* So by seeing what you did to her he would realize what we can do to him. And Robles', angry, During a war no priest is going to give orders in my prison! But *this,* Dio said, is a holy war. When they take a man of God and eat his flesh— Women's hearsay, Robles muttered.

When the door was unbolted and swung open, Pedro and Augustina were lying apart in the far corners. The guards lifted the man up and in that moment he could have seen

Augustina's face, but he looked straight ahead. Dio, eyes gray now, came flying at him for a last time, but Pedro did not blink and they carried him off to a tiny cell where he was kept alone.

Now we must show a second mountain voyage of a second box containing only a single passenger.

In Buñuel's *Las Hurdes* a plain child's coffin is carried down through Spanish passes on the shoulders of a desolate father and perhaps an uncle or brother. The rendition of death is liquid, the camera turns and dances, the river ruffles at the men's legs and the little box is passed, itself relentless, from hand to hand against the course of the water. A coffin reminds us to have fear: it carries inside something which, because it too had volition, we loved as ourselves. And now it has become only a thing in the world, respondent to natural forces only. Look and see how pallbearers' arms strain more than they need to. The men are trying to give some of their human abundance of will to what is dead. Faces fixed, to me they look like little girls who, around twilight, are sometimes discovered in the parlor in the sacrilege of praying to favorite dolls to make them speak.

Hector's great strength, his exactness in performance as long as there was no audience. (Forced to appear in public, he slighted ritual, he slouched, he proved that he was above acting for anyone's sake.) He went alone with only the servants from his own household and he walked the entire day. Four men carried Laura, and the others came behind with rifles and mules and a horse for the master. In spite of the grand excitement in the city, the preparations against the invasion, his brother had offered to come along. But Hector had refused him. With Dio ahead reading from his missal and the rifles canted out ready from the men's hips like vestigial wings, the cortege would have been only caterpillar and military. Even as it was, the procession was darkly festive and gaudy enough to attract attention. He had asked them for a lighter and simpler box, but because he was who he was—and remember also because you were you, he mentioned to the woman inside—they would not allow him anything less than the unwieldy molded object float-ing down the path before him, its silver-painted roses and flourishes, the active industry of its ugliness, casting lights into Hector's eyes. The poisoned wedding cake, he thought. The velvet blue of the mountains today, the way anything dark suddenly fell away, emptied, the shade of a grove of trees down the white trail becoming a morass, a ragged hole in this world through which Hector caught slight visions of the turbulence in the afterworld waiting for him, and more immediately for her, all he knew a product of his having over-fortified himself before setting out.

—and become author of your own visions.

Tell me again, sir?

Nothing, Adáno. I am talking to myself again.

Yes sir. The old servant moved back, leaving his master to speak to himself if he pleased.

They passed through San Lorenzo, which was calm. The Indians in this village, it seemed, had not harkened to Galindo. They crossed themselves when they met Hector's procession. It grew warmer in the sun and the servants begged permission to stop so new men could bear the 'little saint' as they called Laura, and their señor told them also to remove their black jackets. He himself kept on the full coat, which had begun to stink of sweat and, like a cave, alternately to turn him hot and then cold. He wondered what the servants would call her now if they could see her body as he had forced himself to do. Pieces of meat so badly hacked that, overcome with disgust, one could not for the moment even recall the appearance of the animal living.

I wish I could tell you how later, after the war, they discovered Pedro's body, how cold his calves had grown when they held them, yet how alive he felt, and how they cared for it and washed even the dirt from his feet and how they prepared it and about their sustaining grief, and the drying up of the women's tears, but in fact Pedro was shot far away from his followers and his body mutilated and destroyed to keep even his dogs from finding it, so we will have to make do with these small rites for fathers and brothers and wives.

I was wishing, Adáno, that I had loved her more.

The white-haired servant, moving along close behind Hector, said, I understand, sir.

I doubt that. I meant animal love, Adáno. I entered my wife exactly seven times, which means only once in every five years.

Although embarrassed, the servant still noticed the tears in his master's eyes. They had stopped on the path and had brought the procession to a halt. Adáno looked suspiciously at the flowered coffin, covered his mouth with his hand and said, You are still young, sir.

What's wrong here? Hector cried out. Go on! Then remembering Adáno still standing at his side he nodded and said, Yes, younger than I was before.

For all of his years in company with it, Adáno had never learned the smoky shape of the patterns in which his master's mind moved. (Is this perhaps the definition of the difference between servants and masters?) Adáno recognized Hector's absolute courage. But he did not know Hector had no control over what came swimming from his mouth, that there were constraints of knowledge but, at times, none of time or place or decency. Often, as now happened, a few minutes after he had spoken, tears burst from Hector, a pure sorrow for having given himself away.

Later, at twilight, they were met on the road into Chiapa by all of Laura's kinsmen, and Hector's last communion with her abruptly ended. During the Mass and the walk through the old broken streets with the marimba in a cart behind booming out the sad songs she had loved in life, the husband remained silent, dour.

On the return from the cemetery the Governor himself fell in step beside Hector and at one point said, Of course you have my promise they will be made to pay for this. Hector dismissed Dominguez with a wave of his hand. Tomorrow, the Governor went on, I set out myself with troops.

But Hector was listening to the music. On the way back, the marimba was supposed to play the joyful tunes the deceased had loved. Hector cried into his handkerchief because the doleful songs were only being repeated, and for once he was sad for Laura's unending sorrow.

7

Between the eleventh and the fifteenth of June, 1869, over a hundred ladinos were murdered at the ranches in the Tzotzil towns. In the outlying places there was no news. The Indians came suddenly, set fire to the buildings and killed the families. Though the Governor sent thirty more troops to aid the San Cristóbal garrison, Robles was busy trying to calm the city, where people expected an invasion at every minute, and the new captain, Rosas, certainly did not feel he had the strength to go against the Chamulas yet.

In the first days of it, the men returned from each expedition darkened by smoke, drunk, and carrying the precious guns they had seized. They brought the dead on horses and mules, and begged *Htotik* San Mateo to return them to life. He could not, he said, until their Santa Rosha was back and cradled in his arms to oversee the miracle. Some of them took their bodies home to bury them, and others left them out, warped and smelling, to wait.

By Thursday only one party of men, all of them still drunk on captured rum and wearing the hats and trinkets they had stolen, went off to take a ranch where they had once worked together in Larrainzar. Vaguely in search of the tongueless boy Cuscat had asked for, Galindo went walking among the lean-tos pitched on the hillside. The new soldiers sat inside playing with their children or watching their women work. No one remembered seeing the boy since Monday when they had burned the Bermudez place in Chenalhó. There was a middle-aged man following him, and when Galindo paused, the man said in very good Spanish, They think what they have done is a sin, so now they are waiting for the ladinos to come and punish them as the ladinos have always done before.

Coming into his house, Galindo found his wife again in bed, covered with all the blankets that could be gotten her. The poor food and the damp of this place had made her ill. Trejo, who had a good deal of mechanical skill, sat by the fire tinkering with rifles the Indians had captured but were unable to make function. Because Luisa Quevada's two attendant women were watching, her husband first kneeled at her bedside and fervently kissed the hand she held out to him. Then he whispered, If we wait any longer, my dearest, we will lose them. If I get you a litter prepared and bearers, would you be able to go to the city tomorrow?

In civilization it had always been slightly embarrassing to him when she showed her ardent desire to accomplish any task he set for her. Often she seemed to be spurring him to ask impossibilities of her, tests. But now it was pleasing to see her brighten and to feel the clutch of her small hand on his and to hear her breathe, Of course my dearest. I will be ready.

At twilight the drums began sounding in all the parajes where they were stationed. There was no need left for secrecy, for once there was no white man within ten leagues to report on their actions. By the river prayers were recited in half-remembered Latin by former sacristans. Then, imitating Cuscat's method, Galindo appeared suddenly in the circle of torches lit up by his personal guard. In the morning, he told them through translators, we are going to San Cristóbal. There, by my power and the power of Santa Rosha, our gods will be returned to us and the new time will begin. Bring all of your weapons so the ladinos will see what power we now have, but do not worry. I will not let there be fighting!

In the morning boys who had had a little schooling were sent to places above the road to count the men going by. But the excited reports they brought to the front of the march where Galindo and his lady and the *maš* with banners and white flags were, proved unreliable. Many women and children had come along carrying what seemed all their earthly possessions with them, as though they were all bound for Goshen. The commanders were sent into the ranks, but the men laughed and asked, If we send them home, who will cook our suppers tonight? Finally they were persuaded to make the women and children fall back and come at the end of the procession.

By three o'clock when they began trooping by the center of Chamula, Galindo decided there must be four or five thousand men on the road. He had thought of sending the various groups to meet at the fork above the city called La Ventana, but then he had decided that seeing their own numbers they would gain confidence and not be so likely to melt away from him if there were trouble.

Clouds covered the whole sky and the air was wet. The day was losing him and they were moving too slow. But then, reaching the bottom of an incline, Galindo turned back and saw the great warming sight—his own army coming down on him, silent and joyful at the prospect before them, only their bare feet pounding out the sound which proved how many of them there were. They filled the road and overflowed its banks.

Then Galindo passed through a black moment, not of fear because he had betrayed them all, but because for an instant the carefully constructed actual, which was wonderful enough in itself, slipped aside and he recalled what he had dreamed this moment would be. For ten years he had known that if he was ever to have power it would be through such a ragged mob as this, yet he had imagined that somehow he would not only be able to sway them, but would have the time to turn them into instruments as precise and real and as committed to the business of war as those green-uniformed Frenchmen he had seen filing down gangplanks in Veracruz.

The news of the coming onslaught reached San Cristóbal about eleven in the morning. The political chief of the department was locked into yet another meeting of the council, watching flies take the rest of the sugar from his coffee cup. So far they had voted to exclude Hector Estrada from their deliberations because he had sponsored the traitor Fernández de Galindo in the city, subject to a fitting explanation by Estrada on his return from his poor wife's funeral in Chiapa. Silvestre Gutiérrez then undertook to quote at length from a paper the nobles of 1712, the year of the other uprising, had submitted to the mayor of the city, in which they pointed out that they were known to hold honor dearer than life, and their blood was incapable of any debasement. The consternation of the city's lowborn was to be expected, but to take more precautions in order to pander to the low instincts of the rabble, which always include fears, was unnecessary. 'Our fathers,' Silvestre read, 'not bothering themselves with moats and fortifications, and trusting in the ability of their leader Hernan Cortés, beat the savages in over a hundred encounters and filled the civilized world with the fame of their deeds. . . .'

In the last week San Cristóbal had, like a turtle, drawn in on itself. Those who lived outside, mostly the poor and darker people, had boarded up their houses and come to beg places to stay at the great walled establishments in the midst of the city. At first the nobles had taken back their old dependents, but as their courtyards filled with dirty human beings and animals, they began to think of the Trojan Horse and so forth, and to wonder if they hadn't allowed the natural allies of the enemy to lodge in their very heart. The latecomers were turned away and had to camp in the churches. When the churches too became crowded, the rest slept in the parks and in the streets themselves. Robles was asked to take so many Indian servants into custody that he soon had his prison overfilled. Then savage origins long washed over were remembered, and many people were turned in to him as being Indians and sympathizers. *She speaks their language!* one lady kept shouting at Robles, shaking an old woman who had done her laundry for twenty years and who could barely hold herself upright against a staff taller than she was. Robles had had to commandeer houses and post guards at them for the new prisoners.

Personally he was ashamed of the way the city of his birth had responded to the emergency. Not only were houses closed, but the rich had also barricaded their streets and provided bonfires to keep them well-lit at night. Horsemen had trouble threading their way through the city and no coach or wagon could go anywhere. After only four days of it, with no market and no Indians coming to town, the poorer coletos were desperate for food, while the people of Robles' own class held endless parties. The night before a tipsy priest had gotten up and stood in his

chair and treated the guests to his favorite parts of the Book
of Revelations while everyone applauded him.

Robles was about to interrupt Don Silvestre and tell him an
allegiance to Clio was an adornment for an educated man
and then ask exactly how many soldiers the latterday sons of
the conquerors could provide him now, when the bishop himself burst into the room, alb flying from his neck, and drew
Robles out of the meeting. The white flags and the litter in
which Luisa Quevada rode had been spotted. Robles tried to
convince the bishop that his solution to the problem, which was
to summon the people to Mass, would only spread the unrest.

Robles returned and informed the council. He thought the
gentlemen took the news rather well considering their usual
lethargy. Hastily they agreed each of them would draw up a
list of twenty or thirty men personally loyal to him, and these
would be temporarily conscripted and given the remaining government rifles. Before they were through, however, they heard
what sounded like the midday church bells. But it was not yet
noon and the bells continued their slow peal and Robles was
called away to deal with the terrific crush of people filling the
Zócalo and the street to the Plaza de Armas.

The people were permitted to attend Mass in their own barrio
churches, but then were warned to stay off the streets. In the
thundering rain which spread across the valley at midafternoon,
the new tradesmen soldiers with their rifles tried to learn march-
ing and firing orders. Against Robles' specific command the
bells continued, and many older people said how much it was
like times of plague. Separate appeals, from the bishop and
the council and the liberal club as well as from Robles, were
sent out down the mountain to the Governor that day, but
the people of San Cristóbal knew they were being punished for
their loyalty to God's Church in the past and grew convinced
they would stand or fall alone in this matter.

At about five when the rain stopped and a last weak arc of
sunlight rose from the west, the scouts came back with the
word that Galindo and the Indians were stopped at La Ventana
with their white flags set out in the ground before them. The
litter bearing his wife was no longer in the procession, which
Robles thought a bad sign.

Captain Rosas was sent on horseback with three soldiers, one of them bearing a small truce flag. They crossed the bridge below the town and everything was so still around that they could hear the afternoon's rain surging in the river under the planks. In silence they clattered out beyond the last of the houses in San Ramón and past regular fields in delicate green corn, and up under the smoky blue shadow of the great mountain which stands between the two western channels out of the valley. Rosas, who had once been a regular visitor to Hector's library, recognized how beautiful an evening it was and how impressive a page of history or of art this moment would make, in spite of the watery mud splashed up to his horse's withers and onto his own clean white pants.

Where the Indians had stopped at La Ventana, the mountain had already cut off the direct light, and Rosas's corporal had to ride up to their lines on the faith they would be able to see his whipping white flag. In the haze under the trees one could not tell how many men there were. They stretched nearly out of sight up the two forks of the road.

The scout rode back and said the contact had been made according to the etiquettes. Galindo would come out before his troop alone, and Rosas could bring two attachés without weapons.

They saw a man coming on a creamy-white horse and could tell it was Galindo by the red point of his cigar. He did not ride as far out from his line as Rosas would have liked, so he told his men to keep their pistols and swords and galloped out before them.

At about thirty paces, Rosas and Galindo touched their hats to one another and reined up. Galindo called out, Well?

I assume by your flags, Señor Galindo, Rosas shouted, that you come in peace and therefore we can understand one another.

Señor Commandant, I cannot assume anything, Galindo replied in his deep, carrying voice, until I know whether you accept our demands or not.

Demands? I am only a servant of the Governor. I do not deal with demands from anyone.

Then what *is* your job?

Rosas drew himself up in the saddle and his bay thought they were going forward. He pulled in on her and made a tight leftward circle. My job as a soldier is to conquer or to die at my post!

Galindo called back, Then you had better send for your chief, so I can speak to *him*.

The same guarantees?

Of course. Better. Señor Robles's safety I will guarantee on my soldier's honor!

Rosas thought to ask Galindo how much he imagined his soldier's honor was valued among civilized men by now, but did not say it. He sent one of his attachés back to town. Before Robles came, the captain and the renegade sat quietly on their horses and eventually in the dark they could hardly make one another out. Rosas thought for sure the Indians were settled on the wet ground eating. A few small fires even appeared.

When he arrived, Robles spoke briefly with Rosas, introduced himself to Galindo and then asked, And what can *I* do for you, señor?

We want the two saints who belong to us.

Robles laughed. I wasn't aware that we had any celestial visitors incarcerated here in our humble penitentiary. Would you be so good as to name them?

Galindo called out, Augustina Checheb, the Mother of God, and Pedro Díaz de Cuscat!

And what may we call *him*, Señor Galindo? Is he merely the brother-in-law or is this Cuscat to be called the father of the godlings?

There was a long pause. Robles and Rosas heard a horse move off and in the dark they could no longer see the cigar point.

When he lights up his face, he makes himself an easy mark for a rifleman, Rosas remarked.

Yes, but I think he is the stopper in the bottle, Robles replied.

Then they heard Galindo's voice, closer to his lines, but coming clear and loud down the pass. Maybe, señor dear superiors, you think that you can trifle with me because in the blackness you cannot see what you are up against. Here, listen to this!

and then more softly they could hear him calling orders, and at once there was movement among all those men, and the chant Viva Galindo! Viva Galindo! coming first disparately and then, as the echo began and provided a rhythm, again and again, louder, and at the same time bare feet pounding the muddy road.

When at last the sound died, they saw Galindo's face, closer to them again, lit up by a phosphorous match a second, and then the big red coal waving about in the night air as Galindo went on. Our Constitution, gentlemen, is supposed to give all citizens the authority to name who will govern them. Neither I nor these ten thousand men behind me have had even a bit of the say in naming that wonderful jest of a government you two claim to serve so faithfully. So we have no cause to respect you or to continue donating the fruit of all our labor to you, labor forced on us in the first place. If these people were ever given the rights you have taken from them, do you think this fellow Pantaleón Dominguez would be in the governor's seat? No. They would choose a man such as myself who knows their needs and loves them. And I doubt they would stop at making me merely governor of this wretched state. I would be king here!

Even though the night was now damp with misty rain, Robles sat out this hysterical speech. From time to time he could hear the church bells coming across the valley liquid and round and he thought of the people waiting in the city. What is it you want, Señor Galindo? he called at last. What will make you take your men home and leave us in peace?

I want that man and that woman.

I do not have the Checheb girl. She has been sent to Chiapa. But if I give you Cuscat, what security will you give me that your men will go home?

Myself, my wife and Benigno Trejo.

It was unforeseen. Robles started to speak to Rosas, but he knew there was no time. We are sending for him now, Robles said calmly, and he despatched a messenger.

You want me badly, don't you? Galindo said.

It will be a pleasure to play host to you, señor.

While they were waiting, Robles and the captain tried to

imagine what trick this would turn out to be. To their understanding of it, there was no good reason for the successful white
leader to surrender himself for the sake of any Indian.

The inequity of the exchange became more obvious to the
two officials when Pedro was brought. The Indians set torches
to light the space between the two groups. Robles undid the
shackles for Cuscat with a key he kept on his personal keyring,
and placed the box with the clay doll in his arms. Then Galindo
came out of the crowd on the other side with his follower
Trejo. Between them they supported the body of his wife, who
looked sad and bedraggled in her Indian braids and clothing.
Cuscat walked slowly toward the three ladinos. Like the woman,
he seemed to have no strength left. When they met, the white
man bowed and brought the Indian's hand to his mouth. Then,
standing again, he kissed Cuscat's face. They spoke together in
whispers.

Robles called, asking them to hurry, and they broke. When
Galindo reached his line Robles held the handcuffs open to him
and said, I think you made a poor bargain, señor.

Why do you think that?

Because you have surrendered everything and have gotten
no safeguards in return.

No safeguards? If you do anything to me, my people will
come for me.

Do you think they are your people? Look back, Robles said.

Galindo turned. The Indians' torches had been doused, but
even in the darkness they could see the whiteclad figure of Pedro
on the men's shoulders, fading, and hear the thousands of feet
and the high-voiced joyful yelling as the Indians departed on
the run with their prize.

In the afternoon of the twentieth a messenger from the Governor came to La Ventana with a white flag. Pedro went to meet
him there so the ladino would not see the great encampment
at Moshbikil. In the paper the Governor addressed Pedro re-
spectfully as Señor Díaz de Cuscat and said he knew the Indians
had cause for unhappiness with the way they had been treated
by the Department of the Center and the missionary clergy from

San Cristóbal. But in quieter circumstances he, Pantaleón Dominguez, would be prepared to rectify the wrongs the Indians felt. What then was the true reason for their threatening the unarmed city of San Cristóbal and the private and innocent citizens who lived there? And what could be done to make them return to their homes peacefully?

Pedro looked up from the paper into the messenger's rapid eyes. Give us back Señor Galindo, who is our saint, by tonight and tomorrow we will have disappeared again.

While the fireflies were having their hour in the reeds and slight trees all around and below them, by a tallow lamp Panchini? and Andres Joconot, Maria's father, and the others scratched out on the ground a large map they derived from smaller ones, some on vellum, which they had taken from leather tubes.

The long valley of San Cristóbal slopes down easily from east to west. The northern and southern walls are steep descents, too difficult for horses. Behind the northern rim is Chamula land. A hill runs into the valley from the east, where it spreads and flattens the city begins and where it erupts into the little hill of San Cristóbal and finally meets a small river the city stops, and a gradual upward rise begins. Due west is a pass and the village of San Felipe. To the northwest is the great mountain the Indians call *bankilal muk'ta wič* and north of that the valley narrows to the pass called La Ventana where Galindo had met Robles. Beyond lay the road to the Indian town of San Lorenzo or Zinacantán and hot country, Chiapa and Tuxtla and the larger world. The center of Chamula and the northern Tzotzil towns were on the other branch of this road.

They were arguing over the course of the river, whether or not it girded a certain stand of trees or separated them from the town. Andres Joconot said, You cross the river and go *through* the trees and the ladinos' leavings and then out onto the Real. I always come to market that way myself, he said. There are always turds on my feet when I get to the Real. I know it!

One of the other men said, I think you must have been there today. Pedro, what do you think?

He did not answer. Their charts were like what moles would

draw, when they should be like blackbirds'. They were correct in terms of power, the garrison was drawn as a square as large as any three blocks of the town and the cathedral was twice its actual size, but a mole might have more chance than they would. If they came as they planned, all together on the road through San Ramón which the ladinos had already barricaded and thrown up trenches along, they would all be dead before any of them got to that stand of poplars by the river they were fighting over. How surprised they would be when they got to that lovely shade and found themselves in the other world and discovered their new substantialness and their unsuspected reality.

The planners were impatient. Pedro, what do you see?

I see it is true. Andres has proven to us he has been to San Cristóbal more times than any of you.

Andres Joconot proudly reached for a stick, rubbed out the river with his heel and redrew it.

But, Pedro said, I think we would be foolish all to come that way. Look, San Cristóbal is a woman lying with her head on her pillow. We will have Nacho and a lot of men come and tickle her feet where she is ready for us, but then we should have men coming down on both of her shoulders here at the top of the town, in these narrow valleys. And then just for play we should also bother her ribs, as a surprise.

He showed them how the smallest force should descend directly from where they were camped at Moshbikil, cross the river where once he had washed himself on Saturdays, and reach the city through the barrio of Cerrillo. They worked a while at the map, and when they looked up he was staring at all the little fires the people had built in the valley.

Did you send the women home?

Yes. Shall we tell the men to put their fires out?

No, it's too cold.

But if the soldiers come, Nacho said, they could pick them out and shoot them.

They were to him like nerves left from an amputated arm or leg, their human things calling him back again and again. He should explain ladinos would not come to fight at night, he should remind them they had sentries. But his mouth said, The men can be shot when they are cold, but it would be too cruel to the boys.

They did not understand him, so they returned to their map and to trying to figure out what was its center, its heart. The man came to say the word had arrived from the Governor and the messenger was waiting at La Ventana. But Pedro could not be found to speak to him.

He watched them in the firelight passing around k'ok'oš, tortillas cooked a second time so they were hard and bumpy, and bowls of mač', the corn paste mixed with water. He said, It looks as though the women have prepared us to go to hot country to cut corn.

The small group at the fire looked up. The oldest asked if he would sit with them, and they made a place for him. Though he had only a thin old chamarra and was shaking in the night air, he would not come very close to the flame, or eat more than one of the k'ok'oš they offered him or drink more than once from the bowl.

They stared at the scabbed rings around his legs where the shackles had been, and asked if he wasn't cold. No, he said. Look, I have this, and pulled from the bag he carried a beautiful new black coat with sleeves. Would you like it? he asked one boy. I am not going to need it much longer.

The young man stroked the shiny wool and said, No thank you.

Well, since you want to touch it, you want it, just as if you are still doing what you hate you must still like doing it. Devils and angels are the same spirits appearing in the clothes we are ready to see them wearing. But you won't take the chamarra from me, which is your mistake. My wife made that. She has a vagina as big as a gourd.

They tried to cover their laughter, but Pedro encouraged them. Go on, he said, and then imagine the problems I have. What paraje are you from, my boy?

Kuchulumtik, the boy said.

At nearby fires they heard him and they gathered in a larger circle around him. He asked them all their names and where they lived and then he asked if any of them had seen the boy without a tongue. They said no, maybe he had died in the fight against the ranches. Pedro clapped his hands together and said, Good. There we will have time to talk.

He said, The world we are going to is blocked by devils, by ladinos—feeling it was wrong to say so since he had seen white men naked and knew their flesh was vulnerable too, but knowing also that in his absence some of Galindo's words had become necessary food for them, his soldiers, if they were going to do what now had been laid out for them to do.

And again, quietly, as though speaking to them one by one, he told about the green world where things give of themselves to each other and balance, almost exactly as he had written it first in what now seemed an earlier life. He made the older men cry. They remembered at once all the good things of their youth and saw what they might now reachieve.

But the young ones were restless. So Pedro said, Some nights my father would get up after he had eaten and would go outside and I could hear him splash cold water on his feet and then he would scrub them. And my mother would touch her pot there by the fire to see if the water was still warm and call out to see if he didn't want some. I do, he would say, but I'm not asking you for it. I thought she would then take him water, but she never did. And it wasn't until a long time later when I knew what sheep do and dogs, and birds even while they are in the air, that I remembered those nights were the ones my father and my mother made noises in the dark.

The boys laughed. Most grown men did not talk to them about these things which were more important to them than dying.

Now I want you to wash your feet in the morning, Pedro said. Why?

Because at the end of tomorrow an angel is going to come from Santa Rosha and take God's soldiers away with him. And the angel will only be able to tell us by our clean feet.

But they'll be covered with mud before we even get to the town.

Look here. Pedro held his foot up to the fire light. He spat onto his finger and rubbed a circle on his big toe. There, underneath, I'm clean and the angel would know me. But look at this—Pedro extended his other foot, repeated the spitting and rubbing—here's a foot that wasn't washed today. You see how dirty it is underneath? The ladino soldiers are like that.

They stared at their own feet. And at last some asked, But why do you only wash one of your own?

Pedro got up and turned from the fire toward the cold black hills. You see, he said, I have not yet been told whether I will be allowed to go to heaven with you when you go. Bless yourselves and bless me, and try not to die tomorrow, and if you have fear now give it as a gift to our saint, and in return She will give you strength. I'm going.

Go on, many of them replied automatically. Pedro walked away all alone and one or two wanted to start after him, but the others held them back.

On the hill they had kept the messenger blindfolded waiting for Pedro. The Governor's response explained that he was not able to set Fernández de Galindo free, because it appeared Señor Galindo had broken certain laws. After he was tried, if the charges proved untrue, then of course the señor and his wife and his man Trejo would again be at liberty. 'You must understand, Señor Cuscat,' the message concluded, 'that though you and your indigenous followers may have the right to organize an Indian sect, Señor Galindo as a white person and therefore a Catholic, does not have the permission of the state to participate in any such anti-Christian religion.'

Pedro told them to take the messenger back to La Ventana and let him go. His captains showed him their current plan and asked him to work on it.

But you are better soldiers than I am now, he said. You can still gather new things to you, and my satchel has holes in the bottom.

What were you telling the men, Pedro?

I told them about death. Always talk to them about death the night before a fight and convince them not one of them will be alive by tomorrow at this time.

But don't they get afraid?

Of course they do, he laughed. And now a few will run away. But a rope with knots is better than a rope with frays.

What else did you tell them?

I told them not to be like the ladinos.

That took a long time to say.

I know, Nacho. Pedro wanted to sleep, he felt it sucking his life away as a tornado steals the air from us. I never say the same thing to two people, because no two people are the same. With the men it takes a long time, because I have to tell them things you already know.

Pedro's face was dark, flushed. He seemed angry. Nacho Panchini? bowed his head and said, I know nothing myself, Pedro.

Yes you do. I was telling them something we both know, what it is like to make love to your wife—

The others laughed.

—and with my Augustina, Pedro added. Nacho, you look like a little boy who comes home and finds his brother just finishing a lump of sugar. No matter if his mother gives him a piece too, the child is jealous because he will never know how big his brother's was. All of you. I go and tell your soldiers jokes, and all of you are angry in the way a father who must beat his children becomes angry when he sees them with their godfather, whose only job is to bring the children oranges. But none of *you* need to hear jokes.

He looked at them one by one, men who had served the saint from the beginning and who had believed in him even when he was helpless and in prison. He was too hard on them.

I will tell you what I cannot tell them, he said. It is the man in me who wants to take the city. It is a prize we do not really need, and if I were more than I am, we would turn our backs on it now. And I am so ashamed of myself, I cannot make myself look at your maps. Maybe tomorrow it will be better.

He took them to the altar they had set up under the trees and made the saint call each of them by name in Her high voice and She told them She was pleased and that tomorrow in the rain the white soldiers would be beaten.

In the uneasy night, men heard a dog barking, and one or two raised themselves on their elbows and saw him racing up and down along the rim of the hill, stopping and howling at the white city below and the dying bonfires which lit the mazed streets, as though he thought he saw his master coming from far away.

I had made the mistake of leaving the old man for just a few hours. When I came back I found that against his orders his family had brought a curer, and only people who had been in the house when the curer began could reenter it. So, I went to San Cristóbal to spend a day or two.

Juan's second son, who had seemed to dislike me most, came all the way to town to ask me to be with them. We went back on the next truck. On the way he told me what had happened. During the night of the saint's true name day, while the curer and the others were sleeping, Juan had snuck out of his bed, called his grandson to help him down the steep hill into the center one more time, and they had set off in a rainstorm for the mayordomo of Santa Rosha's house. The boy said his grandfather took rum with him because he had a dream that the mayordomo had foolishly allowed himself to run out. And there, in the pine-smelling room before the altar and the little saint's image, with the men and women dancing and shaking their rattles, Juan Tushim had died.

In the night, drunk, I was able to lay my coins with the others on his chest. After a while, when the mourners got tired, they asked would I pray for him in my own language.

I don't remember exactly where I slept, but someone put a blanket over me and I was warm. I saw some general with a waxed mustache, its ends pointing straight out like little arms, come galloping along on a lathered black horse. Beside the dusty road was a kid in the white they wear in the north of Mexico. A new soldier, he had not yet been in a battle or had the chance to scavenge himself a gun, and he was so fresh he hadn't yet heard what principles the leader he had chosen held. Coming on toward him, the general casually pulled out his pistol and shot the boy.

I woke up crying. One of the guitar players was holding up a glass of colorless rum and praying to the soul of the instrument, begging its pardon for the way he played. He took the liquid in his mouth and spat it on the guitar's pegged neck. Juan's daughter was kneeling beside the body, talking to it.

I dreamed the same thing several times. At last, around dawn, again the general came galloping down the road, again the horse's eyes widened and showed white, but now I could see the boy's face clearly. I knew that in the village he came from girls with ribbons braided into their black hair kissed young men who were going to fight and maybe would sleep with them, I knew there had been a band to escort them out of town, and this boy would never otherwise have had a band to escort him anywhere, not even to his grave, and I saw that in only eight days he had traveled farther from home than he ever would have otherwise and, clinging to a burning metal bar, he had actually ridden on a train, and he had heard from the others that at the end of all the war there was going to be land, and he was looking forward to that first fight when he would get himself one of those oiled gray guns which shot more than once, and then it was again the bullet punched into his stomach, and I woke up happy and someone was asking me if I would eat now.

Juan Tushim had said this about Pedro: "Do not ask if he was a man who won or lost. He was a man who took the heaviest of our burdens on his shoulders and put the rope over his forehead and carried us on a way. Most of us, even the strongest, carry only a tiny part of the world's burden and only for a moment. He did more. And if he was broken, and if he died, that does not matter so much."

The ladinos had assumed rightly that the Indians would begin the longest day of the year early, and so at 4:30 La Diana, the morning bugle call, sounded in the Plaza de Armas for the real soldiers and the large group of tradesmen and hostlers and men in from the ranches with black armbands and special reasons for wanting to fight. And though the novice soldiers had been trained for several days and were living a military life now, they took the call as an alarm and rose up with their rifles in their hands, and their suspenders tripping and felling them.

A half hour later a troop, fifty on horse and a hundred and fifty on foot, moved out up the still-dark streets, skirting barricades which rose up suddenly out of the heavy mist. Rosas was their commander, but he had stayed at the town hall with the Governor and the political chief, and would join them later. They were supposed to occupy the heights east beyond the Guadalupe church and above the road to the little village of Kushtitali, now abandoned and locked up.

The ladino captains had not made allowance for the great excitement and energy of the thousands of believers in the saint who had slept the night before in the fields and small pine woods of Moshbikil, men who were convinced they were coming to town for the holy business of wresting an earthly representation of a god from devils. Since three they had been stationed at the head of the valley near what is now the settlement of Piedrecitas. At four, without any light, their leaders allowed some, two thousand men, to start down into the valley, moving not on the narrow road, but above it through the trees and below it through the cornfields.

Encountering no one, by dawn the ladinos were well up the road beyond town. The gray curtain moving ten paces before them and closing in again behind them began to glow first with pink and then with butter yellow light. They could make out the few low white buildings along the way and the coletos among them, having walked this road before in clarity, felt sure they could see the dark ghosts of the trees on the hill to their right beyond the ditch. For some of them, it was like being lost in a whole field of bedsheets left out in the twilight, seeing down corridors which lifted and changed as they moved along them, and knowing there was someone else lost, or worse, hiding there from you. You want to see the face of the other man, and then you do not. There were no birds, even the crowing of the roosters in the city behind them could not come through such fog.

The Indians, invisible for the moment in their white wool, had moved down through the deserted hill barrio, noticing that even the pigs and most of the chickens had been taken into the city, and they crouched under the trees and in the gullies all around and beyond the tight troop of soldiers, waiting.

And then there was a call to ready them, the piercing of the blackbird, and the ones with guns rolled like a ball out of the brush into the middle of the column of soldiers. The Indians fired their muskets, a hundred separate poppings like strung-together firecrackers starting slow and coming more rapidly, to a conclusion, to a few lesser explosions.

When the smoke of this volley, whiter than the rising fog, at last pushed off, the ladinos stood in two sections staring at each other across a red patch of twenty dead men. They ran together over the bodies and the wounded, and would have embraced had they not seen the terrible fear in each other's eyes. Close up! close up! the lieutenant was yelling from the front. He too had turned and was beating his horse back through other horses and the men, whipping them away from him into the ditches and up onto the hill.

But there, now they could see, it was also death. In the trees and ditches and in the corn the savages were waiting for them, and way in the back an Indian was calling, for those who could understand him, It is cutting brush, brothers! it is cutting sugarcane!

While those with guns were pushing new shot in and ramming it, the men armed with only their field tools went to work. They came on the horse-soldiers with the long-handled luques, reaching up and grabbing into the flesh at the shoulder or just the uniform and pulling them to the ground so their friends could have them. Even for people who had used the machete all their lives, it took time and the ladinos were firing on them now, but at least among the stepping riderless horses there was cover from the rifles. And they found it was best to get a man standing and with both hands to swing so the head came flying off like a button, better than to wound him and have to waste time hacking at him to make sure he would die afterward.

The Indians worked away at both ends of the disorganized cluster of ladinos. They were not hunters and not accustomed to killing, but the soldiers were hardly men, they fell like trees, and the biting smoke and the terrible racket and the speed of it all and the blood was to their taste. It was an awesome fiesta they had come upon and they meant to enjoy it to the end.

The center of the column of ladinos had closed over the first dead, and held. The trained soldiers managed to get there, and using each other for cover, shot away at the Indians. The rifles were invaluable. The townsmen with only muskets died against the machetes, but the repeating rifles could stop them.

And it was worse too for the coletos because they knew the people they fought. Pressed back, one poor man looked down into the ditch he had decided he must cross and there he saw the grim, smoke-charred face of an old Chamula who had slept a hundred nights on the ground in the ladino's courtyard. The ladino shot point blank in the old man's face, and he thought, His name is Salvador Méndez. The smoke cleared and the Chamula still smiled up diffidently as he had done when the ladino had lent him money against his corn. The ladino then leaped the ditch, and as he flew down the embankment what seemed a sharp woman's hand reached up his leg and hooked his hip, drew the cloth and flesh away, and brought him down in the dirt, upended, screeching.

About seven o'clock, the fog lifting quicker and quicker now from the floor of the valley, Captain Rosas and the Governor finished deploying the other men and came riding up east from the city with a small personal guard. Rosas noticed what looked like single-file columns of ants moving down the face of the northern mountains, estimated them at five hundred, and sent an order off for his last free unit, a disreputable group hired for the defense of the main streets by wealthy citizens, to come and defend the barrio of Cerrillo. When he sent the order, Rosas was not even sure these men would obey. It would depend on the decision of the frightened hidalgos who paid them. Then, as he and Pantaleón Dominguez rose higher, he could see the ants were the last of an army to descend. The rest, perhaps fifteen hundred Indians, were already in the valley, most of them on the near side of the river, and coming warily up the back side of the hill toward the first buildings. Rosas could do nothing more than remark them and the small group with the colored flags above them on the mountain.

Ahead where they expected the troop to be stationed, there was only silence. The Chamulas seemed to have broken through.

They met an occasional shot from behind a wall, and as they rode through intersections, they could see Indians a block or so away running for cover like mice when a room is suddenly lit up.

At last they found the contingent, far short of the place on the Kushtitali road where they were supposed to be. The lieutenant, his hand wound up in a cloth, had managed to get the men and the ten remaining horses back to the east edge of town, but when he tried to rally them, they had refused to return and instead had broken into the house of a man who made his living selling liquor, and had used their bayonets to force their way into the rooms where the barrels were kept.

It was a pitiful sight, not the merely drunk and scared who by now had found the liquor did nothing to erase the picture in their minds of a far-away moment in the dawn when others had died around them and they for some reason had not, but the hurt sprawled together and forcing bottles to each others lips, trying to wash the subtle, deep, bonecracking machete wounds with rum, bringing pain and confusion on themselves and calling in the dark for the others, the whole ones, to come and help them.

In his felt hat and long coat and violet cravat Pantaleón Dominguez went about hitting at his own soldiers from Chiapa, forcing them to their feet with the flat of his sword. He got the professionals and a few of the coletos together and led them up the road to the place where the actions had taken place in the shadow of the trees.

At least here it was calm, though from other parts of the valley there came echoes of gunfire and from time to time the boom of a cannon. Buzzards had already settled on the bodies of the dead, and only when the Governor himself advanced on them and fired his pistol, did they take leave and reluctantly flap up into the trees to wait. There were no firearms or Indian bodies remaining. The corpses of the ladinos had all been turned face up, the eyes gouged and the tongues pulled out. Most of them had great fleshy red gashes in the fork of their legs.

Once the road was secured, Dominguez made the mistake of ordering civilians out from the city to bring in the wounded and the dead to the convents and great houses like the Estradas'.

By noon flocks of women in black ran tormented through the streets, beating on locked oak doors and asking for their men. They gave out the details of the massacre, fed one another the stories of atrocity and dismemberment, and the knowledge of the soldiers' cowardice spontaneously grew inside the city.

In the west beyond the river bridge, the ladinos had wagons overturned in the road and slight trenches extended out into the fields. Nacho Panchini? had about three thousand men, including most of those from the other Tzotzil towns. They found that in small numbers they could get around the fortifications, but they took losses because a mobile group of thirty horsemen would chase them back. Panchini? had received no word all day from Pedro in Moshbikil. He could hear the battle going on elsewhere and he was alone and useless.

At about midafternoon, a small rainstorm came flowing down from the east, cutting through the gun-smoke haze which filled the valley. There had been no firing for an hour or so, and Panchini? was sure that behind their barricades the ladinos were eating their lunch. So he went around and told the leaders of the little groups what they would do. Light-colored and shushing very softly as it came, the rain wound down on the ladinos. On their stomachs or darting across the broken fields, the Indians then got within twenty paces of the ladino line and were on them before the bugler got his horn to his lips to blow attack.

It did not last long. The ladinos broke and the Indians chased them through the smoke all the way back to the river, yelling Will you die? and The dear saint lives! Horses clogged the bridge itself and many of the soldiers clammered down the banks among the creamy lilies which grow there and into the brown water. Some Indian boys jumped in after them. They dragged the soldiers to the white stone pilings of the bridge and beat their heads open there, laughing all the while and asking the soldiers if they were getting enough to drink.

The ladinos regrouped on the town side of the bridge and eventually fought their way back to their first position. There they stayed until nightfall, when the Indians slipped away from them, back into the mountains, carrying extra arms and all the ladinos' drums and flags.

San Cristóbal is at such an elevation that a rain cloud may drench one part of the valley and elsewhere it will remain clear. Thus while Panchini? was having his fun at the bridge, in the southeast a privately formed group of young men from San Cristóbal's best families were unloading a fifty-year-old field cannon in the bright sun. Their older advisors, including Hector Estrada, submitted that it was not the best idea to place a cannon at the bottom of an arroyo, but they could not get their wagon up the hill and they had noticed what they thought were Indians around the houses at the top, so they unlimbered the piece according to correct procedures and fired a ball. The walls of one of the houses crumbled, the roof frame tilted and the tiles came skittering down into the arroyo. The artillery students cheered themselves and loaded another of their precious balls. There were only twenty. But then two ladino women, both clutching their bloody heads, came running down to them begging them to stop. They had killed five old people in the house.

Indians hidden in the corn below the arroyo were firing on them. So they turned the cannon around, redirected it, and produced a number of great satisfactory explosions of dirt. Cornstalks which looked like men blew out of the earth and spun away.

In two hours they had run out of both powder and shot and had to send back to town for more. Outside the arroyo the Indians intercepted the wagon and killed the driver.

The students began to grow nervous. They could see the Indians in the field were resurrected and were firing on them. While one fellow was talking to his friends, a red flower bloomed on his forehead and he sank to the ground and died. The boys fired off what was in their pistols, but the enemy continued.

Indian women in black shawls and long skirts appeared at the top of the arroyo. They were led by a man Hector recognized. Not wanting to frighten the students, he did not say anything. The women, their faces heavily rouged, danced along the edge, swaying their hips in grotesque imitation of the way women dance. The Indian man called down, Don't you want some of this? Don't you want to come up and get it? Here, I'll show it to you. The women turned and, bending over, pulled their skirts up to their waists, exposing themselves. The man with them laughed and called again, It's very sweet, my friends. You *should* want it. His face contorted and his elbows went tight against his sides, fists to his chin. Some sort of fit or ecstasy, Hector imagined. We've had yours by now, the man called, all of them, even the girls so small they were hard to get inside, and I can tell you now this stuff is better!

Remembering the Niños Heroes, the students wanted to organize a charge up the arroyo with swords. Hector wondered if they even realized that the Indians dancing above them were not women. He and the other advisors managed to persuade them to go into a safer side channel, and from there shepherded them into a small grove of trees where they waited for night and, helpless, watched the Indians come and drag away their precious cannon.

In the Indian accounts of the war of Santa Rosha, they tell how at first the saint won, She took away all of the arms of the ladinos, even their flags and trumpets and their drums, and her power became very great. And how did She accomplish this? She sent the women and the women turned up their skirts, they showed their buttocks and their vaginas to the ladino soldiers, and witched the whites' firearms so they would not work.

The stories have their own truth. The Indians won the June 21st battle against the city. They did not gain the center of town or free their San Mateo, and perhaps it was only their numbers and the paucity of the ladino soldiers and the poverty of their leadership which gave the Indians their victory, but still they had that day, and when they withdrew in the dark, they were better-armed and prepared for continuing the siege than they had been in the dawn.

In the city they counted over a hundred white and only forty savage bodies. Of course many of the Indian dead had been removed by the saint's retreating soldiers. But still there was reason for the panic which possessed the city that night. Dominguez was closeted with one or two of his officers, fighting off with brandy the anguish he felt at having allowed the situation to reach such a calamitous point. He tried to think where he might get additional troops and arms, and knew there were none close enough.

And Pedro went about for a while among his people with the

saint in his arms, asking after his boy and blessing them and taking drinks and begging them to bury their dead brothers here in Moshbikil. Don't take them home, he said. Now our land is wherever we are walking. Then he was somewhere by himself crouched under a tree, eye to eye with the little broad-faced figure, crying, searching past Her eyes into the other world for his Augustina, like a small boy again, wanting to find her and to tell her how he had killed two white men with a machete and maybe a third would die of wounds. The weight of the dead ones pressed in on him suddenly now, he said, each one a stave in his own body. He wanted to lay before her so she would forgive him the story of the strange woman he had slept with, the one he had always longed for, and to tell how he had pissed on her marble altars and had driven into her and learned everything her blood and heart and smell could teach him, and that he found now, sadly, there was nothing more worth knowing in her. Her alien's secret, costly to discover, was that she had no secret. Her mystery was that she could live with no heart, no center at all.

8

From the hill they occupied the Indians from Chenalhó had a clear view of the road which wound out of the valley east toward the ladino town of Comitán. They stayed there without orders, suspecting the others had pulled back, but not knowing for sure. Steady rain began in the middle of the night and they found earthen ledges to crawl under and some dug out little holes to sit in. When the light came back, they saw some black-cloaked ladino women inching up the hill, hiding a minute in one doorway before moving on to the next. When they got near enough, the Indians fired the last of their shot. They killed one woman in the road and hit another in the foot. She hobbled away calling out to her friends in a high soft voice, For the love of God wait for me! Wait!

The mute was gone. When he had joined up with them ten days ago, they had been a little afraid of him. Somewhere he had appropriated himself a red velvet coat with gold lace at the collar and a tight-buttoned waist, and a watch which he consulted like a religious medallion in moments when he was worried, as ladinos did, although the watch had died about a day after its owner was killed. But he had an old gun with a slightly flaring barrel and loaded it with round stones he picked up when they were short of balls for their own guns, so the men had come to like him and had given him food when they had it.

About eight o'clock they saw they were not alone. The Chamulas in their white had returned to the hills and the positions of the day before. Then the boy came up the road with a barrel on his shoulder and a turkey held by the neck flapping against his side. The barrel unfortunately had liquor instead of powder, and they decided they could not risk even a small fire, so they wrenched the turkey's neck and plucked it, and ate the meat still bloody and warm.

Twenty ladino horsemen came trotting along the road with rifles ready. The Chenalheros slid down the hill and ran after them with their machetes, but the troop just took a few shots at the Indians and moved off faster.

With his gun badly hidden under his coat, Primavera sauntered down past the church of Guadalupe and into deserted San Cristóbal where water was running ankle deep along the stone streets. The houses were boarded up, but putting his ear close to doors he could tell there was life inside some. In spite of the dangers, people had snuck back to their own places to prepare the dead and have their sorry wakes. The boy sang to himself in his language and crossed directly through the town he did not know, not aware of the danger, thinking only he had news now to give to Pedro, and going along as direct a line as the labyrinth streets would allow. Coming out into the open on the northeast side of the town, he encountered two soldiers with rifles and white cloth flaps on the back of their caps. They had spent the night guarding empty houses and both were in a bad mood. From nearly a block away they ordered him to put up his hands, but he came on directly at them, one arm close to his side to hold the gun, the other out to them and his empty mouth going, the sounds hurtling forth at a tremendous rate. Had they been natives of the town they would have known he was not one of the regular beggars of the place and they would have shot him. But in the last two days the two soldiers from Chiapa had seen a good deal of the awful madness of these cold people, and though they pushed the boy by with their rifles and refused to give him anything, they half-seriously decided he must be the son of some syphilitic San Cristóbal noble with a captain's commission in the town guard and a uniform of his own private design.

He crossed the drenched fields and waded the river with his precious gun cushioned on the velvet coat bundled on top of his head, and then rapidly made his way up the steep red paths through the trees to the top. He searched through Moshbikil for his master, and all along the northern rim where the leaders had again stationed themselves to supervise the day's action.

They found him naked and huddled in some bushes in the early morning. They warmed him and put him down to sleep in a little hutch they made by throwing pine boughs over the cleft between two rocks. In a little while he came out, staggering like a drunk man, and told them they must get him a woman. They talked for a long time about what to do and finally one man, whose house was nearby in Oshbotik, sent for his wife and his eldest daughter. They made her wash and watched her comb her hair, and then the men descended on her, tugging at her skirt, cleaning mud from her feet with their own hands and spittle.

Soon after they fed her into Pedro's little cave, they heard him grunting and moving on her and they were first satisfied with themselves and relieved. Then they moved off a way so they would not have to hear. When the girl came out at last to be taken home by her mother, her mouth was swollen and there was a tiny speck of blood on her lip. She would not answer any of their questions.

Panchini? and the others went off by themselves to plan, nervous as they worked because they knew they needed him and that there was something wrong in repeating the sallies and attacks of yesterday. But they had grown up believing San Cristóbal was a deep well of riches and good things to eat, and did not know about the desperation and hunger there. They could not, in so short a time, induce the principles of conducting a siege, and they did not imagine that the Governor believed he was risking everything when he sent his best remaining cavalry out that morning with orders to get to hot country in any way possible and to bring back every armed man in the state.

Nacho Panchini?'s father knew what confusion Pedro was causing his son, so when he noticed Primavera he grabbed him firmly by the arm and ran with him to the hutch. He left the boy before the opening and, withdrawing, called, Sir? the one you were asking for is waiting here for you.

A hoarse voice replied, Why do you think you can still tempt me with things of the world?

But then after a bit the old man saw an arm snake out of the hutch and draw the boy inside. He waited.

Pedro put his hands under the fancy coat and felt all over his body for wounds. Satisfied, he kissed the boy and tugged at the tail of hair running down into the lace collar. He examined the old gun and the blue stones used for shot, and made the watch come back to life for a while. Then he had Primavera tell him what had happened since Pedro had been lost. The rain came down on the boughs over their heads.

Father? he called out, I have finished eating this one and am ready for another. So would you bring me your son?

The old man waiting in the rain said he would.

When Panchini? arrived, Pedro told him about the horsemen who had gone to Comitán. Go yourself, Nacho, and follow them. I want all the best to go. There are Indians in the villages you will pass. Tell them what we have done, and how they have spit on Christ's children and how good it feels to kill them when they kill us and they will join you. Ask them to find a high place above the road, so when the soldiers come back you can finish them.

Pedro's captains went away pleased, with enough work to occupy them for several days. But now that they had seen the fierceness of the ladinos and the danger to the women and children waiting for them and to the fields about to ripen, many of the men were unwilling to give up the places they had won in the hills. So half remained and only the stronger ones set out by the eastern paths down toward hot country. It was hard to speak the language of the Indians in the warmer villages. They lived more exposed to roads and were more accustomed to working at the ranches and to the whites running their lives. But even these people had heard the news and they sent along their young men armed with slingshots and what hunting pieces there were.

Three days later, the Indians met three hundred soldiers under Captain Rosas and fought them, slowly retreating up a road into the dark of a forest above Teopisca where they vanished.

The Chamulas were losing their chance. The reenforcements from Comitán got through to San Cristóbal. With them they brought slung across the back of a horse the body of an Indian Rosas believed to be Cuscat. Robles looked at the face, which had been half blown away by a bullet, and agreed. To make sure, he sent for the Estrada brothers. Hector gazed a long time at the rigid body, the legs drawn up and the hands curling in on themselves like paws, and then simply nodded. Dio, who was sleepless and energetic from having tended the wounded and comforted those he could for five days and nights, made a complete inspection, pulling open the shirt to the bloated belly and ripping down the pants. He announced finally that he too was convinced.

As they were walking home, Hector asked, What were your reasons?

It was the man, Dio said.

Oh come. You looked at the neck particularly. I saw you do it, and the collar was not there.

One can outgrow such birthmarks.

Never.

Then why did *you* say it was Pedro?

Hector smiled. I think my reason is less devious than yours, Brother. The people here should calm themselves, and if they can now believe the Devil is dead, so much the better for them. You, on the other hand, want still to save his life for some purpose or old love all your own.

Dio waved off his brother's words.

Pantaleón Dominguez had found out who his real friends were. The liberal state of Oaxaca responded to his plea for troops with a letter saying they could lend him no one. But the garrison of Huehuetenango across the border in Guatemala, where the bishop of San Cristóbal still had many supporters, spontaneously offered its services.

By the twenty-fourth, the name day of San Juan, patron given the Chamulas in another century, there were fourteen hundred soldiers in San Cristóbal. The valley was secured and people began to move back to their own houses in the outlying districts.

And finally on the twenty-sixth, the day of the execution of Ignacio Fernández de Galindo and Benigno Trejo, they began to let Indians, especially the Tzeltals who had remained loyal, back into the city. As always, the poor were the ones who had to go out and buy from them. In bitter silence they plucked the potatoes and small fruits away from the frightened Indians, and dropped the little coins into the yellow flat hands.

The soldiers inspecting bundles did not stop the white-haired blind man in the tatters of a Tenejapa chamarra, though they wondered about his 'eyes,' an absurd, feral child in an obviously stolen red velvet coat. They stood on the steps under the portal, and in some tongueless talk people in the crowd could hear the boy describing it to his master, the nobles of San Cristóbal lined up on fine horses along one side, the women in black and girls again in their white lace at the windows and on the balconies which overlooked the square and the fountain. Like wakened children brought to witness the gaiety of a party, Indian prisoners in chains were made to stand near the priest. He barely moved his lips as he read to the condemned men, contemptuous of them and only in the abstract desiring their salvation.

Galindo and Trejo were chained to what had once been the public whipping posts. They had been removed from the plaza fifty years before, but in the morning an old man had found them in the prison storeroom and had come running to the Zócalo just to see if the fingerholes and the removable stone flags still existed, which they did.

Robles read the findings of sedition and treason against the two ladinos, and then they were blindfolded. Galindo was also gagged, since during the trial the previous day he had repeatedly shouted obscenities at the military judge. When the twelve soldiers lined up and aimed and the officer raised his sword, the old beggar made a cross of his thumb and index finger, kissed it and held it above the heads of the people near him. The boy in red began to cry. The smoke billowed out and rolled across the square, forcing the ladies across the way to take their fingers from their ears and cover their mouths with their handkerchiefs. A surgeon came forward quickly to put the knife through Galindo's heart. When he had claimed that right, no one had wanted to grant it. But Robles had dutifully looked it up in a military manual, and had found that, since Galindo had been an officer in a recognized army, he was entitled to the privilege.

As they were going away from the crowd, Pedro said, There is no reason for you to cry for San Mateo. In his way he was a person, like you and me, allowed to see how it might be. And for people such as us, it is always possible to live in our dreams. We cross back and forth over the borders with ease. It becomes harder when we try to carry other people along with us, either for their own good or for our own selfish comfort. But we do it, in minutes, sometimes for hours and whole days. And so we are expended, and dying is only a just price for what we see and make others see.

Except for you, my boy, they are all gone now. Yet I remain here with only small impatience. Once a man said he had taught me all he could, except for one thing—the sadnesses and impossibilities that living his life had given him the right to know but not the right to pass on. I have no such sadnesses to give to you.

They stopped to beg at the gates behind one of the great houses and were handed two stale pieces of white bread which they ate sitting along the wall outside.

Pedro said slowly, I am fighting up a hill. Already I am under the head of it where there is purple and the black. And for my own reasons, for the sake of my brother, I go on. There is a town somewhere, somewhere I have a house, and I am fighting toward it, untouched in the swarm of bullets so great the leaves are being torn out of the trees. Behind me I look and see that they, all those I have loved, are dying. But at the top of the hill I am permitted life, and even allowed to see the sun. It sinks away from me, orange when it goes toward the blue world where everything is fine. At my back night is cold and there is the field, the pit filled with all the dead I own. And then my oldest enemy, the only man who ever made my soul start, he comes fighting up that hill too, and touches me lightly on the shoulder. We hug each other like men in danger of dying from ice and we dance along the ridge drunk and our eyes are so wet from laughing we cannot see anything and we fall down together. All I care for now is to be alive.

That afternoon when Pedro and his Primavera returned to the place the men were camped beyond the center of Chamula, they passed on the word that in the morning the soldiers would come. Before dawn, before many who had gone home could be brought back by the drums, the ladinos were seen on the road.

They slept out in a field, and when Nacho Panchini? approached, the boy jumped up and began barking and growling at him. Pedro agreed to speak to the men gathered in loose units on the hill. Seeing him, they knelt, and he spent a good deal of the precious time they had walking among them, gently touching them and asking them please to stand. He told them they should not worry, trouble here meant nothing in the world to which they were going. He knew how they must think now the city of San Cristóbal and the whites were indestructable as their fathers had always told them. You think that I have tricked you, and maybe I have. He looked up the hill and was counting with his eye while he talked. But we are the lucky ones, he said. Now we are back in our own land which was given us by our dear saints, and here we cannot be beaten. For you cannot win out over the dirt itself. And we are God's dirt. But think of your friends who did not come today, who found no reason good enough to die here. They must not love the little saint, or even their women and their children and the land. And when *they* die, even the forgiving saints will not find it easy to take your neighbors into their place.

The tales say that when the people of San Cristóbal understood they could never beat the saint by themselves, they went to the people of Chiapa, known to have great fighters and magicians for ancestors, and begged them to help out. And the Chiapa people came, and they won out over the saint's followers, but only by a trick. Because, they say, the Chiapa people were women, and they tantalized the saint's soldiers and slept with them and so defeated them in the end by sorcery.

The ladinos arrive on the twenty-seventh in a force of over fifteen hundred, with two cannon. For a while it went well for Pedro's men, they could hide in the corn from the charges of the cavalry and from the bullets and there in the deep green tangles pull the whites down and kill them. But steady lines of soldiers advanced on them, trampling everything, firing again and again, and flushing the Indians from their cover, and at last they had to withdraw. Yet only thirty died.

The whites had finally learned. In the future they would fight only pitched battles with rapid-moving troops sent to places they were informed the Indians were holding a meeting.

There were many spies. The people who had held power in Chamula before had paid some court to the popular saint in Tzajalemel and to Pedro in his ascendancy, but now they saw who was bound to win, and they came regularly to San Cristóbal to be paid for their news and for the lists of the families which had gone with the saint. A new president was named for Chamula. Robles told him the only way to punish the people was to burn their houses and rip their crops from the ground, and the new president agreed. To prove their loyalty men went to work destroying their neighbors' fields. Then in the night they returned and lit candles and cried and drank and prayed, explaining to the saints that it wasn't their doing, they did not mean to give offense to the corn, but they were powerless to stop the ladinos.

Those who had been changed by the war and could not give up fighting or had no reason to go back to their own ruined places, retreated farther into the mountains, beyond Tzajalemel where it had begun and where the cross remained upright by the river, into Larrainzar and Santa Marta, and even into the plantations and jungle plains north toward Yahalon. They carried the little saint which Pedro had given to them, but She was sad over what had happened and no longer spoke. One night, knowing that at dawn they would have to flee down a steep open hill to get away from the soldiers, they buried Her box in the woods in a grave scratched only knee deep into the earth.

Although they had lost the saint's body, late in August they held a meeting at an abandoned ranch in Chenalhó in honor of Her day. Many people said that Cuscat himself would be there. Those who still believed wanted only to see if he was really alive, and others came because they heard he was at last going to bring the dead back to life.

They say he came that day, so feeble he had to lean on his red-coated boy, and that his hair had turned nearly white. They had been living in caves and eating the wild growing things Pedro taught Primavera how to gather.

In the late afternoon they laid out in a row seven or eight men who had been killed the day before. Pedro went down the line smiling and asking for the story of how each had died. This man went home to Cruzton to catch just a glimpse of his family, they said, and found his house burned over his people, and when he came back he could not sleep thinking how starved his wife and children had looked, so he borrowed a gun from his friend and shot himself.

Pedro made a face. They asked him what was wrong and he said, Nothing. But I will miss having him with me in the other place.

Then he spoke to the people. You came to see me raise the dead, to have me show off my power. You want me to prove to you that I am still someone. But I am not going to do that. God does not give us His miracles to win us over, but as gifts. You will not fight the ladinos as my men do, but you want to see miracles. Death is no miracle. Only life is a miracle. Stay with the ladinos, do it! And when the time comes, God will raise mine and the ladinos can raise you! If you have loved things which grow here, then you will be put among growing things in the next world. But if you have loved death, then you will have a long time to embrace it there.

That night while the fugitives were burying their friends, the soldiers came back and killed most of them. The next day people said they found Pedro's body and his boy's red coat.

But who knows? One afternoon in late October, a broadside appeared on the walls of churches and at streetcorners in San Cristóbal. Hector Estrada, coming from the yellow temple of Santo Domingo where he had said a prayer for his wife's soul, saw soldiers pushing a small group of Indians toward the place where a curate would read them the message. Though he was already acquainted with the document, Hector moved into the crowd.

The broadside was in two columns, Spanish on the left and a translation into Tzoztil which the curate read aloud on the right. It was called 'For All the Rebellious Indians to Hear.'

'The Government of this state is disposed to punish severely Indians who have disrupted the public order and to bring them back under the rigor of the law.

'But because you are so many and because in our fatherly hearts we hate to take the full measure against you, and because we consider you guided by ignorance and perhaps by terror your leaders instilled in you, the Government has given you eight days to surrender yourselves.

'And since you may not understand this, we the undersigned have sent you this letter in your own speech, making the following observations:

1. If you surrender within eight days, you will be forgiven, and if not then you will be persecuted and you will die, either by gunshots or by hunger in your flight.

2. If you do not surrender, not only you but your wives and your children will die. Not because the Government would kill *them*, but because fleeing into the mountains the poor

women and children will suffer terrible hunger, and from hunger will follow death.

3. Pursued, you will be unable to plant, and with no one tending them you will lose your stores of corn, so even those who are not shot will simply die with nothing at all to eat.

4. What you demand is unjust. God, the Most Holy Virgin of Rosario, your Patron San Juan, San Mateo and Santa Rosha are angry with you, and have brought about the fall of your religion.

5. You were cheated by your leaders. This Galindo cheated you. Many died in your war, but who has come to bring them back to life?

6. The President of the Republic now knows what you have done and he is angry with you, and though there are enough soldiers here, now he is going to send us many more, and then you will be brought to an end. Those who are coming do not know you, they do not love you as we do. The proof of our love is that so far we have sent so few soldiers against you.

7. Everyone in this city is begging the Government to pardon you, but only if you surrender at once and lay down your arms so we can believe you.'

The broadside was signed by two priests. Hector had spoken at length to his brother about it. There are certain things which, I suppose, must be done, he had said. At least they always have been done in history. But they should be accomplished only in the dark of a night when even the most beloved of chroniclers is dead drunk or has been farmed out among his lord's women. This is a perfect case in point. If we must destroy them, at least we could avoid leaving documentation.

At the last minute Dio had decided against adding his name.

The Indian standing next to Hector was shaking his head.

What is wrong? the ladino asked.

No one will understand it, the man said. That's not our language, it's their *idea* of how we talk and how we care only about our stomachs. And since they are men of God why can't they be more happy? more courageous and playful?

I don't understand what gives *you* the courage to continue, Hector said.

It is no longer a matter of that, señor. It's the pleasure. I eat the excitement of it. When you have no place to run away to, you run instead at the soldiers and embrace them and stick your knife into the space between their ribs, and you feel as weak in the legs as you did before that first time with a girl.

But how can you risk coming here?

That is also easy now. They know I am dead, so I can go wherever I like. And besides, I want my son to learn this town. I was often happy here. The Indian took the hat off his boy's head and pushed him down to kiss Hector's hand. There, ask the blessing of the señor.

Primavera looked up at the gaunt, paperskinned white man, and the sounds came from his throat.

Hector frowned and then smiled and pulled a coin from his pocket. Does he understand? Hector asked, his hand closing on the copper.

A good deal.

I am sorry for you.

Don't be, señor. I am not sorry for myself.

Neither of us ended up with children who could, by their love, keep us alive for even a little while after we are dead.

But mine learns. He has learned.

Learned what?

If you hold that coin out to him and ask him whether he would like to have it or whether he would like to see the baby Jesus, he will take the coin. And then when Christ appears to him, he will lie to you about it and only his eyes will tell you he has seen the Señor.

Hector laughed and then, since the two soldiers were coming to disperse the small crowd, he was afraid for Pedro, so he touched his hat to him and started home.

The Indian came running after Hector. A moment, señor!

Hector stopped. What is it?

Is your brother well?

He has the gout. But otherwise yes, Dio is fine.

If you think it is wise, will you tell him I pray for his health?

Of course.

In November the ladinos burned corn in Chamula where the ears were still on the stalks turned down to dry, and there was land for sale to people who had the courage to come back to the ranches. Indians died of hunger or went to scratch out a life in the mountains.

A young man named Victoriano Gómez who had been a soldier for the saint escaped the persecution because what he had was so little and because his neighbors protected him. Coming home one evening after the turn of the year to his house in Kuchulum-tik he saw from the distance a man in a black chamarra crucified on his door. He went closer, his heart running fast, and saw in fact the chamarra had no man inside. It was nailed to his door, new and lovely and thick.

Only a year later did this Victoriano Gómez meet the woman who told him Pedro had come to her after the war and had given her the money to weave the finest coat she could and have it dyed and to leave it for him.

By then, because they saw the tongueless boy moving through the countryside all alone, even the most faithful people decided Pedro was dead.

And they did not think of the possibility that the child had only, for a while, come to doubt in the man.

NOTES

Many people have given me material or suggestions which were of important help in writing this novel. The dream a man in Chamula has before taking a cargo was first written out for me by Salvador Gusman Bakbalom of Peteh. Salvador Gómez Oso of Cruz Obispo told me a history of the War of Santa Rosha, and additional texts taken by Gary M. Gossen and Robert M. Laughlin were also helpful. Several years ago Duane Metzger informed me of the honey gatherers who still work the circuit of haciendas in Yucatán. Gertrudis Duby de Blom and Prudencio Moscoso Pastrana lent me the use of their fine libraries of Chiapas and their time. I received various kinds of help from my friends Jay Cantor, George Collier, Monroe Engel, John and Leslie Haviland, Ulric Köhler, Robert M. and Mimi Laughlin, Alan and Ann Lebowitz, Pam Matz, Timothy Mayer, Priscilla Rachun Linn and Evon Z. and Catherine Vogt.

None of these people need assume any special responsibility for my work, and the anthropologists among them will necessarily feel a little uncomfortable with the ethnographic material. Dealing with events a hundred years ago and more, for the sake of the story I meddled with some of the 'historical' facts. I also assumed that we cannot know for sure which customs had currency in which towns at that time, so I was willing to be eclectic. I was lucky to have available to me the rich body of work accomplished in the Tzotzil and Tzeltal areas in the last few years.

Following the notes, I have added a list of books which were more indirectly helpful.

I consider this novel a stopgap, a marker to be erased when a Tzotzil is ready to write a more true version of the story.

An account of the realities of a popular uprising can rightly only be dedicated to the people who made the fight and to their heirs. But the part of this novel I possess through creation, the 'fiction' with all its faults, I would like to think is for my brothers David and Tono, and for my nephews David and Ben.

San Cristóbal Las Casas, January 1971

PART I: THE FLOWER BEARER, 1836–1856

22. Vogt, Evon Z., *Zinacantán, a Maya Community in the Highlands of Chiapas* (Cambridge, Massachusetts, 1969), pp. 523-4. A myth from the town of Zinacantán, which borders Chamula. The bull ". . . was present when the Christ Child was born. The child was dying from the cold and the other animals would not stay to warm the hut with their breath and body heat. The bull, however, at the request of Joseph and Mary, agreed to stay, and this is the reason it is honored at this fiesta [Nativity]."

Morley, Sylvanus Griswold, *The Ancient Maya*, 3rd ed. (Stanford, California, 1956), p. 37. For the Maya, "certain dreams and omens are regarded as sure forerunners of death. . . . To dream that a black bull is trying to push its way into one's home or to dream of breaking a water jug indicates that a member of the family will die."

25. Vogt, p. 367. In Zinacantán it is believed that *ryoš* (the sun or God) stops each day in the middle of 'heaven' to "sit down at a desk and make a list of the sins of men."

26. Prokosch, Erik, "Field Notes," 1962 (Harvard Chiapas Project). These notes include an account of a case tried before the president of Chamula in which a man gained entry to a woman's house by asking her if he couldn't just warm himself at her fire.

31. Robert M. Laughlin, personal communication, January 1964. A woman in Zinacantán was reported to have been given the punishment for murder of digging up the body and carrying it to a proper place for burial.

32. Ricard, Robert, *The Spiritual Conquest of Mexico*, trans. by Leslie Byrd Simpson (Berkeley, California, 1966), p. 32. This baptism prayer comes from the Aztec area. The ritual was probably performed either with water or pulque.

34. In Mitontic, a small Indian town in Chiapas, new civil officials make their entry into the center on January 1 carried on the shoulders of their helpers.

40. Kenneth Carson, personal communication, August 1970. In one Chamula explanation of the legend of Saint Christopher, Jesus is the large figure and the child on his shoulder is his son, the little Saint Christopher.

42. His mother's story, which Pedro tells his father, about the building of the church is a variation on several myths. In Chamula I have been told that the stones for the church of San Sebastián, the shepherd, were originally sheep. They willingly turned themselves into rocks. In the Zinacantán story of San Sebastián (Robert M. Laughlin's Tale 85, quoted in Vogt, pp. 326–30), the saint took away the light so the people would not be afraid while his temple was being built.

48. Shah, Idries, *Tales of the Dervishes* (London, 1967), p. 56. In a Sufi story about the young Jesus, the boy made clay birds on the Sabbath. When the elders came to see if the law against work on the Sabbath had been broken, the clay birds flew away.

49. Ricard, pp. 106–7. The painting Pedro sees is like a canvas used by the Dominican fathers in the sixteenth century to bring Indians to a knowledge of heaven and hell and to a desire for their baptism and salvation.

52. Bricker, Victoria R., "The Meaning of Laughter in Zina-cantán: An Analysis of the Humor of a Highland Maya Community" (Ph.D. Dissertation, Harvard University, 1968), p. 271. (Also in Vogt, p. 542.) Bricker gives more full examples of the ritual joking cargoholders must submit to.

53. Interview with Mariano Wakaš, conducted by Robert Ravicz, August 1966. Such acts of shriving cargoholders seemed to have been performed in extreme cases in the Tzeltal municipio of Tenejapa.

57-60. Menget, Patrick J., "Death in Chamula," *Natural History*, 77:48–57. This article contains information on funeral rites in Chamula, and photographs of the celebration of the Day of the Dead.

69-71. Calderón de la Barca, Madame, *Life in Mexico*, 2 vols. (Boston, 1843). It is unfortunate that the famous clear-sighted diarist never reached Chiapas, since she would have described the place so precisely.

71. Thompson, J. Eric S., ed., *Thomas Gage's Travels in the New World* (Norman, Oklahoma, 1958), especially p. 138ff. Also, Ricard, p. 86, quotes a speech to the Indians from the *Pláticas* of Fray Bernardino de Sahagún, which demonstrates the best of the early missionaries' intent: "Do not believe that we are gods. Fear not,

we are men as you are. We are only messengers sent to you by a great lord called The Holy Father, who is the spiritual head of the world, and who is filled with pain and sadness by the state of your souls. These are the souls he has charged us to search out and save. We desire nothing better, and for that reason we bring you the book of the Holy Scriptures, which contains the words of the only True God, Lord of Heaven and earth, whom you have never seen. That is why we have come. We do not seek gold, silver or precious stones. We seek only your health."

78. Simpson, Leslie Byrd, *Many Mexicos*, 4th ed., rev. (Berkeley, California, 1967), p. 90. The folk tale about the provisionary cat originally grew up around the figure of Fray Francisco Tembleque, a sixteenth-century Franciscan and architect. Because cats were believed to be servants of Satan, a board of inquiry was sent to visit Fray Francisco. On the day they came, the industrious cat provided enough game to feed them also, and the monk was cleared of the suspicion of consorting with the Evil One.

81. Reed, Nelson, *The Caste War of Yucatán* (Stanford, California, 1964), p. 34ff.

85-87. Calcott, Wilfred Hardy, *Church and State in Mexico, 1822–1857* (New York, 1965), p. 65. Calcott discusses the reason for the absolute decline in the number of the clergy following the liberation from Spain. During most of the 1820s Chiapas, a highly religious state, did not even have a bishop.
Ricard, pp. 99–101, has a description of the regimen in the earlier monasteries which devoted themselves to the training of Indians.

89. Ricard, p. 168. From the *Códice Franciscano*.

90-92. Low, Colin, *Circle of the Sun* (National Film Board of Canada, 1961).

95. Ricard, p. 131. In the sixteenth century a Fray Antonio de Roa was particularly zealous about converting Indians. "As he preached he had himself scourged in the sight of all, and, as the Indians, he said, give little weight to words without deeds, once, while speaking of hell, he threw himself upon some burning coals, where he stayed for some time and then rose abruptly, calling their attention to the fact that, if he could not stand such pain any longer, what must be the pain of eternal fire! To demonstrate that the body is a slave, he had his skin burned by bits of torch. Every time he saw a cross he had himself cruelly scourged, insulted and spit upon. All that, he told the Indians, God had suffered in order to redeem the sins of men."

96-98. Neihardt, John G., *Black Elk Speaks, Being the Life Story of a Holy Man of the Oglala Sioux* (Lincoln, Nebraska, 1961), pp. 82–7. Black Elk describes what his cousin Crazy Horse would see in visions. "He dreamed and went into the world where there is nothing but the spirits of all things. That is the real world that is beyond this one, and everything we see here is something like the shadow from that world. He was on his horse in that world, and the horse and himself on it and the trees and the grass and the stones and everything were made of spirit, and nothing was hard and everything seemed to float. His horse was standing still there and yet it danced around like a horse made only of shadow, and that is how he got his name, which does not mean that his horse was crazy or wild, but in his vision that it danced around in that queer way."

Vogt, pp. 222–3, decribes Zinacanteco beliefs about what happens to the souls of the dead.

104. Ricard, pp. 270–1. The Indians and curers of an earlier day told their people much the same stories about the Domincans as the ones Mesha tells Pedro.

110. When Hector refers to the "Marquis himself," he is speaking of Hernán Cortés.

111. Vogt, p. 451. "We cannot beg if there is no pardon, we cannot beg if there is no forgiveness," comes from a Zinacanteco curer's prayer.

Vogt, p. 411. In one form of Zinacanteco witchcraft, people leave their clothes on the crosses in their yards at night and then turn into goats.

PART II: THE HONEY MAN, 1856–1860

125. Dadant, C. P., *First Lessons in Beekeeping*, rev. and re-written by Dadant, M. G. and J. C. (Hamilton, Illinois, 1968). A generally useful book.

135. Dunn, Henry, *Guatimala* (sic) or, *The United Provinces of Central America, in 1827–8; Being Sketches and Memorandums Made During a Twelve Months' Residence in that Republic* (New York, 1828), p. 159. Unable to find accounts of beekeeping in Chiapas in the nineteenth century, I used the Reverend Dunn's. He found that the Guatemalan honey, "has an agreeable scent, is much softer, and in taste not so pleasant as that of the European insect."

138-142. The tricks Pedro and the old man play on each other are at least as old as the mutual deceptions in *Lazarillo de Tormes*.

143. Pozas, Ricardo, *Chamula, un pueblo indígena en los altos de Chiapas* (Mexico, 1959), p. 19. The talking saint appeared to the men of Guatemala to chastize them for not raising corn.

149. Neihardt, p. 183. Black Elk describes how he felt when his guiding spirits deserted him. ". . . I was alone there among my people. They seemed heavy, heavy and dark, and they could not know they were heavy and dark. I could feel them like a great burden upon me, but when I would go through all my vision again, I loved the burden and felt pity for my people."

151-152. "Quita de vergüenza" (relief from shame) is a piece of folk magic still performed in Chiapas. It may have been brought from Spain, but today both Indians and ladinos make use of some form of the central action. A ladino woman told me that quita de vergüenza had saved her life after not even penicillin had been able to cure her fevers and the eruptions on her face. In Chamula ceremonies, at regular intervals the musicians are given additional glasses of rum so they can perform ꞌšiꞏꝑel apun. Taking the liquor in their mouths, they spray it over the neck and wooden pegs of the guitar and harp, and then say a prayer begging pardon of the souls of the instruments for their bad playing.

PART III: GOD'S PLAY, 1867–1870

170. Molina, Cristóbal, "War of the Castes: Indian Uprisings in Chiapas, 1867–70." Middle American Series, Tulane University, pamphlet 8, publication 5 (New Orleans, 1934), p. 365. Molina disagrees with the other historians, who believe the first saints were made of clay. He is quite specific about the first appearance: "On the 22nd of December of the year 1867, while the Indian girl Augustina Gómez Checheb, a native of the town of Chamula, was tending her sheep in the hollows of Tzajalemel, she selected three round, bluish-black stones and laid them on the ground beside her. When her mother came to see her, Augustina said to her: 'Look, mother, three stones fell from the sky.' Her mother asked 'Where?' and she replied 'Look, here they are.' "

190. Oso, Salvador Gómez, *"kwenta yuꝑun hmuk'tot Biktoryano Gómes,"* interview in Tzotzil and Spanish, August 1970:

"Many people came to speak to the saint, to ask for medicine for sickness. The saint provided medicines, gave herbs as medicine for sickness. Yes, so the people who wanted medicine for sickness were given it, but all alone the saint did this for a long time, giving orders for medicine the saint alone, without the permission of the president in the center.

"There the saint was giving orders all alone, not only for medicine and for curing people. Boys without wives asked the saint if it was possible to join with the girls they wanted in their hearts. It was all right, the saint said, you can have her because I say it. The saint ordered the girl to come, even if she didn't want the boy, and the saint obliged her to go with the boy and so they were married. Other boys heard of these arrangements, 'The saint gives us our wives,' said the people. And so they came to the saint for their wives. The saint made them join [get married] even if the girl did not want it. And so they accepted it."

Also, Méndez Tzotzek, Mateo, "*loʔil yuʔun soltaro čaketa leva*," interview in Tzotzil and Spanish, transcribed by Salvador López Castellanos, from Gary H. Gossen, Text 162:

"They had there in Tzajalemel a saint in their house. For this they made fiestas there in their paraje. Each time they made a fiesta they went to the river with their guitars and skyrockets. There they began to dance in the river, with the saint and the music [guitars]. In the night they made their fiestas in the midst of the river. They carried the saint on their backs. While they were dancing they carried the saint on their backs. There they danced in the river at night. On the riverbank the musicians played their guitars. At the water's edge they set off their skyrockets. While they danced they said 'Samataluʔisha, shalatapérez, shalatagómez.'"

197. There seem to be few known facts about the life of Ignacio Fernández de Galindo. For a short time he ran a technical academy in San Cristóbal called the Colegio Científico y Literario. In *El Espiritu del Siglo, Periodico Oficial del Gobierno del Estado Libre y Sobreano de Chíapas*, the official newspaper for state business published in Chiapa, appears a copy of Galindo's December 24, 1868 examination, and his students' marks. The problems involve trigonometry and algebra. In one, the student is asked to do a piece of figuring about a viaduct to bring water to fields, and then to consider the good viaducts will do for farmers.

In Flavio A. Paniaguas's romance about the Cuscat Rebellion, *Florinda* (Chiapas, 1889), the character equivalent to Galindo has fought with Maximilian's troops in the north and has gained his revolutionary ideas among the French soldiers. Paniaguas was a native of San Cristóbal and perhaps this is one of the 'facts' in his novel. It is true that Galindo did arrive in Chiapas soon after the collapse of the French-sponsored Empire.

198. In Dunn, p. 132, a Guatemalan ladino tells the English clergyman about his confessor: "I am a plain man of business and have had no opportunity of study. He is my spiritual adviser; I have confidence in him, and if he leads me into error, my blood is upon his head."

198. Reed, p. 99. When Galindo tells Pedro not to begin any military action until after the planting, he is referring to the rebellion in Yucatán. In 1847 the Indians there were about to take the city of Mérida when they noticed winged ants filling the sky, a sign of approaching rain, and they went home to prepare their milpa.

199. Trens, Manuel B., *Historia de Chiapas desde los tiempos mas remotos hasta la caída del Segundo Imperio* (Mexico, 1957). When the separation of Church and State laws of the Juárez Government were finally promulgated in Chiapas in 1861 and 1862, the bishop pronounced himself against the laws and, taking the religious treasures along, closed the churches and removed himself to Huehuetenango in Guatemala.

200-202. Pineda, Vicente, *Historia de las sublevaciones indígenas habidas en el estado de Chiapas* (San Cristóbal de las Casas, 1888), pp. 72–3. Also in Molina, p. 366ff.

208-216. Pineda, pp. 76–7. "In the church of Santo Domingo," says Pineda, "there is an image named 'El Santo entierro de Cristo,' much-loved by the Chamulas, and visited always in Lent, and especially on Good Friday. In 1868 it was noted they did not come. It seems Pedro Díaz Cuscat had told them it was not necessary to worship figures not of their own race, since they had their own and since those in the church were made by ladinos; [he told them] that in ancient times the ladinos had chosen one of their own to name 'El Señor' and they had nailed him on a cross and the crucifixion was always repeated in Holy Week, and so the Indians should have one of their own to worship, of the same soul and blood. Domingo Gómez Checheb was chosen, son of Juan Gómez Checheb and Manuela Pérez Jolcogtom (sic).

"They put him on the cross already well-tied, and began their barbarity. He gave out the most painful shouts, overwhelmed by the hubbub of the infernal furies, drunk on liquor and blood. The 'saints' caught the blood of the crucified, while others incensed him.

"We do not know (or will ignore) what the new jews did with the body and blood of the martyr of savagery, although it is not improbable that they drank the blood."

220-221. Molina, pp. 366–7.

Reed, p. 139, mentions that at the church of the 'True Cross' of the Yucatec rebels, there was a pit dug out behind the altar, "and there crouched a hidden spokesman who used a wooden cask as an echo chamber to amplify, project his voice, and give it resonance."

222. Niehardt, p. 145. The leader Crazy Horse was told he would have to go to Washington to see the Great Father. Black Elk says, "He told them that he did not need to go looking for his Great Father. He said: My Father is with me, and there is no Great Father between me and the Great Spirit."

226. Pineda, pp. 74–5, believes that the Governor's release of Cuscat caused the Indians to think they had Dominguez's approval of their actions.

226-228. Molina, p. 367, and Pineda, p. 74.

Reed, pp. 48–9, includes a declaration made by the Indians of Yucatán against the whites there. "We poor Indians are aware of what the whites are doing to injure us, of how many injuries they commit against us, even to our children and harmless women. So much injury without a basis seems to us a crime. Indeed, therefore, if the Indians revolt, it is because the whites gave them reason; because the whites say they do not believe in Jesus Christ, because they burn the corn-field. . . . But even these things, now that they have begun, will not discourage us, even if they last twelve years and always go against us, for we are God's sacrifices. They will have to say whether God gave them permission to slaughter us all, and that we have no will in the matter. . . . Therefore, if we die at the hands of the whites, patience. The whites think that these things are all ended, but never. It is so written in the book of Chilam Balam, and even so has said Jesus Christ, our Lord on earth and beyond, that if the whites will become peaceful, so shall we become peaceful."

229. Pineda, pp. 78–9, contains the information about Galindo bringing the military manual and knowledge of the Yucatec and Apache revolts.

231-232. Molina, pp. 368–70.

234-236. Molina, p. 370. Only Molina mentions that Galindo brought the small animals to "deceive" the Indians, and the hypnotizing of the children.

236-237. Ulric Köhler, personal communication, August 1970. Old men in the town of San Pablo Chalchihuistán remember the existence of a written threat from San Mateo to them. They also say that they gave Cuscat his name, *hkus kʔat* (I wipe my penis), a reference to his sacrileges with the saints.

239. Martínez, J. Pedro, "La Guerra de Chamula, 1869," 8 lithographs (San Cristóbal, undated). The only set of these I know of belong to Professor Prudencio Moscoso P., and I studied them with his kind permission. They appear to be handtinted with watercolor. The first of the series, 'El 12 de Junio de 1869 fué asecinado el cura de Chamula, el maestro y dos mas por los indigenas en el camino de San Pedro Chenaló (sic)' shows Galindo in Indian dress, the dead priest in a frock coat and boots, and the Indians wearing black chamarras.

Pineda, pp. 81–2.

In January 1971, I was talking with an older Chamula. He claimed to know nothing about the War of Santa Rosha, but after I mentioned a few historical facts, he leaned close to me and asked softly, "And did they really kill a priest?"

242-243. Reed, p. 101. Although this was perhaps not done in the Tzeltal Rebellion of 1712, it did occur in the Yucatec War a century and a half later.

244. Niehardt, p. 129. Black Elk describes taking a watch from a dead soldier's belt. "It was round and bright and yellow and very beautiful and I put it on me for a necklace. At first it ticked inside and then it did not anymore. I wore it around my neck for a long time before I found out what it was and how to make it tick again."

245. Buñuel, Luis, *Las Hurdes* (Spain, 1932).

251. Pineda, pp. 46–7, contains this document from 1712.

252-256. Pineda, pp. 86–92.

Klein, Herbert S., "The Tzeltal Rebellion of 1712 and the Tzotzil Rebellion of 1869." Klein believes the conversation between Rosas and Galindo reported in Pineda is "fanciful." But he agrees that it is correct in its assumption that Galindo was primarily a social revolutionary.

Martínez lithograph No. 3, 'Los traidos del 17 de Junio de 1869 en el labor denominada Esquipulas.' Galindo appears to have a cigar.

256-262. Pineda, p. 95, contains the messages sent between Pedro and the Governor.

262. Niehardt, p. 140. Black Elk says that toward the end, ". . . the people noticed Crazy Horse was queerer than ever. He hardly ever stayed in the camp. People would find him out in the cold and ask him to come home with them. He would not come,

but sometimes he would tell the people what to do. People wondered if he ate anything at all. Once my father found him alone like that, and he said to my father 'Uncle, you have noticed me, the way I act. But do not worry; there are caves and holes for me to live in, and out here the spirits may help me. I am making plans for the good of my people.' "

264-272. Pineda, pp. 95-104.

Reed, p. 242. In battles, "machetes could be used against single-shot muzzle-loaders if losses were accepted, but not against repeating rifles."

Martínez lithograph No. 4, "Batalla con los indígenas de Chamula el 21 de junio de 1869." The man in charge of the ladino soldiers, perhaps the Governor himself, is wearing a frock coat and waistcoat.

271. Reed, p. 92. At the siege of Ticul, when the whites began running out of ammunition, "sensing their predicament, the Maya taunted them, performing their traditional X-tol dances in plain view: dressed in captured uniforms, or as women, with their faces painted black, they shouted insults and threats, inciting wasteful volleys of artillary."

All the stories of the battles in the War of Santa Rosha tell how by exposing themselves Chamula women tried to charm or "cool off" the ladino guns. People from Zinacantán did not take part in the war, but they too have the story, here in a concise and mocking form. Robert M. Laughlin Tale 65, "The War of Saint Rose," interview in Tzotzil with M. P. K., August 1960:

"Once there used to be a Saint Rose, long ago. But she was the mother of dissension, Saint Rose. There was strife. The Chamulas gathered together. Lots of women joined in. They were going to make war. They were going to wage war.

"There next to the Quinta is a bridge. The bridge is named Saint Rose. The trouble reached there, because they were fighting there. They went. There used to be cannons here (in San Cristóbal). They went. They went to fire cannons there.

"The women—first the women came. They came with their skirts (lifted high and wide) so that the cannons would grow cold, so that they would not fire.

"But the cannons did fire! All the women were left in heaps like chickens. They were all killed by the cannons.

"The men came on. They didn't enter (San Cristóbal). They never entered. They were just finished off like the others. . . ."

275-278. Pineda, pp. 105–7.

Martínez lithograph No. 5, "Ejecucion de Galindo y Trejo en la plaza principal de S. C. 26 de junio."

Reed, p. 63. In the Yucatán, whipping posts which had been taken down at the time of the liberation from Spain were replaced during the War of the Castes.

In January 1971 I was sitting with an older ladino woman who has made her life as a corn and coffee trader in a Tzeltal town near Chamula. She remembered that I had worked in Chamula and then, to amuse her granddaughter, began to sing in imitation of the Chamula prayer-songs, "San Juan Fiador, San Mateo, Santa Rosha." Then she asked me, "Do you know about that Galindo, the one who stirred them up?" We had not previously talked about the War of Santa Rosha. I imagine that Galindo's name hangs on in the memory of many ladinos simply because he was the outstanding and dangerous traitor to his own race.

280. Martínez lithograph No. 6, "Batalla en la loma de Chamula el 30 de junio de 1869."

In Pineda, p. 108ff.

281-282. Reed, p. 223. The True Cross in Yucatán spoke to the Indians who no longer adhered to it. "Is there perhaps another God? Tell me because I am the Owner of the sky and the earth, because, my children, maybe you can postpone the judgment over you here in the world, the last day of Final Judgment, when I will raise all those to whom I have given life and you can raise those that you want to judge, o creatures of the world."

282-283. Lazos, Feliciano J., and Solorsano, Manuel L., "Aguaiic Iscotol Lumalic Te Indioetic" (sic): "Oid Los Pueblos Todos de Indios Sublevados" (San Cristóbal, October 1869).

ADDITIONAL BIBLIOGRAPHY

Brinton, Daniel G., *Maria Candelaria* (Philadelphia, 1897). A drama about the 1712 Tzeltal uprising.

Castellanos, Rosario, *Oficio de Tinieblas* (Mexico, 1962). A beautiful novel which resets many of the events from the War of Santa Rosha in a later period.

Cosio Villegas, Daniel, ed. *Historia Moderna de Mexico,* 4 vols. (Mexico, 1956).

daCunha, Euclides, *Rebellion in the Backlands,* trans. by Samuel Putnam (Chicago 1944).

Gossen, Gary H., "Chamula Traditional Narrative," Harvard Chiapas Project, 1965.

Gutieras-Holmes, Calixta, *Perils of the Soul, The World View of a Tzotzil Indian* (Glencoe, Illinois, 1961). An excellent single-informant ethnography of the town of Chenalhó.

Lawrence, D. H., *Mornings in Mexico* (London, 1956). Lawrence's reportage of U.S. and Mexican Indians contains little ethnography, but his intuitions seem to me excellent.

Metzger, Barbara, "Notes on the History of Indian-Ladino Relations in Chiapas," Harvard Chiapas Project, 1960.

Olson, Charles, *Mayan Letters,* ed. and with a Preface by Robert Creely (London, 1968).

Pozas, Ricardo, *Juan Pérez Jolote: Biografía de un Tzotzil* (Mexico, 1952). Also, trans. by Lysander Kemp as *Juan the Chamula* (Berkeley, California, 1962).

Raynaud, Georges, Gonzales de Mendoza, J. M., y Asturias, Miguel Angel, trad. y notas, *El Libro del Consejo,* 3rd ed. (Mexico, 1964).

Thompson, J. Eric S., *The Rise and Fall of Maya Civilization* (Norman, Oklahoma, 1954).

Villa Rojas, Alfonso, *The Maya of East Central Quintana Roo*, Carnegie Institution of Washington Publication 559 (Washington, D.C., 1945).

Vogt, Evon Z., ed., *Los Zinacantecos: un pueblo Tzotzil de los Altos de Chiapas* (Mexico, 1966).

Ximenez, Francisco, *Historia de la Provincia de San Vicente de Chiapas y Guatemala de la orden de predicadores* (Guatemala, 1929–31).